DOLPHIN GIRL

Eye of the
BALONEY STORM!

Eye of the
BALONEY STORM!

WRITTEN AND ILLUSTRATED BY
ZACH SMITH

COLOR BY LETICIA LACY

PIXEL+INK

PIXEL✛INK

PIXEL+INK IS A DIVISION OF TGM DEVELOPMENT CORP.
PRINTED AND BOUND IN SEPTEMBER 2021 AT C&C OFFSET, SHENZHEN, CHINA.

IMAGES, CLOCKWISE ON PAGE 35: EARTH — IXPERT/SHUTTERSTOCK.COM
SMILING DOLPHIN — NATASNOW/SHUTTERSTOCK.COM
LEAPING DOLPHIN — NEIRFY/SHUTTERSTOCK.COM
SPACE SHUTTLE — DIMA ZEL/SHUTTERSTOCK.COM
LEAPING DOLPHINS — MURATART/SHUTTERSTOCK.COM
LIGHTNING, PAGE 48: JEEDY_JOY/SHUTTERSTOCK.COM
FIRE, PAGE 116: WEERACHAI KHAMFU/SHUTTERSTOCK.COM
YEARBOOK BACKGROUND, PAGE 207: SECOND BANANA IMAGES/SHUTTERSTOCK.COM

WWW.PIXELANDINKBOOKS.COM

FIRST EDITION
1 3 5 7 9 10 8 6 4 2

LIBRARY OF CONGRESS CATALOGING-IN-PUBLICATION DATA
NAMES: SMITH, ZACH, AUTHOR. | LACY, LETICIA, COLORIST.
TITLE: EYE OF THE BALONEY STORM! / WRITTEN AND ILLUSTRATED BY ZACH SMITH;
COLOR BY LETICIA LACY.
DESCRIPTION: FIRST EDITION. | [NEW YORK] : PIXEL+INK, 2021. |
SERIES: DOLPHIN GIRL; [2] | AUDIENCE: AGES 8-12. | AUDIENCE: GRADES 4-6. |
SUMMARY: "SUPERHERO-IN-TRAINING DOLPHIN GIRL MUST TEAM UP WITH A RIVAL
TO STOP AN ENEMY FROM CREATING A COLD-CUT CATASTROPHE IN DEERBURBIA."
IDENTIFIERS: LCCN 2021014201 (PRINT) | LCCN 2021014202 (EBOOK) |
ISBN 9781645950196 (HARDBACK) | ISBN 9781645950202 (PAPERBACK) |
ISBN 9781645950974 (EBOOK)
SUBJECTS: CYAC: GRAPHIC NOVELS. | SUPERHEROES—FICTION. |
DOLPHINS—FICTION. | LCGFT: GRAPHIC NOVELS.
CLASSIFICATION: LCC PZ7.7.S6427 EY 2021 (PRINT) | LCC PZ7.7.S6427 (EBOOK) |
DDC 741.5/973—DC23
LC RECORD AVAILABLE AT HTTPS://LCCN.LOC.GOV/2021014201
LC EBOOK RECORD AVAILABLE AT HTTPS://LCCN.LOC.GOV/2021014202

FOR THE TEACHERS IN MY LIFE:
MRS. MONIQUE SMITH OF MOUNTAINVIEW
ELEMENTARY (MY WIFE/SPIRIT GUIDE),
MRS. KRISTIN TURNWALD OF GRAND VIEW
ELEMENTARY (MY EXTREMELY FUNNY SISTER),
MRS. DEBBIE SMITH WHO IS NOW RETIRED FROM
LAKELAND HIGH SCHOOL (MY #1 ALL-TIME
MOM), AND TO ALL THE TEACHERS
WHO HELD THE WORLD TOGETHER
DESPITE BRATTY PARENTS
DURING THE COVID-19 PANDEMIC.

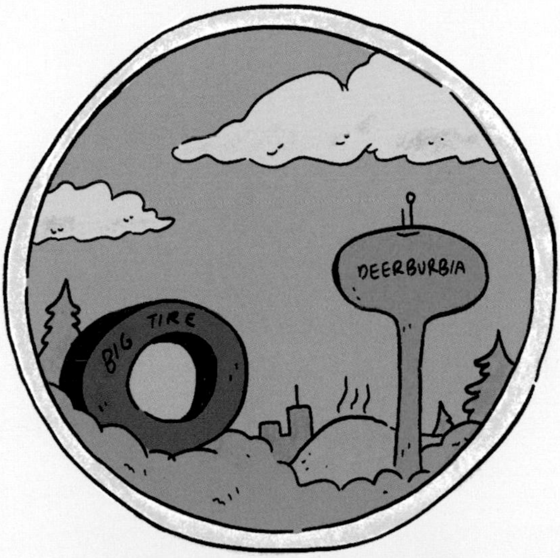
BIG TIRE
DEERBURBIA

PART ONE

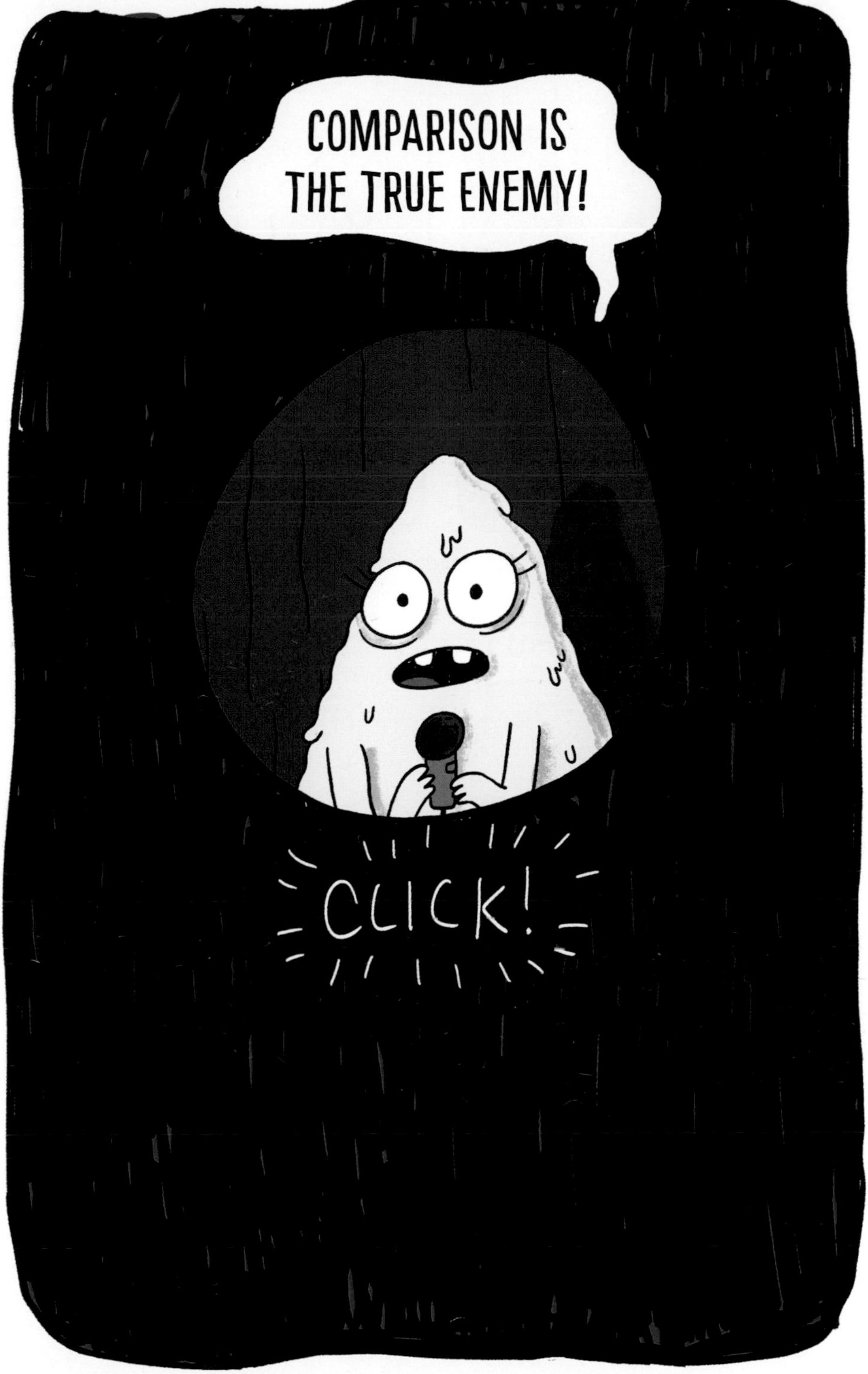
COMPARISON IS THE TRUE ENEMY!
CLICK!

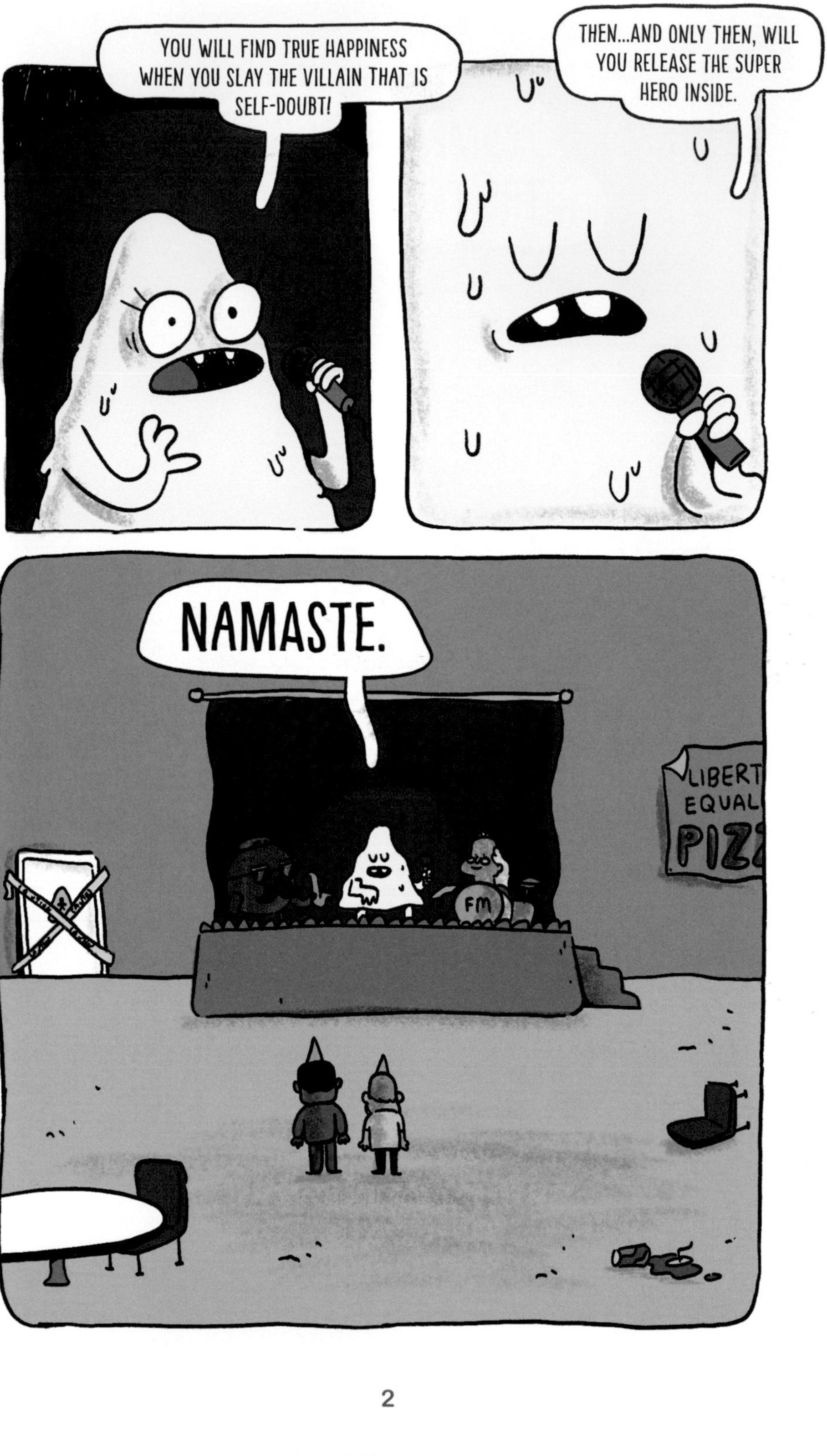
YOU WILL FIND TRUE HAPPINESS WHEN YOU SLAY THE VILLAIN THAT IS SELF-DOUBT!
THEN...AND ONLY THEN, WILL YOU RELEASE THE SUPER HERO INSIDE.
NAMASTE.
FM

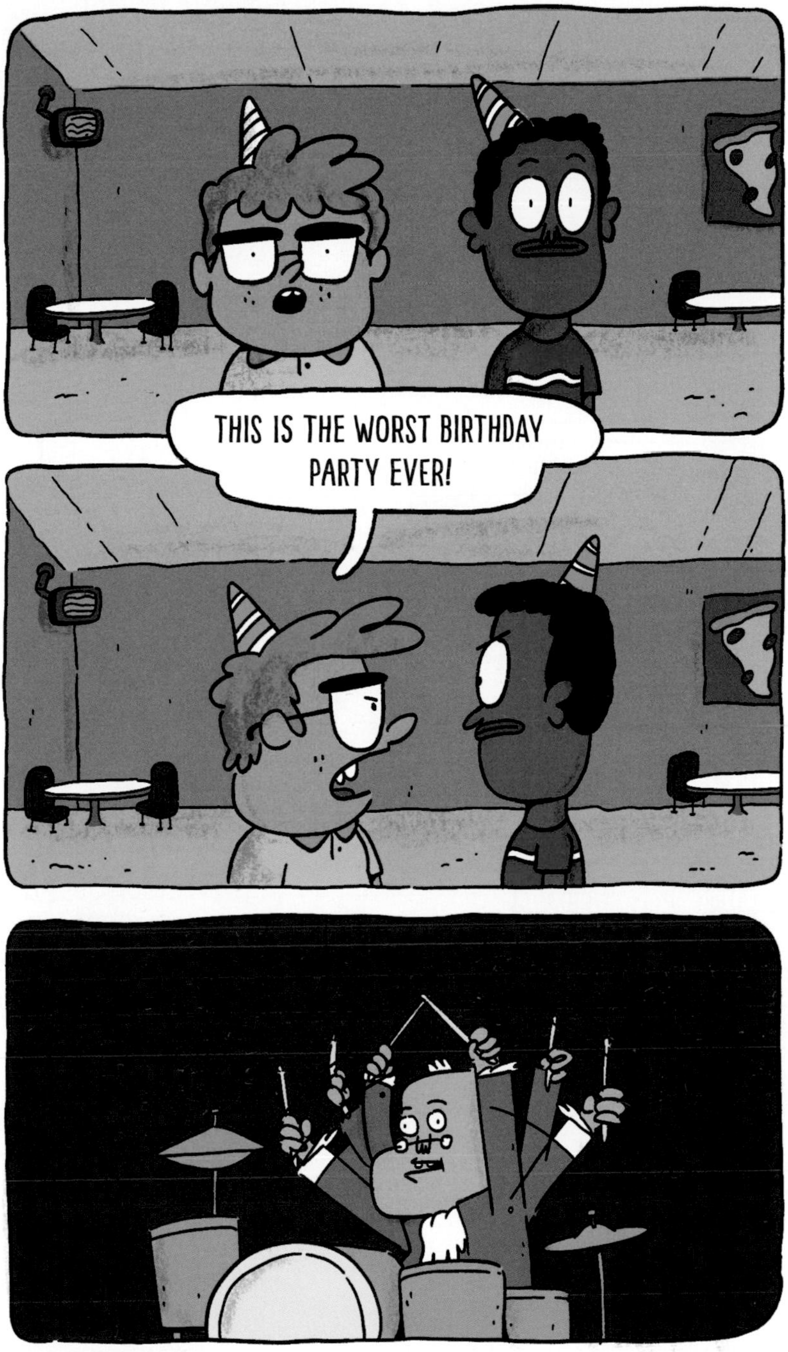
THIS IS THE WORST BIRTHDAY PARTY EVER!

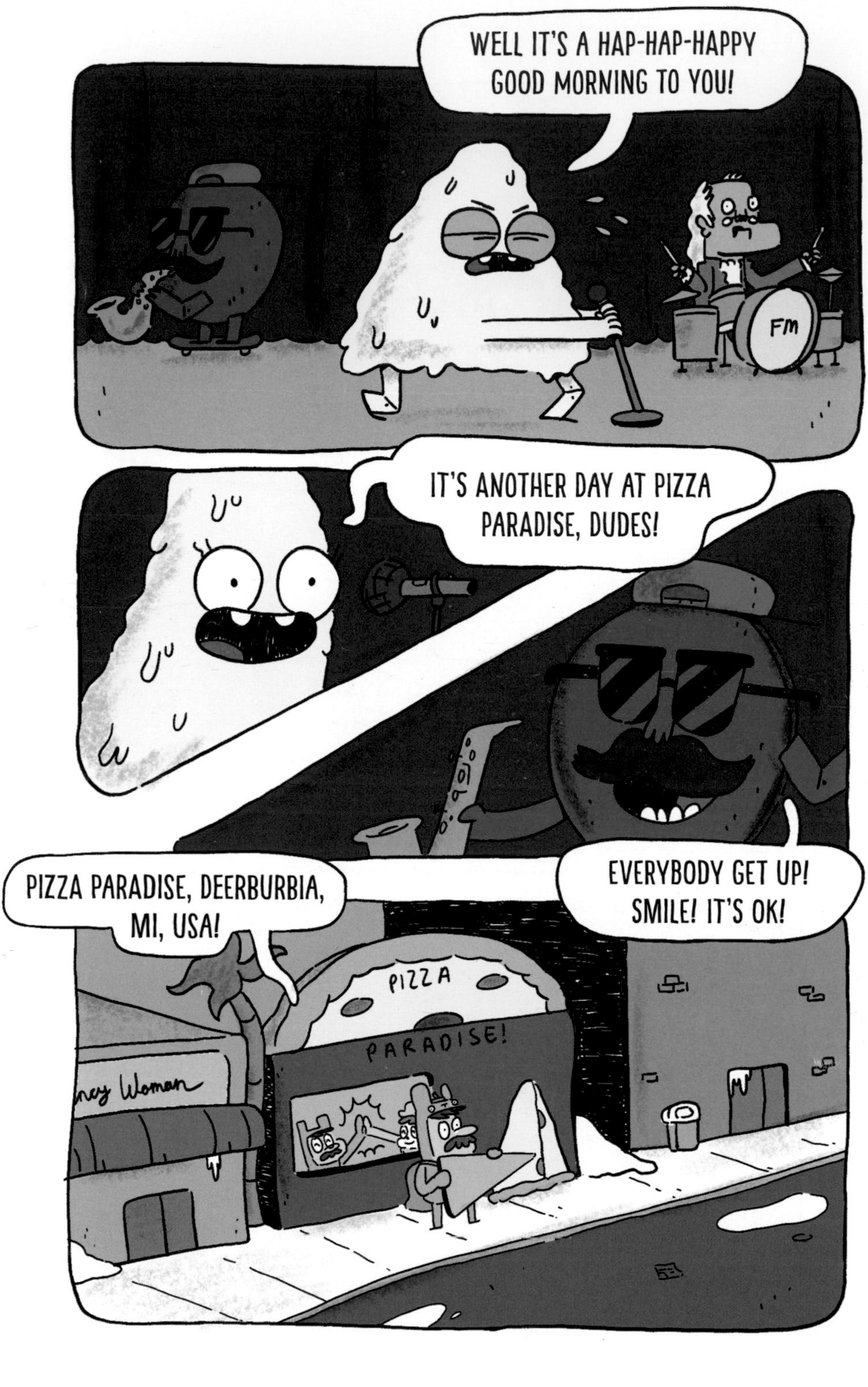
WELL IT'S A HAP-HAP-HAPPY GOOD MORNING TO YOU!
FM
IT'S ANOTHER DAY AT PIZZA PARADISE, DUDES!
PIZZA PARADISE, DEERBURBIA, MI, USA!
EVERYBODY GET UP! SMILE! IT'S OK!
PIZZA
PARADISE!

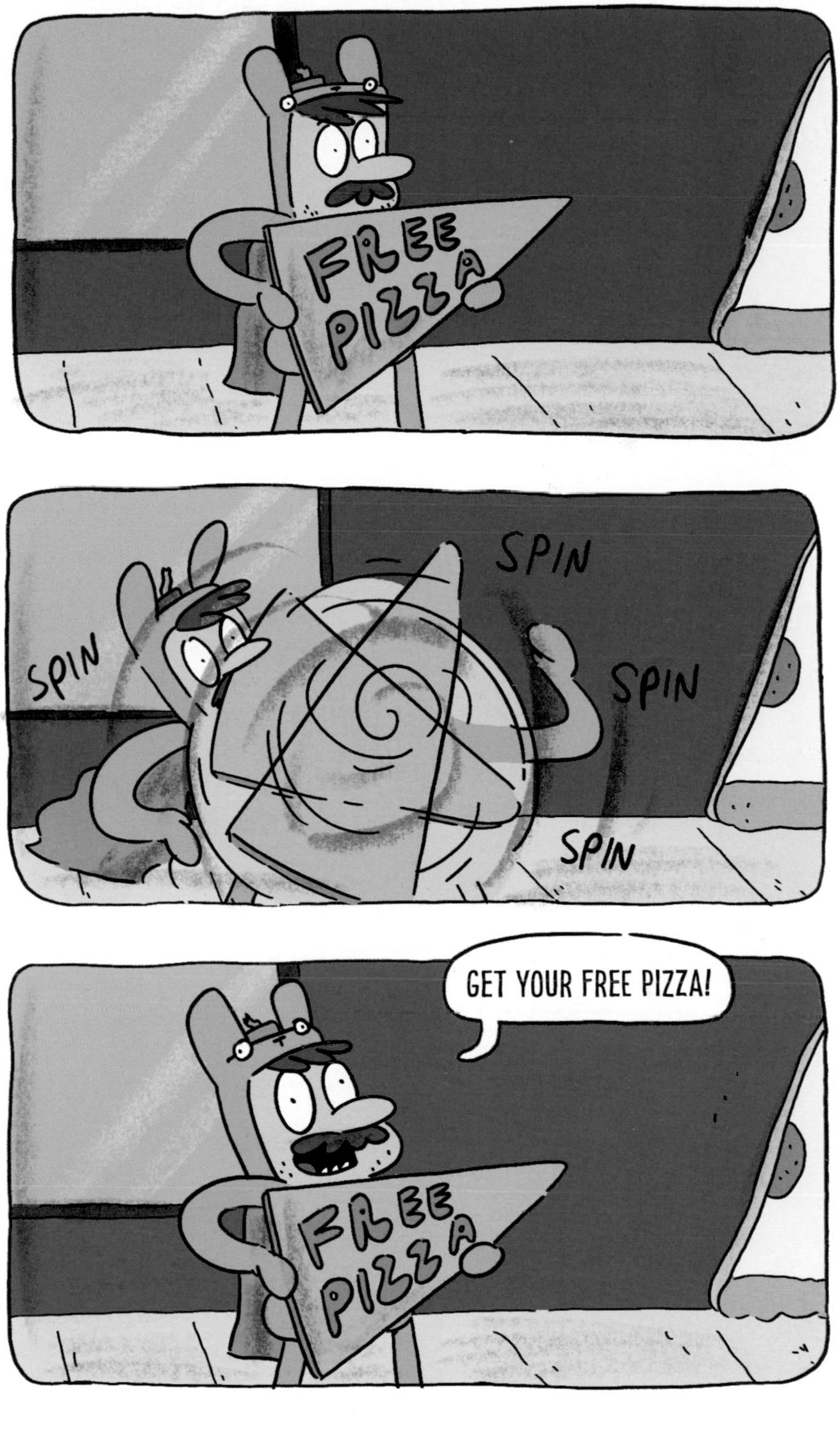
FREE PIZZA
SPIN
SPIN
SPIN
SPIN
GET YOUR FREE PIZZA!
FREE PIZZA

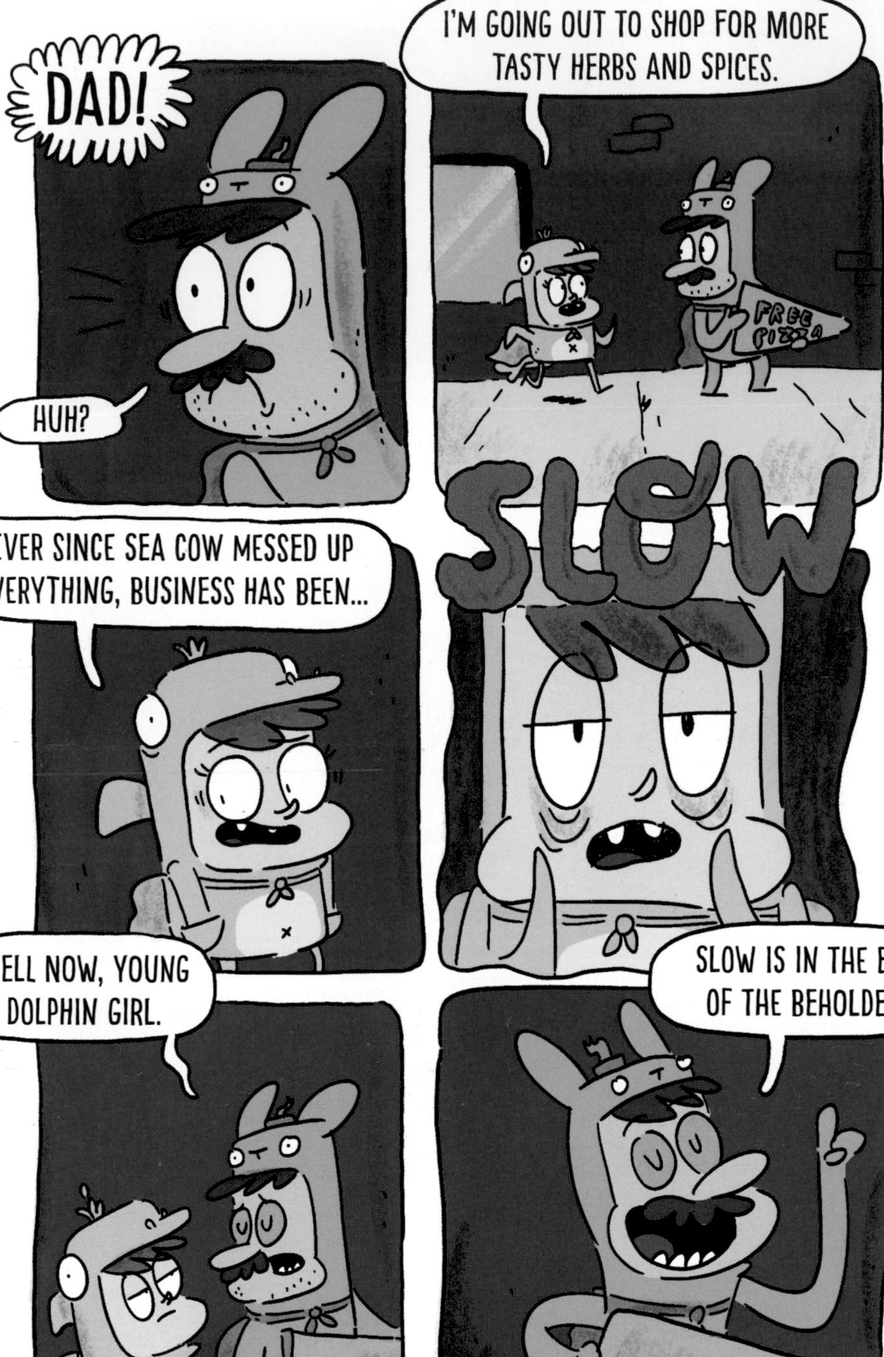
DAD!
HUH?
I'M GOING OUT TO SHOP FOR MORE TASTY HERBS AND SPICES.
FREE PIZZA
EVER SINCE SEA COW MESSED UP EVERYTHING, BUSINESS HAS BEEN...
SLOW
WELL NOW, YOUNG DOLPHIN GIRL.
SLOW IS IN THE EYE OF THE BEHOLDER.

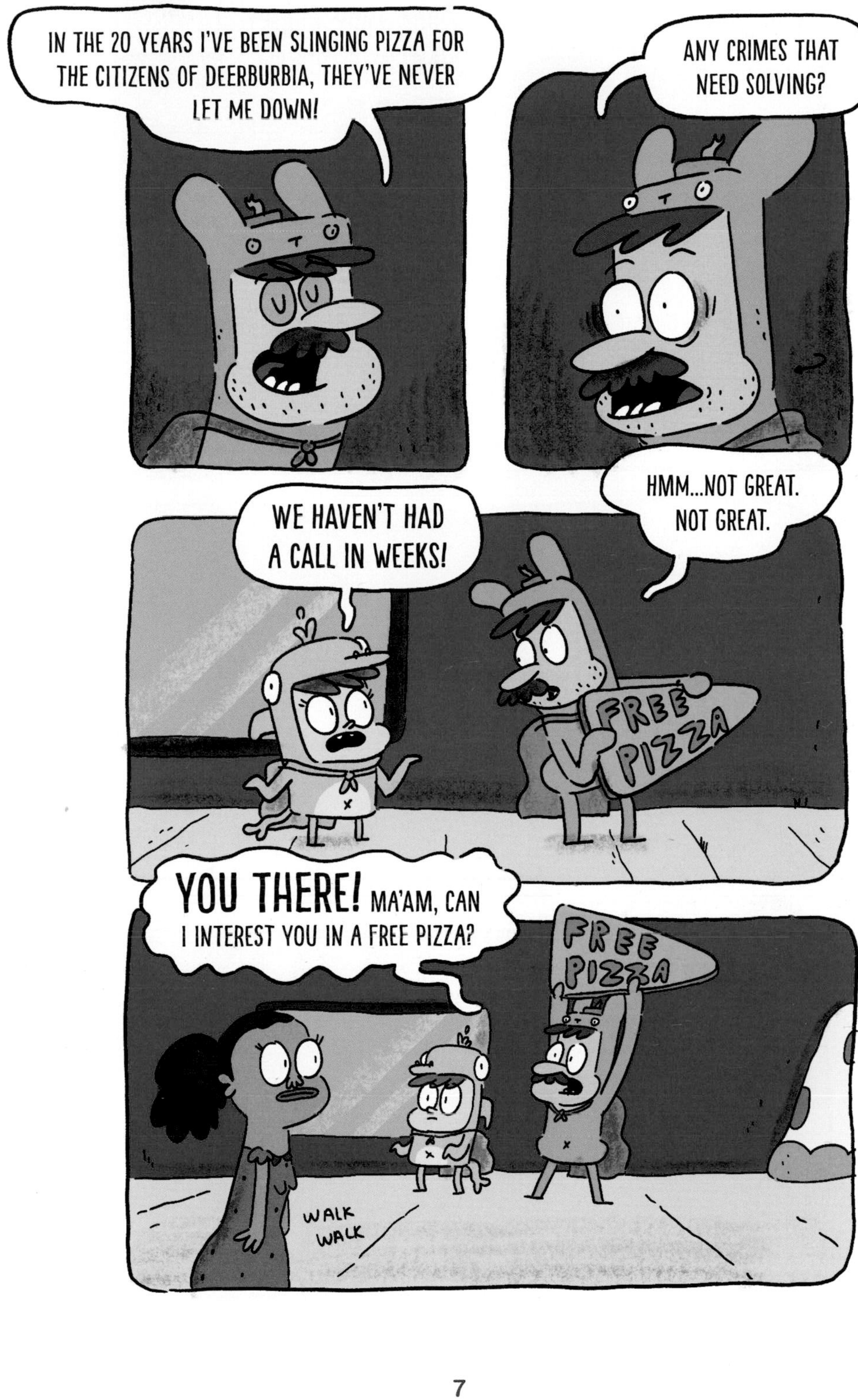
IN THE 20 YEARS I'VE BEEN SLINGING PIZZA FOR THE CITIZENS OF DEERBURBIA, THEY'VE NEVER LET ME DOWN!
ANY CRIMES THAT NEED SOLVING?
WE HAVEN'T HAD A CALL IN WEEKS!
HMM...NOT GREAT. NOT GREAT.
FREE PIZZA
YOU THERE! MA'AM, CAN I INTEREST YOU IN A FREE PIZZA?
FREE PIZZA
WALK
WALK

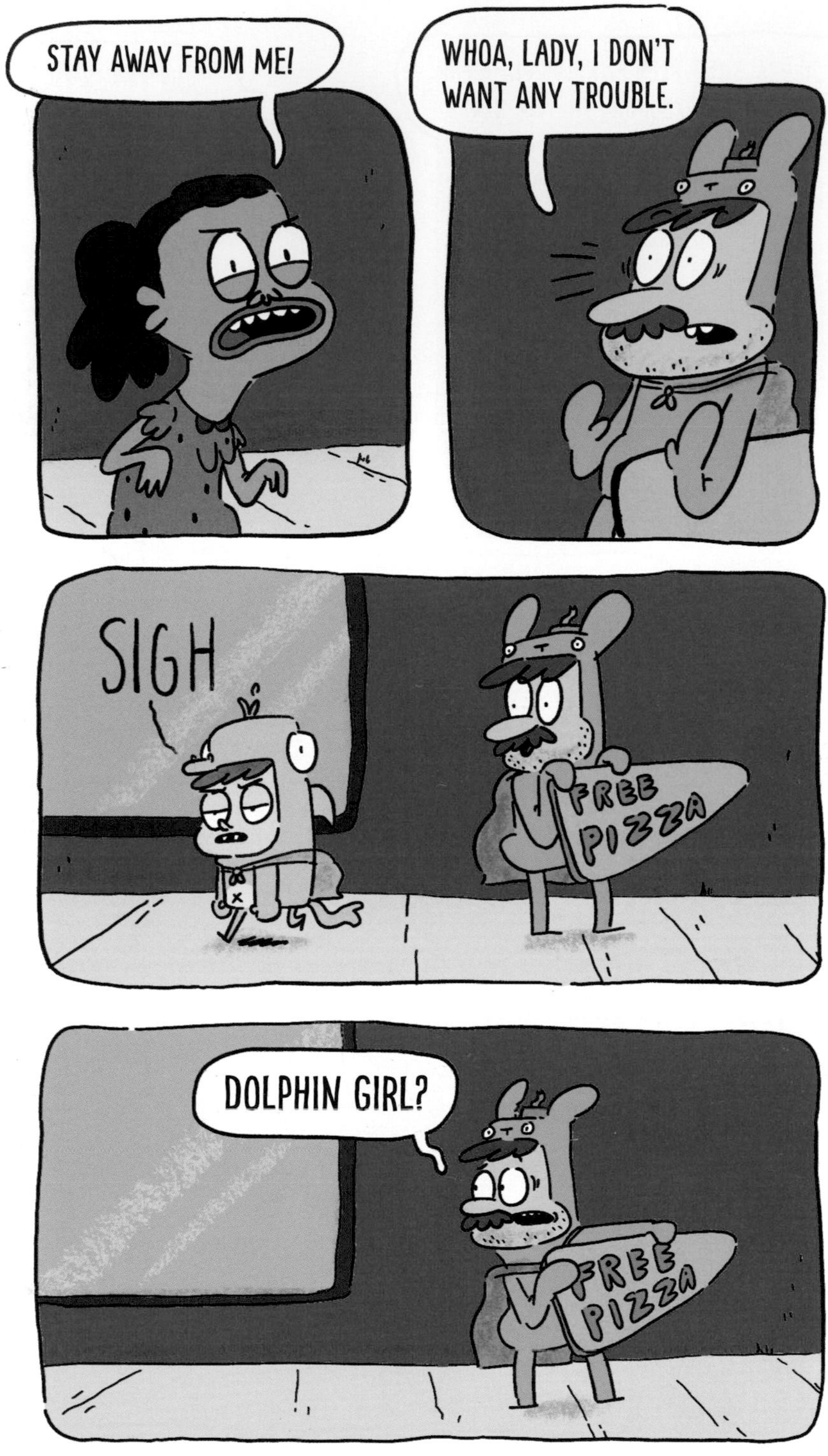
STAY AWAY FROM ME!
WHOA, LADY, I DON'T WANT ANY TROUBLE.
SIGH
FREE PIZZA
DOLPHIN GIRL?
FREE PIZZA

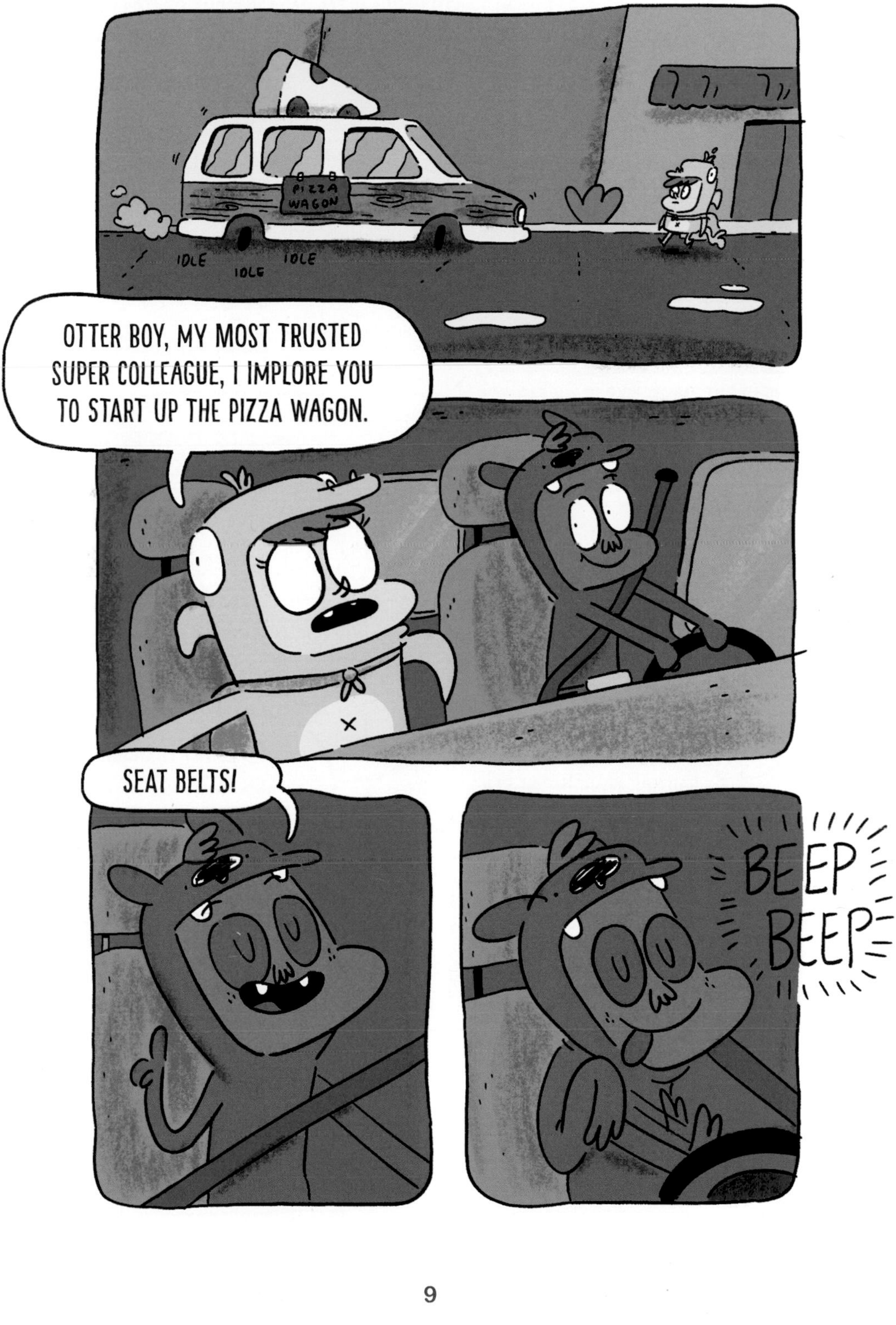
PIZZA WAGON
IDLE
IDLE
IDLE
OTTER BOY, MY MOST TRUSTED SUPER COLLEAGUE, I IMPLORE YOU TO START UP THE PIZZA WAGON.
SEAT BELTS!
BEEP BEEP

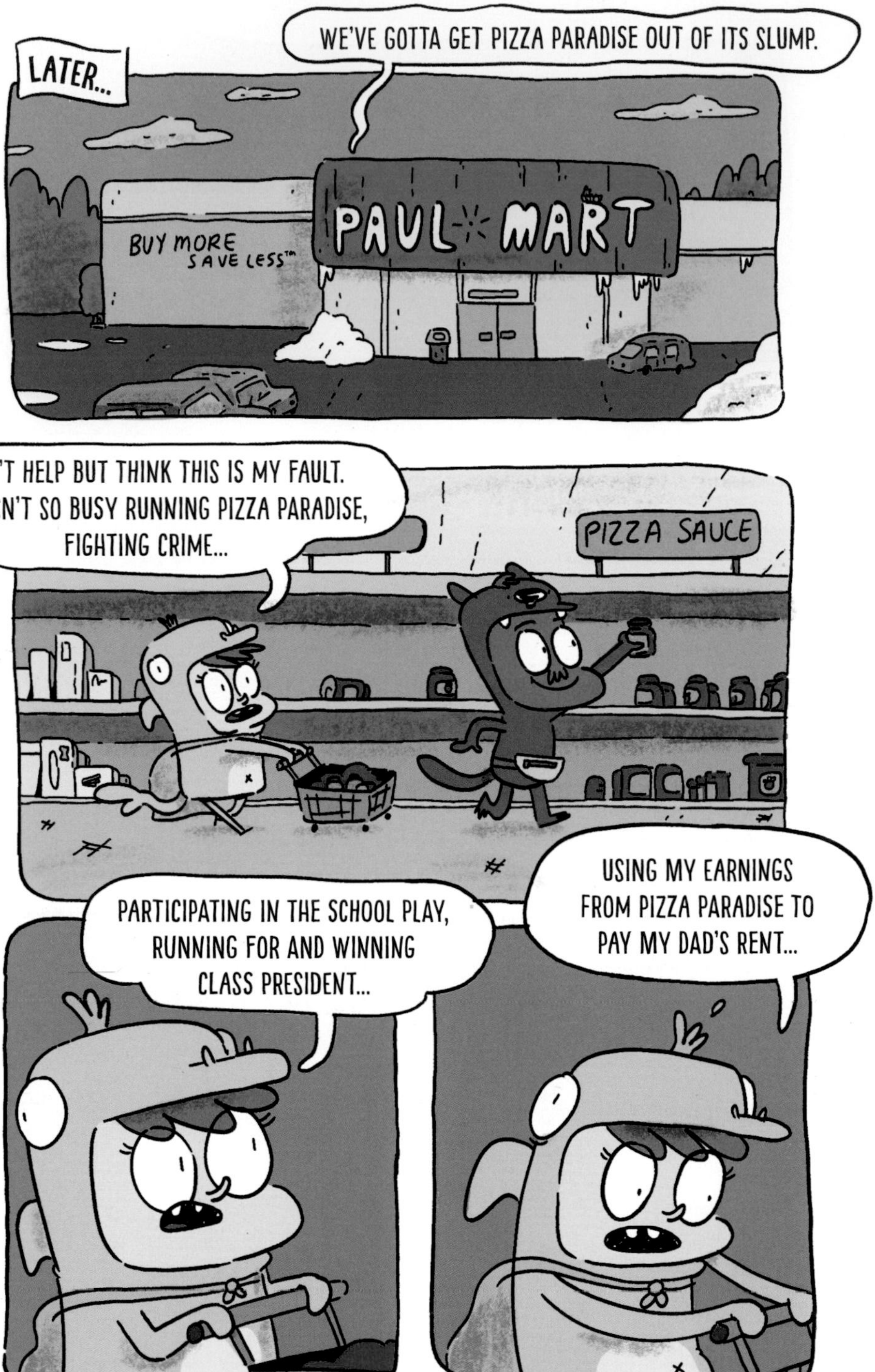
LATER...
WE'VE GOTTA GET PIZZA PARADISE OUT OF ITS SLUMP.
PAUL MART
BUY MORE SAVE LESS™
I CAN'T HELP BUT THINK THIS IS MY FAULT. IF I WASN'T SO BUSY RUNNING PIZZA PARADISE, FIGHTING CRIME...
PIZZA SAUCE
PARTICIPATING IN THE SCHOOL PLAY, RUNNING FOR AND WINNING CLASS PRESIDENT...
USING MY EARNINGS FROM PIZZA PARADISE TO PAY MY DAD'S RENT...

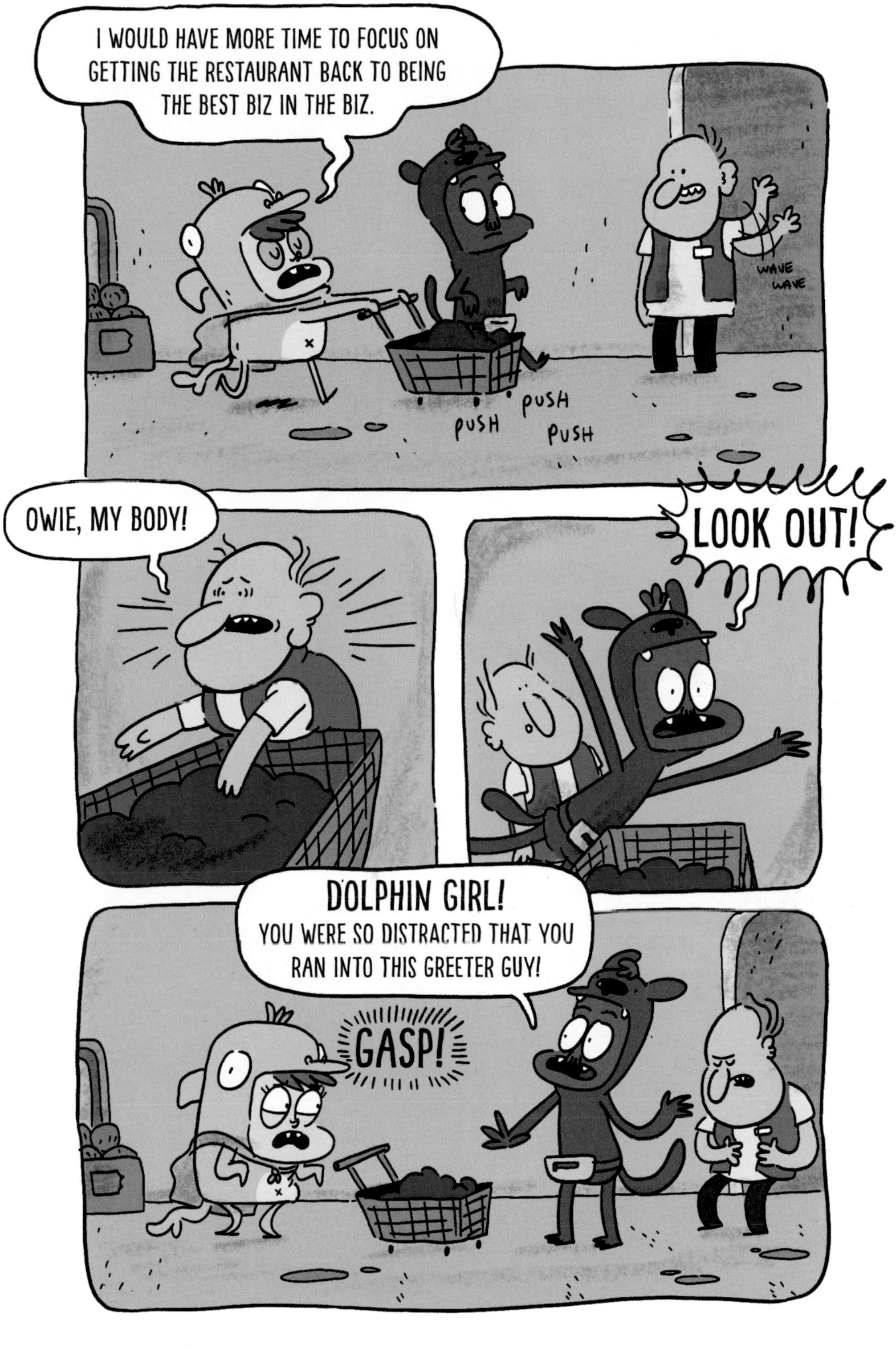

I WOULD HAVE MORE TIME TO FOCUS ON GETTING THE RESTAURANT BACK TO BEING THE BEST BIZ IN THE BIZ.
WAVE
WAVE
PUSH
PUSH
PUSH
OWIE, MY BODY!
LOOK OUT!
DOLPHIN GIRL!
YOU WERE SO DISTRACTED THAT YOU RAN INTO THIS GREETER GUY!
GASP!

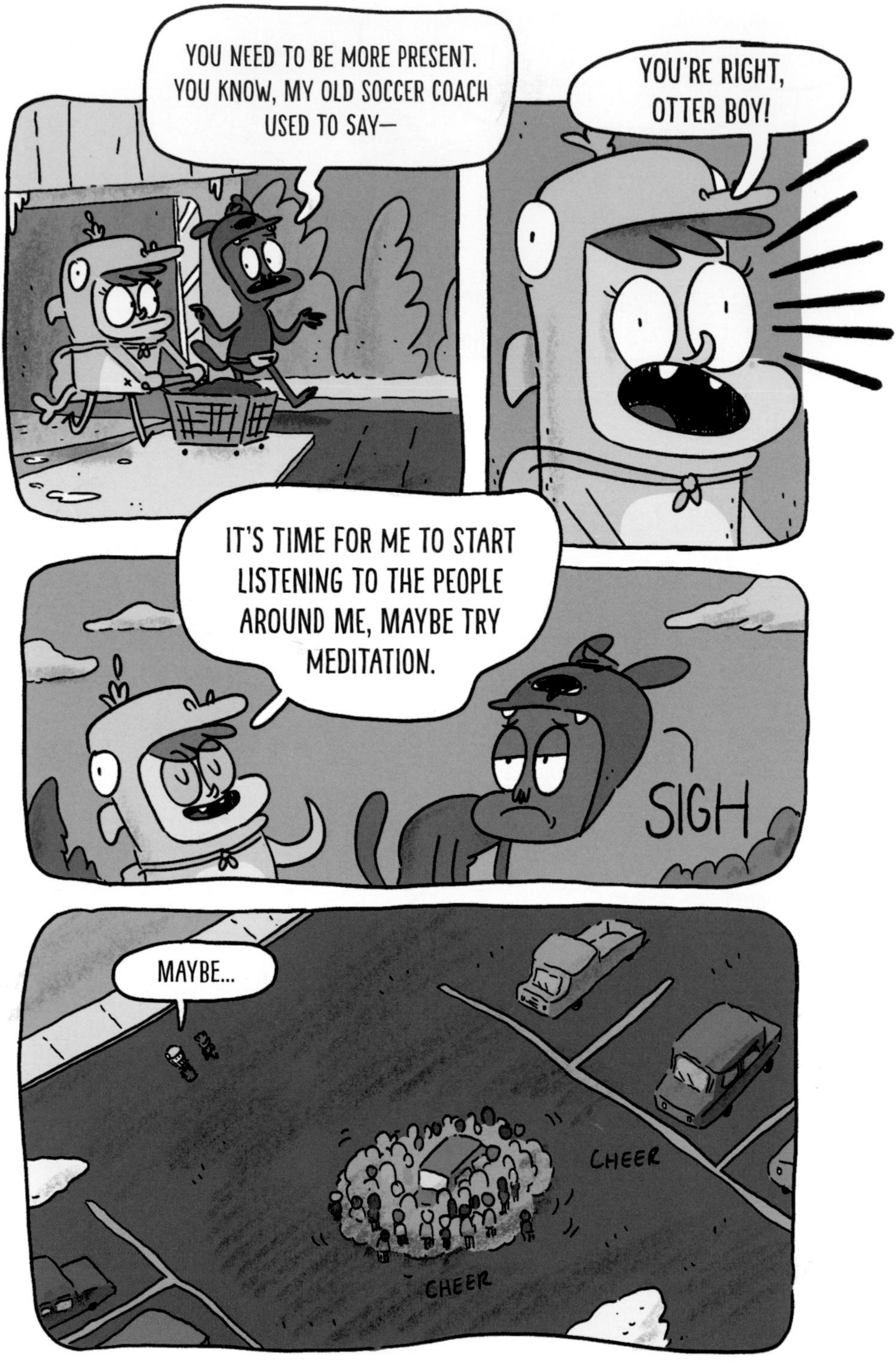
YOU NEED TO BE MORE PRESENT. YOU KNOW, MY OLD SOCCER COACH USED TO SAY—
YOU'RE RIGHT, OTTER BOY!
IT'S TIME FOR ME TO START LISTENING TO THE PEOPLE AROUND ME, MAYBE TRY MEDITATION.
SIGH
MAYBE...
CHEER
CHEER

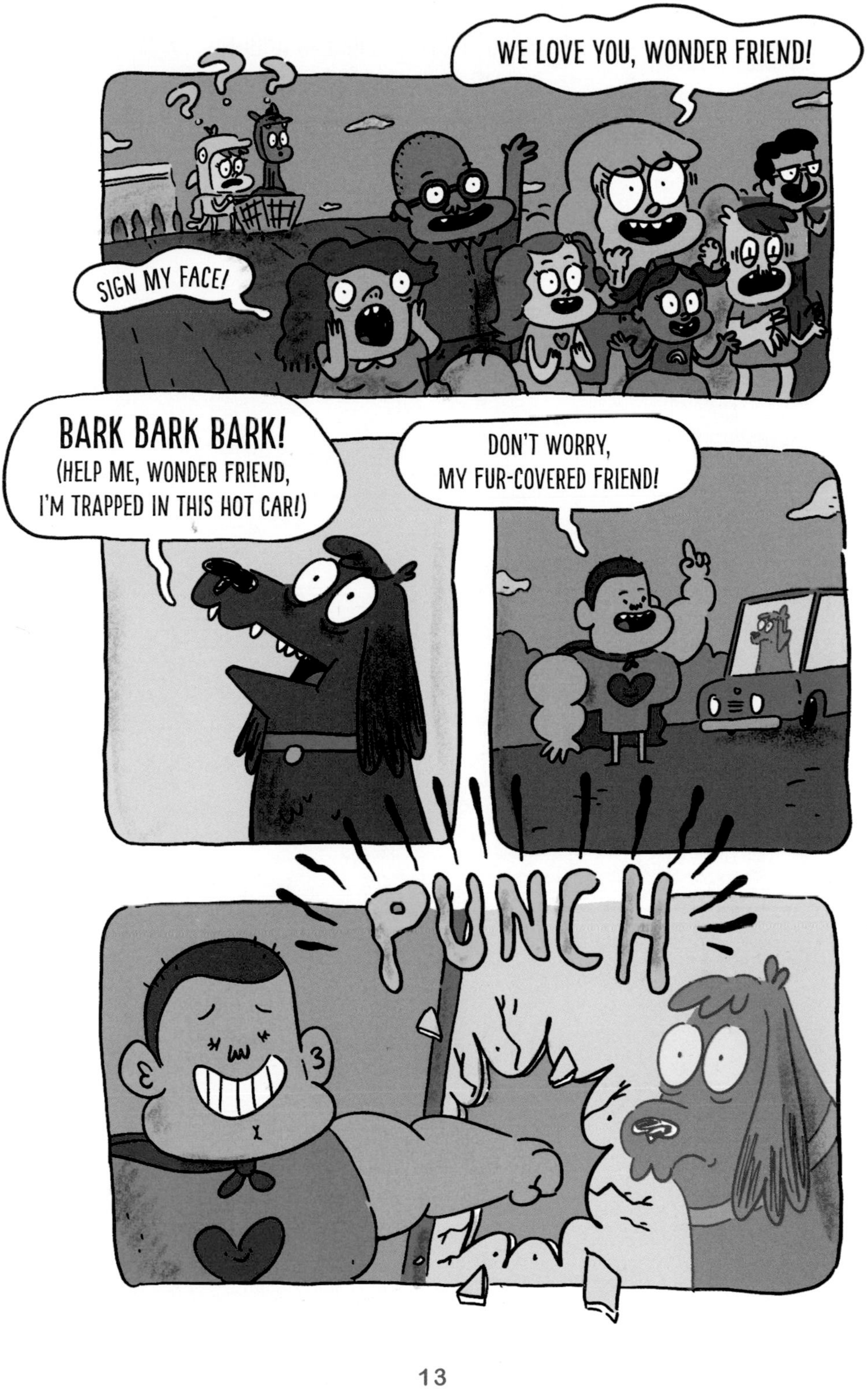
WE LOVE YOU, WONDER FRIEND!
SIGN MY FACE!
BARK BARK BARK!
(HELP ME, WONDER FRIEND, I'M TRAPPED IN THIS HOT CAR!)
DON'T WORRY, MY FUR-COVERED FRIEND!
PUNCH

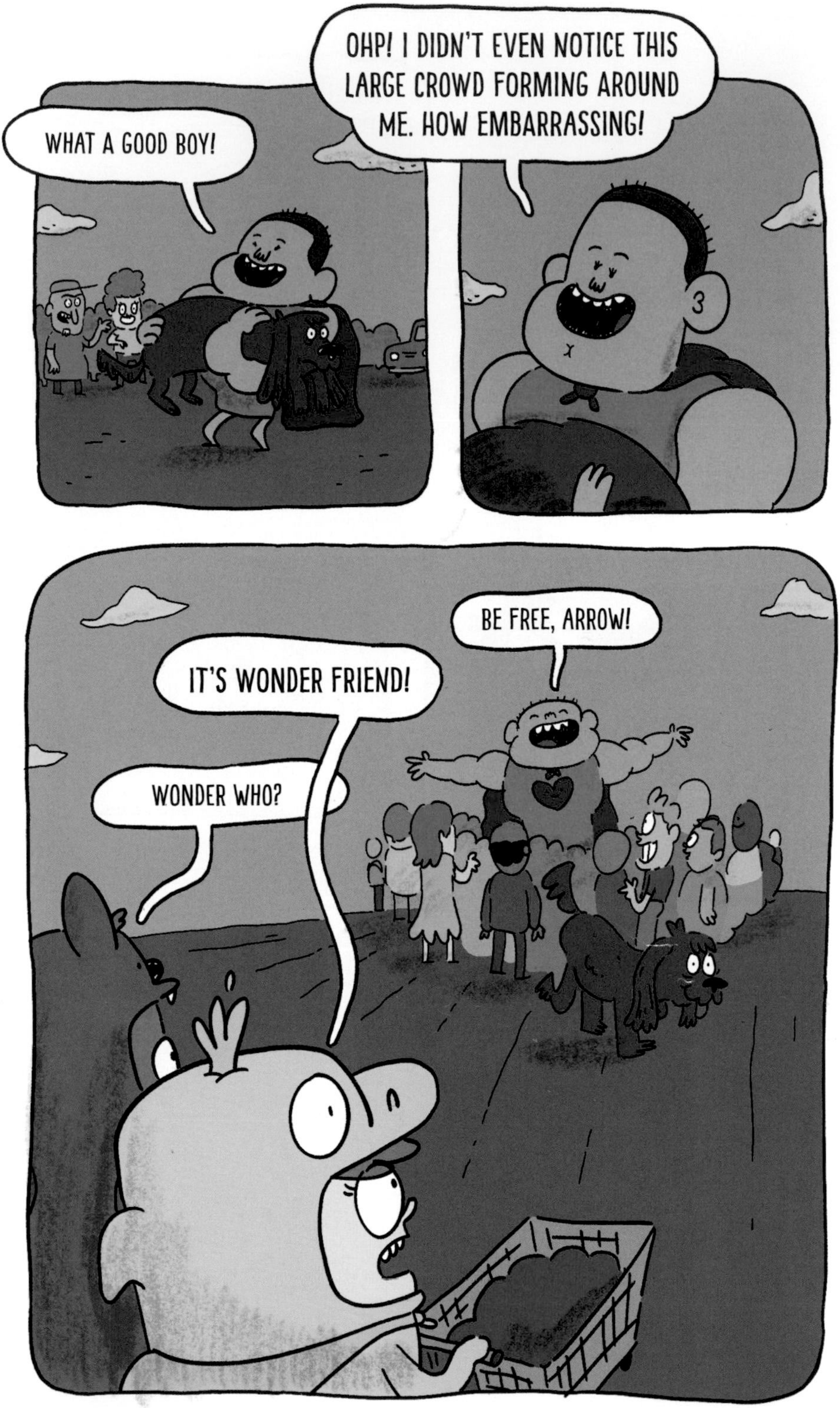
WHAT A GOOD BOY!
OHP! I DIDN'T EVEN NOTICE THIS LARGE CROWD FORMING AROUND ME. HOW EMBARRASSING!
IT'S WONDER FRIEND!
WONDER WHO?
BE FREE, ARROW!

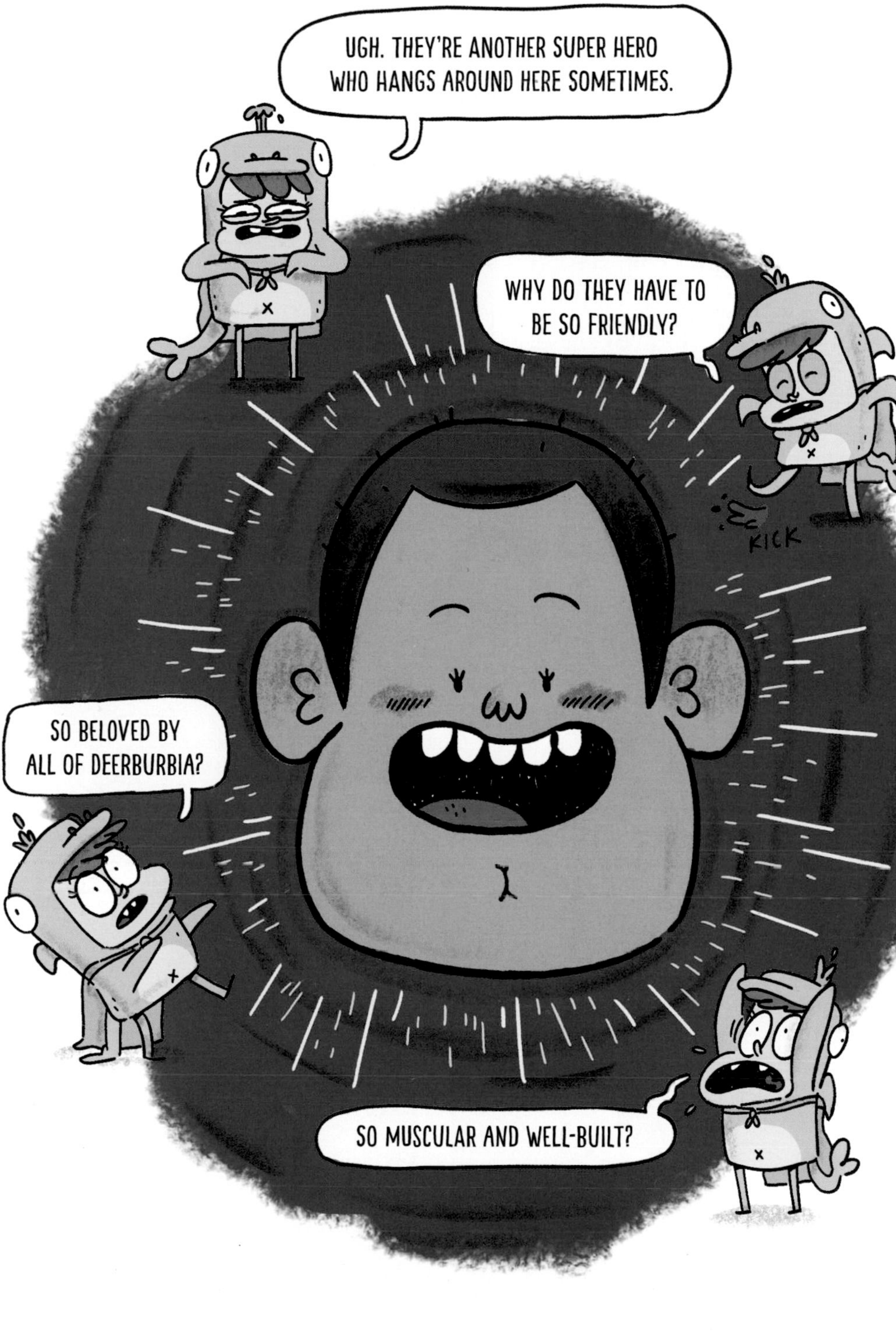
UGH. THEY'RE ANOTHER SUPER HERO WHO HANGS AROUND HERE SOMETIMES.
WHY DO THEY HAVE TO BE SO FRIENDLY?
KICK
SO BELOVED BY ALL OF DEERBURBIA?
SO MUSCULAR AND WELL-BUILT?

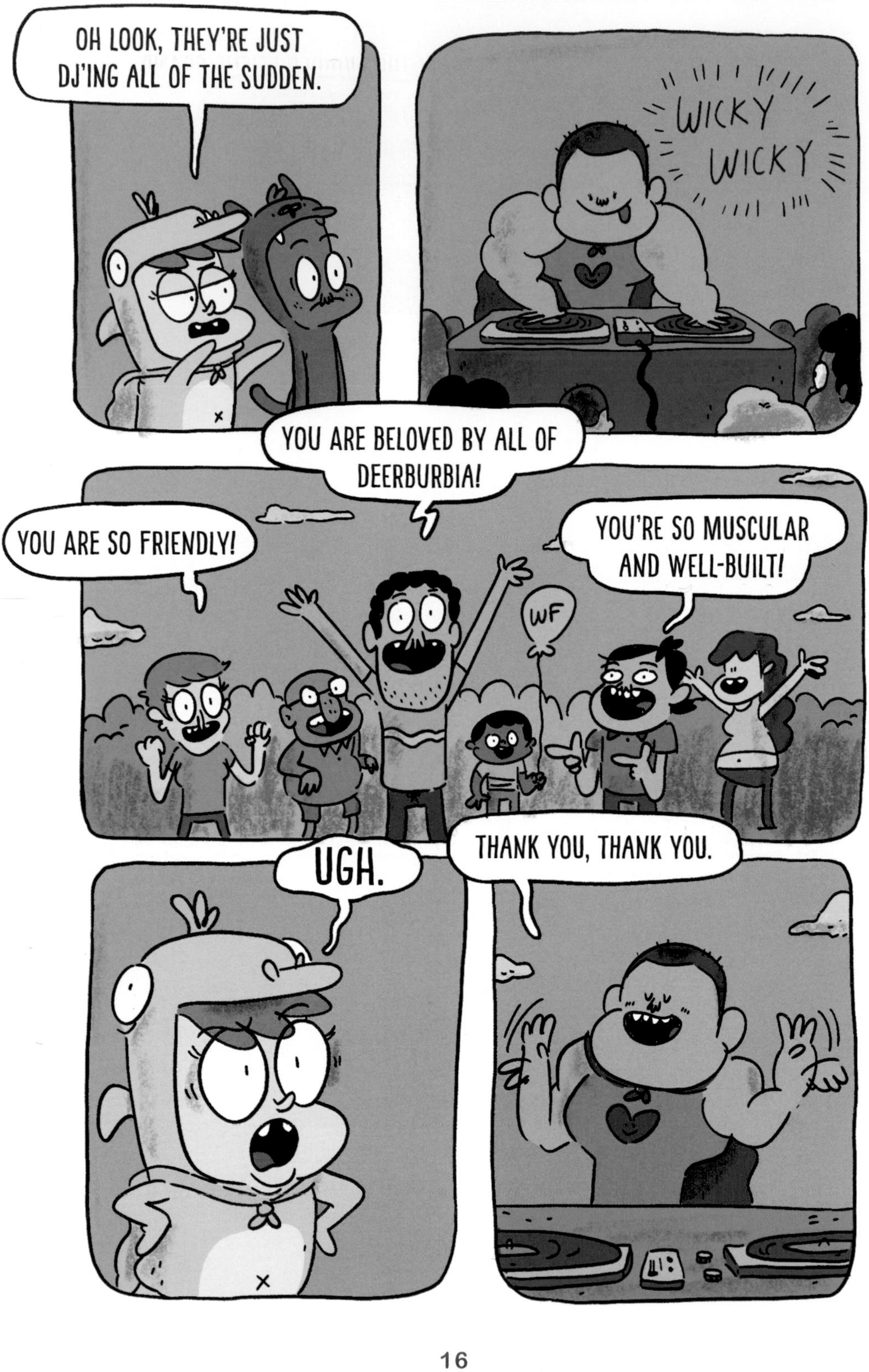
OH LOOK, THEY'RE JUST DJ'ING ALL OF THE SUDDEN.
WICKY WICKY
YOU ARE BELOVED BY ALL OF DEERBURBIA!
YOU ARE SO FRIENDLY!
YOU'RE SO MUSCULAR AND WELL-BUILT!
WF
UGH.
THANK YOU, THANK YOU.

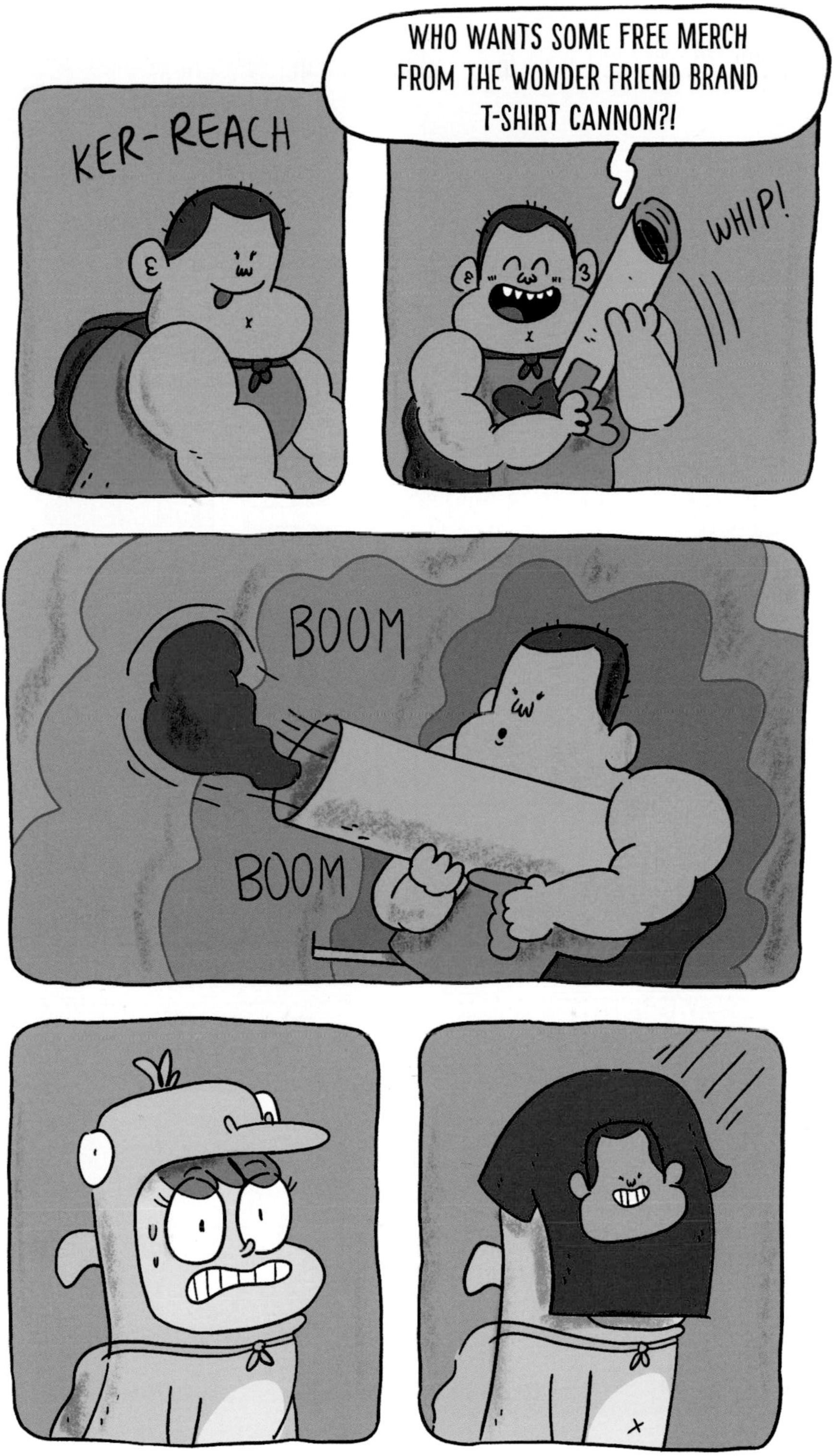
KER-REACH
WHO WANTS SOME FREE MERCH FROM THE WONDER FRIEND BRAND T-SHIRT CANNON?!
WHIP!
BOOM
BOOM

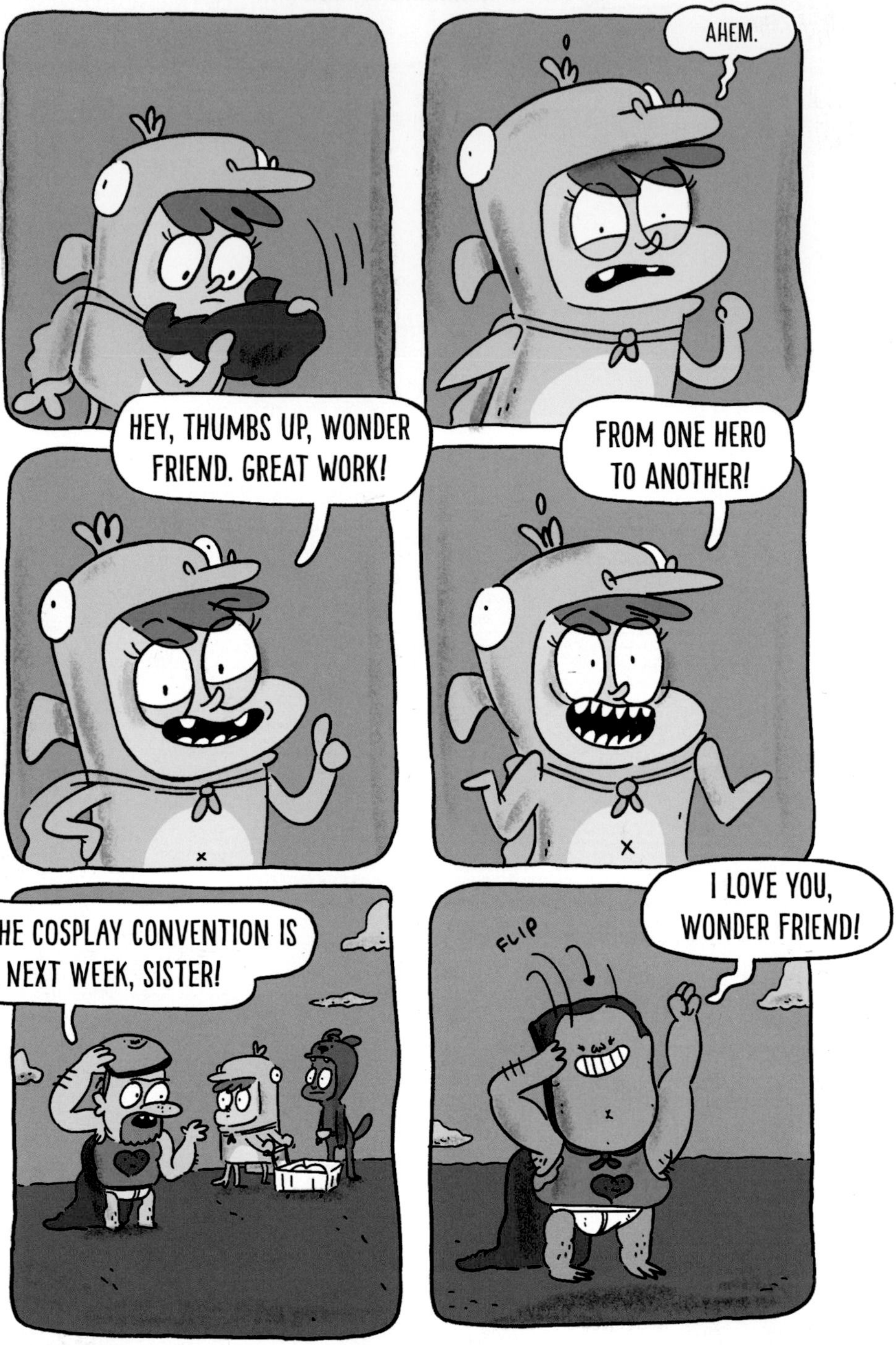
AHEM.
HEY, THUMBS UP, WONDER FRIEND. GREAT WORK!
FROM ONE HERO TO ANOTHER!
HEY, THE COSPLAY CONVENTION IS NEXT WEEK, SISTER!
FLIP
I LOVE YOU, WONDER FRIEND!

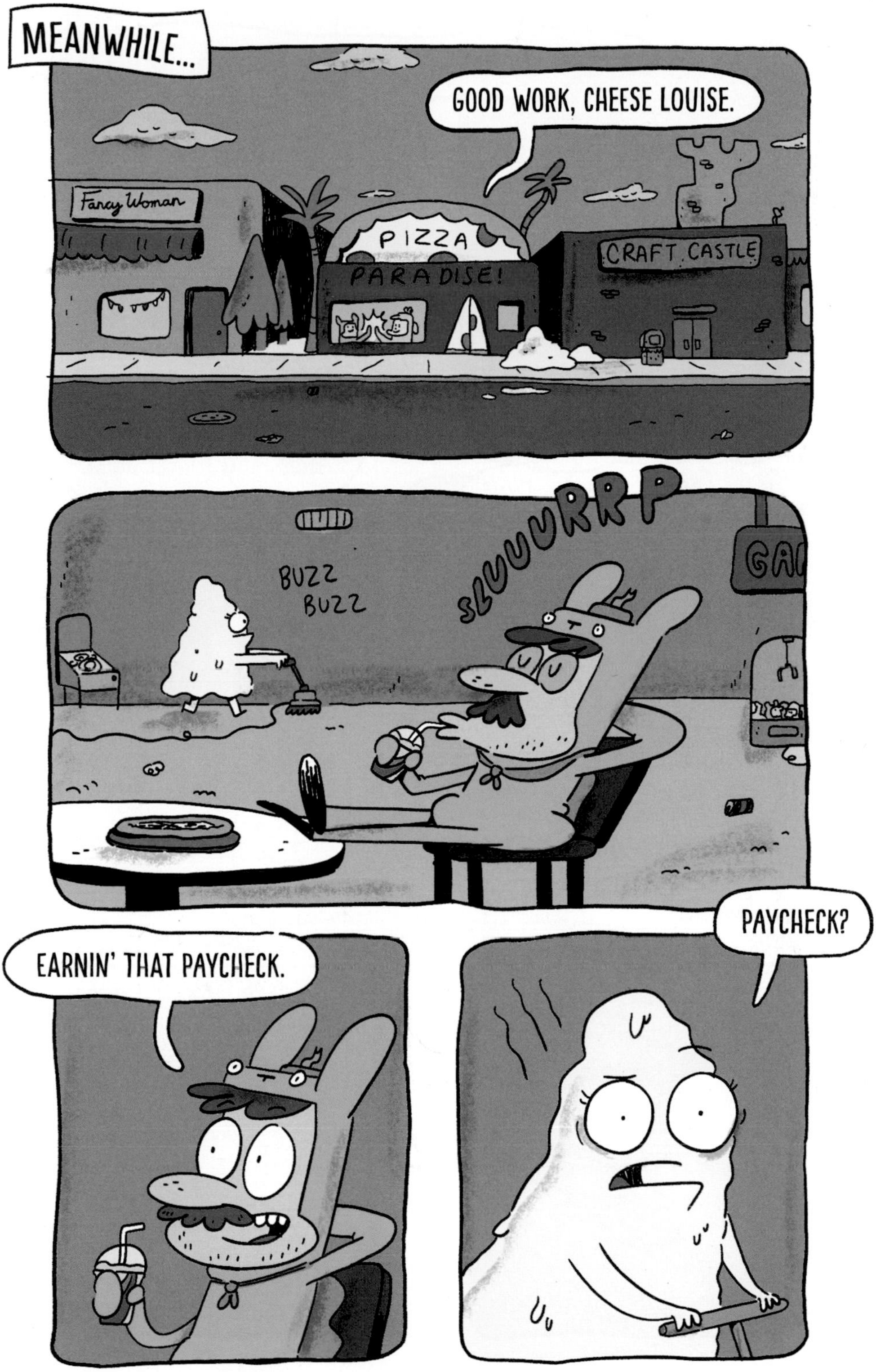
MEANWHILE...
GOOD WORK, CHEESE LOUISE.
Fancy Woman
PIZZA
PARADISE!
CRAFT CASTLE
BUZZ
BUZZ
SLUUURRP
EARNIN' THAT PAYCHECK.
PAYCHECK?

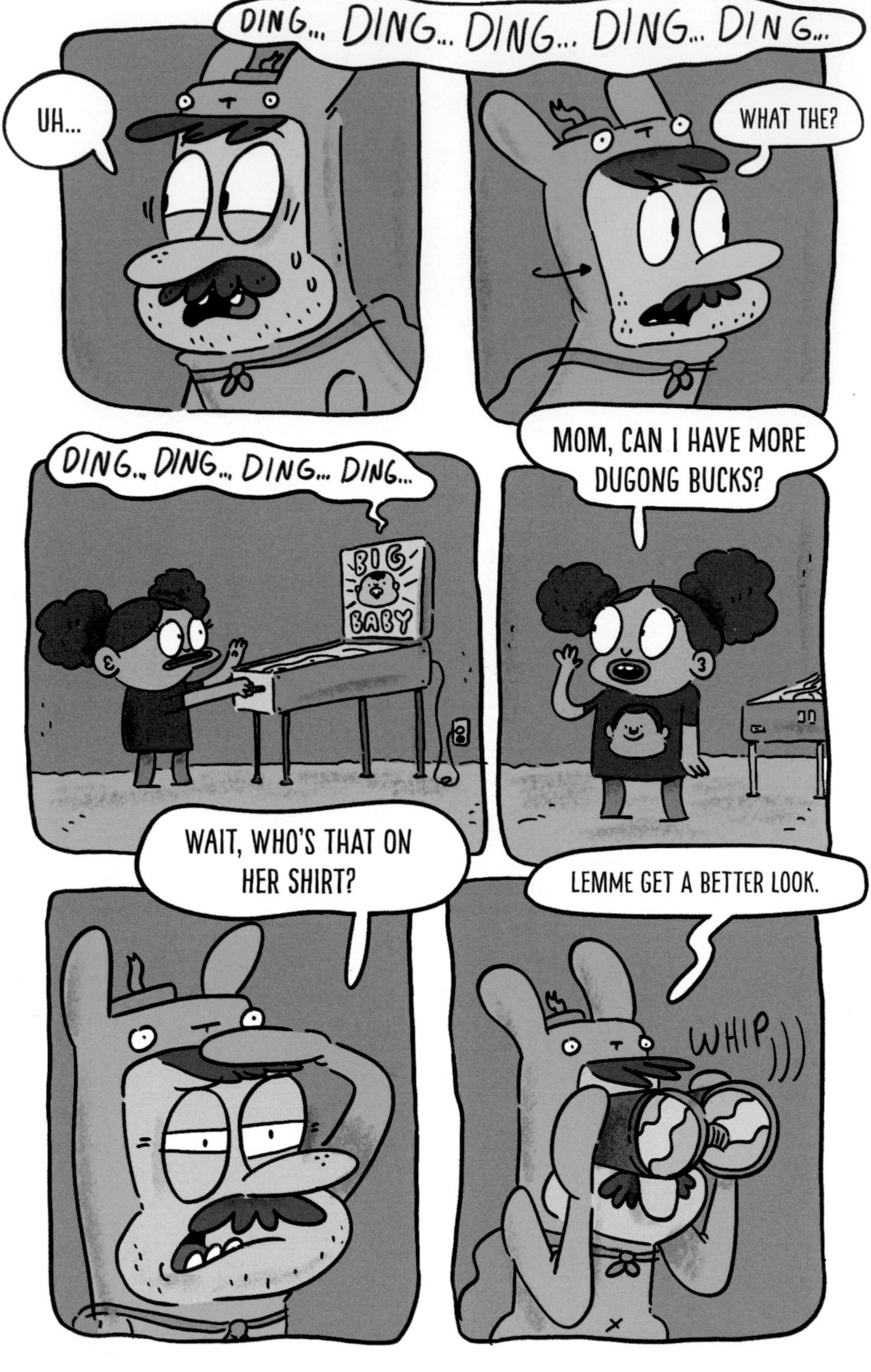
DING... DING... DING... DING... DING...
UH...
WHAT THE?
DING... DING... DING... DING...
BIG BABY
MOM, CAN I HAVE MORE DUGONG BUCKS?
WAIT, WHO'S THAT ON HER SHIRT?
LEMME GET A BETTER LOOK.
WHIP

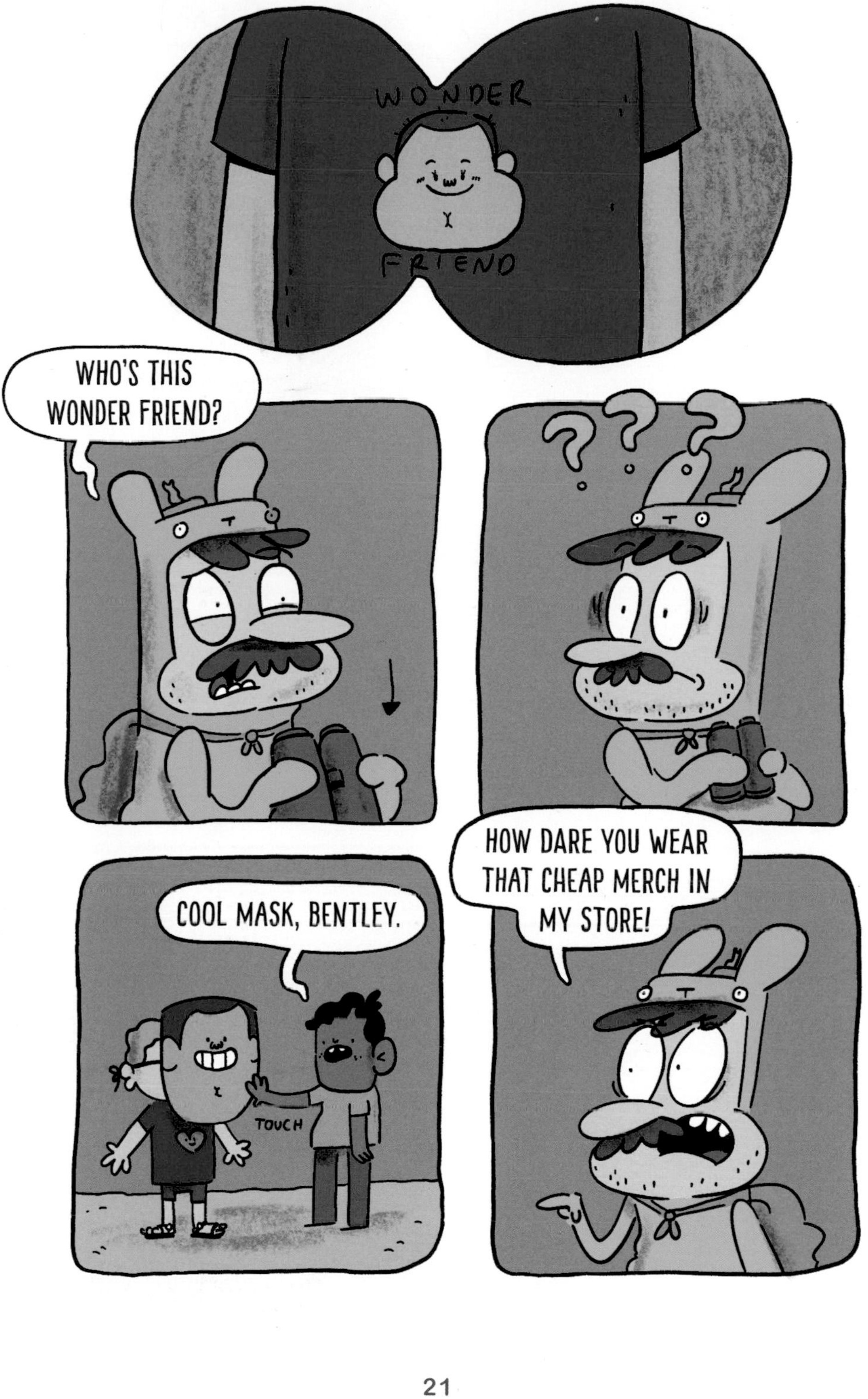
WONDER
FRIEND
WHO'S THIS WONDER FRIEND?
COOL MASK, BENTLEY.
TOUCH
HOW DARE YOU WEAR THAT CHEAP MERCH IN MY STORE!

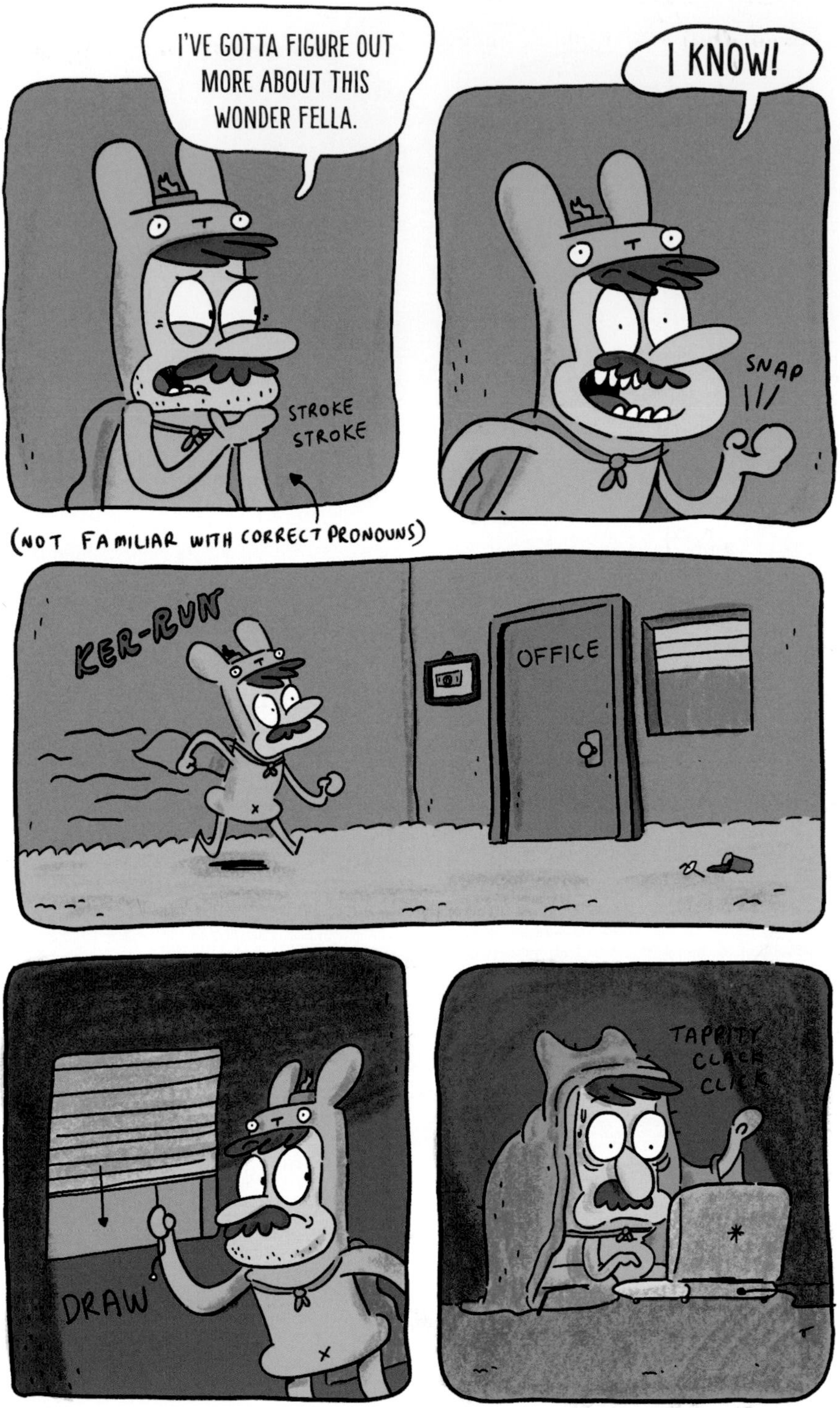
I'VE GOTTA FIGURE OUT MORE ABOUT THIS WONDER FELLA.
STROKE STROKE
(NOT FAMILIAR WITH CORRECT PRONOUNS)
I KNOW!
SNAP
KER-RUN
OFFICE
DRAW
TAPPITY CLACK CLICK

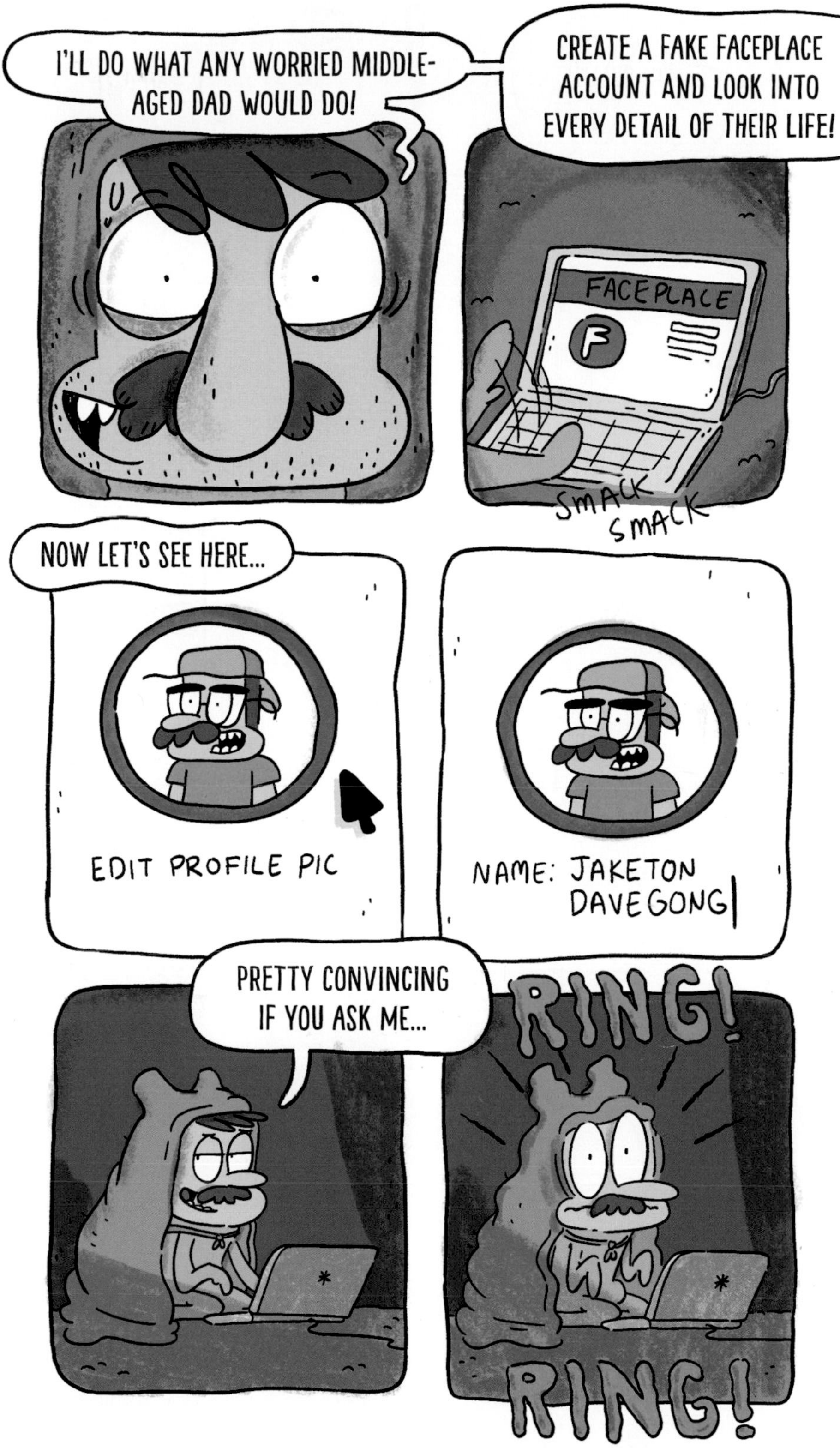
I'LL DO WHAT ANY WORRIED MIDDLE-AGED DAD WOULD DO!
CREATE A FAKE FACEPLACE ACCOUNT AND LOOK INTO EVERY DETAIL OF THEIR LIFE!
FACEPLACE
F
SMACK SMACK
NOW LET'S SEE HERE...
EDIT PROFILE PIC
NAME: JAKETON DAVEGONG
PRETTY CONVINCING IF YOU ASK ME...
RING!
RING!

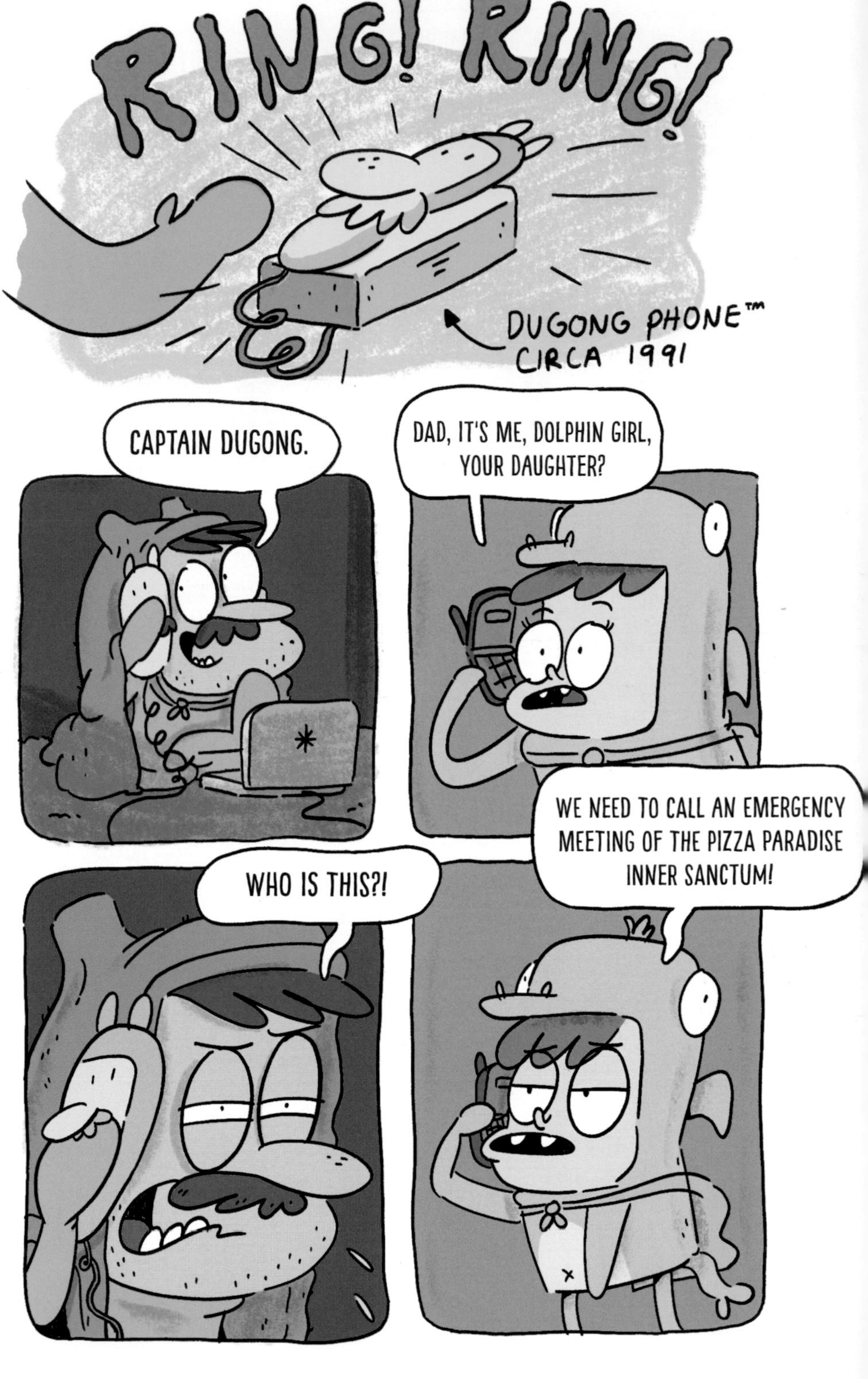
RING! RING!
DUGONG PHONE™ CIRCA 1991
CAPTAIN DUGONG.
DAD, IT'S ME, DOLPHIN GIRL, YOUR DAUGHTER?
WHO IS THIS?!
WE NEED TO CALL AN EMERGENCY MEETING OF THE PIZZA PARADISE INNER SANCTUM!

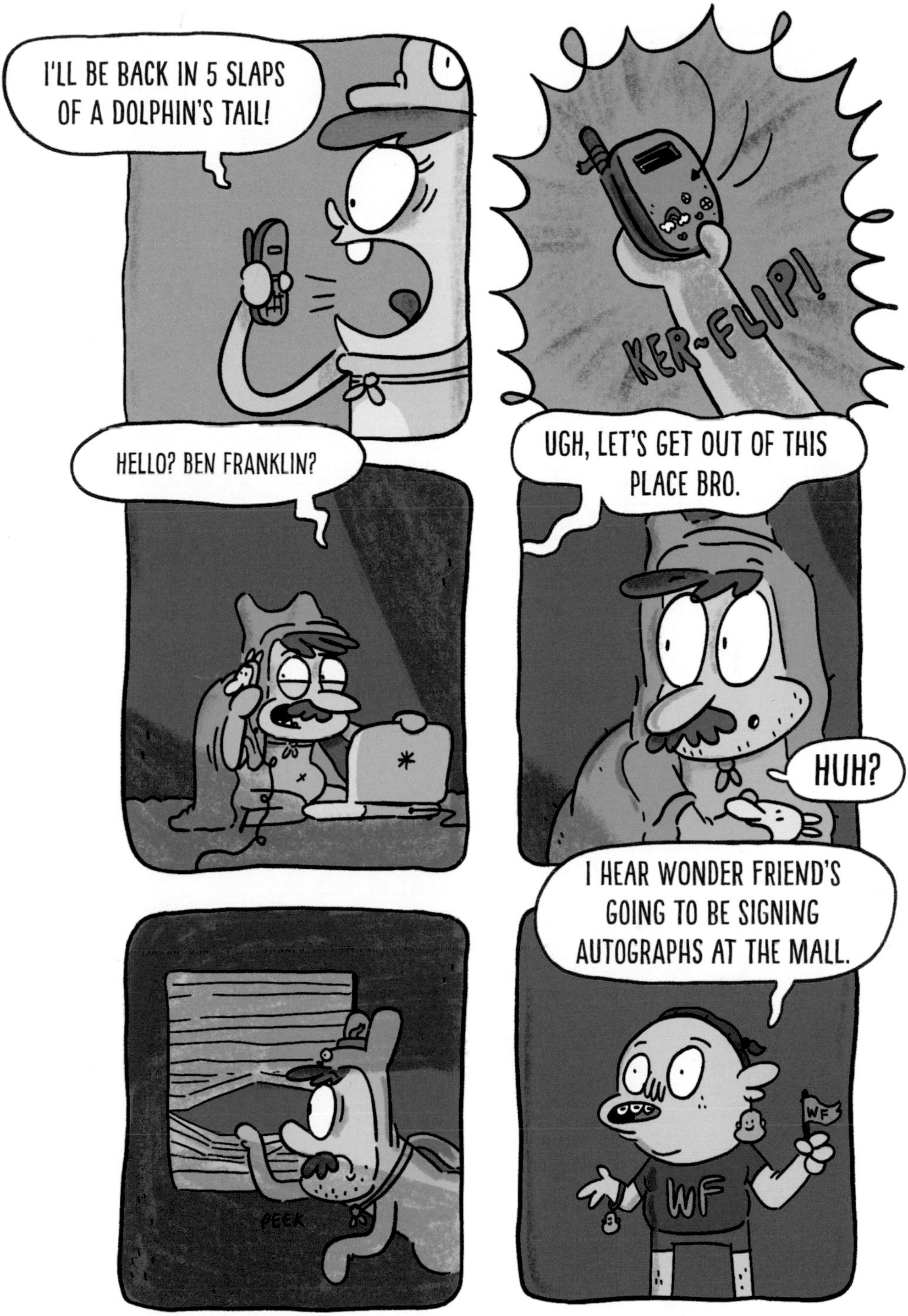
I'LL BE BACK IN 5 SLAPS OF A DOLPHIN'S TAIL!
KER-FLIP!
HELLO? BEN FRANKLIN?
UGH, LET'S GET OUT OF THIS PLACE BRO.
HUH?
PEEK
I HEAR WONDER FRIEND'S GOING TO BE SIGNING AUTOGRAPHS AT THE MALL.
WF
WF

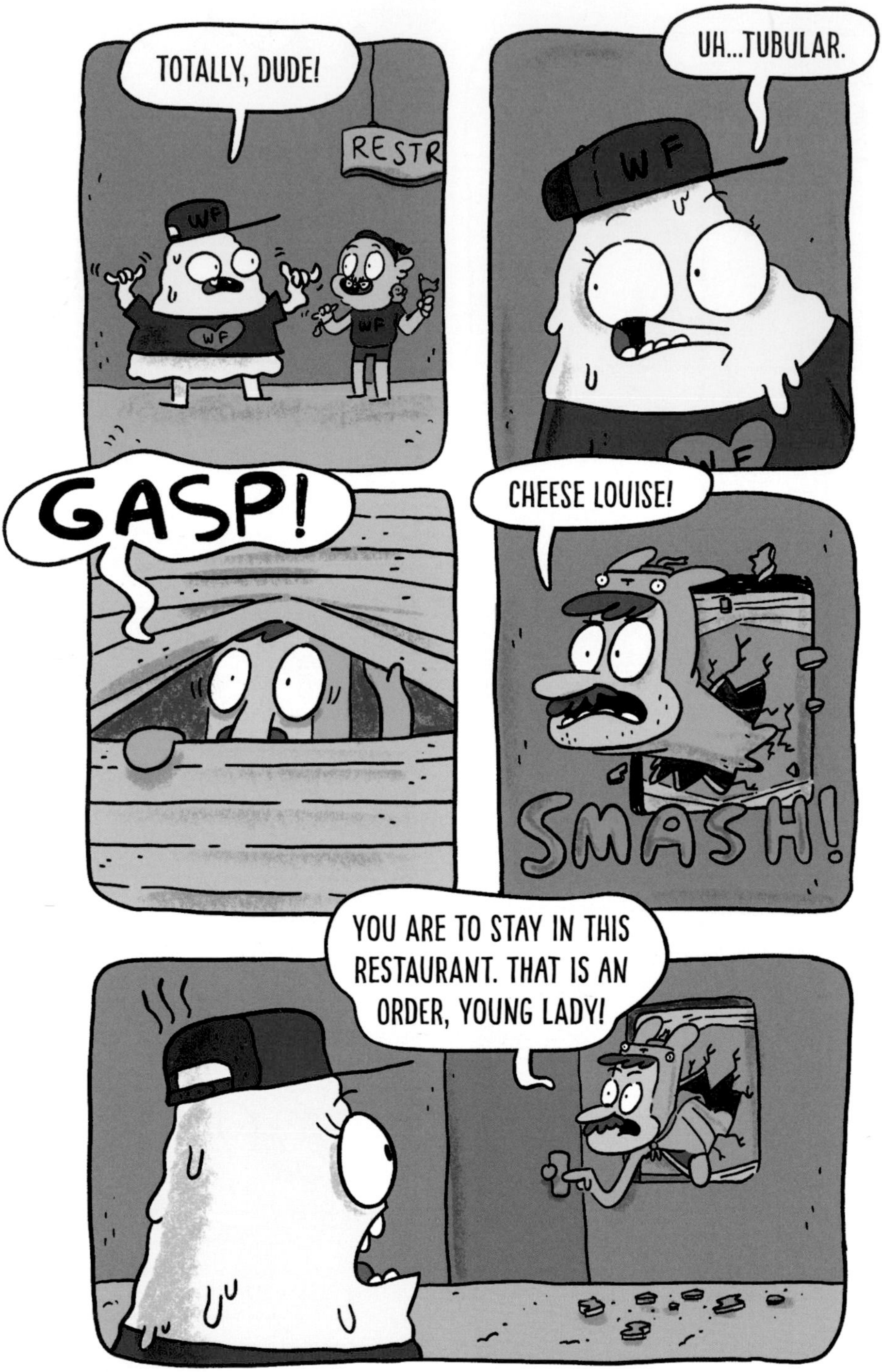
TOTALLY, DUDE!
RESTR
WF
UH...TUBULAR.
GASP!
CHEESE LOUISE!
SMASH!
YOU ARE TO STAY IN THIS RESTAURANT. THAT IS AN ORDER, YOUNG LADY!

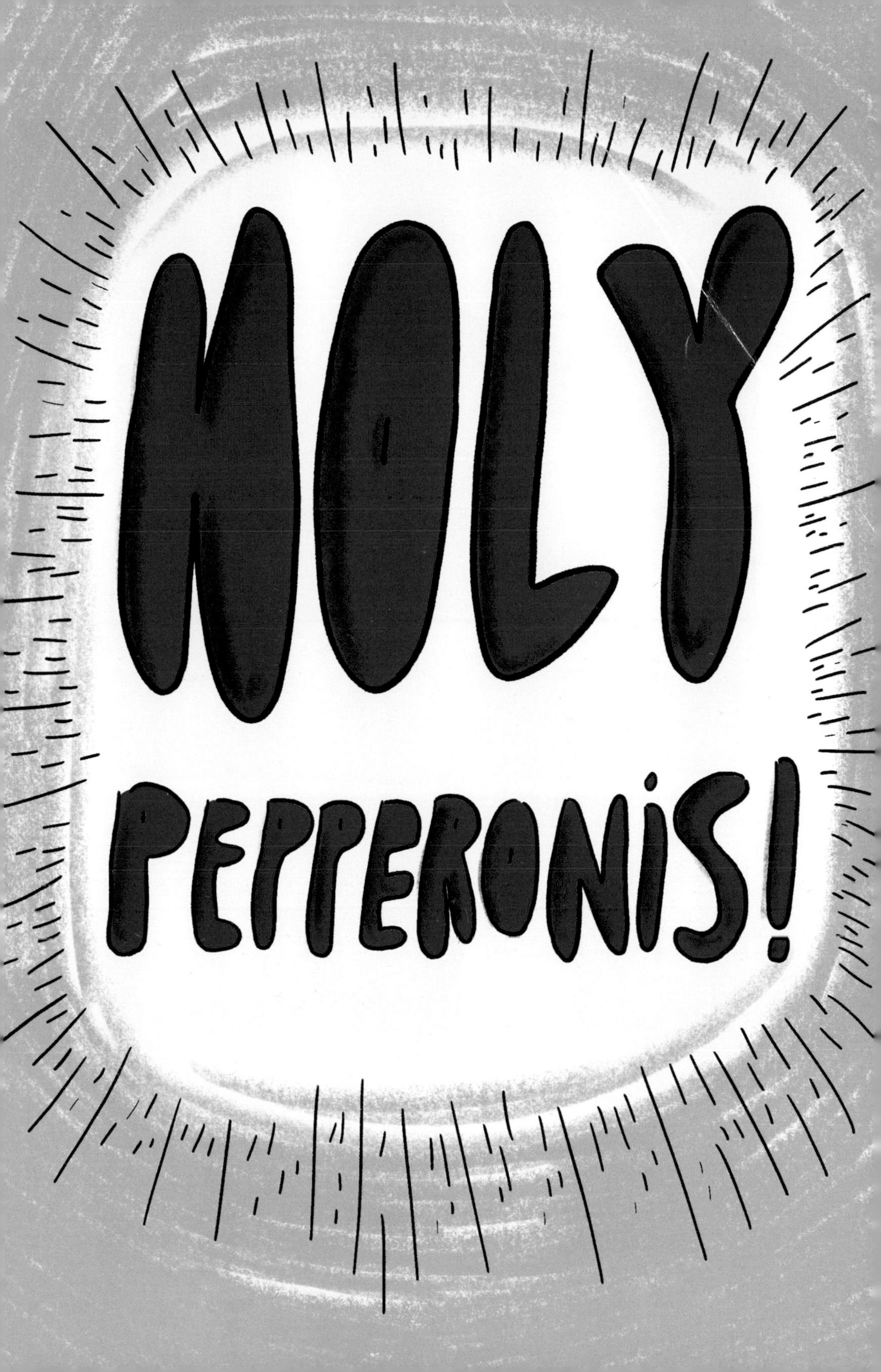
HOLY
PEPPERONIS!

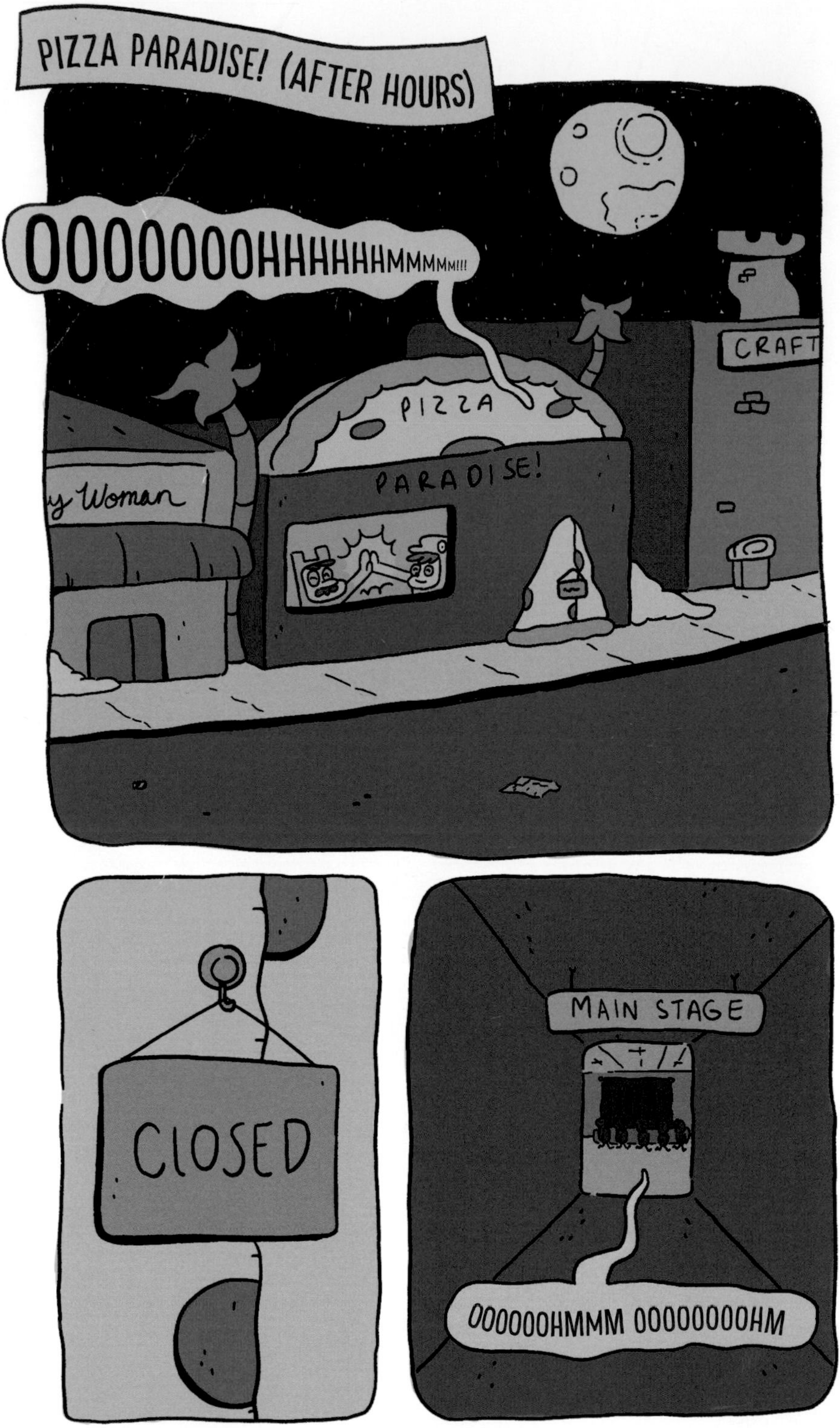
PIZZA PARADISE! (AFTER HOURS)
OOOOOOOHHHHHHMMMMM!!!
CRAFT
PIZZA
PARADISE!
y Woman
CLOSED
MAIN STAGE
OOOOOOHMMM OOOOOOOOHM

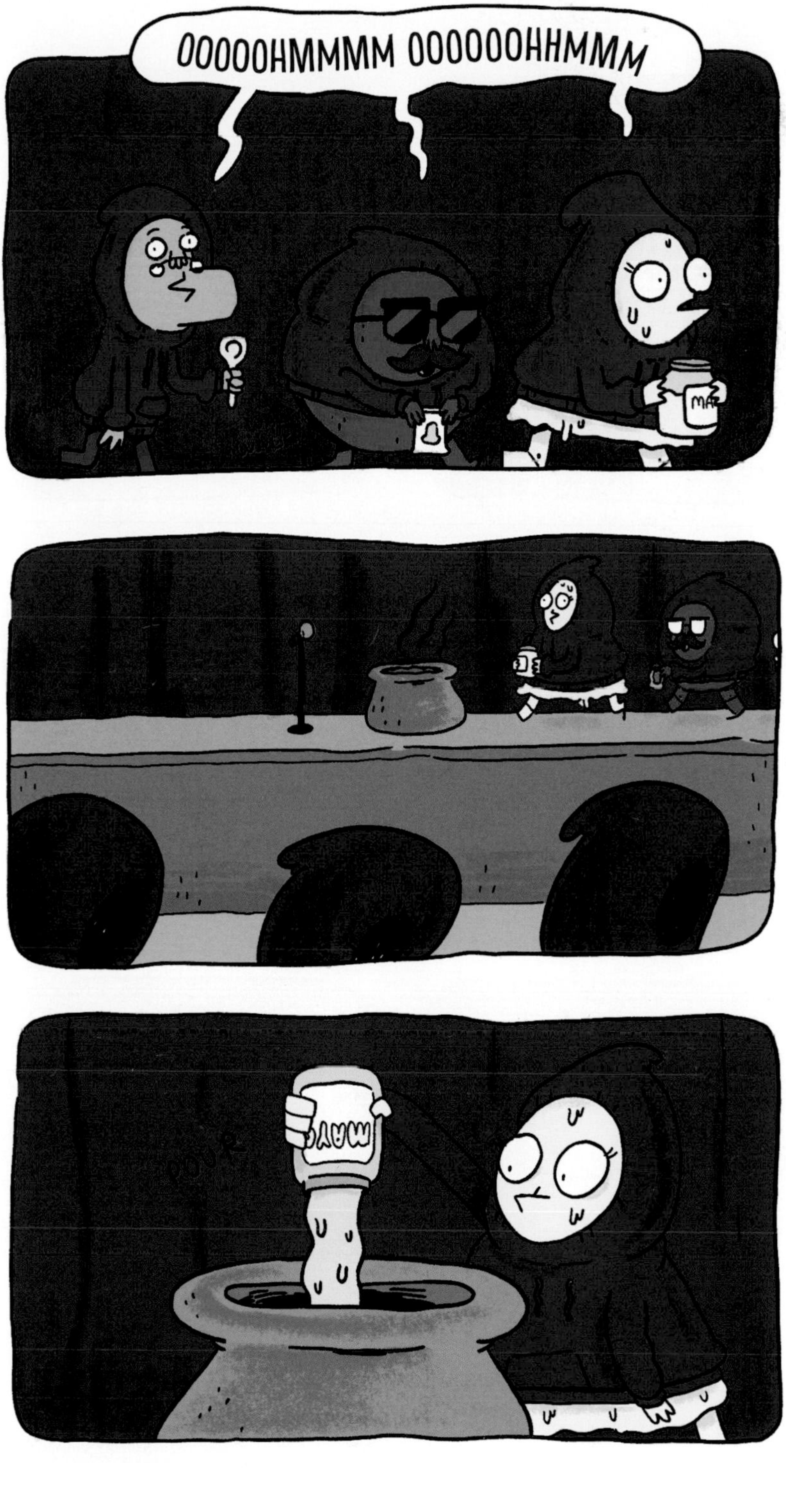
OOOOOHMMMM OOOOOOHHMMM
MA
MAYO

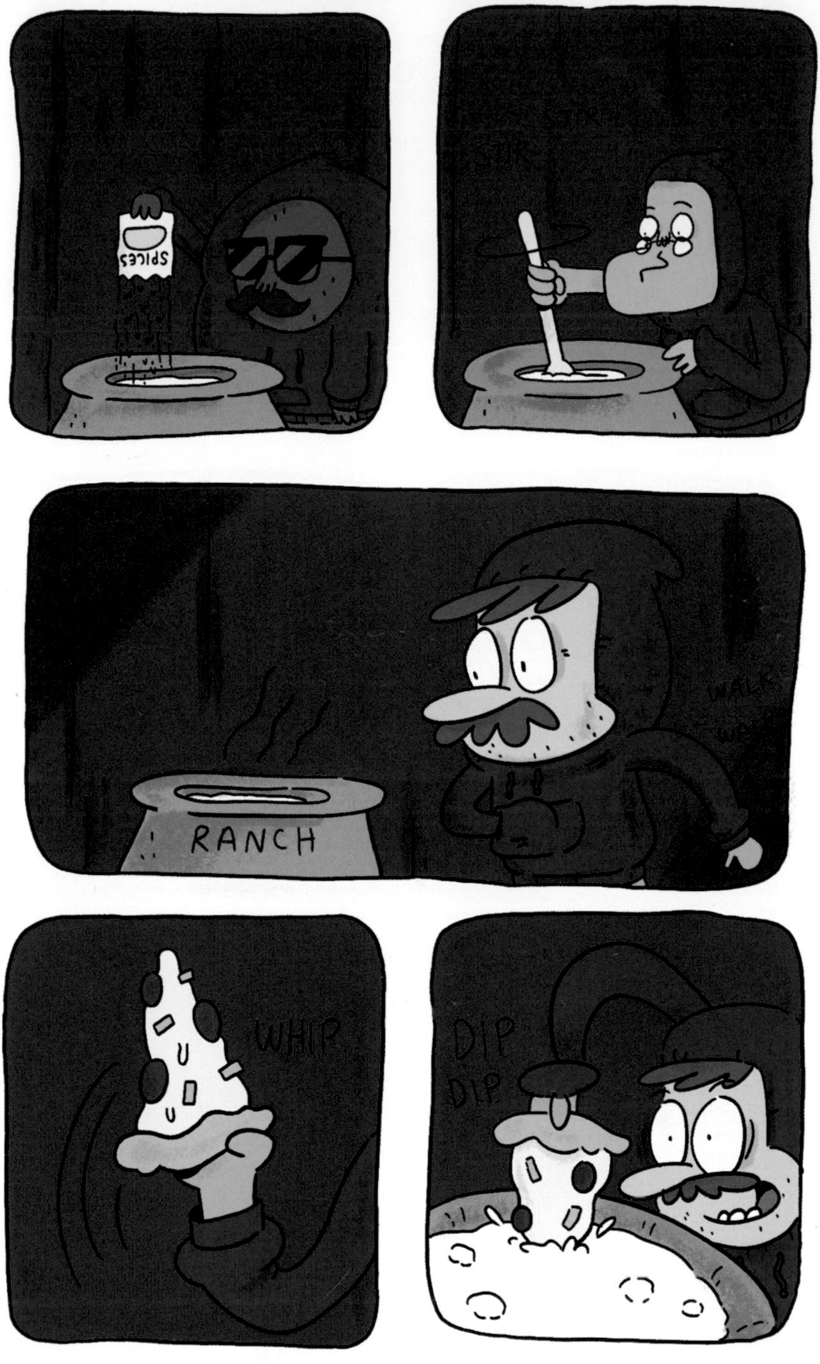
STIR
STIR
RANCH
WALK
WHIP
DIP
DIP

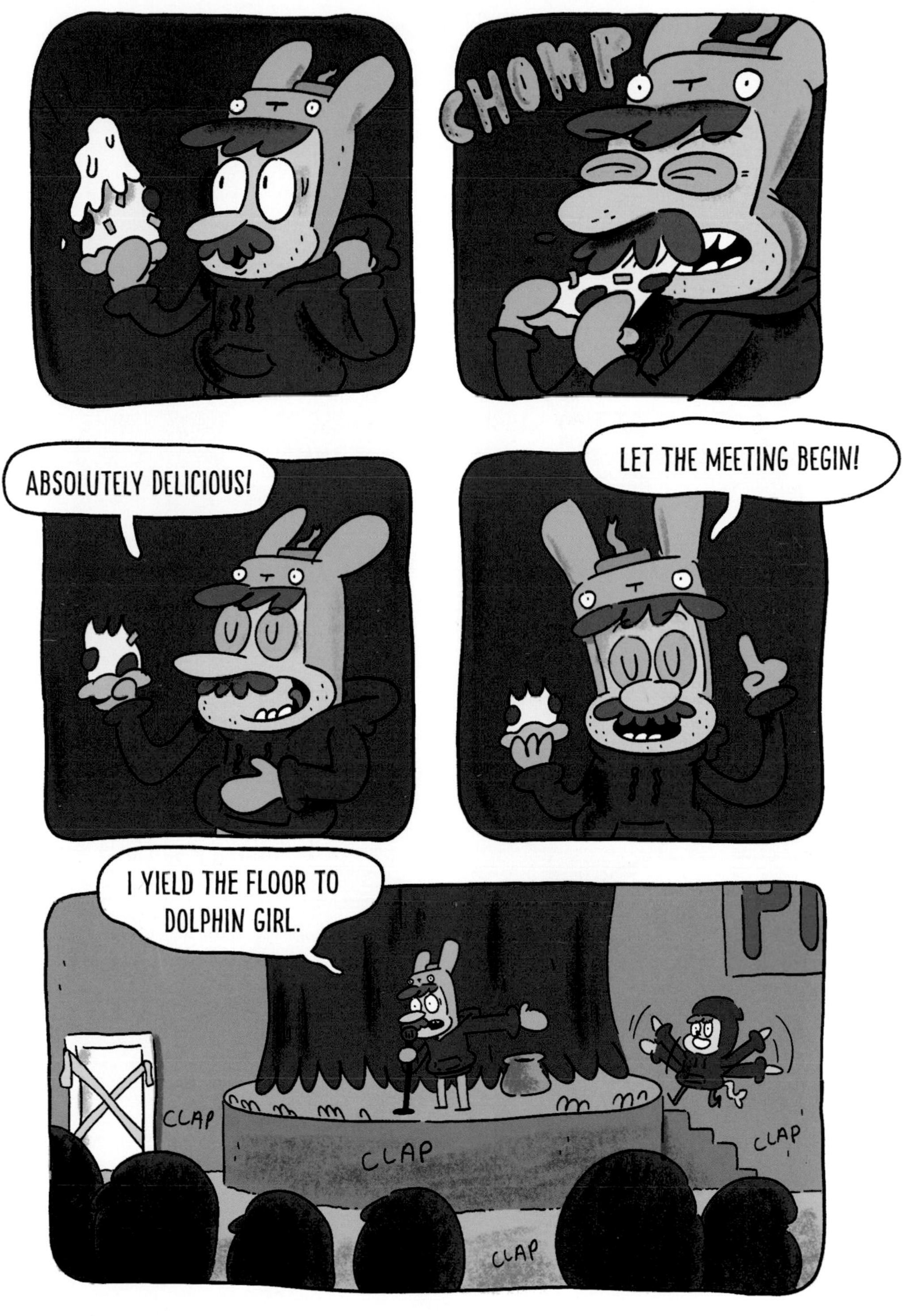
CHOMP
ABSOLUTELY DELICIOUS!
LET THE MEETING BEGIN!
I YIELD THE FLOOR TO DOLPHIN GIRL.
CLAP
CLAP
CLAP
CLAP

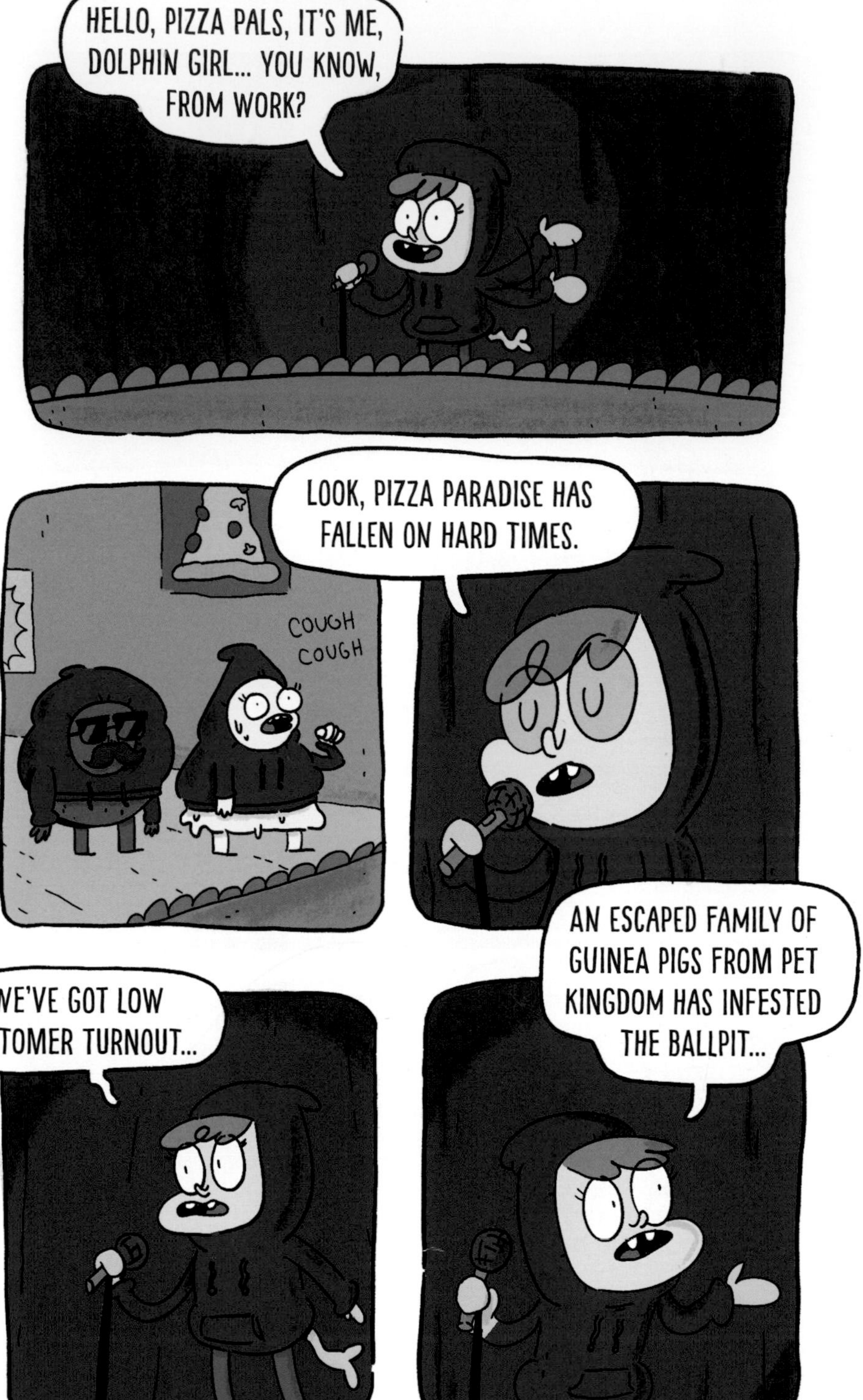
HELLO, PIZZA PALS, IT'S ME, DOLPHIN GIRL... YOU KNOW, FROM WORK?
LOOK, PIZZA PARADISE HAS FALLEN ON HARD TIMES.
COUGH COUGH
WE'VE GOT LOW CUSTOMER TURNOUT...
AN ESCAPED FAMILY OF GUINEA PIGS FROM PET KINGDOM HAS INFESTED THE BALLPIT...

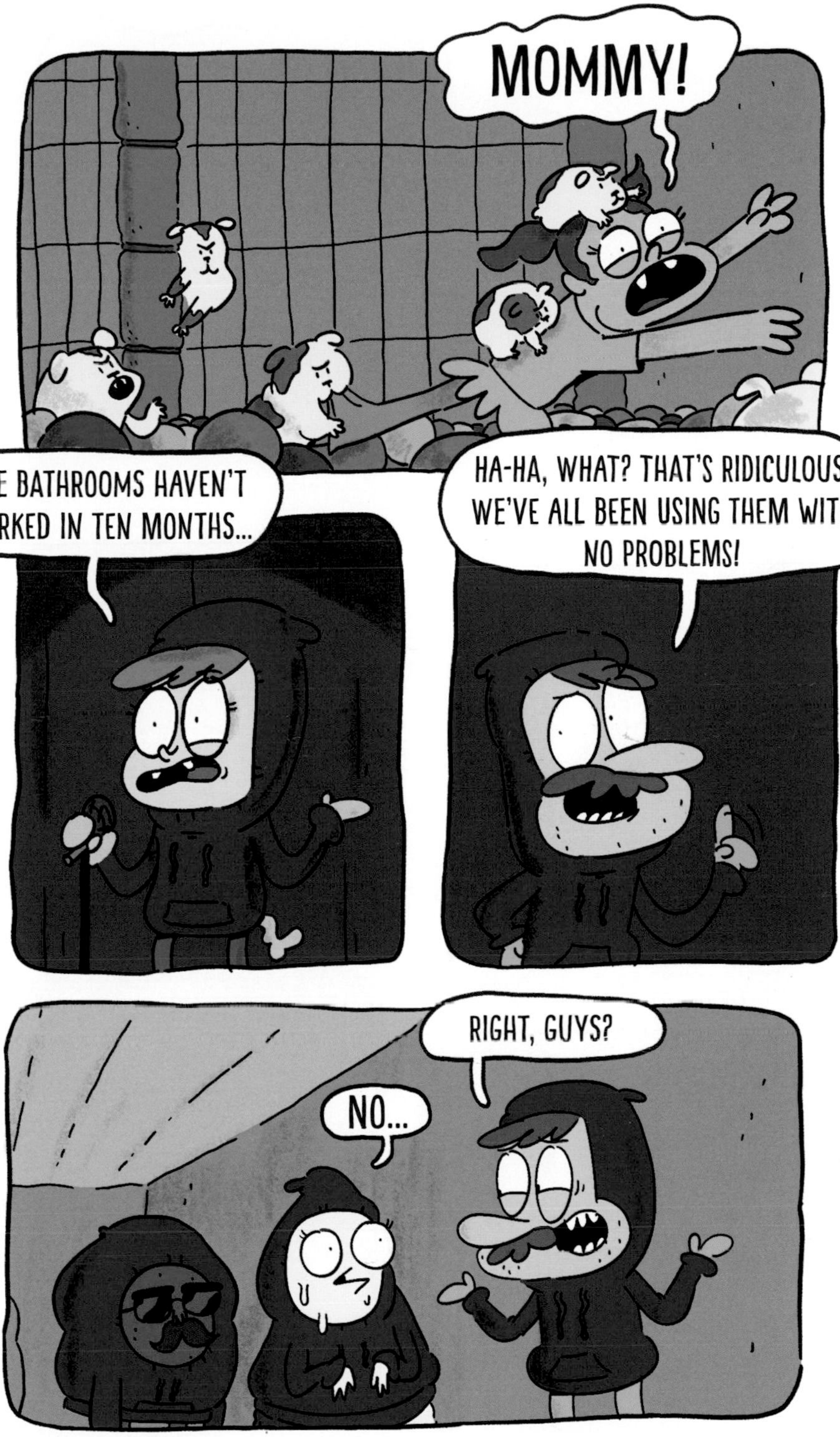
MOMMY!
THE BATHROOMS HAVEN'T WORKED IN TEN MONTHS...
HA-HA, WHAT? THAT'S RIDICULOUS, WE'VE ALL BEEN USING THEM WITH NO PROBLEMS!
RIGHT, GUYS?
NO...

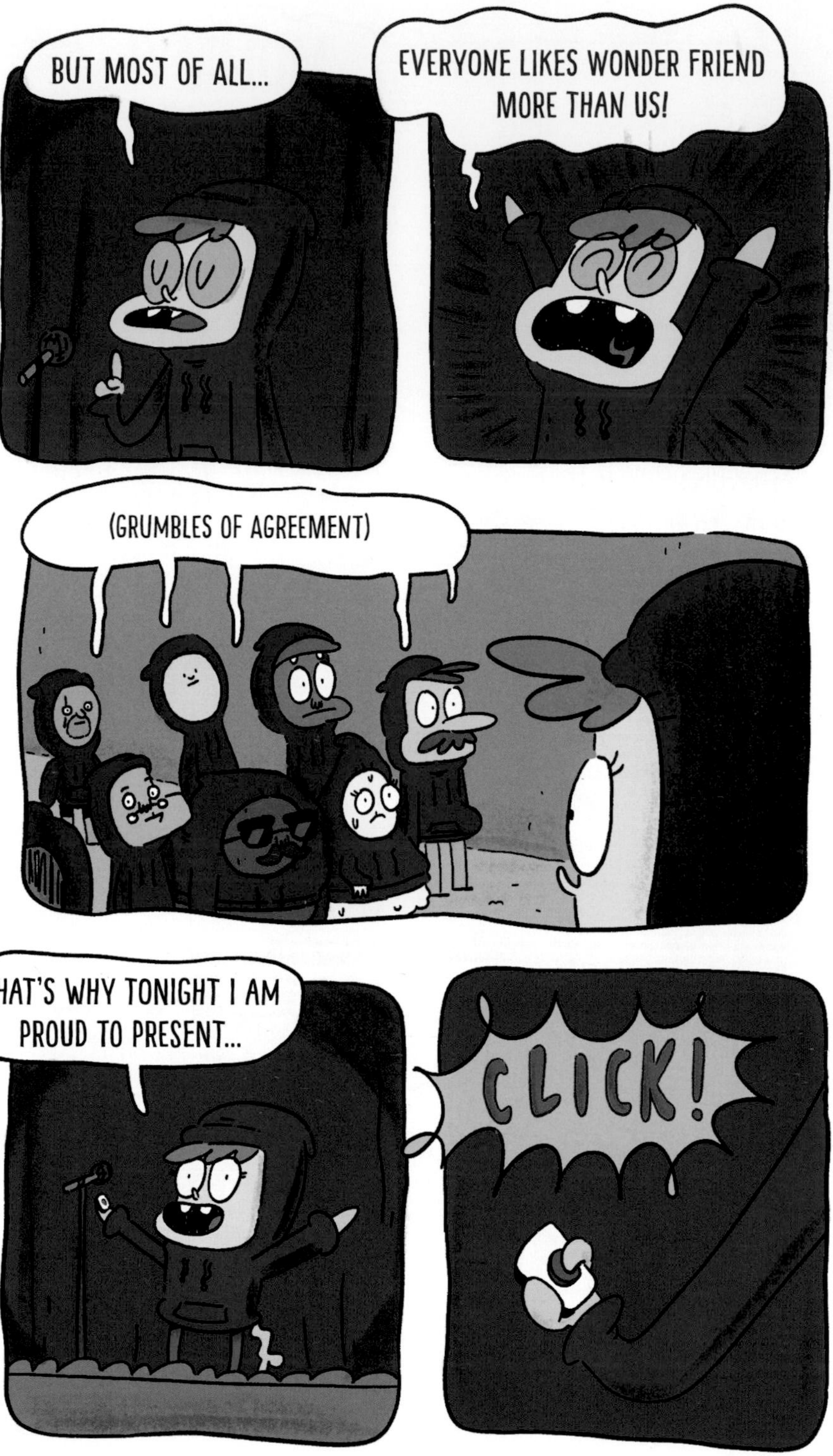
BUT MOST OF ALL...
EVERYONE LIKES WONDER FRIEND MORE THAN US!
(GRUMBLES OF AGREEMENT)
THAT'S WHY TONIGHT I AM PROUD TO PRESENT...
CLICK!

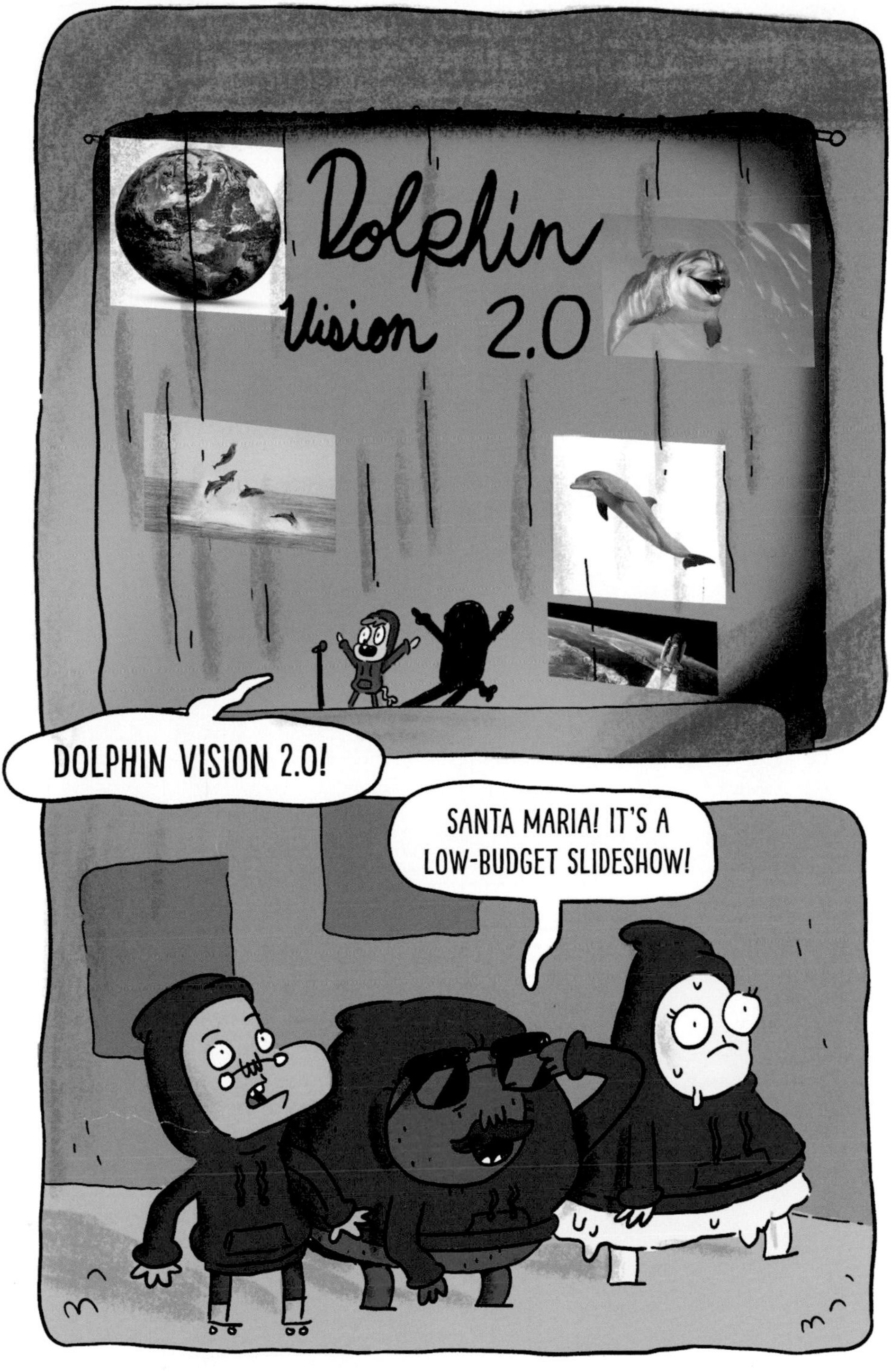
Dolphin Vision 2.0
DOLPHIN VISION 2.0!
SANTA MARIA! IT'S A LOW-BUDGET SLIDESHOW!

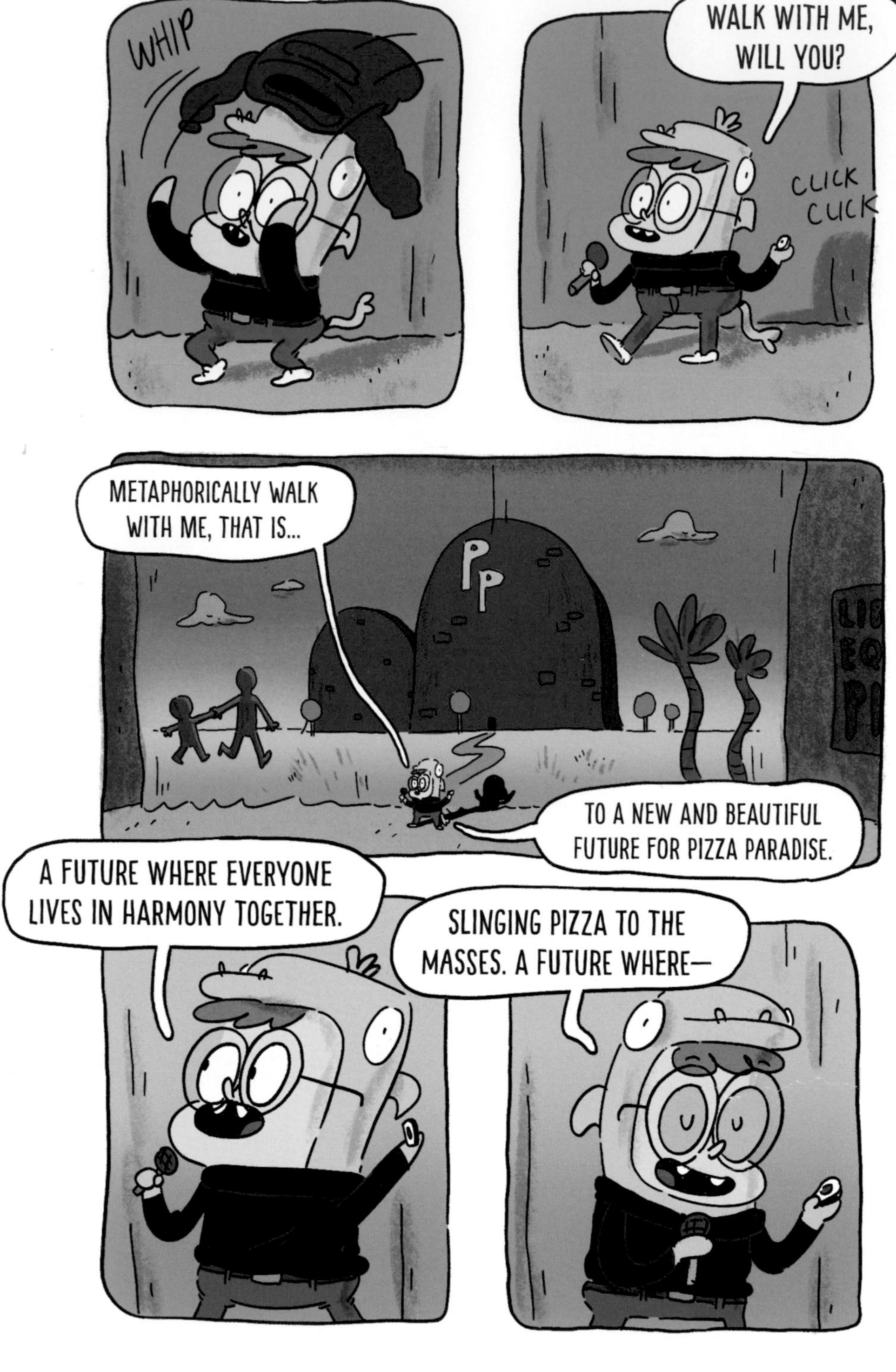
WHIP
WALK WITH ME, WILL YOU?
CLICK CLICK
METAPHORICALLY WALK WITH ME, THAT IS...
PP
TO A NEW AND BEAUTIFUL FUTURE FOR PIZZA PARADISE.
A FUTURE WHERE EVERYONE LIVES IN HARMONY TOGETHER.
SLINGING PIZZA TO THE MASSES. A FUTURE WHERE—

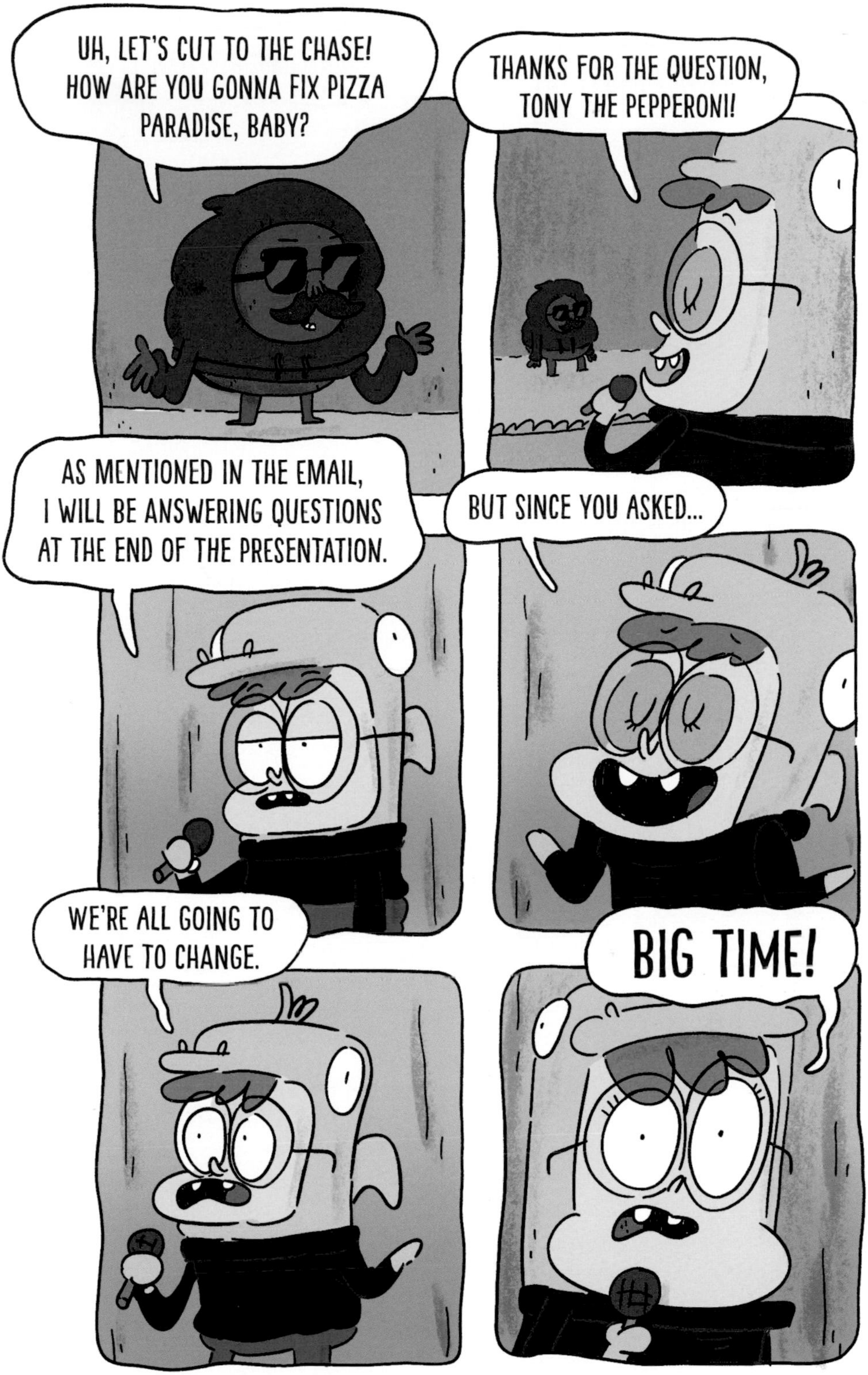
UH, LET'S CUT TO THE CHASE! HOW ARE YOU GONNA FIX PIZZA PARADISE, BABY?
THANKS FOR THE QUESTION, TONY THE PEPPERONI!
AS MENTIONED IN THE EMAIL, I WILL BE ANSWERING QUESTIONS AT THE END OF THE PRESENTATION.
BUT SINCE YOU ASKED...
WE'RE ALL GOING TO HAVE TO CHANGE.
BIG TIME!

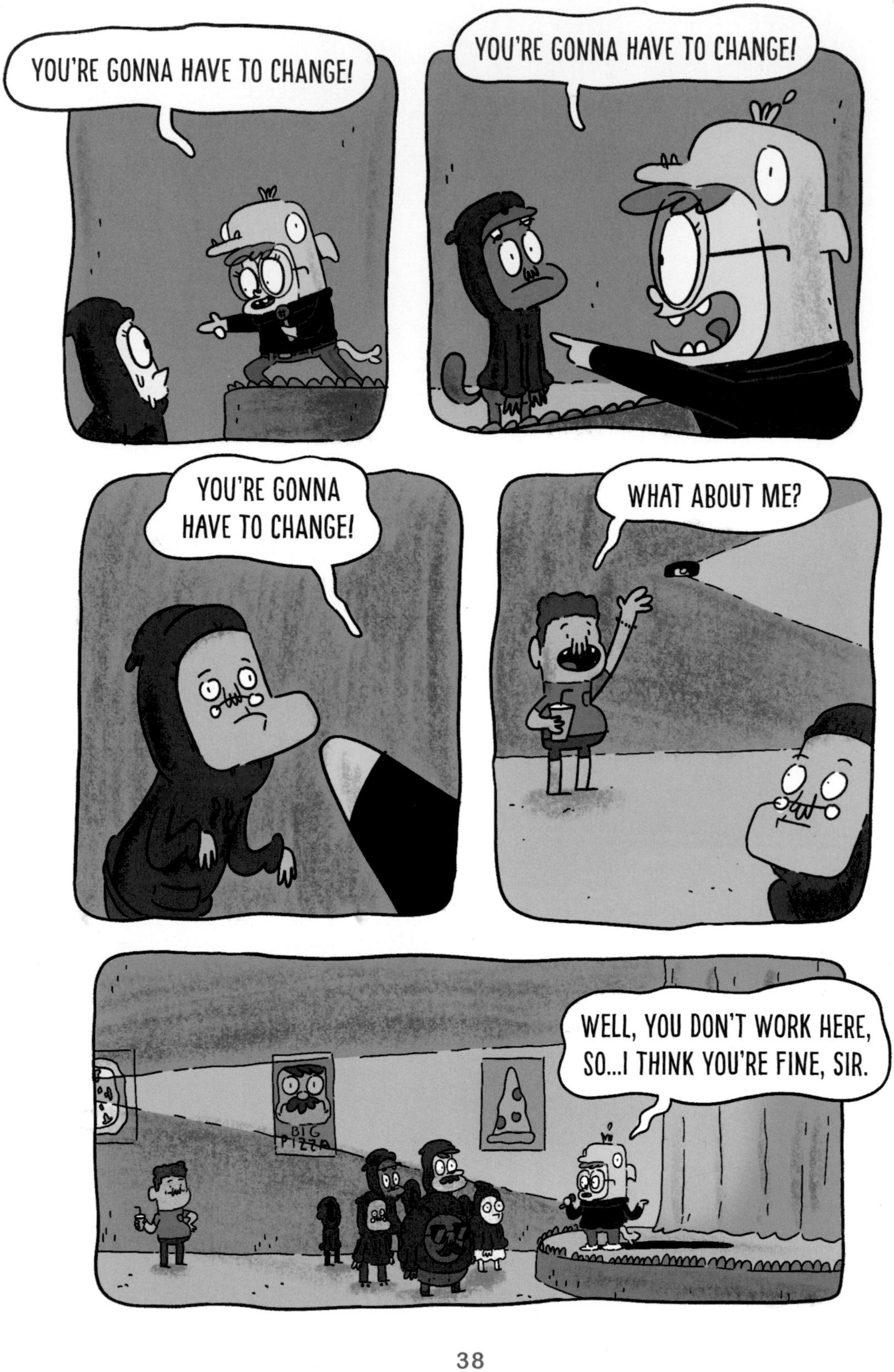
YOU'RE GONNA HAVE TO CHANGE!
YOU'RE GONNA HAVE TO CHANGE!
YOU'RE GONNA HAVE TO CHANGE!
WHAT ABOUT ME?
BIG PIZZA
WELL, YOU DON'T WORK HERE, SO...I THINK YOU'RE FINE, SIR.

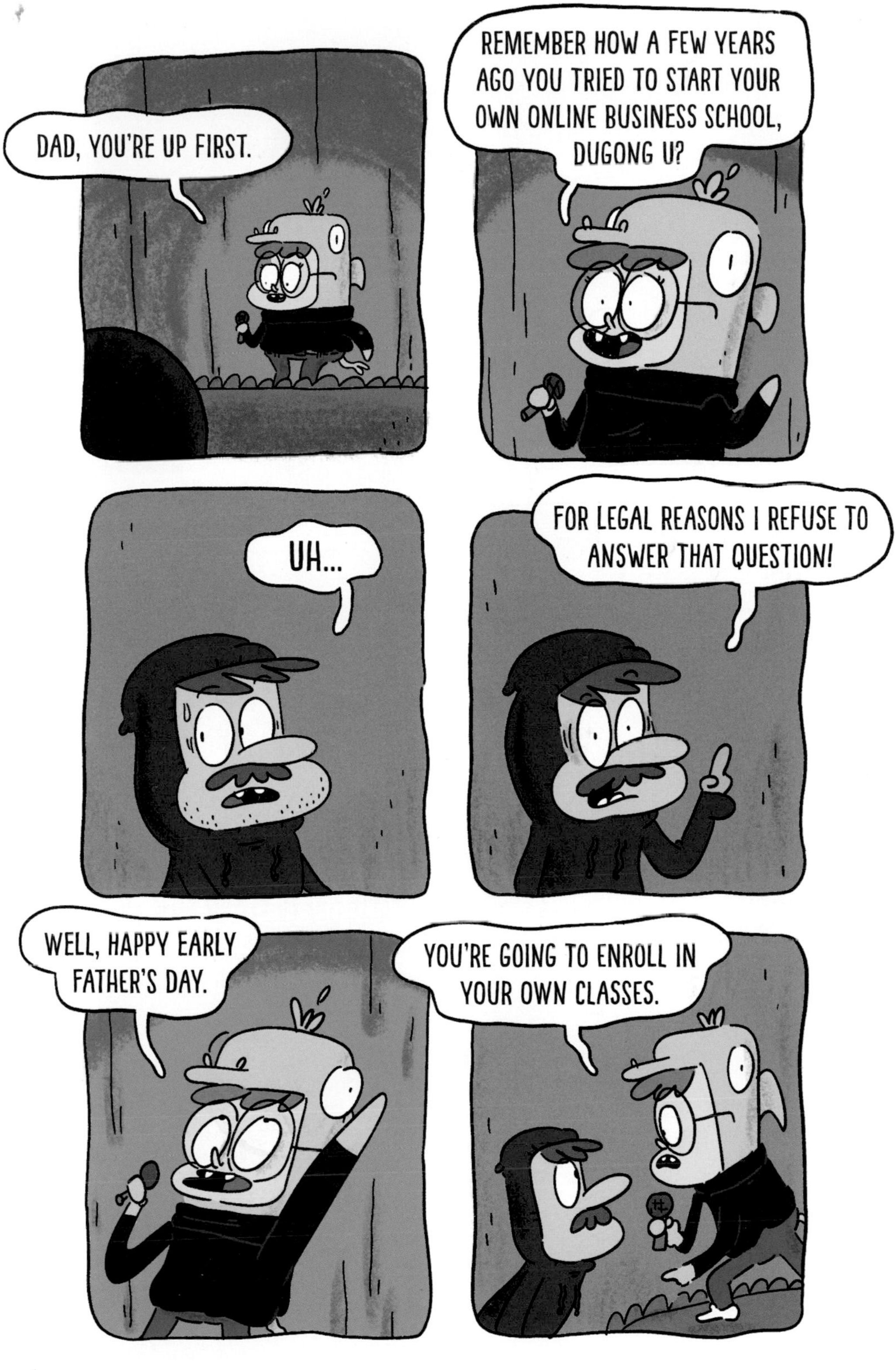
DAD, YOU'RE UP FIRST.
REMEMBER HOW A FEW YEARS AGO YOU TRIED TO START YOUR OWN ONLINE BUSINESS SCHOOL, DUGONG U?
UH...
FOR LEGAL REASONS I REFUSE TO ANSWER THAT QUESTION!
WELL, HAPPY EARLY FATHER'S DAY.
YOU'RE GOING TO ENROLL IN YOUR OWN CLASSES.

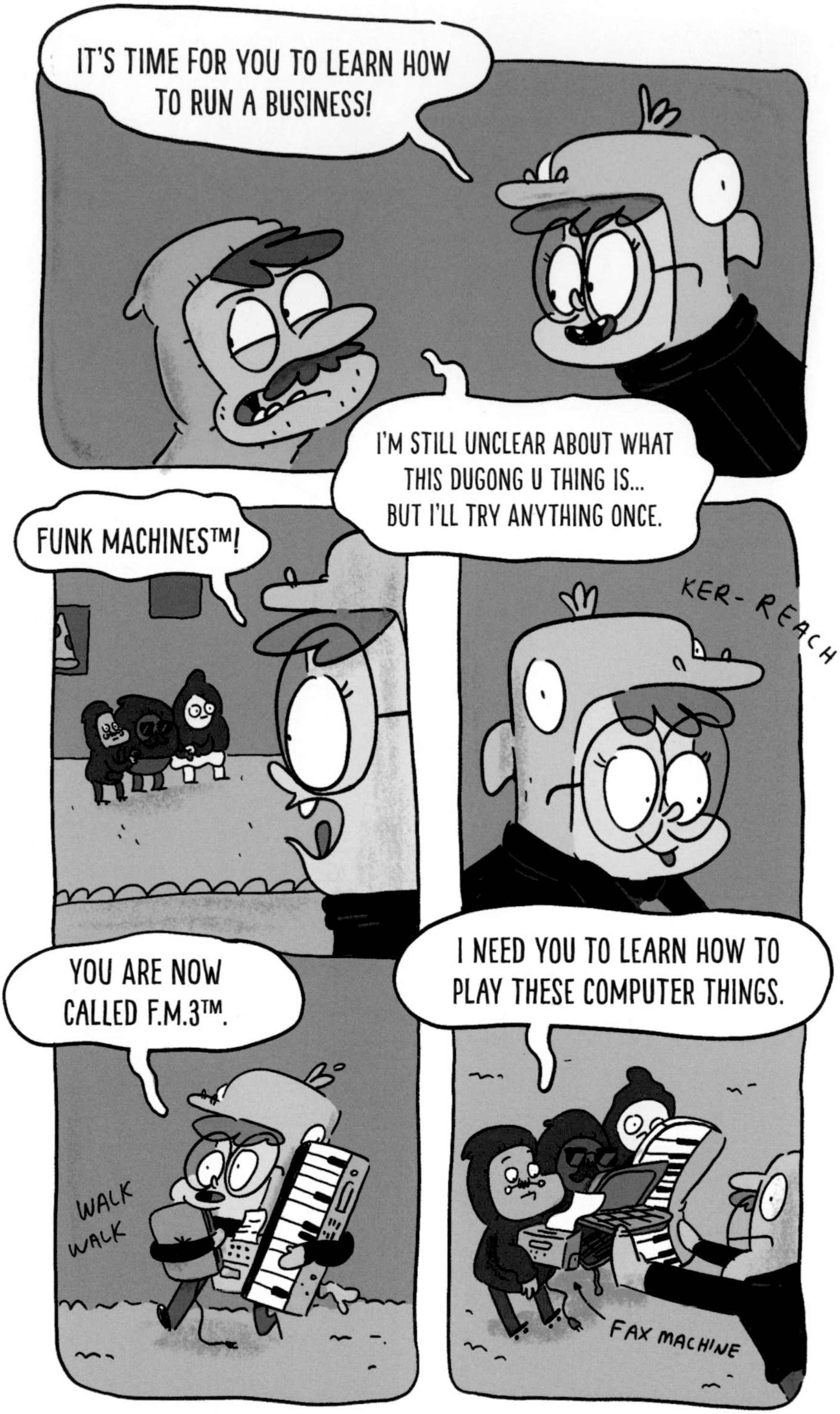
IT'S TIME FOR YOU TO LEARN HOW TO RUN A BUSINESS!
I'M STILL UNCLEAR ABOUT WHAT THIS DUGONG U THING IS... BUT I'LL TRY ANYTHING ONCE.
FUNK MACHINES™!
KER-REACH
YOU ARE NOW CALLED F.M.3™.
WALK WALK
I NEED YOU TO LEARN HOW TO PLAY THESE COMPUTER THINGS.
FAX MACHINE

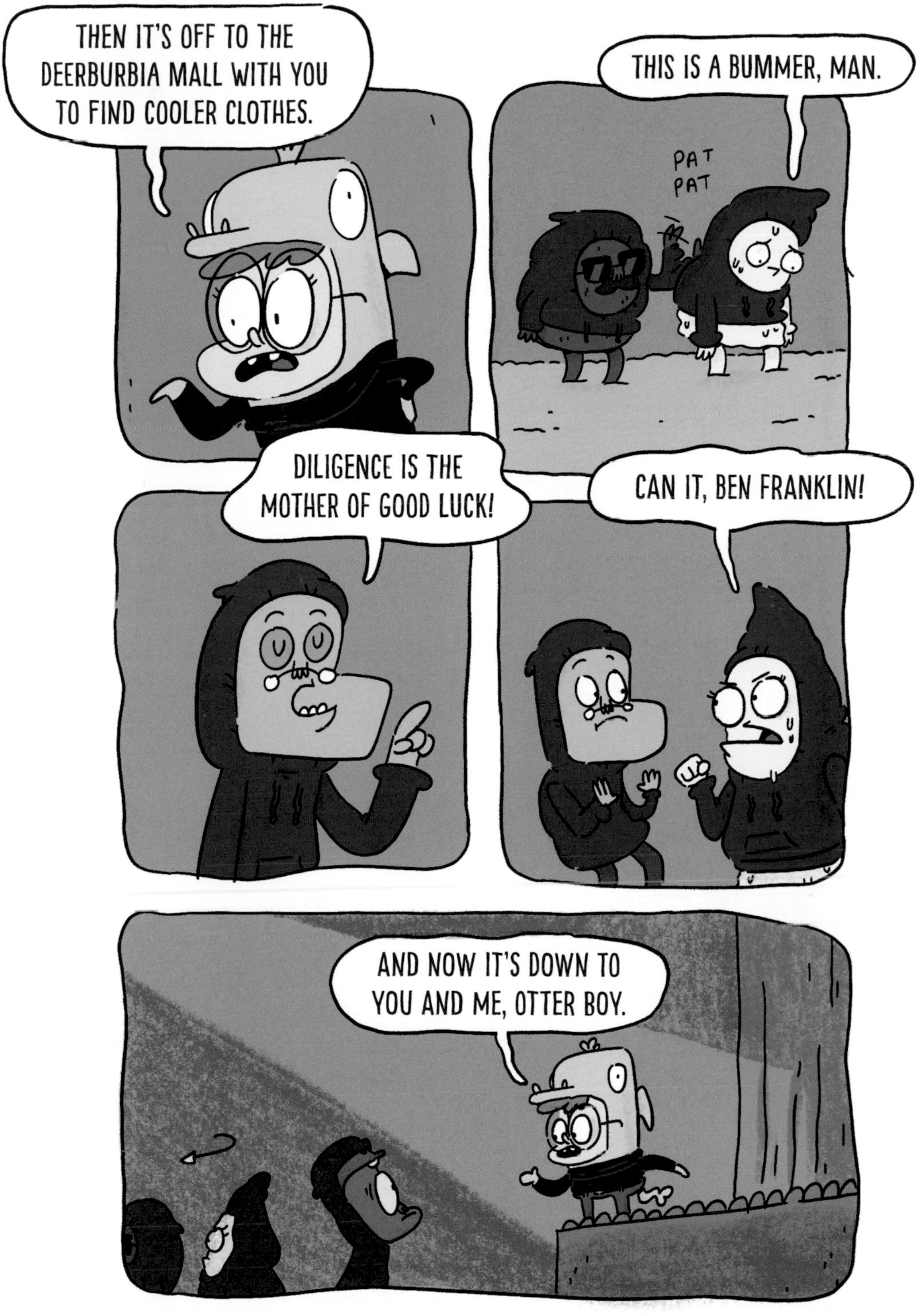
THEN IT'S OFF TO THE DEERBURBIA MALL WITH YOU TO FIND COOLER CLOTHES.
THIS IS A BUMMER, MAN.
PAT PAT
DILIGENCE IS THE MOTHER OF GOOD LUCK!
CAN IT, BEN FRANKLIN!
AND NOW IT'S DOWN TO YOU AND ME, OTTER BOY.

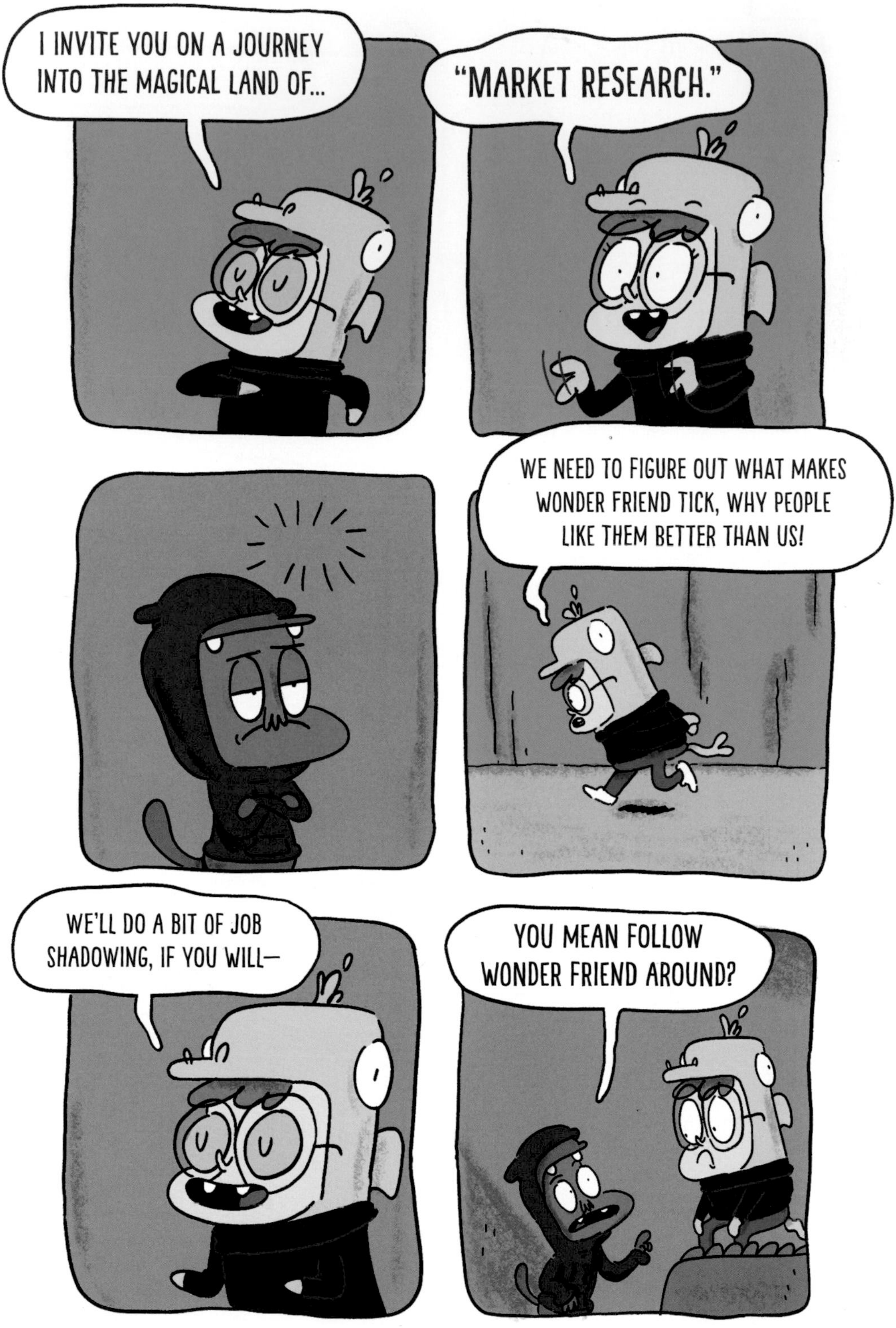
I INVITE YOU ON A JOURNEY INTO THE MAGICAL LAND OF...
"MARKET RESEARCH."
WE NEED TO FIGURE OUT WHAT MAKES WONDER FRIEND TICK, WHY PEOPLE LIKE THEM BETTER THAN US!
WE'LL DO A BIT OF JOB SHADOWING, IF YOU WILL—
YOU MEAN FOLLOW WONDER FRIEND AROUND?

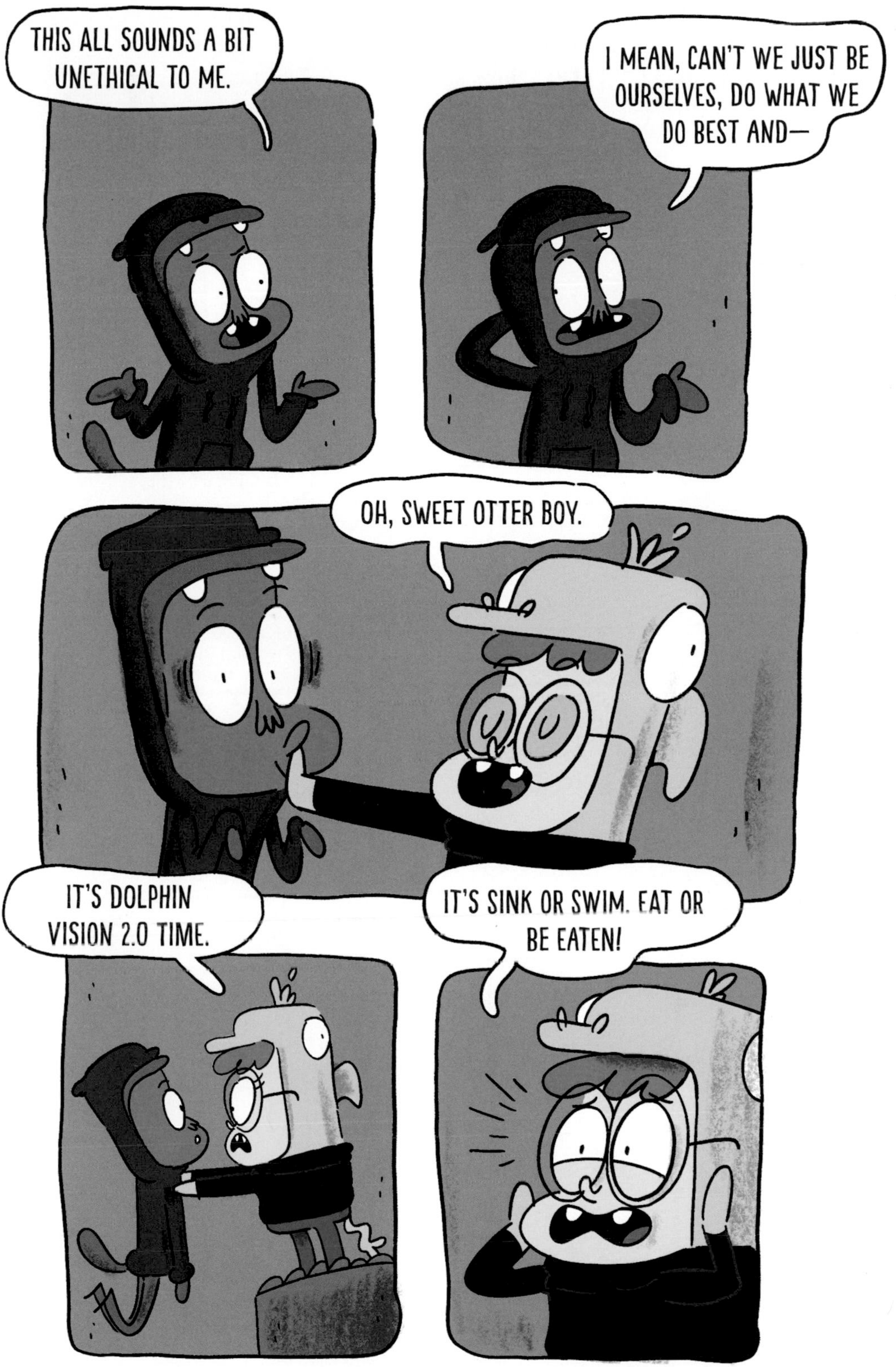
THIS ALL SOUNDS A BIT UNETHICAL TO ME.
I MEAN, CAN'T WE JUST BE OURSELVES, DO WHAT WE DO BEST AND—
OH, SWEET OTTER BOY.
IT'S DOLPHIN VISION 2.0 TIME.
IT'S SINK OR SWIM. EAT OR BE EATEN!

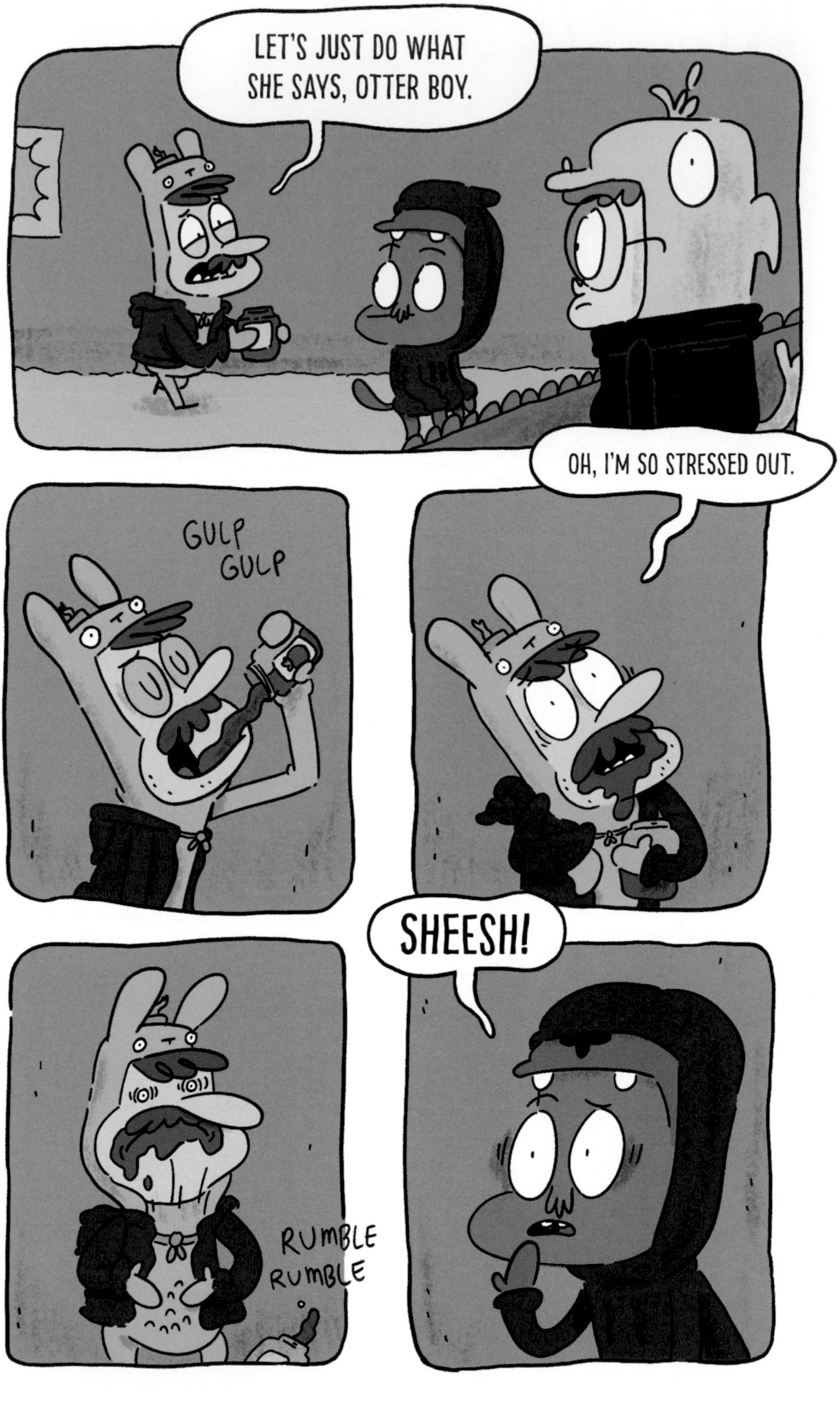
LET'S JUST DO WHAT SHE SAYS, OTTER BOY.
OH, I'M SO STRESSED OUT.
GULP
GULP
SHEESH!
RUMBLE
RUMBLE

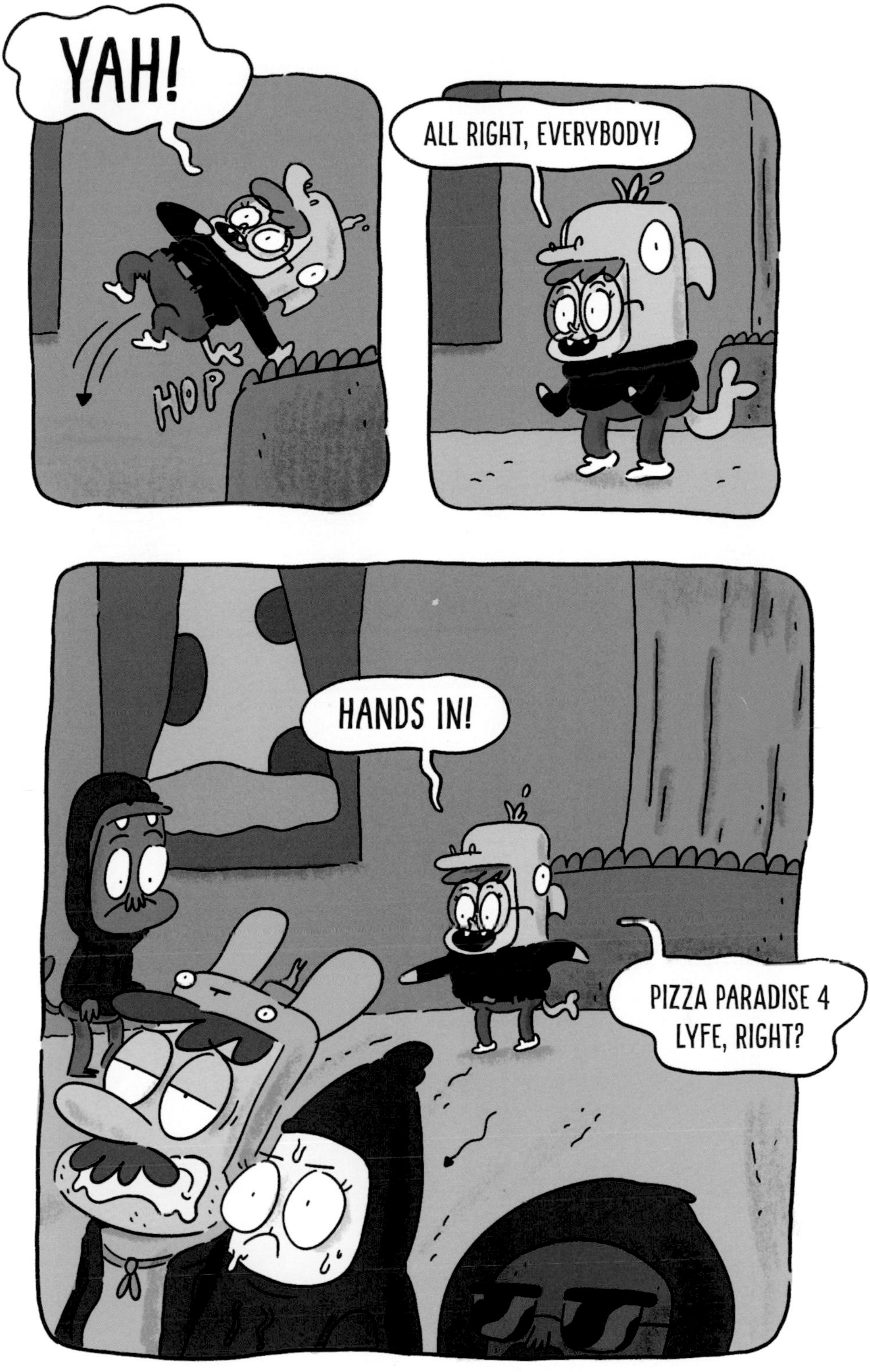
YAH!
HOP
ALL RIGHT, EVERYBODY!
HANDS IN!
PIZZA PARADISE 4 LYFE, RIGHT?

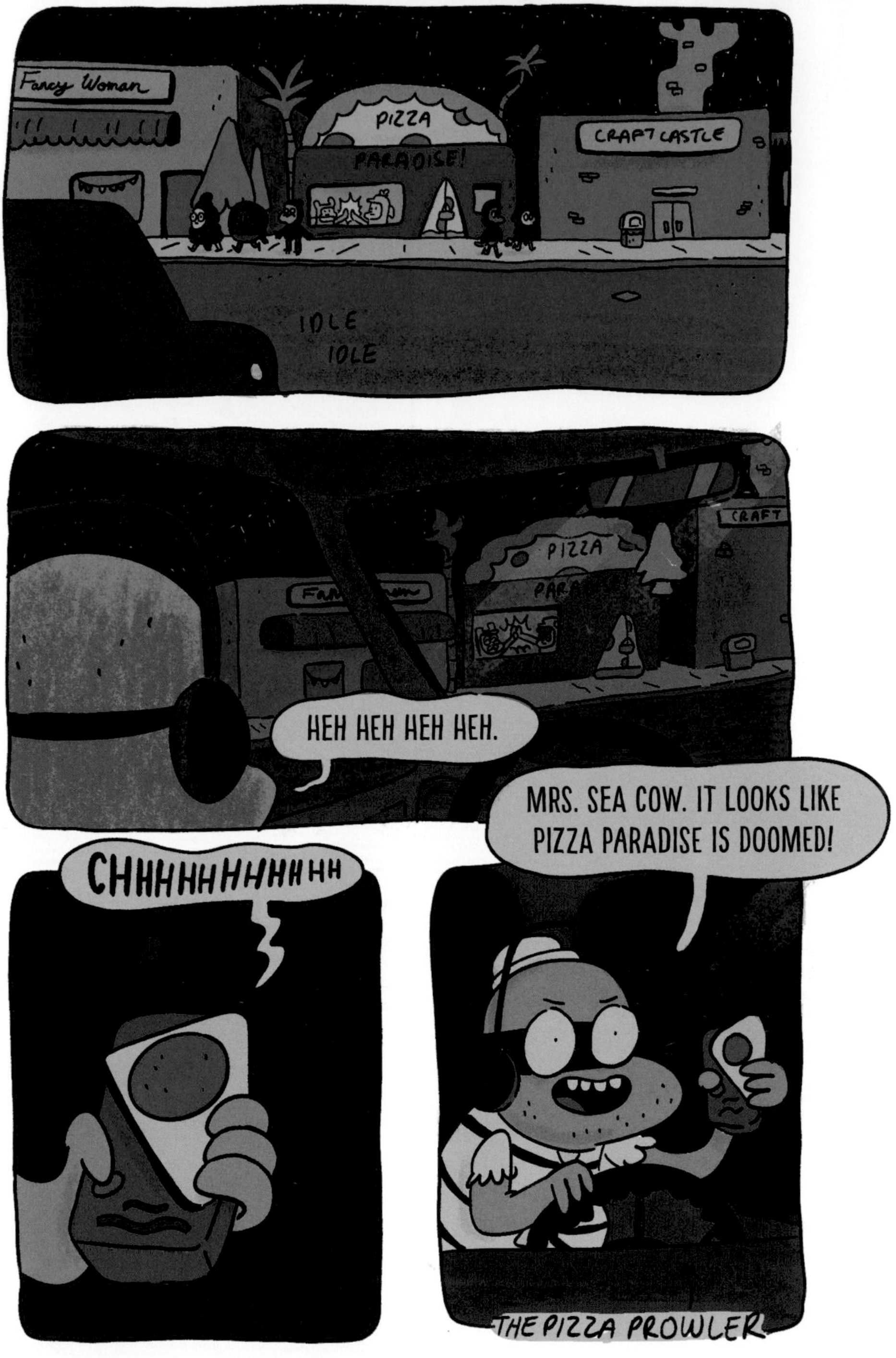
Fancy Woman
PIZZA
PARADISE!
CRAFT CASTLE
IDLE
IDLE
PIZZA
CRAFT
HEH HEH HEH HEH.
CHHHHHHHHHH
MRS. SEA COW. IT LOOKS LIKE PIZZA PARADISE IS DOOMED!
THE PIZZA PROWLER

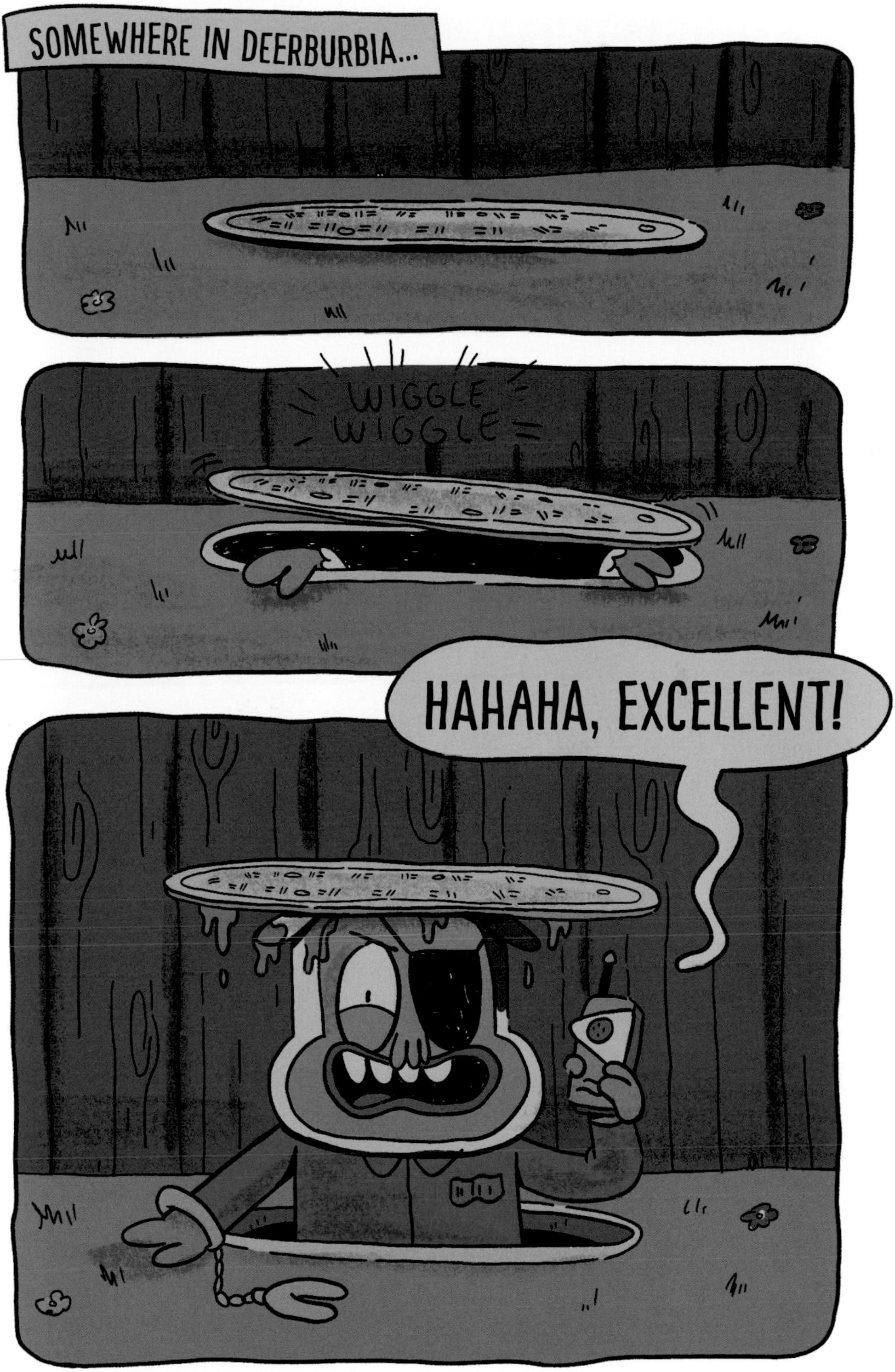
SOMEWHERE IN DEERBURBIA...
WIGGLE WIGGLE
HAHAHA, EXCELLENT!

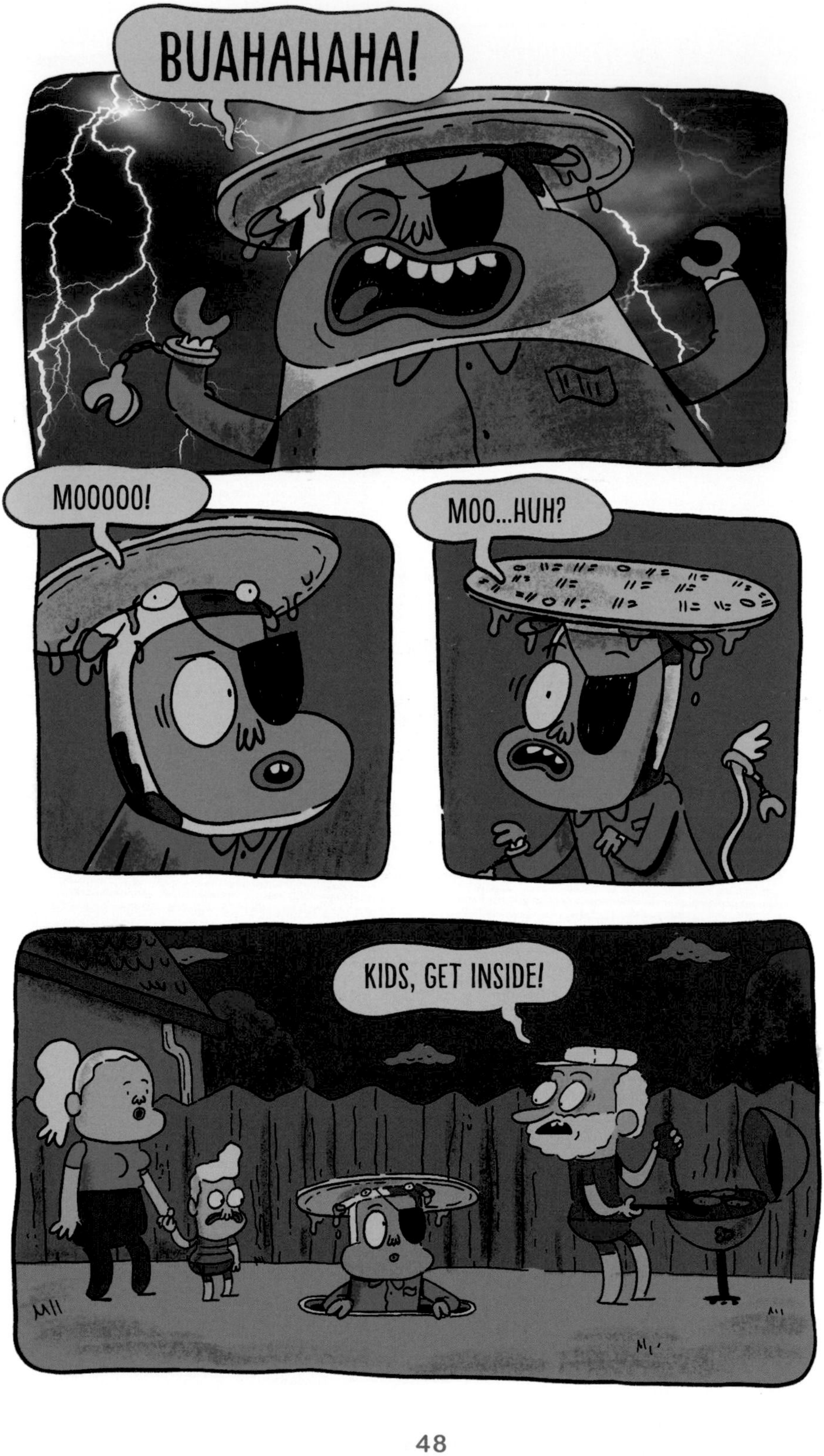
BUAHAHAHA!
MOOOOO!
MOO...HUH?
KIDS, GET INSIDE!

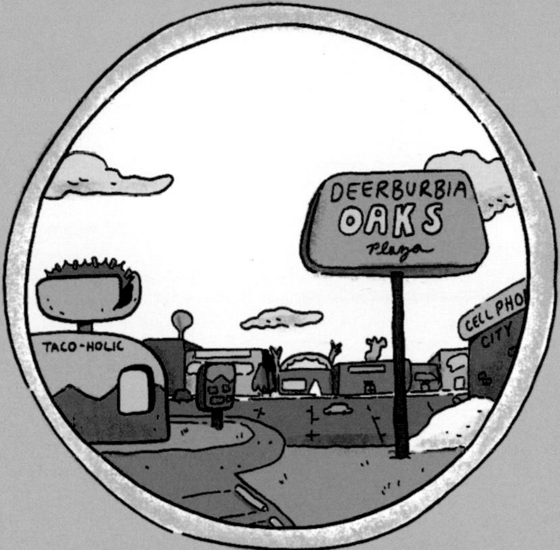
DEERBURBIA
OAKS
Plaza
TACO-HOLIC
CELL PHO
CITY

PART TWO

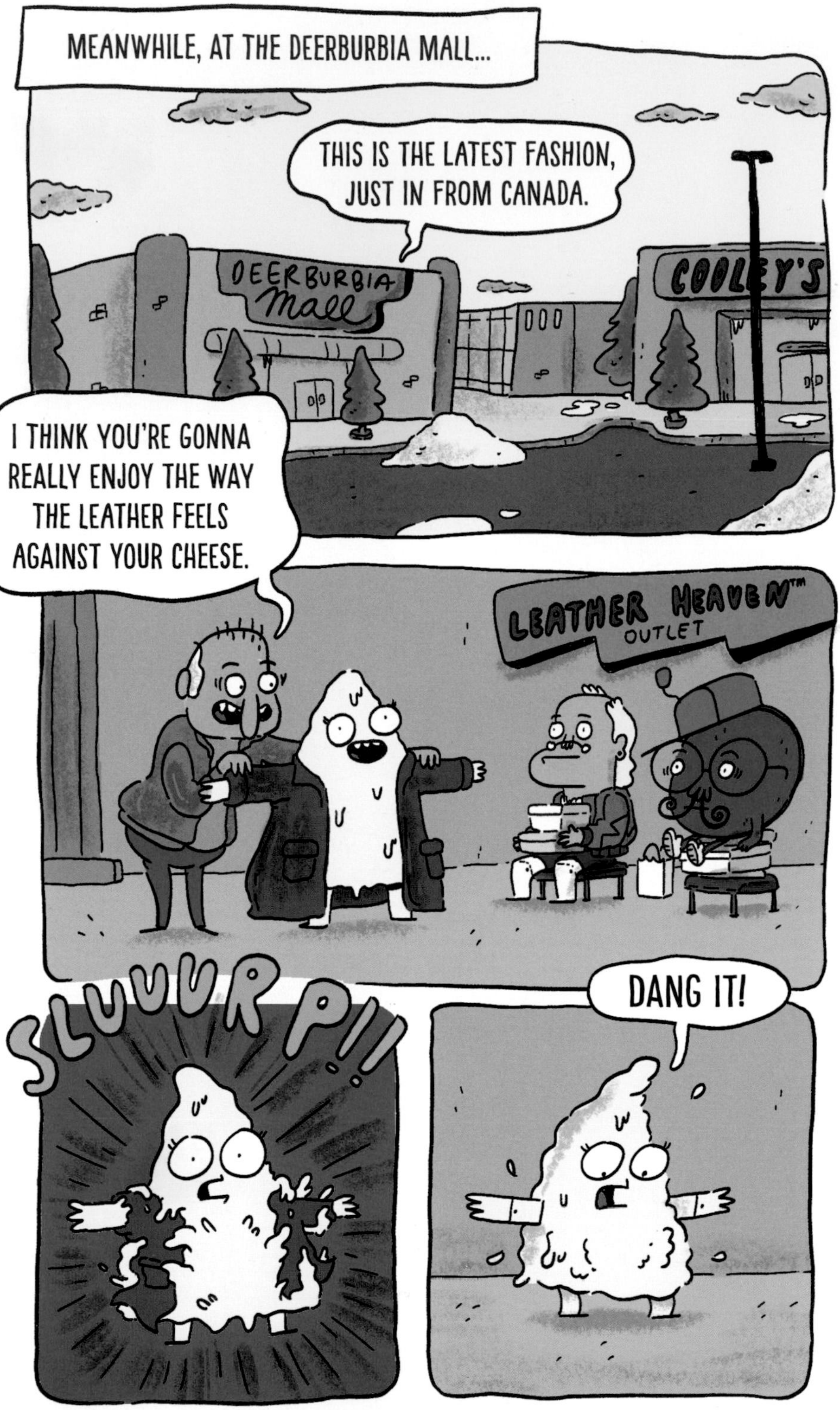
MEANWHILE, AT THE DEERBURBIA MALL...
THIS IS THE LATEST FASHION, JUST IN FROM CANADA.
DEERBURBIA
Mall
I THINK YOU'RE GONNA REALLY ENJOY THE WAY THE LEATHER FEELS AGAINST YOUR CHEESE.
LEATHER HEAVEN™
OUTLET
SLUUURP!!
DANG IT!

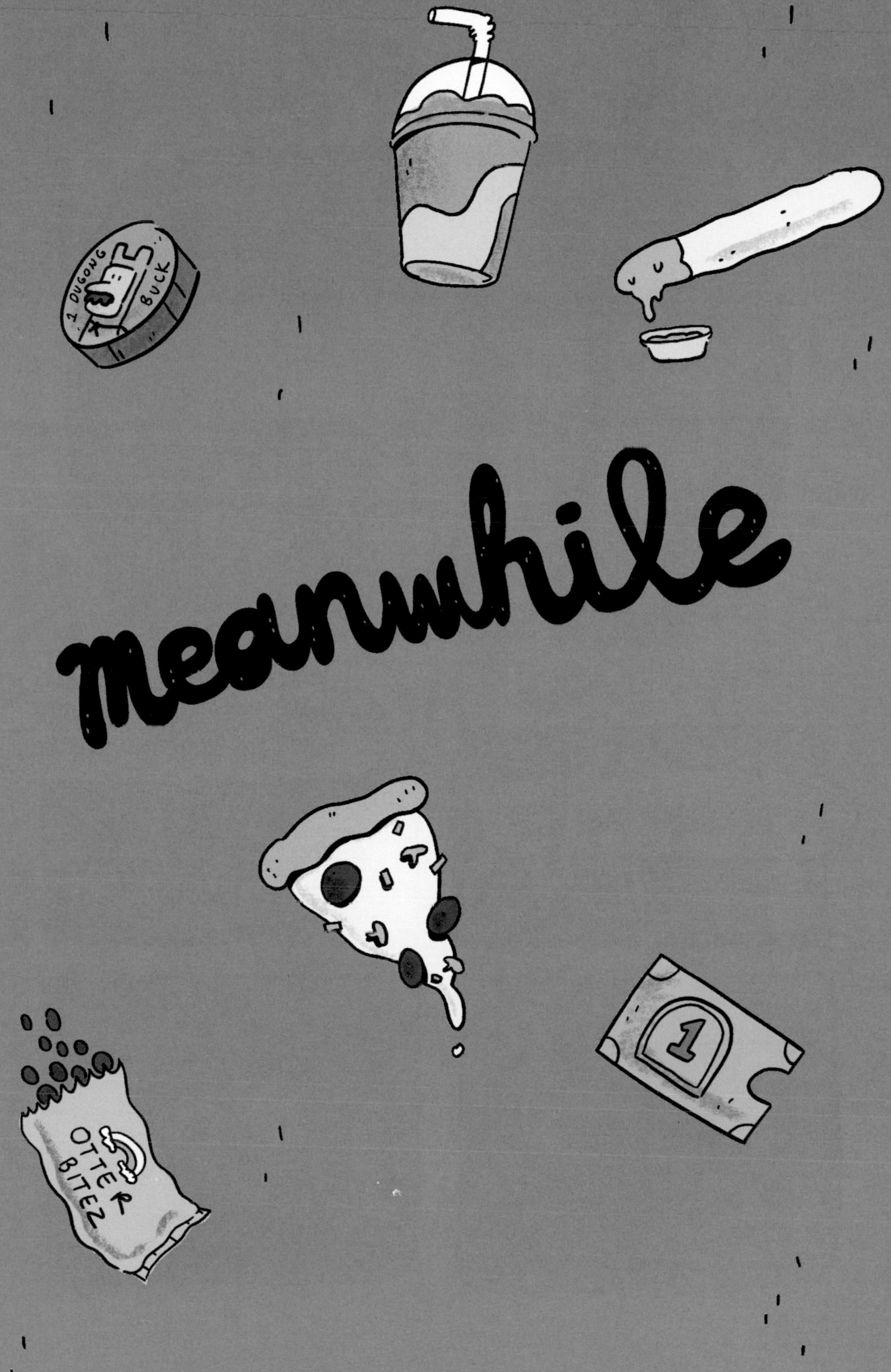
1 DUGONG BUCK
meanwhile
OTTER BITEZ
1

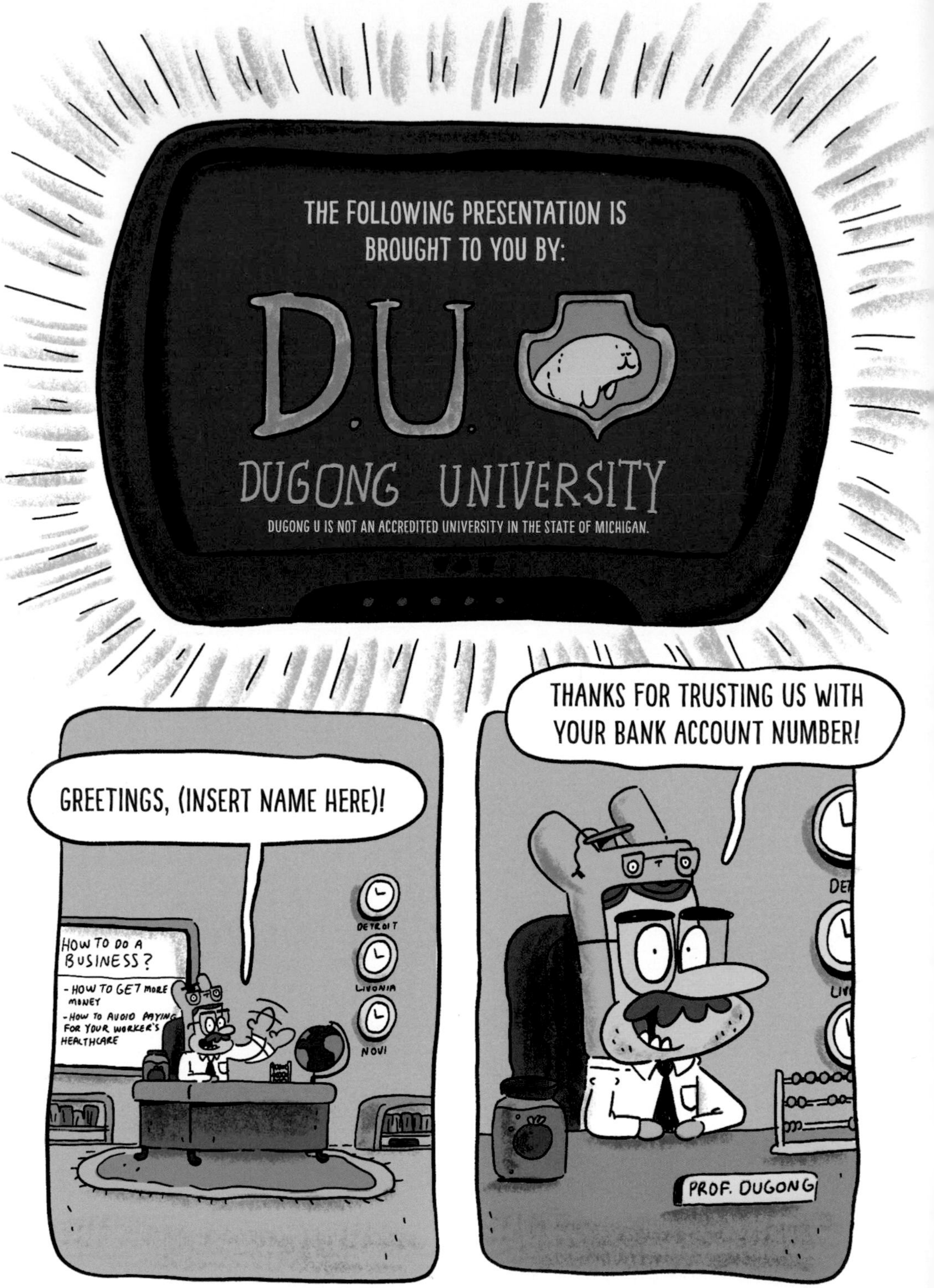
THE FOLLOWING PRESENTATION IS BROUGHT TO YOU BY:
D.U.
DUGONG UNIVERSITY
DUGONG U IS NOT AN ACCREDITED UNIVERSITY IN THE STATE OF MICHIGAN.
GREETINGS, (INSERT NAME HERE)!
HOW TO DO A BUSINESS?
- HOW TO GET MORE MONEY
- HOW TO AVOID PAYING FOR YOUR WORKER'S HEALTHCARE
DETROIT
LIVONIA
NOVI
THANKS FOR TRUSTING US WITH YOUR BANK ACCOUNT NUMBER!
PROF. DUGONG

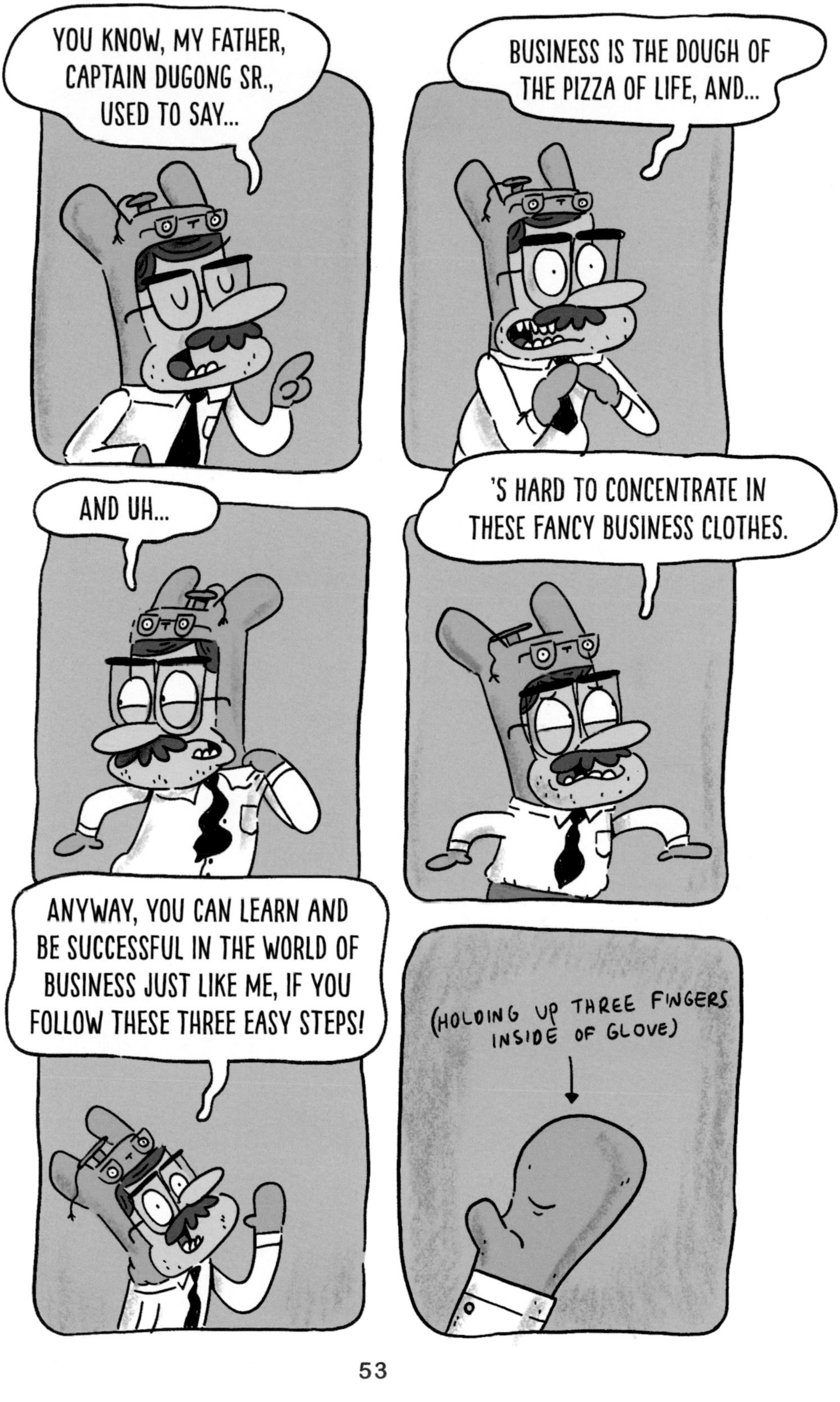
YOU KNOW, MY FATHER, CAPTAIN DUGONG SR., USED TO SAY...
BUSINESS IS THE DOUGH OF THE PIZZA OF LIFE, AND...
AND UH...
'S HARD TO CONCENTRATE IN THESE FANCY BUSINESS CLOTHES.
ANYWAY, YOU CAN LEARN AND BE SUCCESSFUL IN THE WORLD OF BUSINESS JUST LIKE ME, IF YOU FOLLOW THESE THREE EASY STEPS!
(HOLDING UP THREE FINGERS INSIDE OF GLOVE)

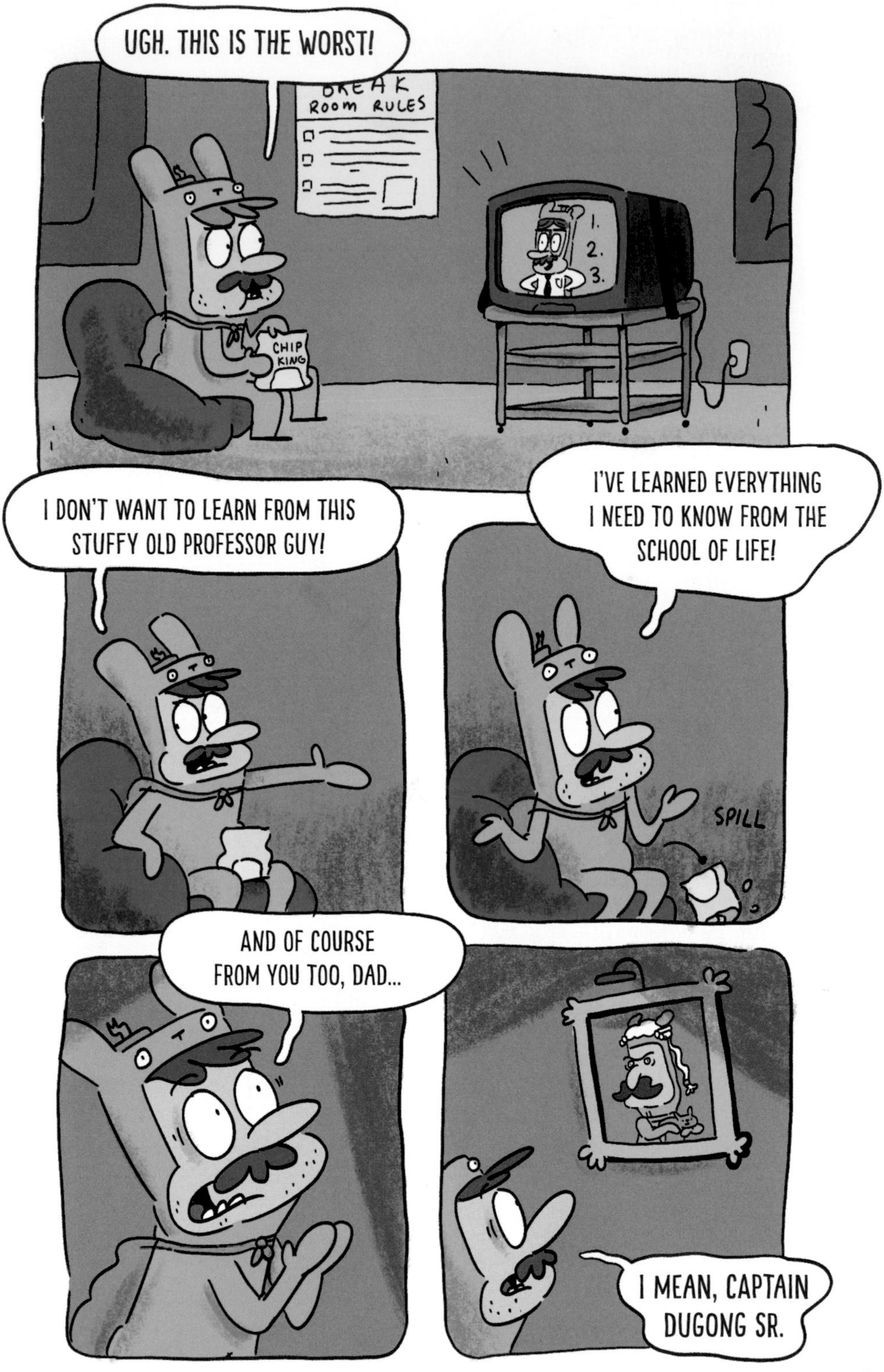
UGH. THIS IS THE WORST!
BREAK ROOM RULES
1.
2.
3.
CHIP KING
I DON'T WANT TO LEARN FROM THIS STUFFY OLD PROFESSOR GUY!
I'VE LEARNED EVERYTHING I NEED TO KNOW FROM THE SCHOOL OF LIFE!
SPILL
AND OF COURSE FROM YOU TOO, DAD...
I MEAN, CAPTAIN DUGONG SR.

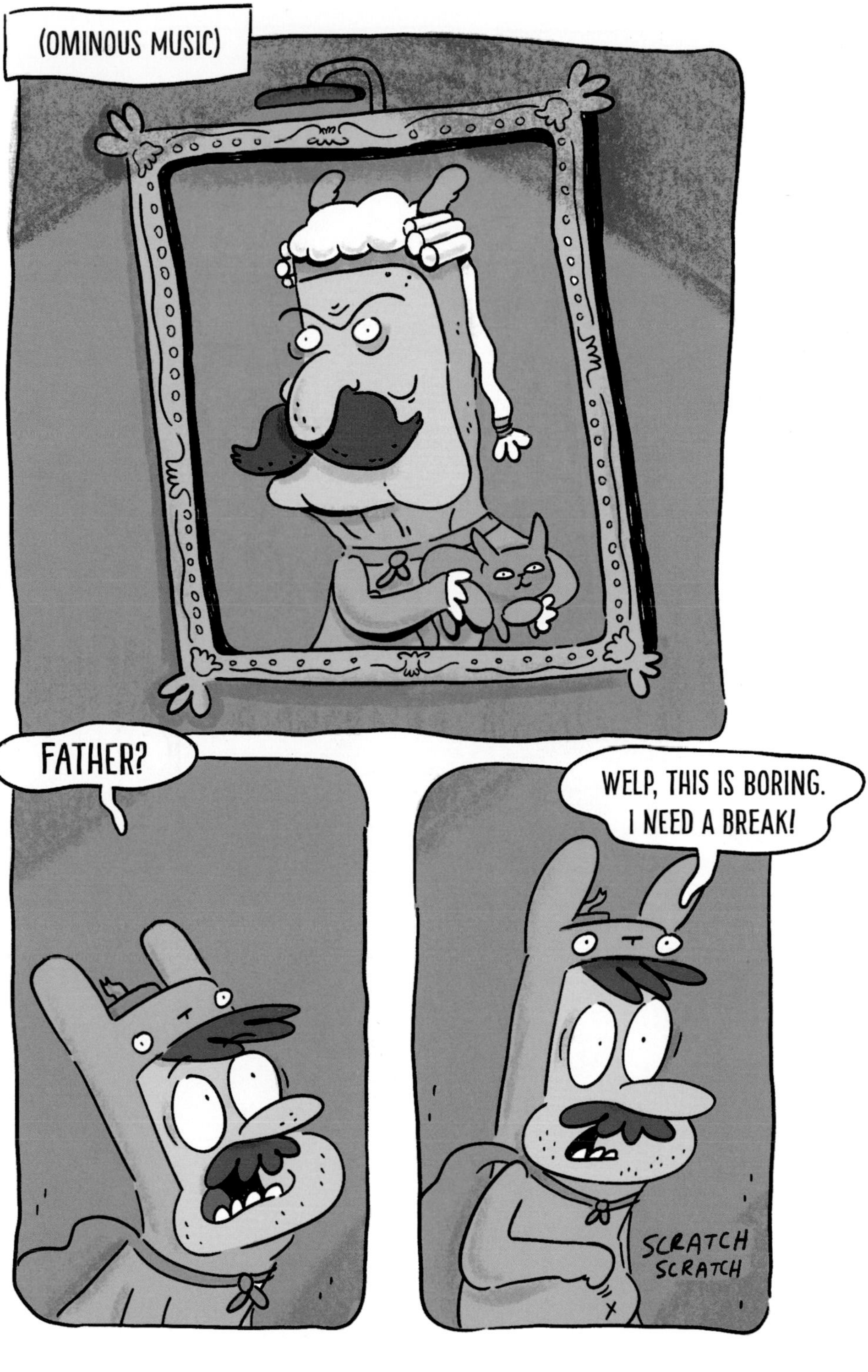
(OMINOUS MUSIC)
FATHER?
WELP, THIS IS BORING. I NEED A BREAK!
SCRATCH SCRATCH

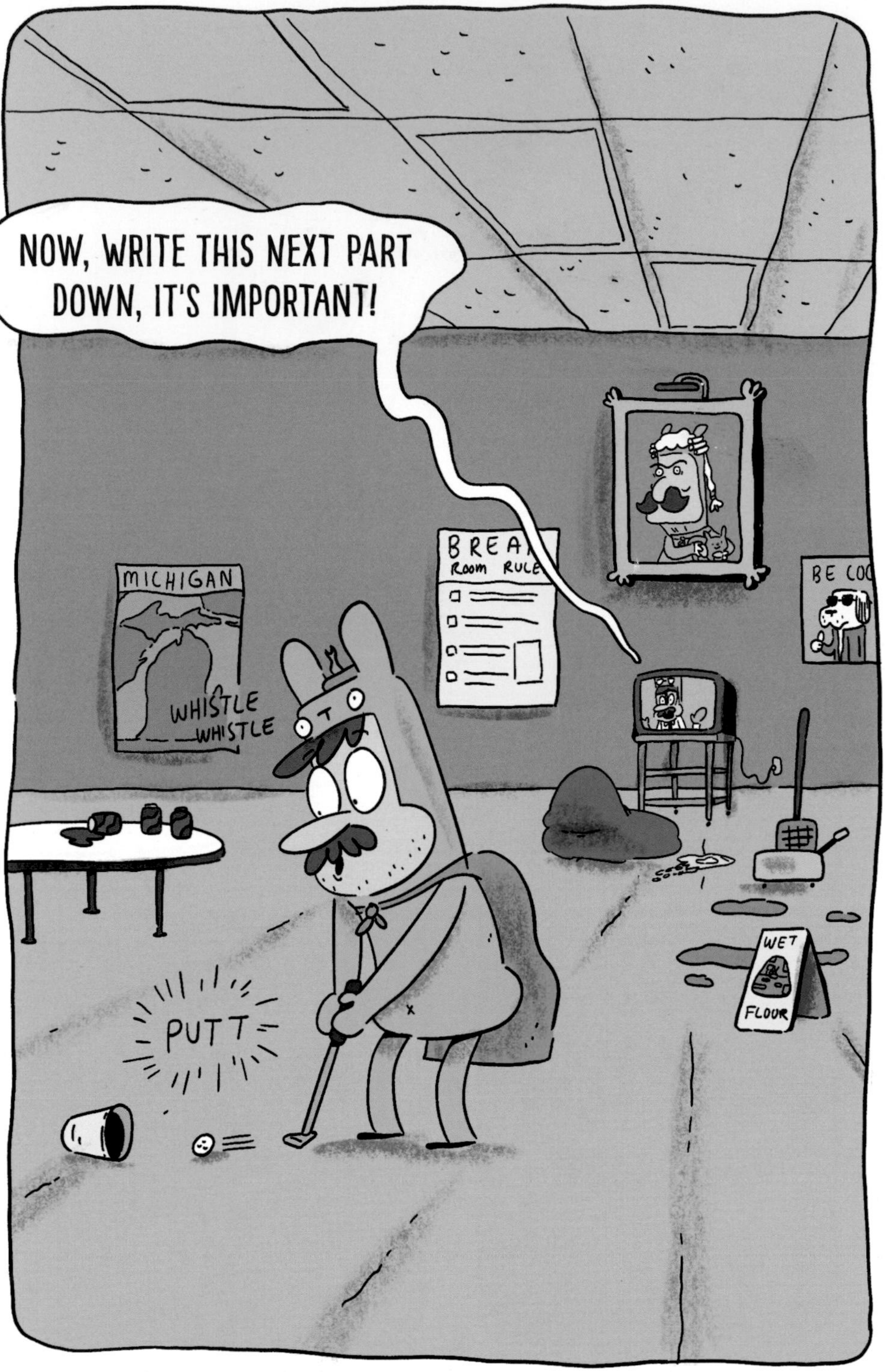
NOW, WRITE THIS NEXT PART DOWN, IT'S IMPORTANT!
MICHIGAN
WHISTLE
WHISTLE
Room RULE
PUTT
WET
FLOUR

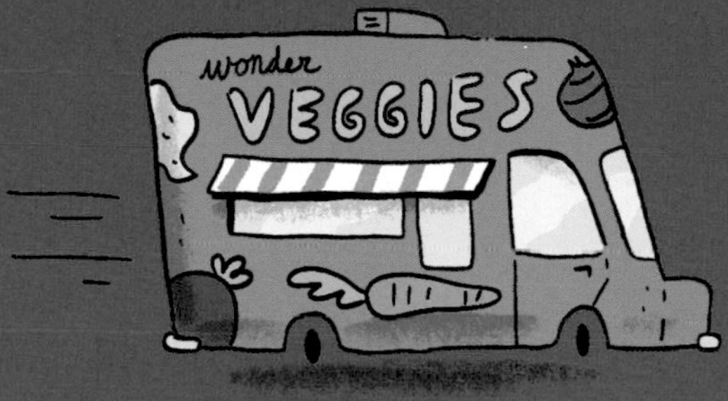
wonder
VEGGIES

ALSO meanwhile

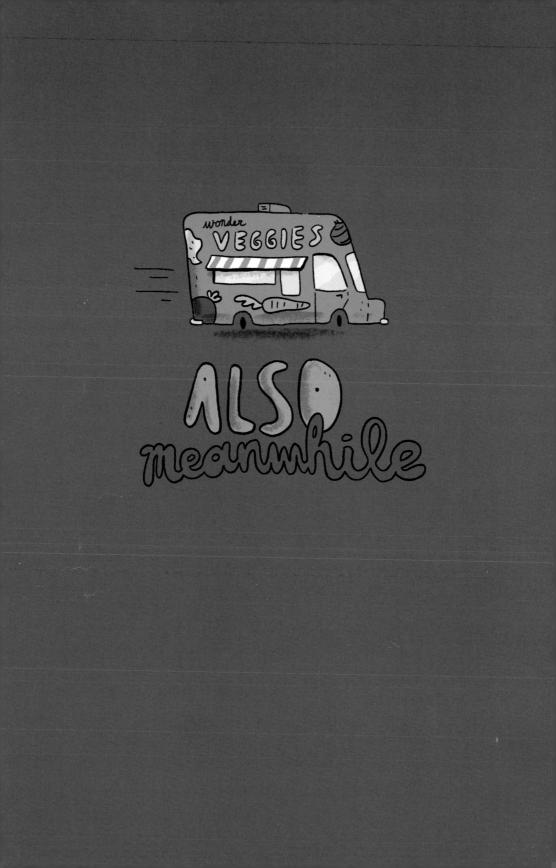

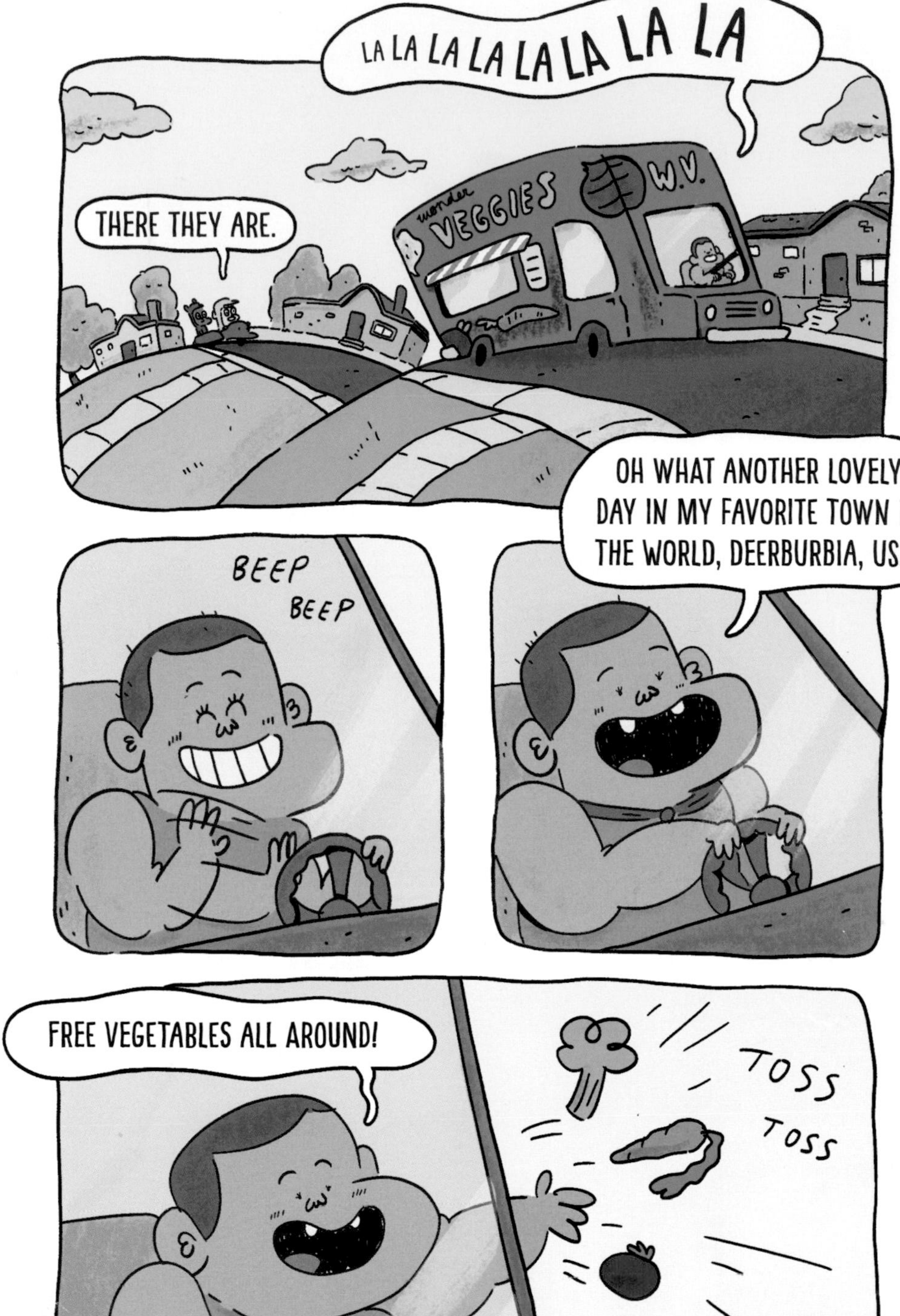
LA LA LA LA LA LA LA LA
THERE THEY ARE.
wonder VEGGIES
W.V.
BEEP
BEEP
OH WHAT ANOTHER LOVELY DAY IN MY FAVORITE TOWN IN THE WORLD, DEERBURBIA, USA!
FREE VEGETABLES ALL AROUND!
TOSS
TOSS

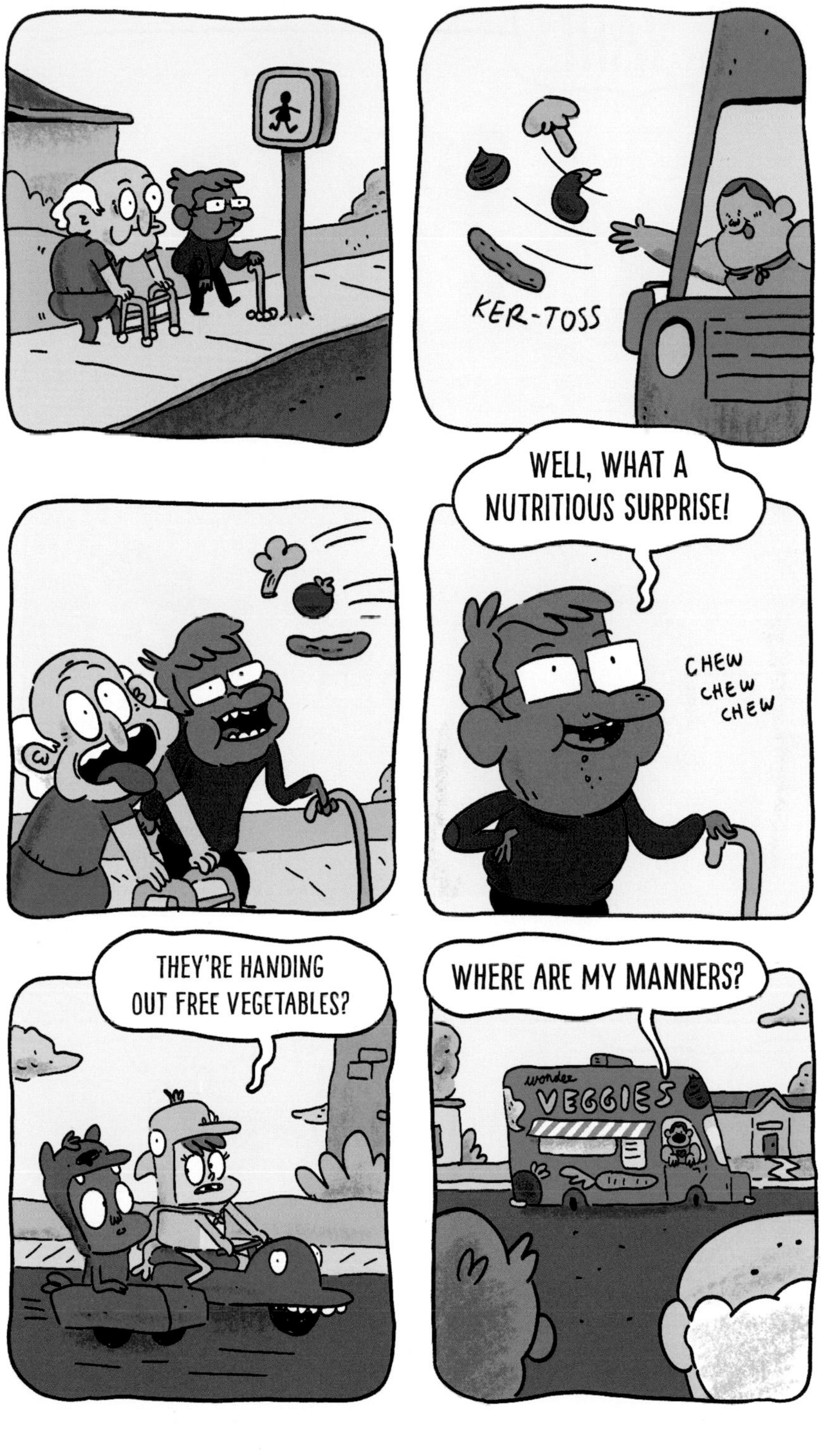
KER-TOSS
WELL, WHAT A NUTRITIOUS SURPRISE!
CHEW CHEW CHEW
THEY'RE HANDING OUT FREE VEGETABLES?
WHERE ARE MY MANNERS?
wonder VEGGIES

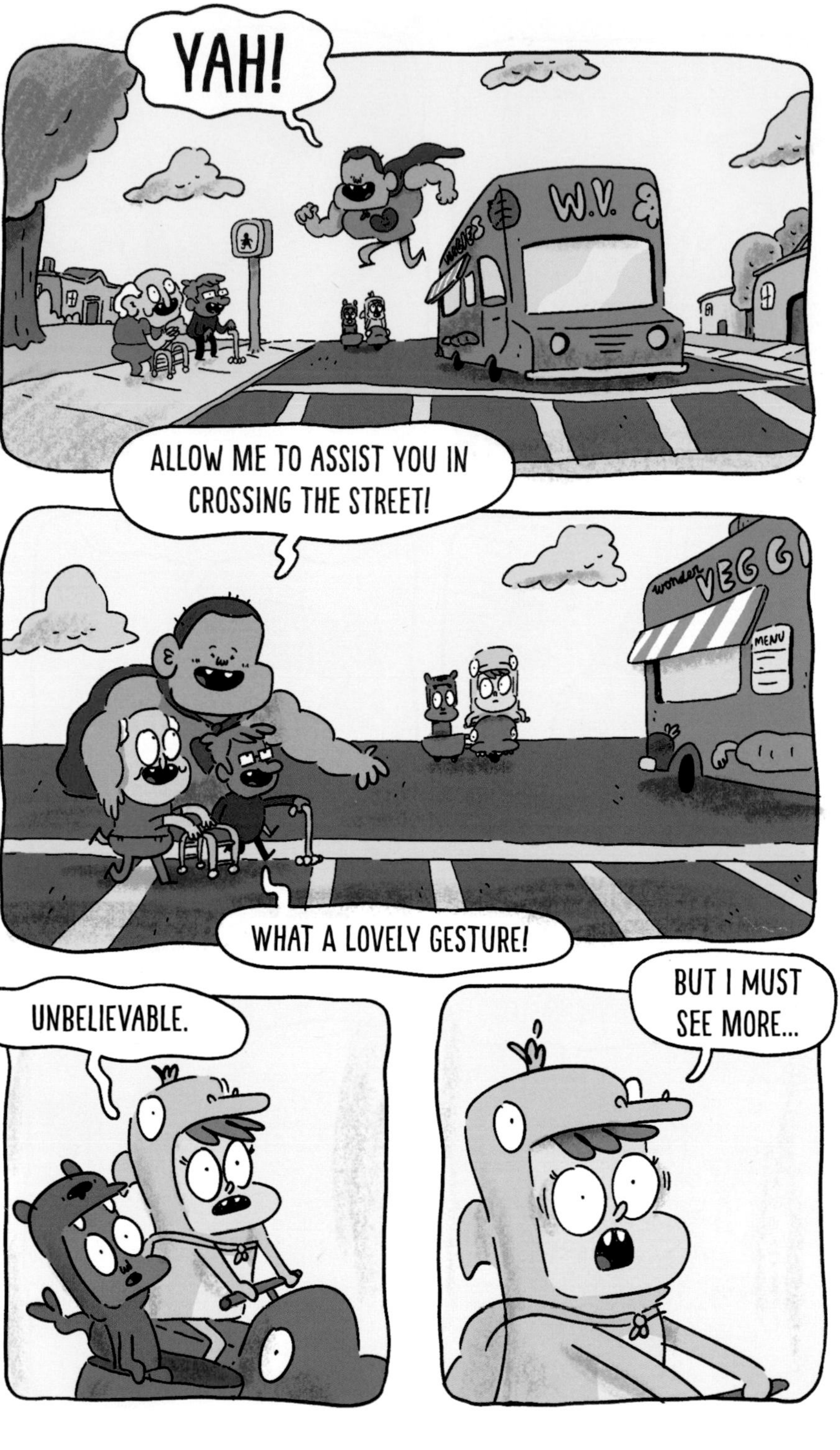
YAH!
W.V.
ALLOW ME TO ASSIST YOU IN CROSSING THE STREET!
VEGGI
MENU
WHAT A LOVELY GESTURE!
UNBELIEVABLE.
BUT I MUST SEE MORE...

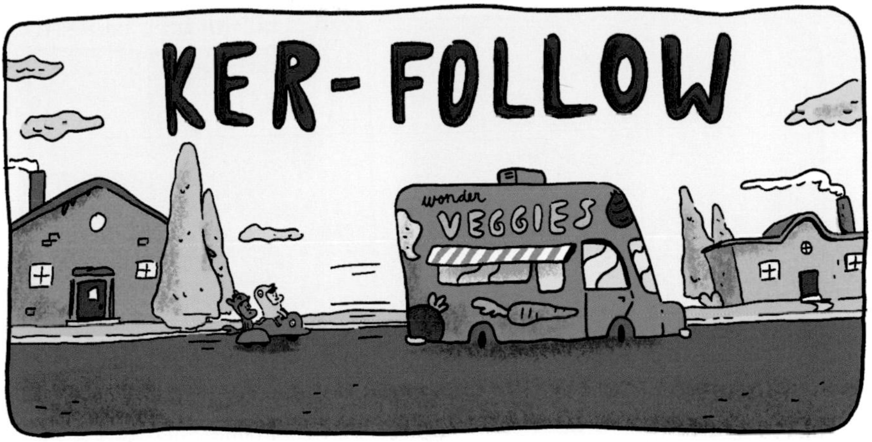
KER-FOLLOW
wonder
VEGGIES

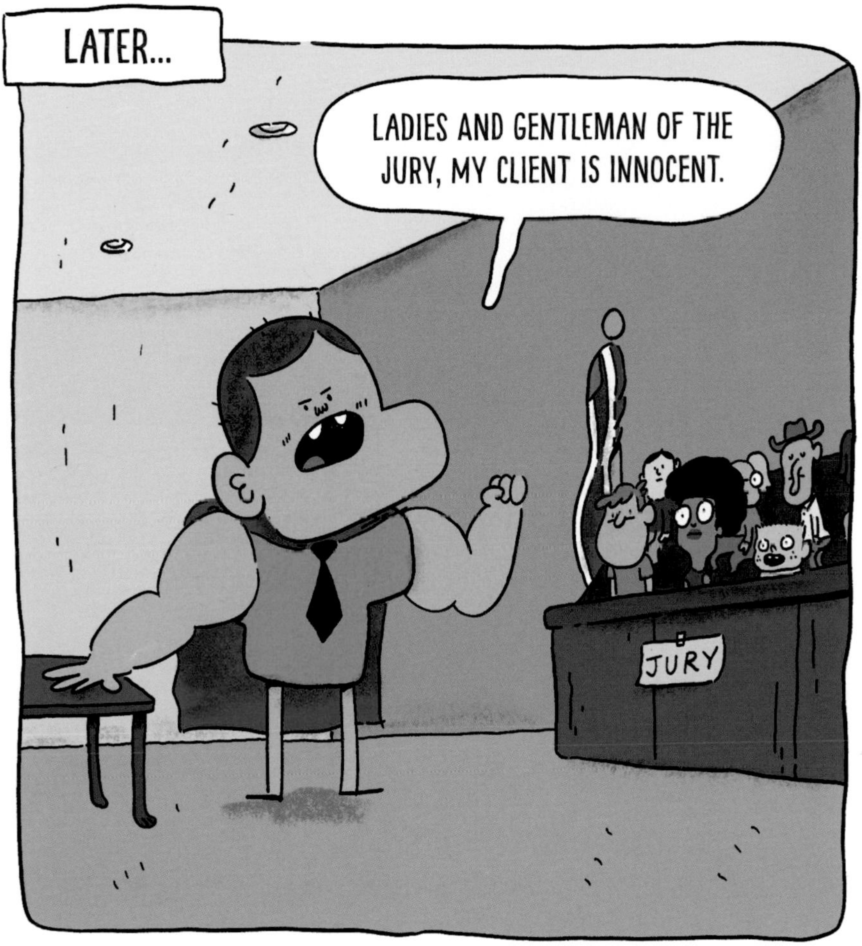
LATER...
LADIES AND GENTLEMAN OF THE JURY, MY CLIENT IS INNOCENT.
JURY

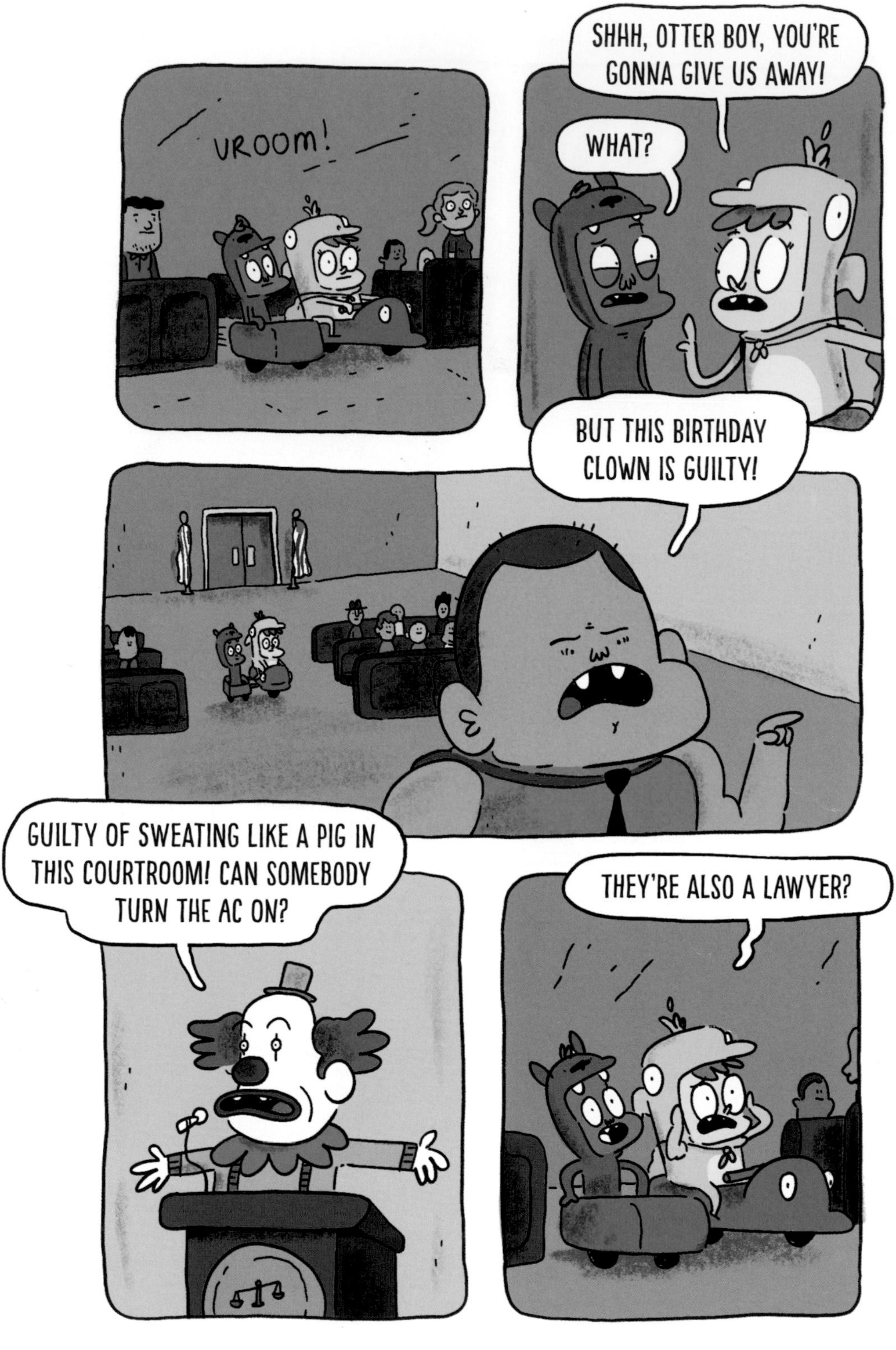
VROOM!
SHHH, OTTER BOY, YOU'RE GONNA GIVE US AWAY!
WHAT?
BUT THIS BIRTHDAY CLOWN IS GUILTY!
GUILTY OF SWEATING LIKE A PIG IN THIS COURTROOM! CAN SOMEBODY TURN THE AC ON?
THEY'RE ALSO A LAWYER?

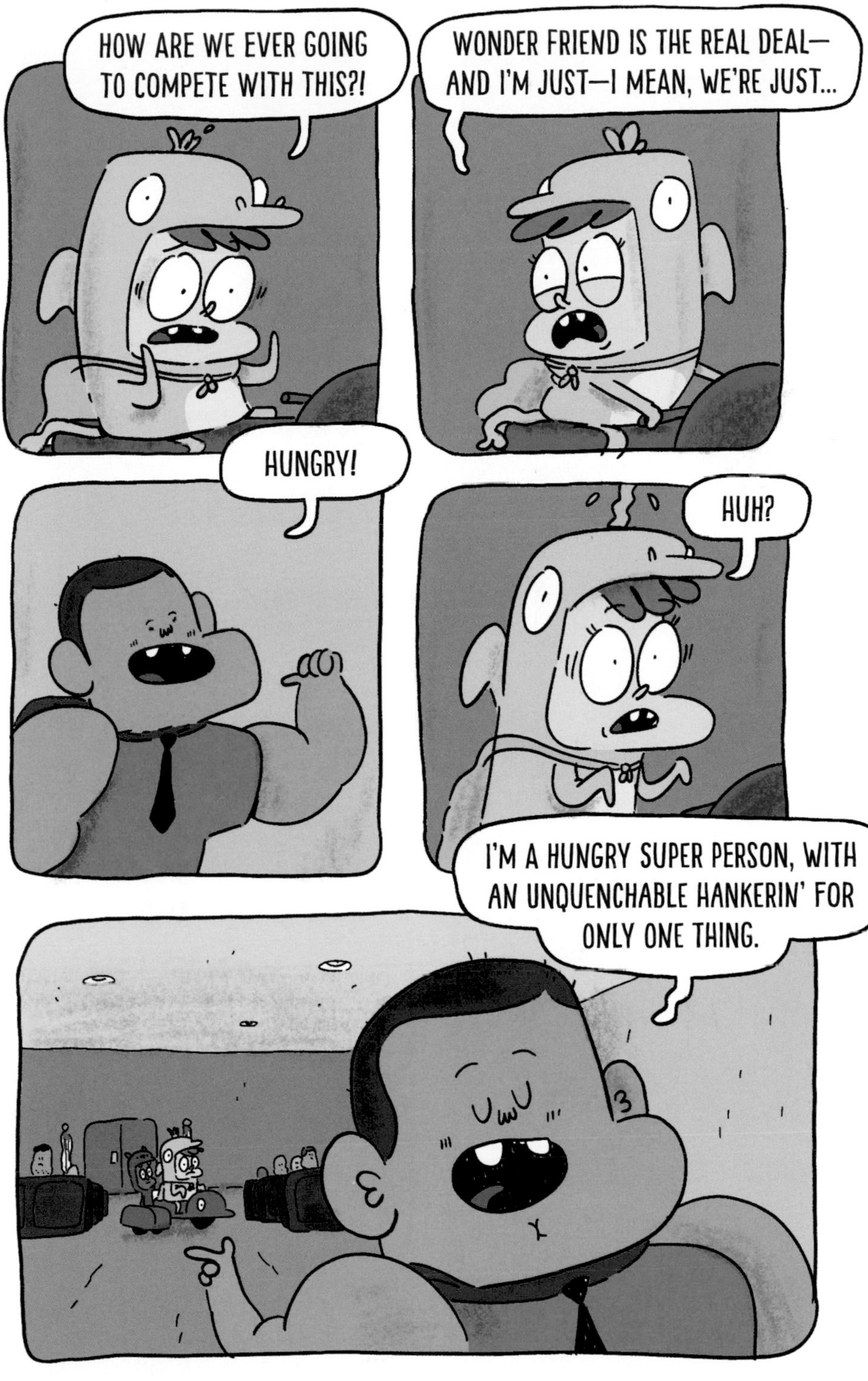
HOW ARE WE EVER GOING TO COMPETE WITH THIS?!
WONDER FRIEND IS THE REAL DEAL—AND I'M JUST—I MEAN, WE'RE JUST...
HUNGRY!
HUH?
I'M A HUNGRY SUPER PERSON, WITH AN UNQUENCHABLE HANKERIN' FOR ONLY ONE THING.

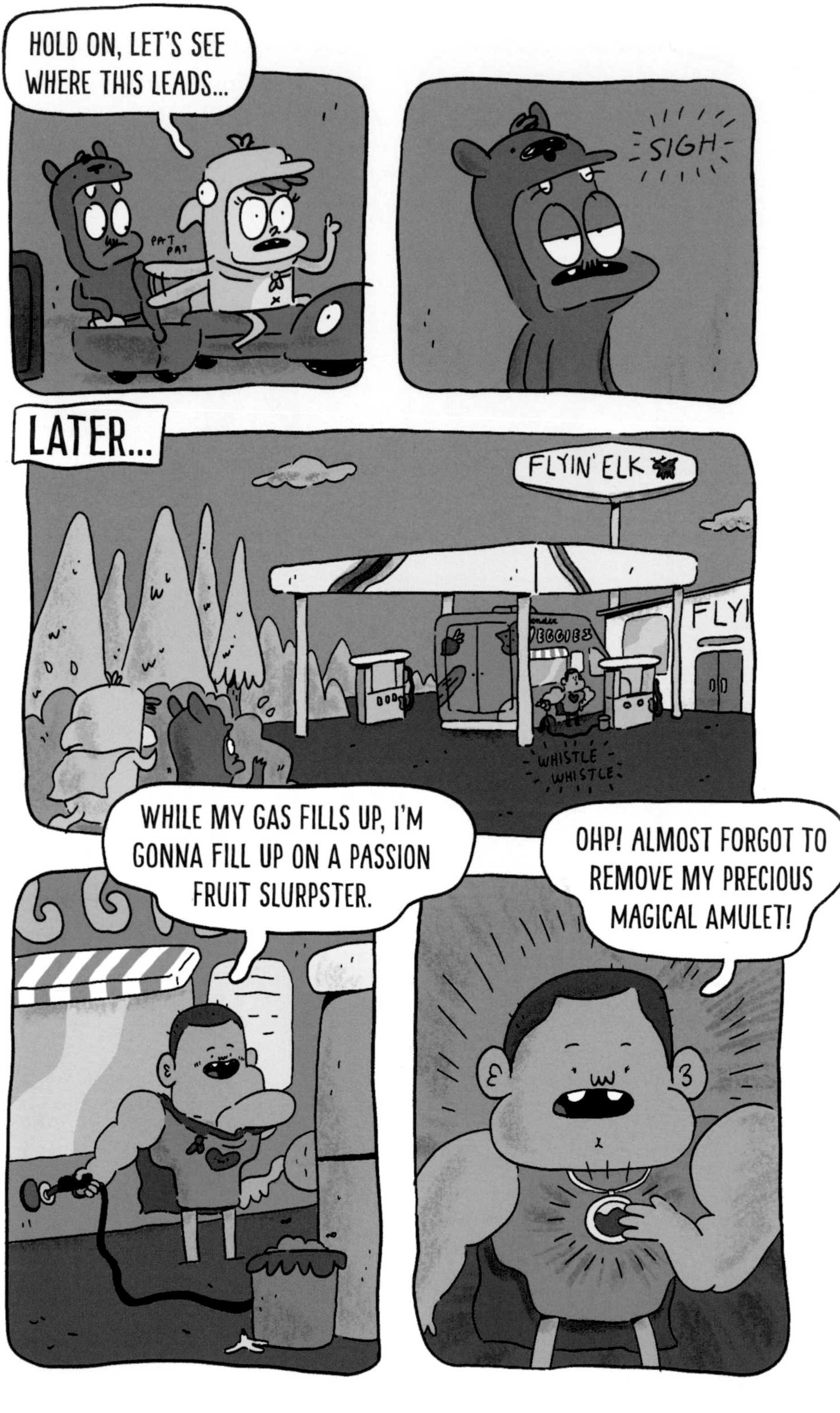
HOLD ON, LET'S SEE WHERE THIS LEADS...
PAT PAT
SIGH
LATER...
FLYIN' ELK
FLYI
VEGGIES
WHISTLE WHISTLE
WHILE MY GAS FILLS UP, I'M GONNA FILL UP ON A PASSION FRUIT SLURPSTER.
OHP! ALMOST FORGOT TO REMOVE MY PRECIOUS MAGICAL AMULET!

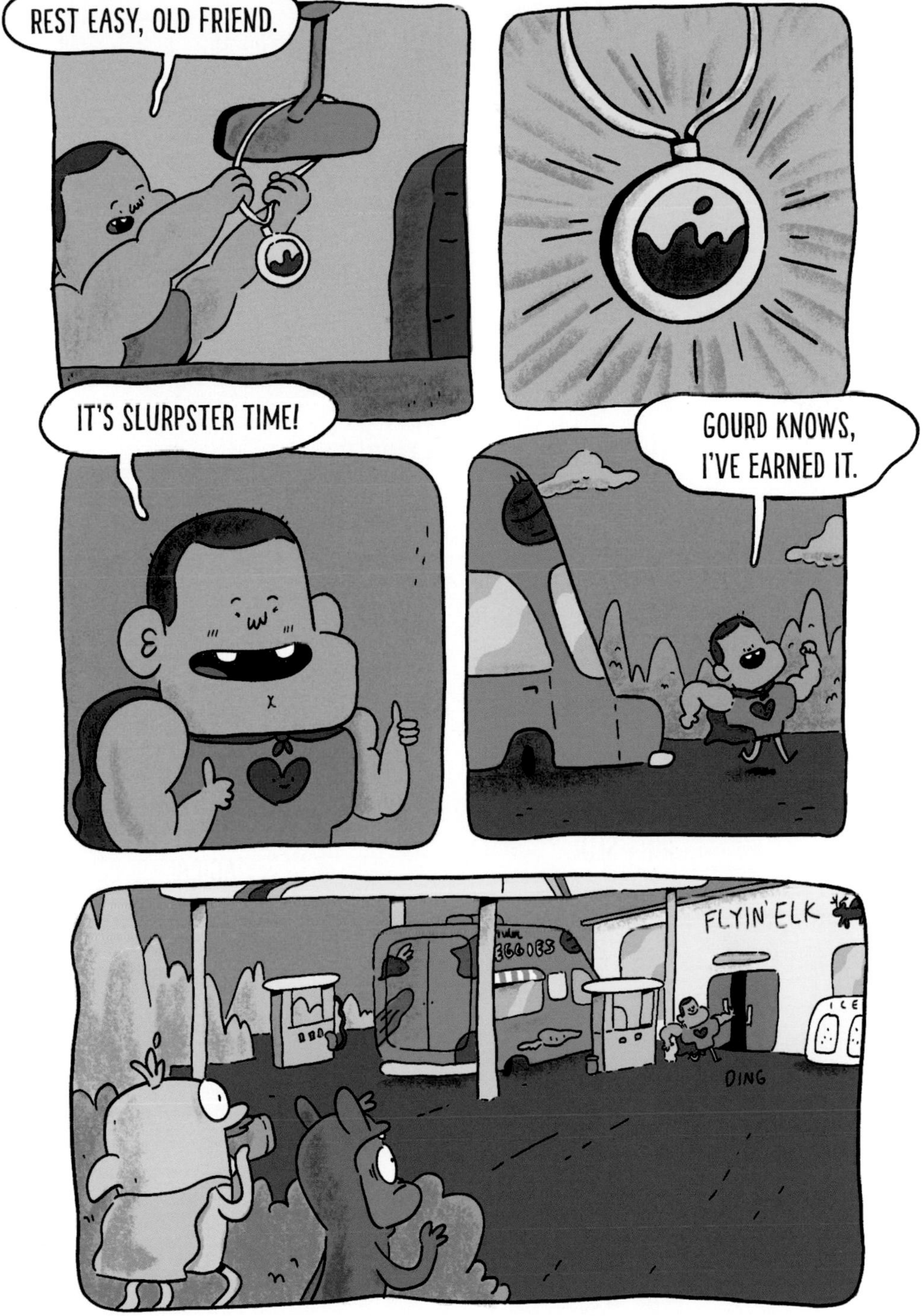
REST EASY, OLD FRIEND.
IT'S SLURPSTER TIME!
GOURD KNOWS, I'VE EARNED IT.
FLYIN' ELK
ICE
DING

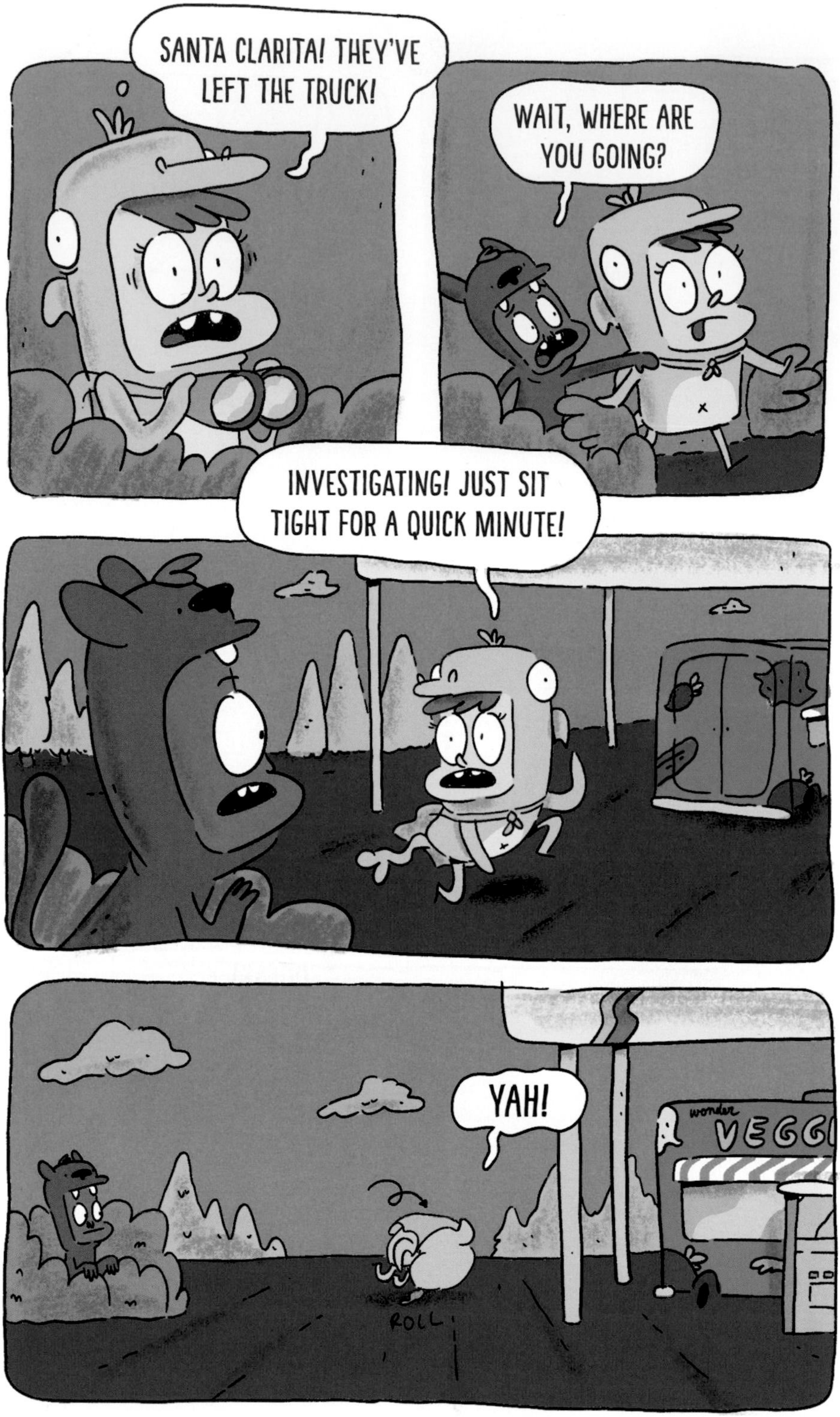
SANTA CLARITA! THEY'VE LEFT THE TRUCK!
WAIT, WHERE ARE YOU GOING?
INVESTIGATING! JUST SIT TIGHT FOR A QUICK MINUTE!
YAH!
wonder VEGG
ROLL

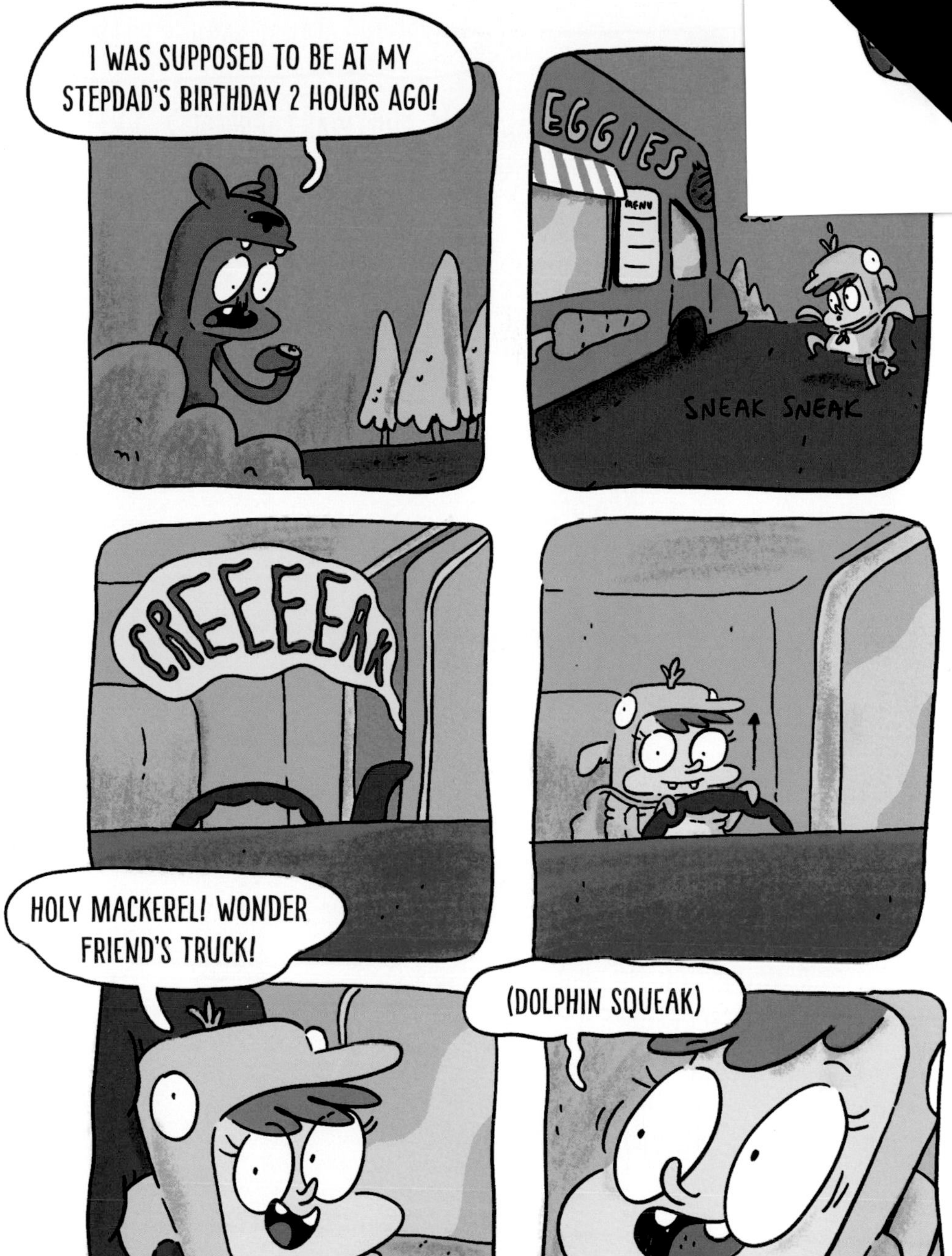
I WAS SUPPOSED TO BE AT MY STEPDAD'S BIRTHDAY 2 HOURS AGO!
EGGIES
MENU
SNEAK SNEAK
CREEEEAK
HOLY MACKEREL! WONDER FRIEND'S TRUCK!
(DOLPHIN SQUEAK)

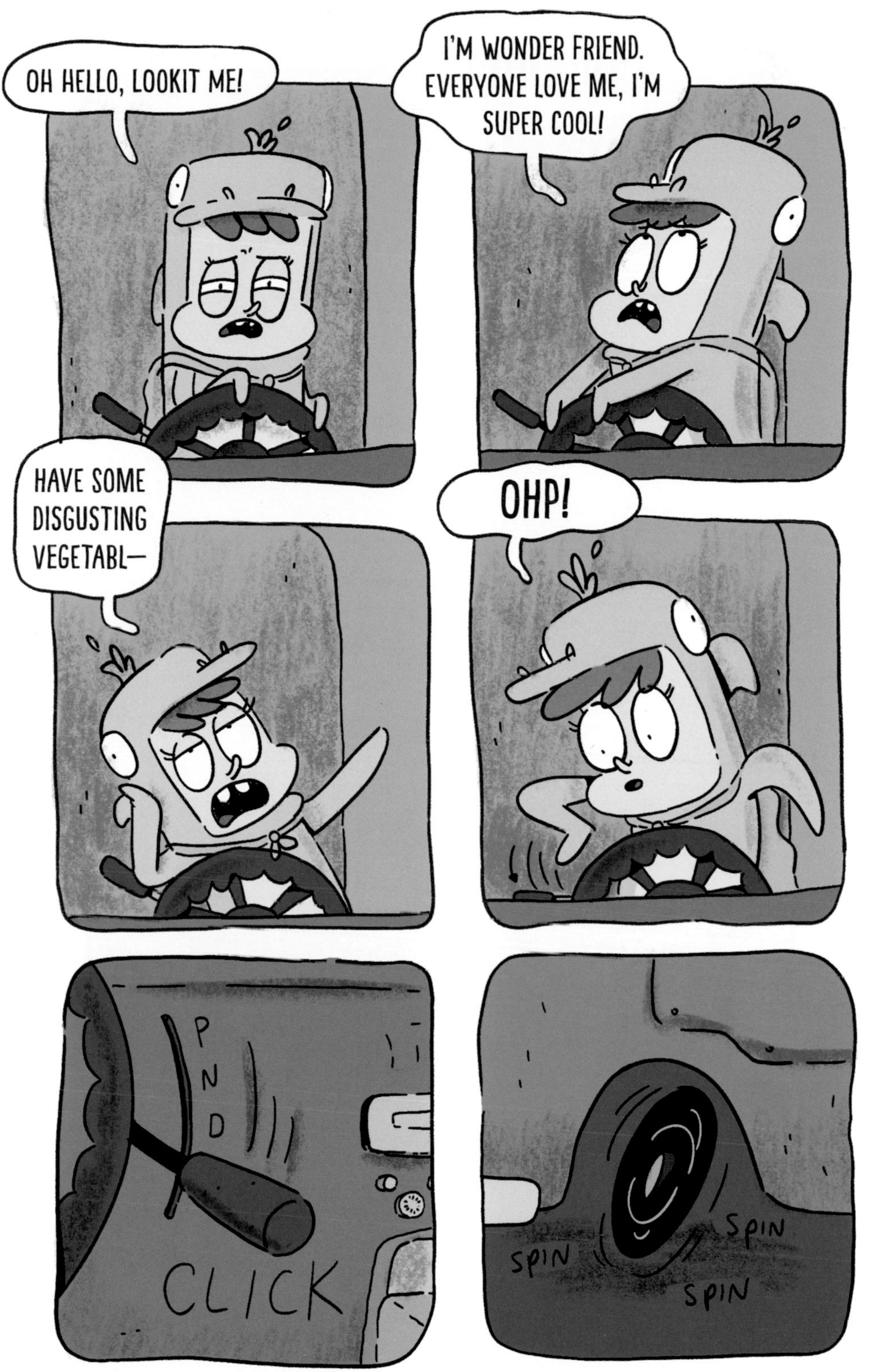
OH HELLO, LOOKIT ME!
I'M WONDER FRIEND. EVERYONE LOVE ME, I'M SUPER COOL!
HAVE SOME DISGUSTING VEGETABL—
OHP!
P
N
D
CLICK
SPIN
SPIN
SPIN

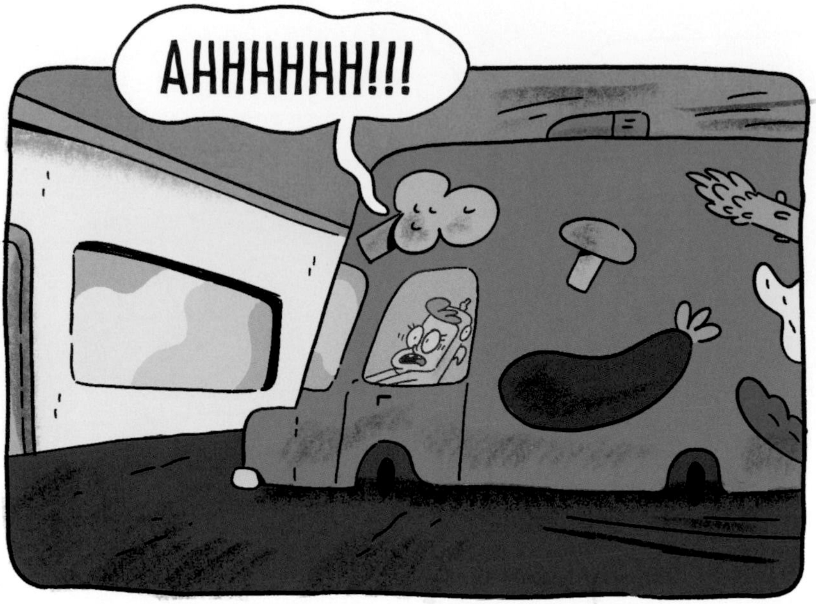
AHHHHHH!!!

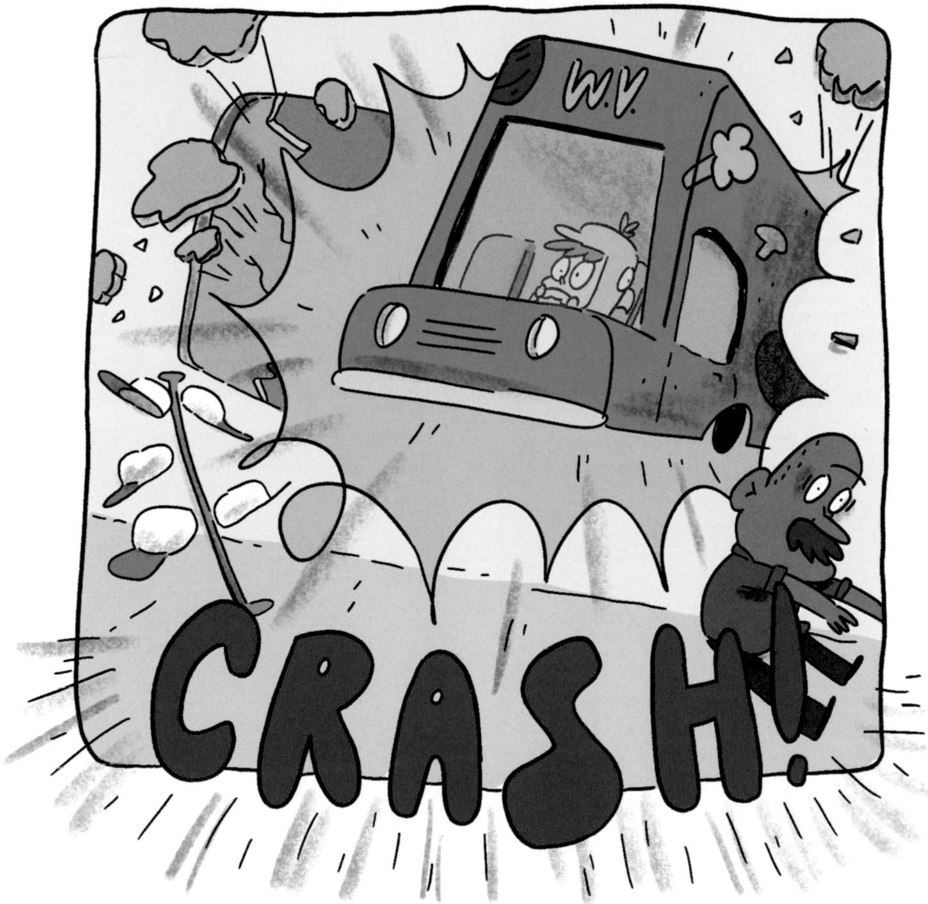
W.V.
CRASH!

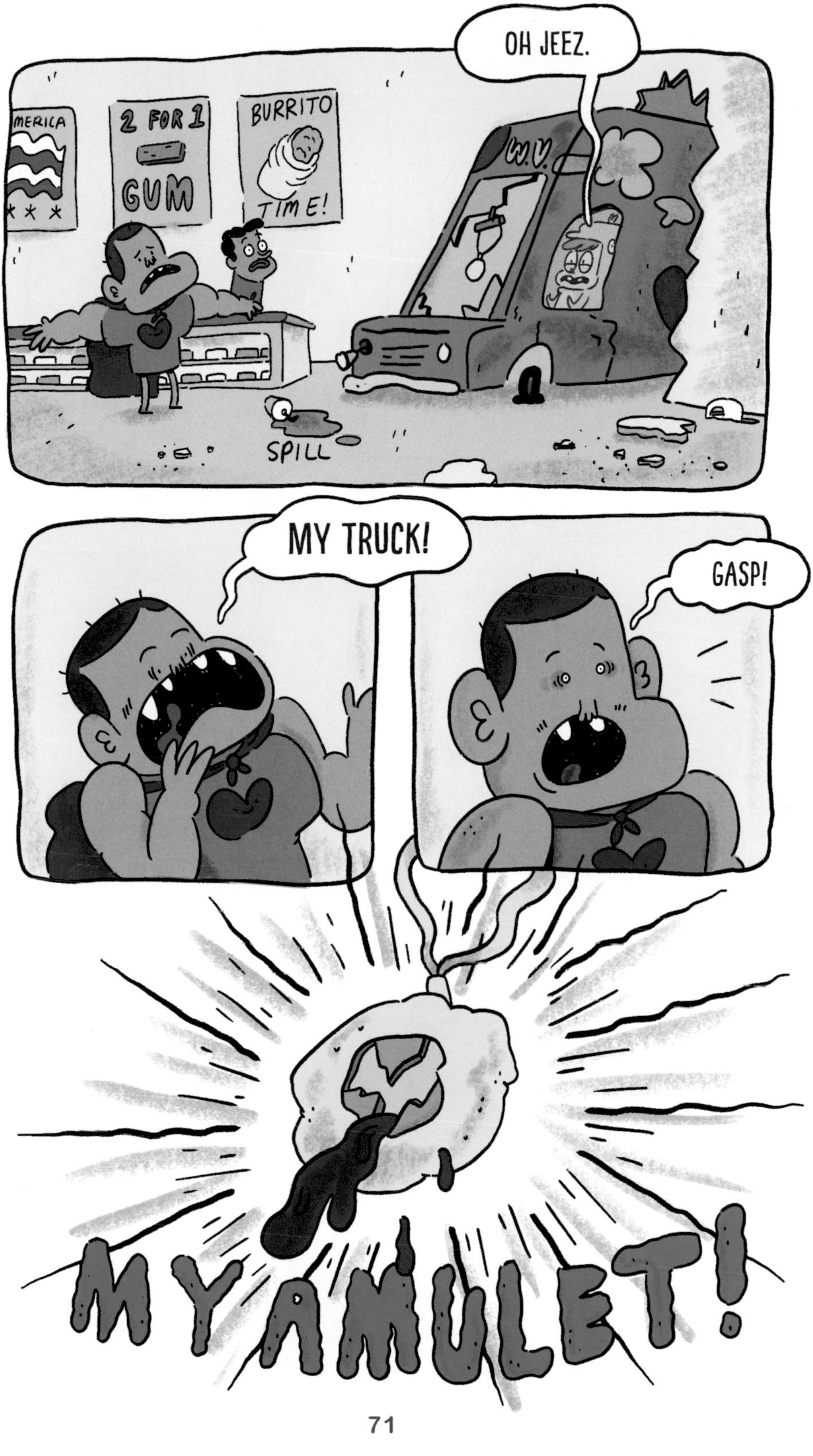
MERICA
2 FOR 1
GUM
BURRITO
TIME!
OH JEEZ.
W.V.
SPILL
MY TRUCK!
GASP!
MY AMULET!

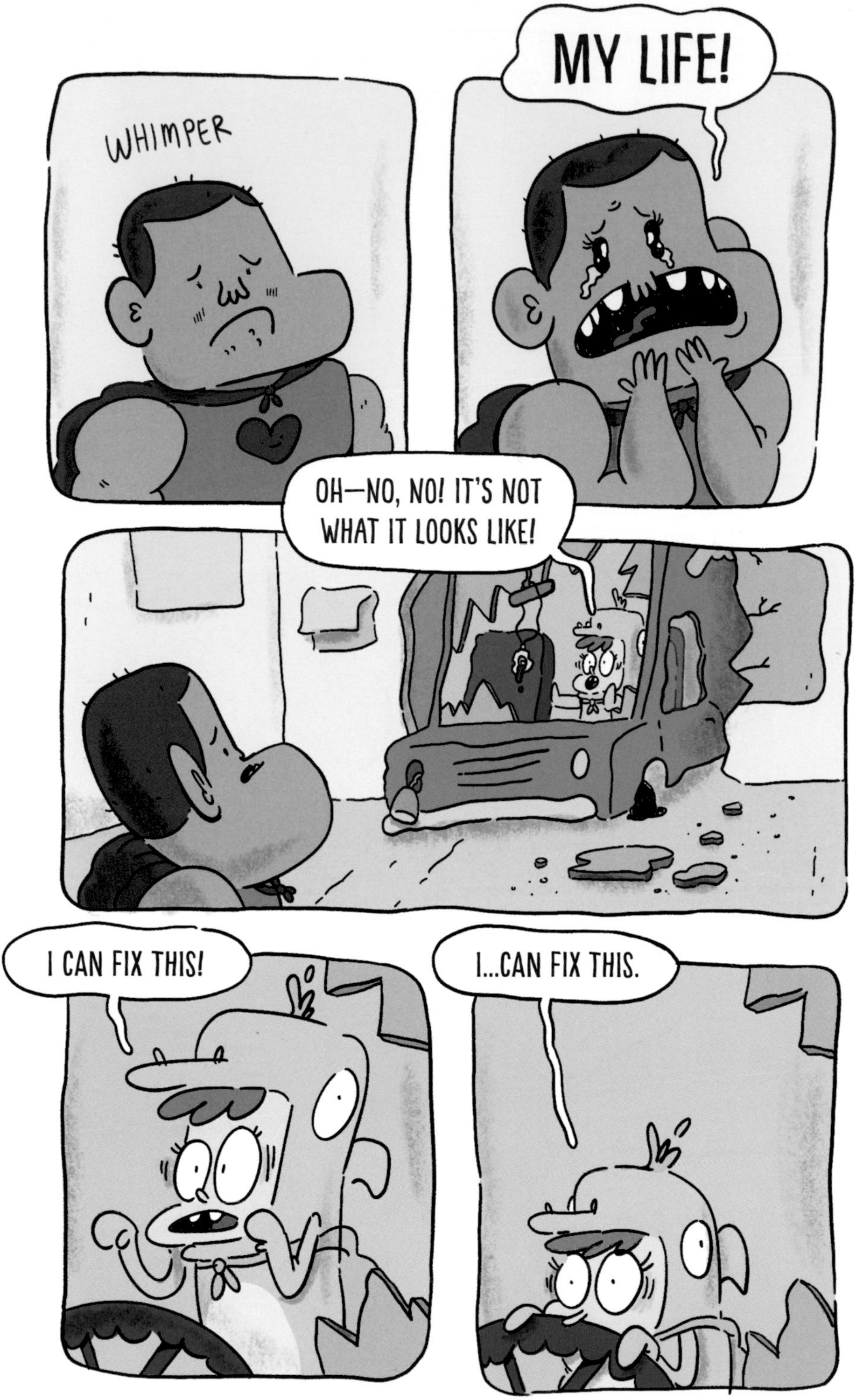
WHIMPER
MY LIFE!
OH—NO, NO! IT'S NOT WHAT IT LOOKS LIKE!
I CAN FIX THIS!
I...CAN FIX THIS.

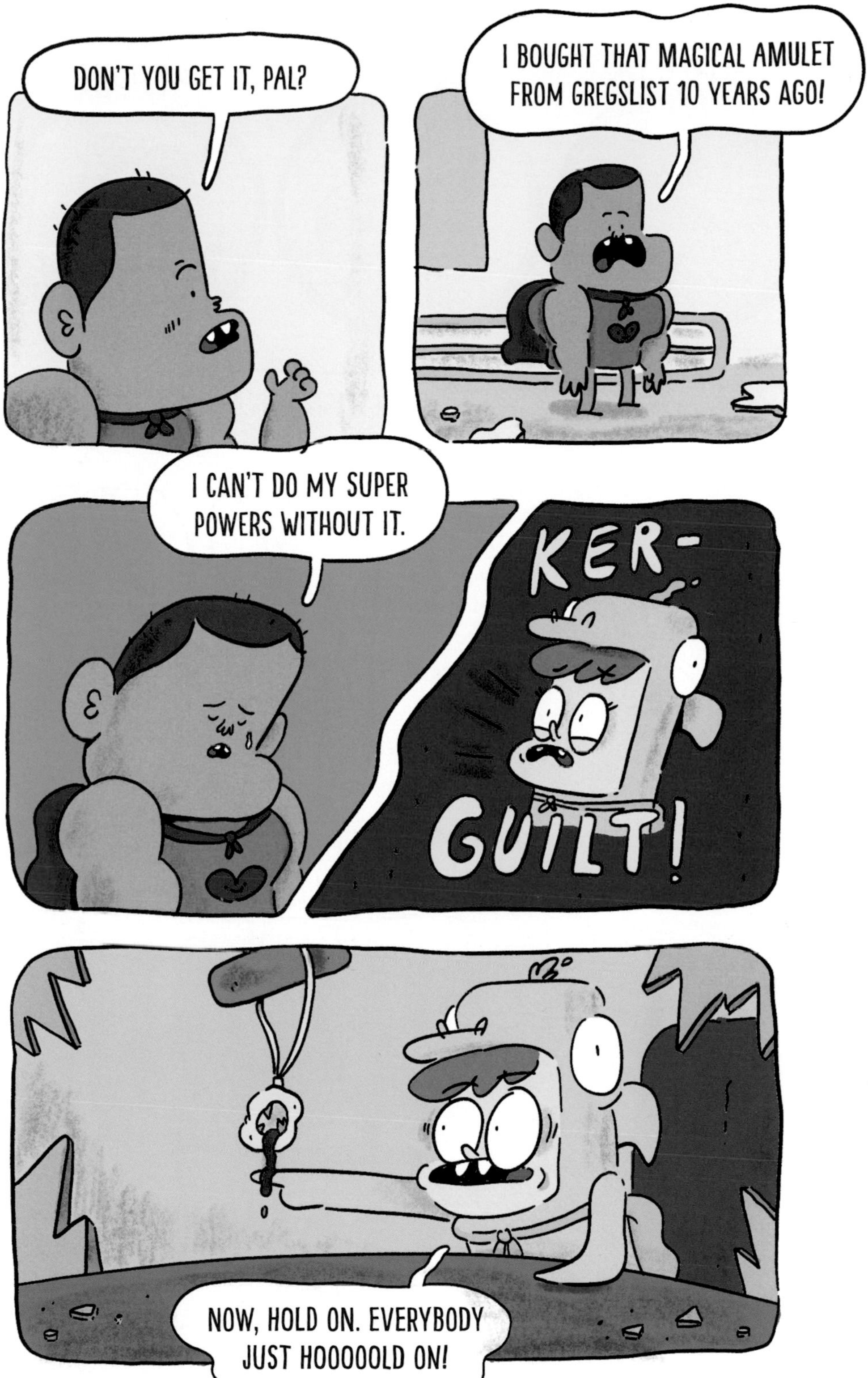
DON'T YOU GET IT, PAL?
I BOUGHT THAT MAGICAL AMULET FROM GREGSLIST 10 YEARS AGO!
I CAN'T DO MY SUPER POWERS WITHOUT IT.
KER-GUILT!
NOW, HOLD ON. EVERYBODY JUST HOOOOOLD ON!

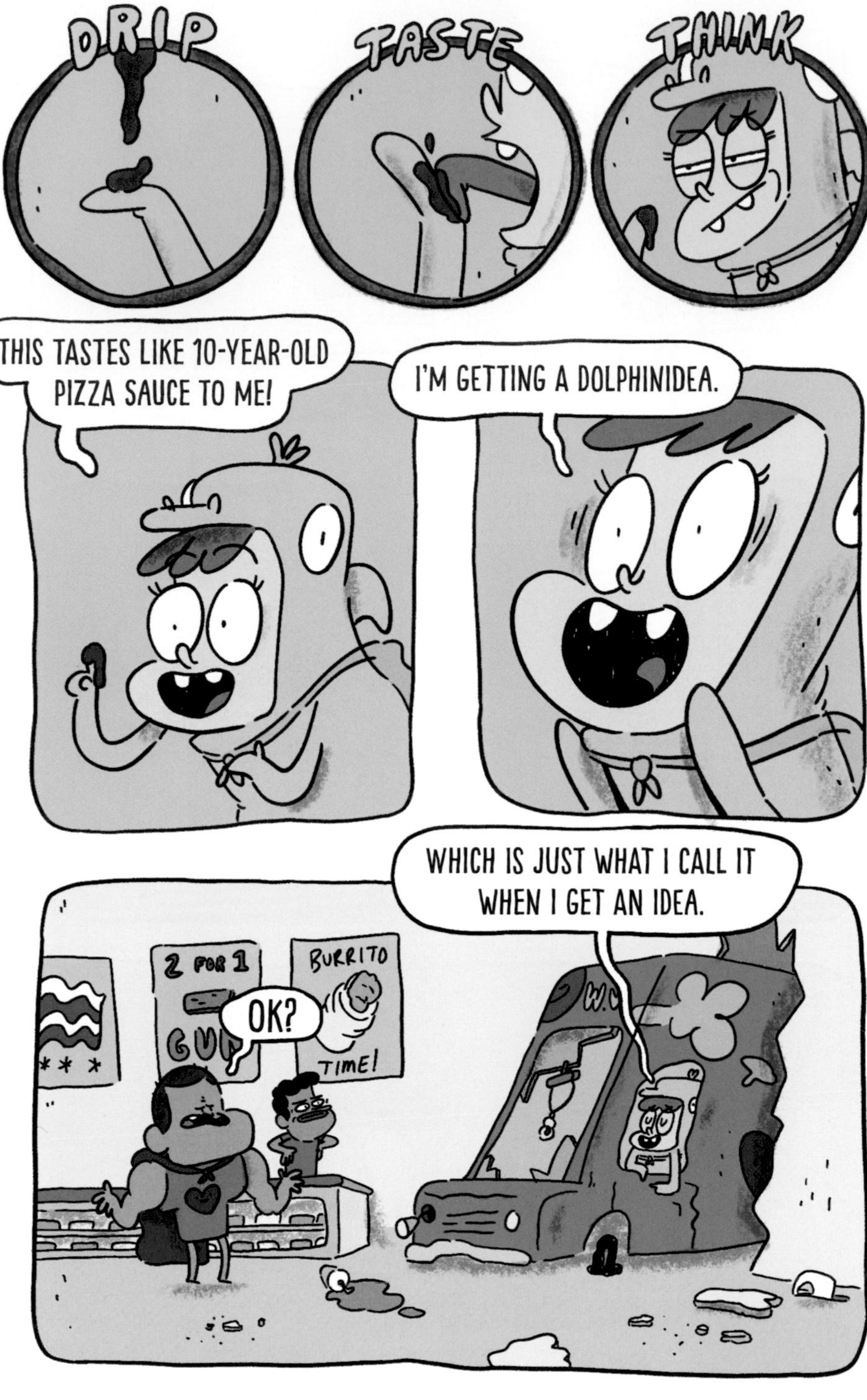
DRIP
TASTE
THINK
THIS TASTES LIKE 10-YEAR-OLD PIZZA SAUCE TO ME!
I'M GETTING A DOLPHINIDEA.
WHICH IS JUST WHAT I CALL IT WHEN I GET AN IDEA.
2 FOR 1
BURRITO TIME!
OK?

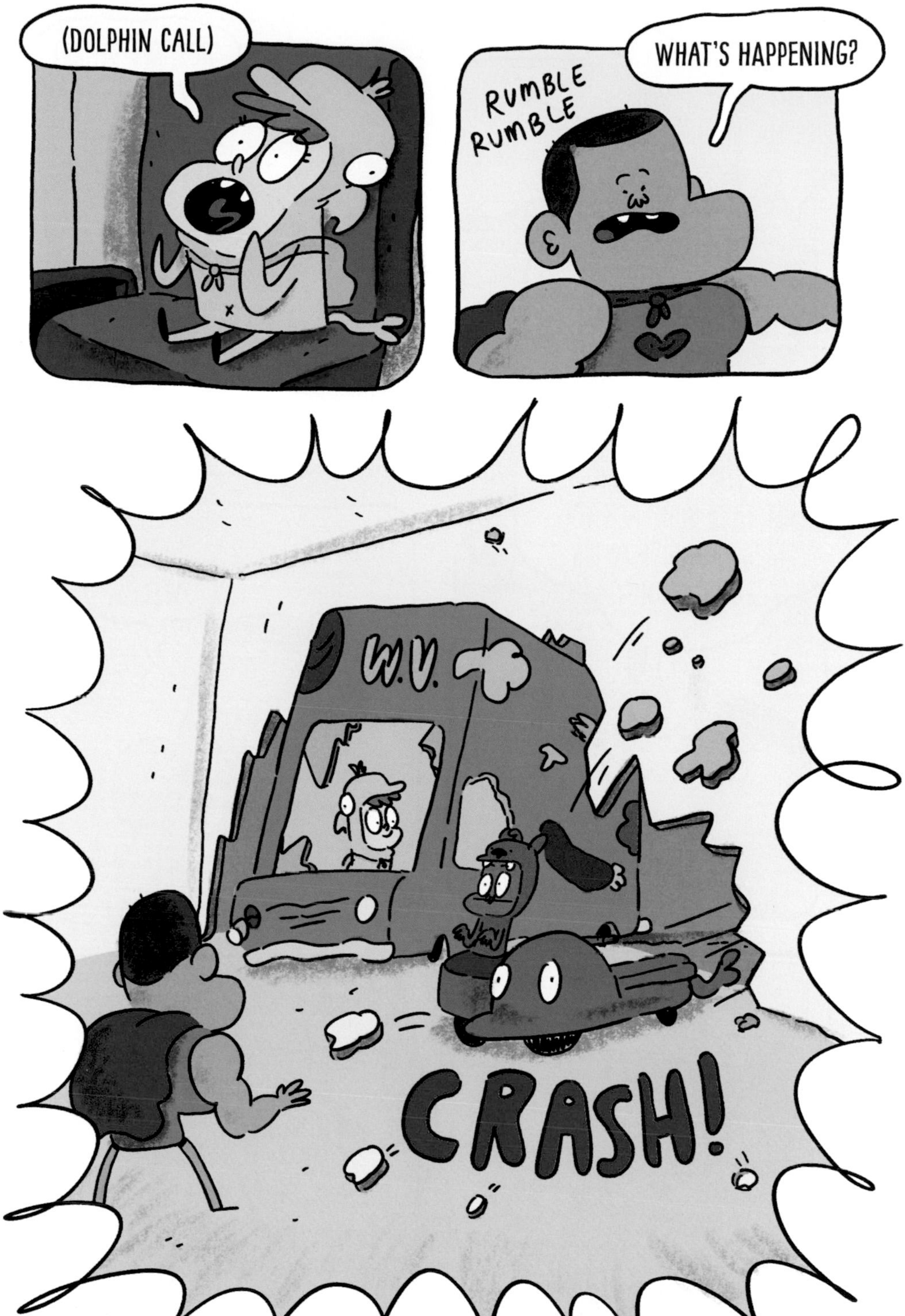
(DOLPHIN CALL)
WHAT'S HAPPENING?
RUMBLE RUMBLE
W.V.
CRASH!

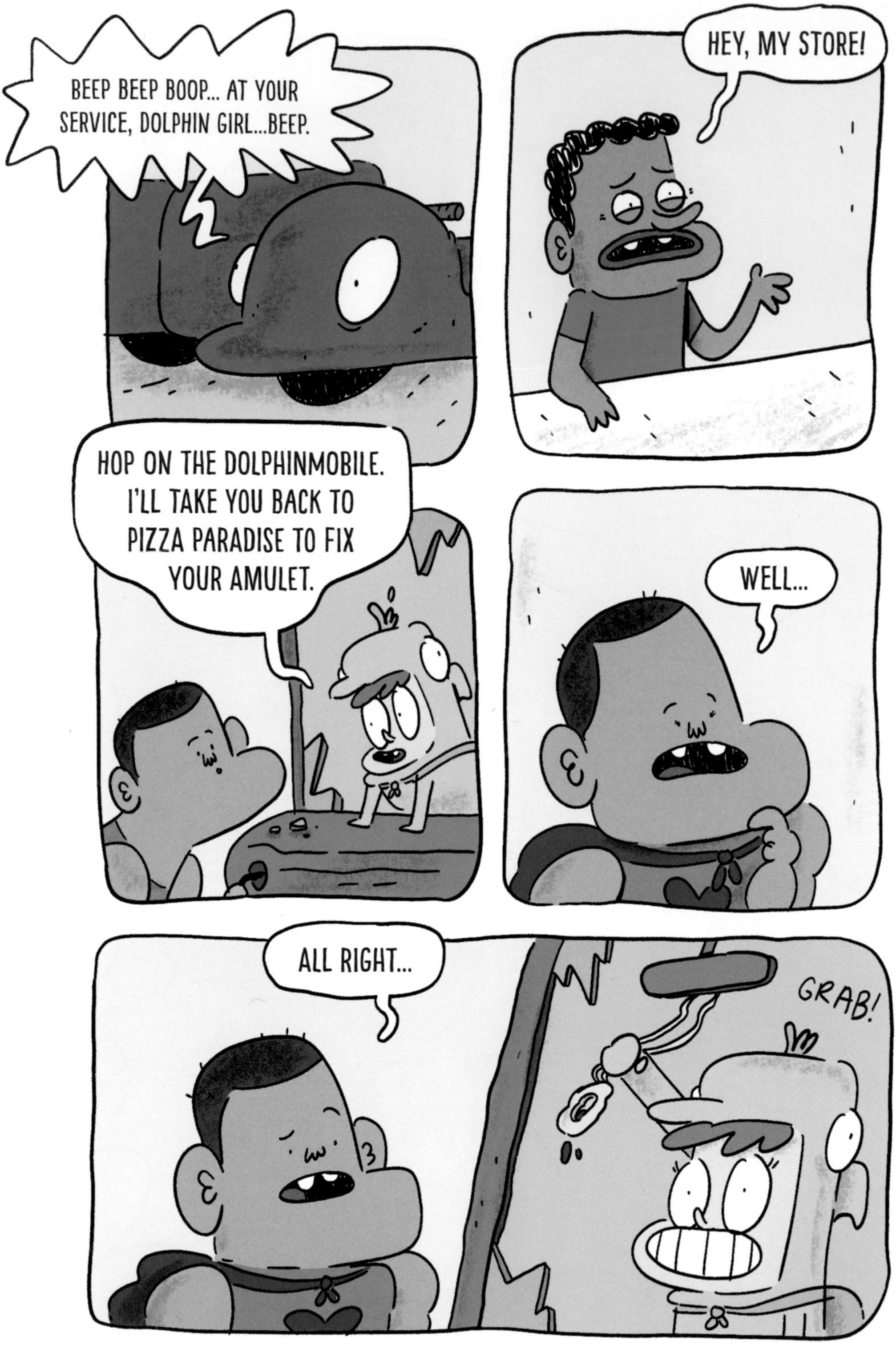
BEEP BEEP BOOP... AT YOUR SERVICE, DOLPHIN GIRL...BEEP.
HEY, MY STORE!
HOP ON THE DOLPHINMOBILE. I'LL TAKE YOU BACK TO PIZZA PARADISE TO FIX YOUR AMULET.
WELL...
ALL RIGHT...
GRAB!

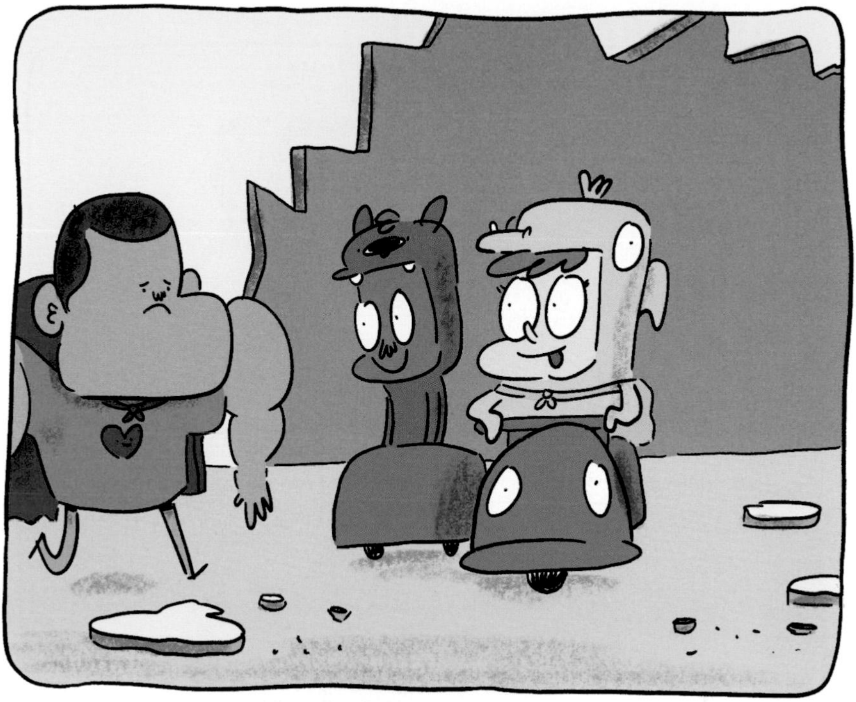

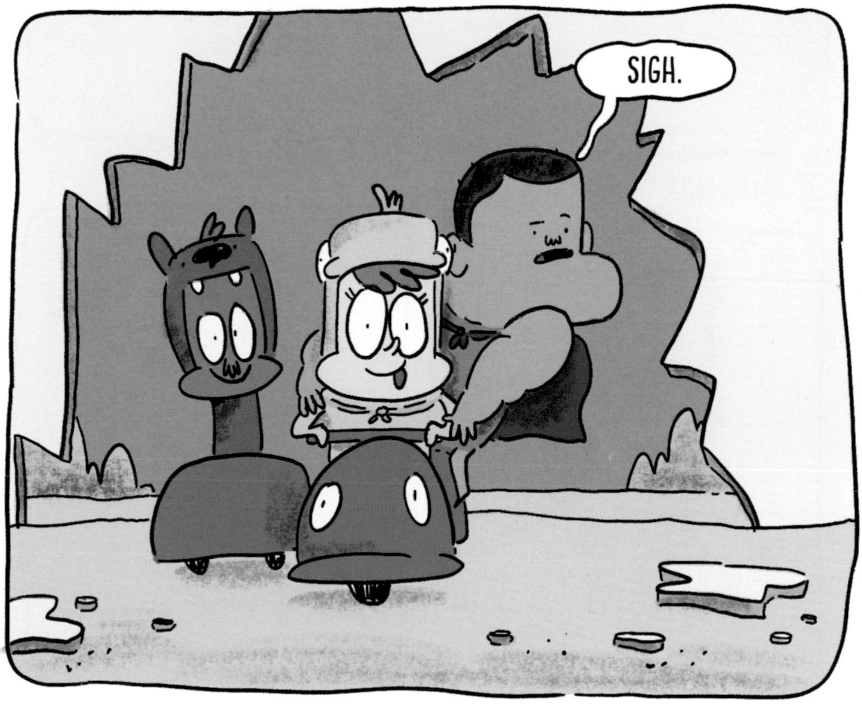
SIGH.

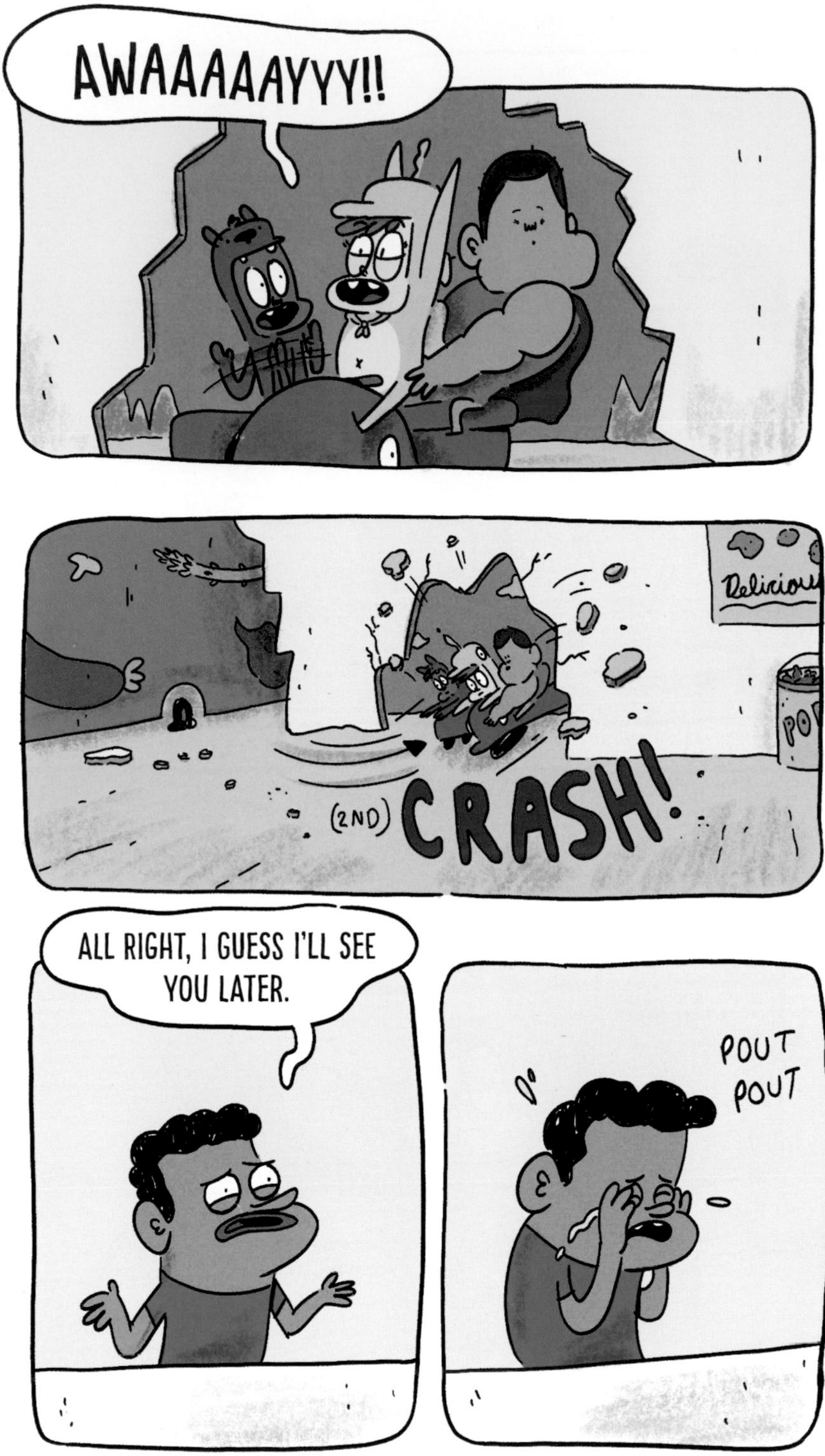
AWAAAAAYYY!!
Delicious
POP
(2ND) CRASH!
ALL RIGHT, I GUESS I'LL SEE YOU LATER.
POUT
POUT

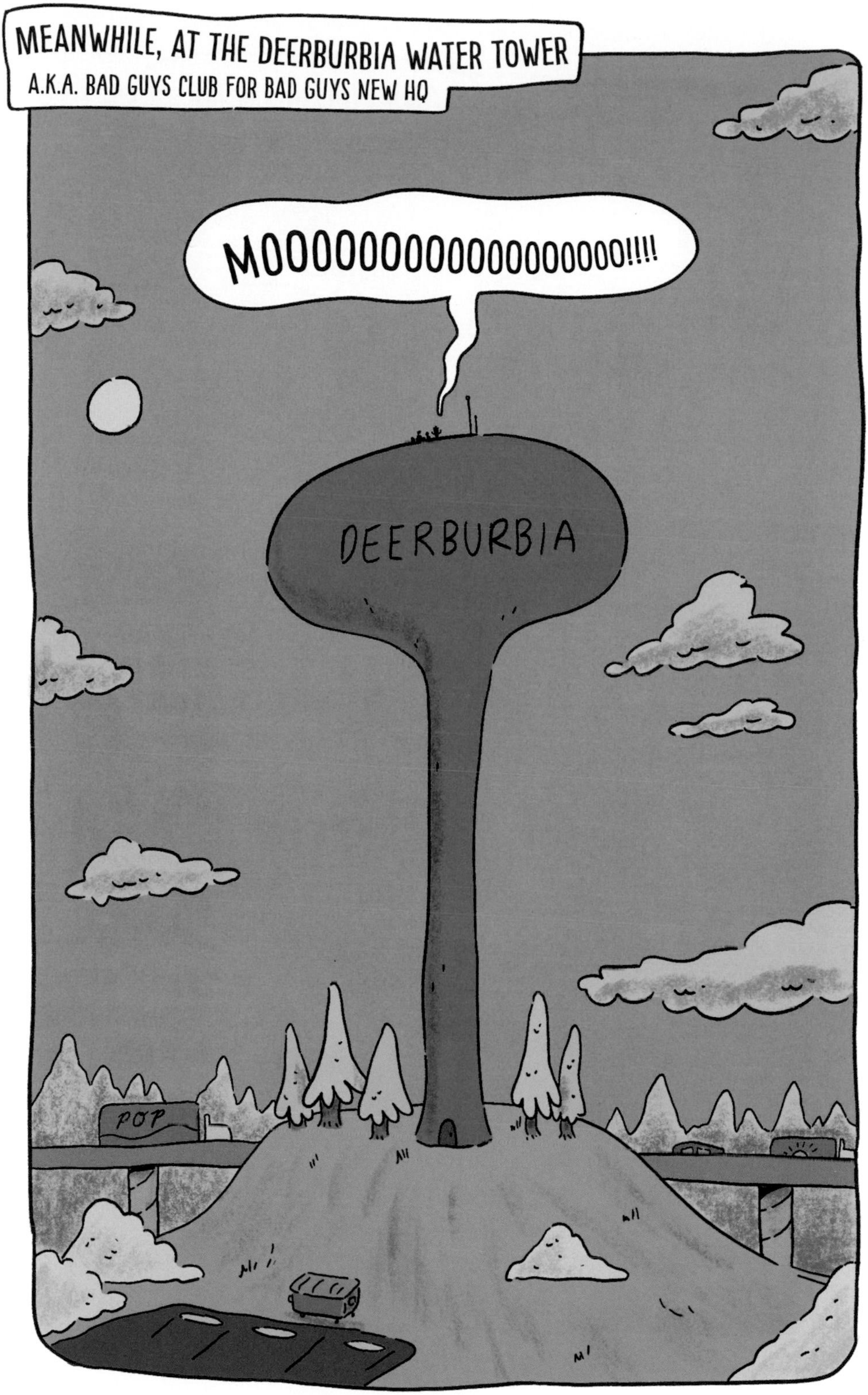
MEANWHILE, AT THE DEERBURBIA WATER TOWER
A.K.A. BAD GUYS CLUB FOR BAD GUYS NEW HQ
MOOOOOOOOOOOOOOOOOOO!!!!
DEERBURBIA
POP

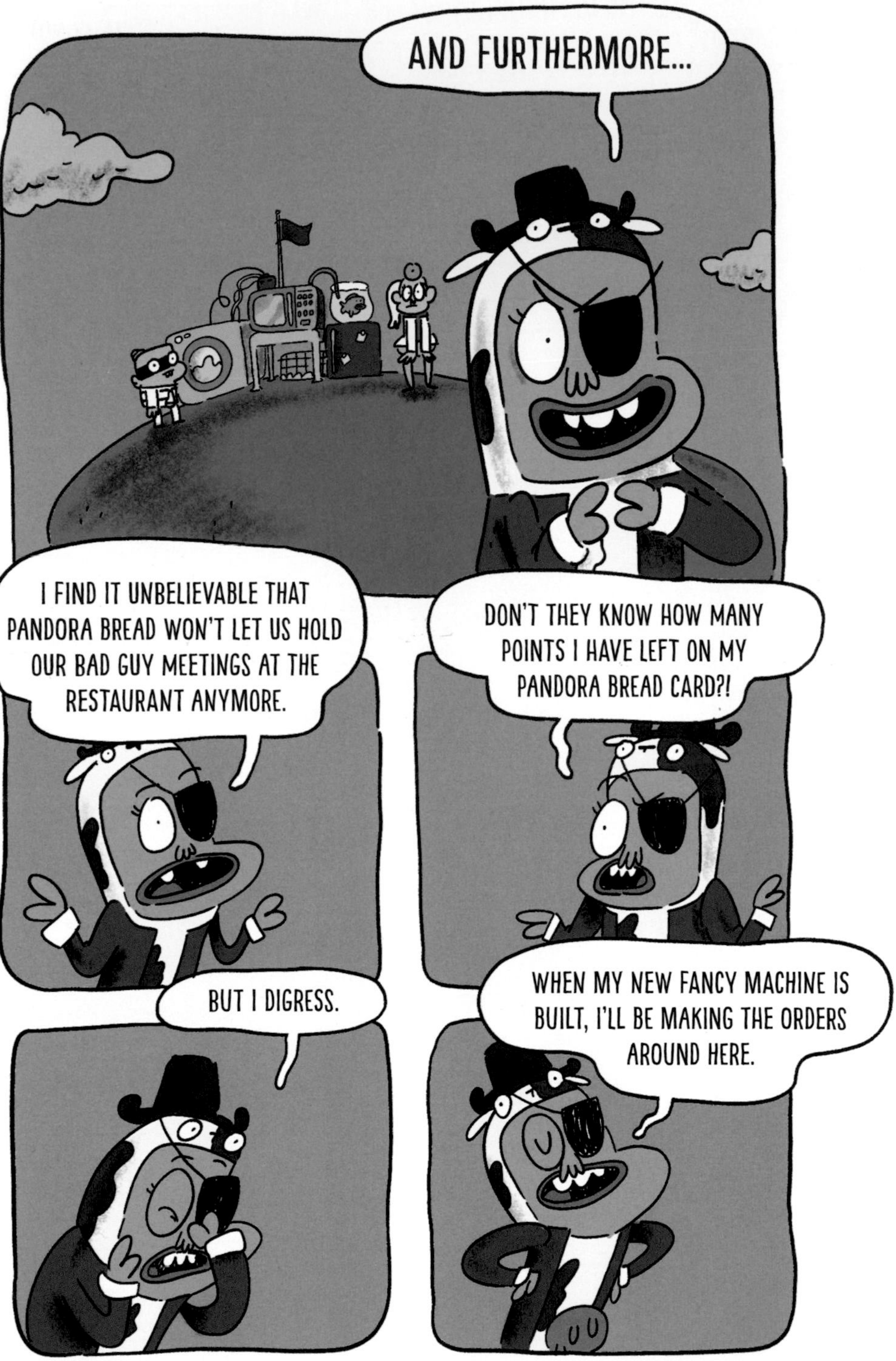
AND FURTHERMORE...
I FIND IT UNBELIEVABLE THAT PANDORA BREAD WON'T LET US HOLD OUR BAD GUY MEETINGS AT THE RESTAURANT ANYMORE.
DON'T THEY KNOW HOW MANY POINTS I HAVE LEFT ON MY PANDORA BREAD CARD?!
BUT I DIGRESS.
WHEN MY NEW FANCY MACHINE IS BUILT, I'LL BE MAKING THE ORDERS AROUND HERE.

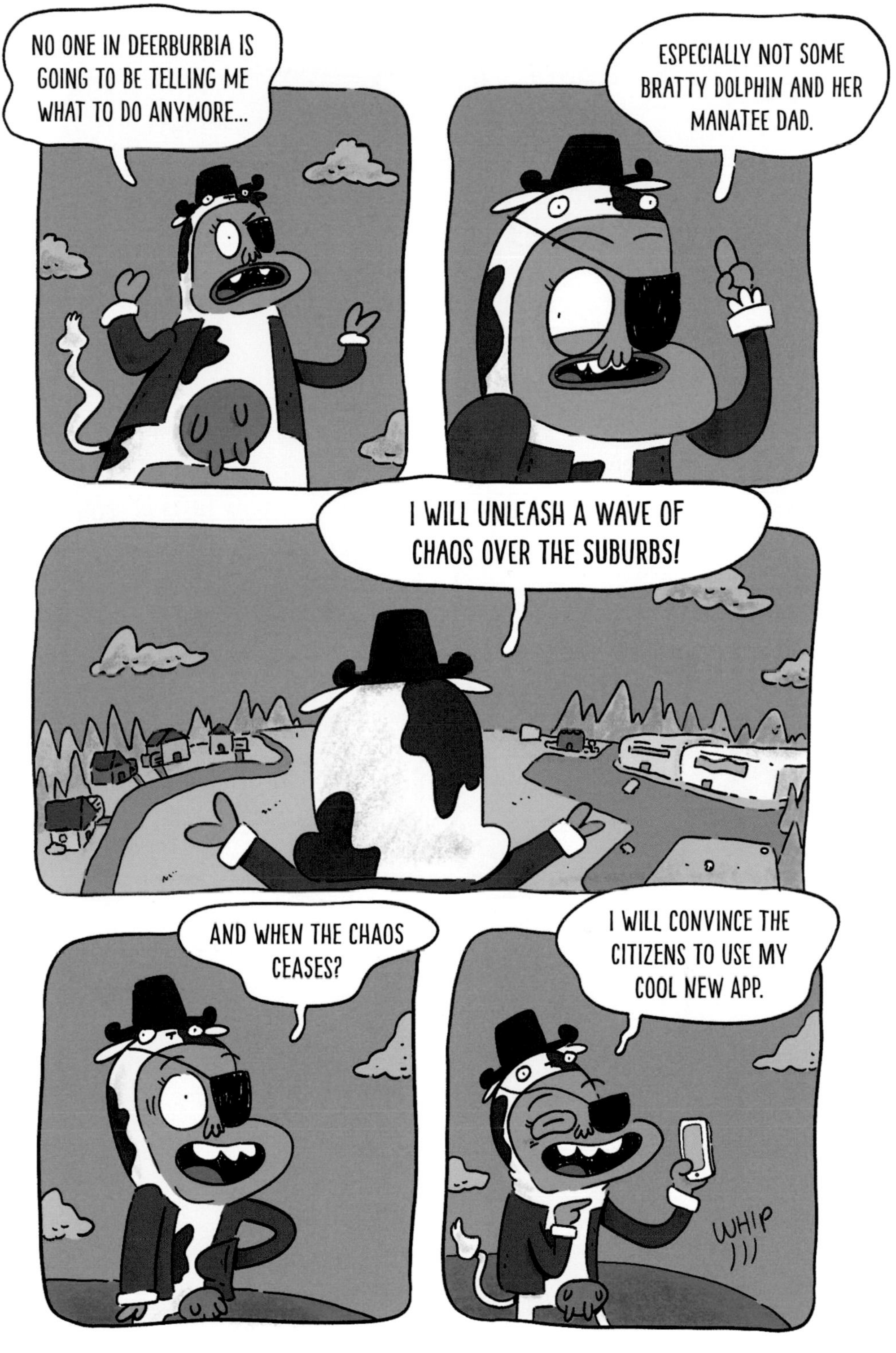
NO ONE IN DEERBURBIA IS GOING TO BE TELLING ME WHAT TO DO ANYMORE...
ESPECIALLY NOT SOME BRATTY DOLPHIN AND HER MANATEE DAD.
I WILL UNLEASH A WAVE OF CHAOS OVER THE SUBURBS!
AND WHEN THE CHAOS CEASES?
I WILL CONVINCE THE CITIZENS TO USE MY COOL NEW APP.
WHIP

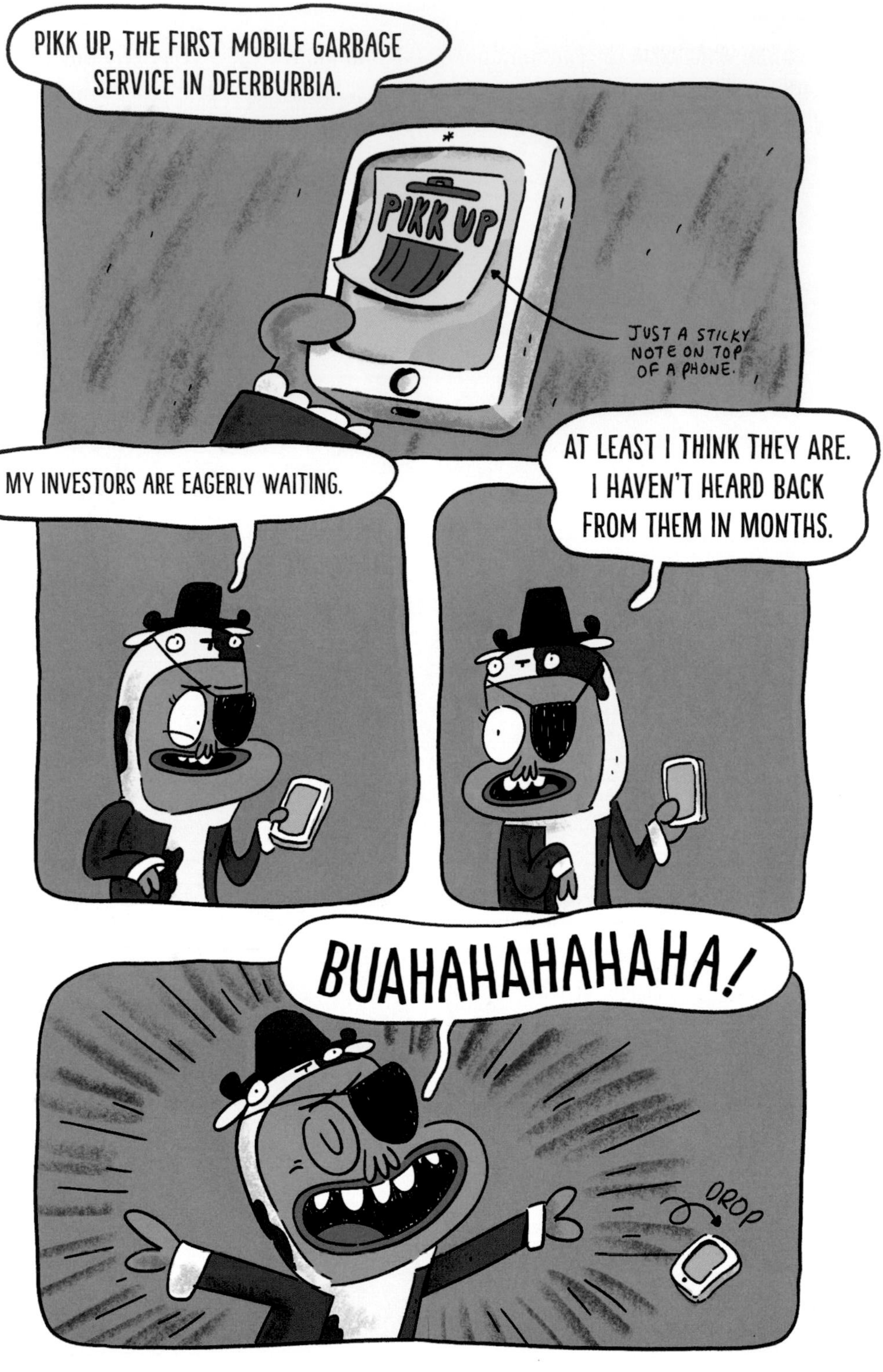
PIKK UP, THE FIRST MOBILE GARBAGE SERVICE IN DEERBURBIA.
PIKK UP
JUST A STICKY NOTE ON TOP OF A PHONE.
MY INVESTORS ARE EAGERLY WAITING.
AT LEAST I THINK THEY ARE. I HAVEN'T HEARD BACK FROM THEM IN MONTHS.
BUAHAHAHAHAHA!
DROP

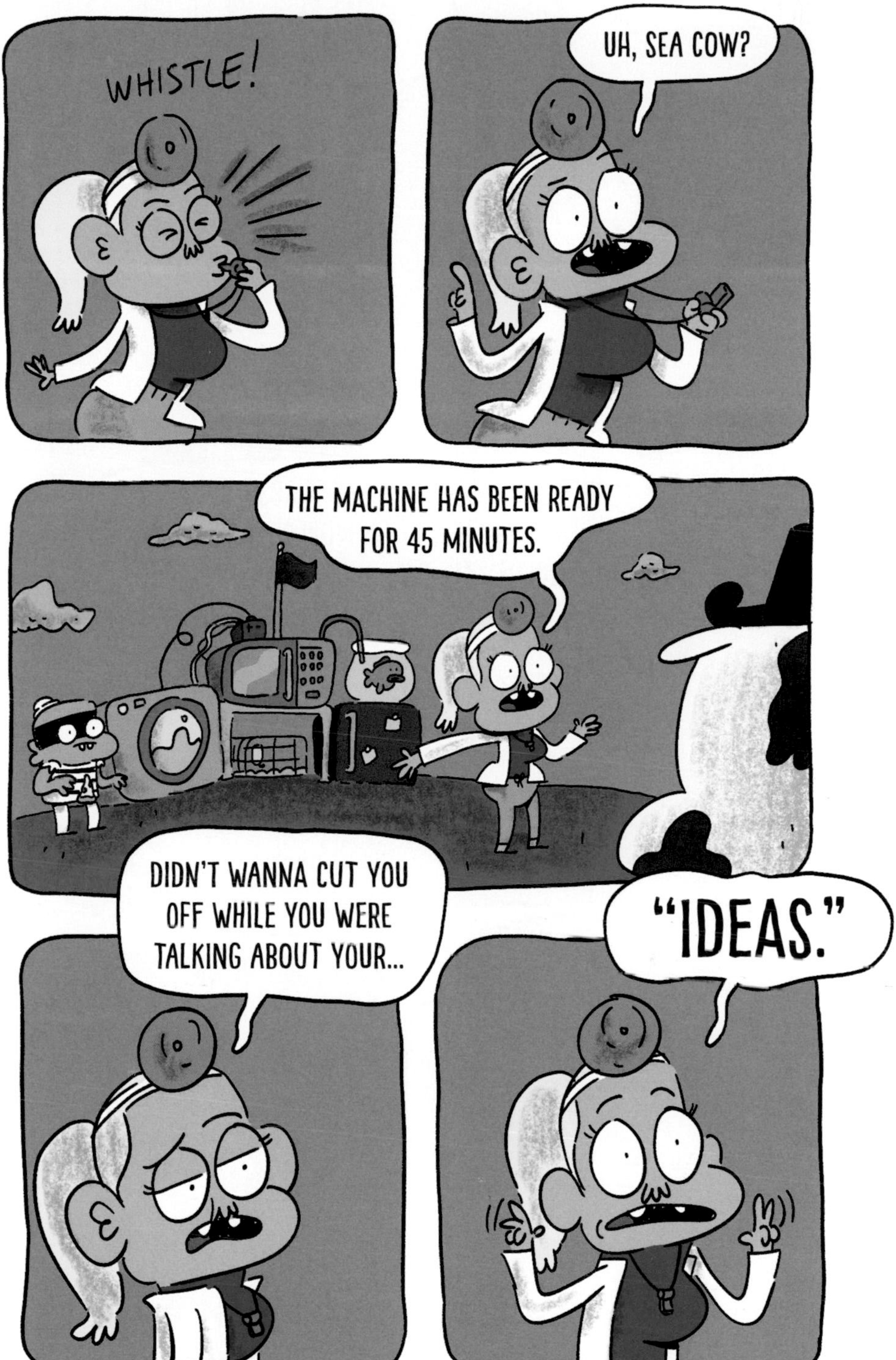
WHISTLE!
UH, SEA COW?
THE MACHINE HAS BEEN READY FOR 45 MINUTES.
DIDN'T WANNA CUT YOU OFF WHILE YOU WERE TALKING ABOUT YOUR...
"IDEAS."

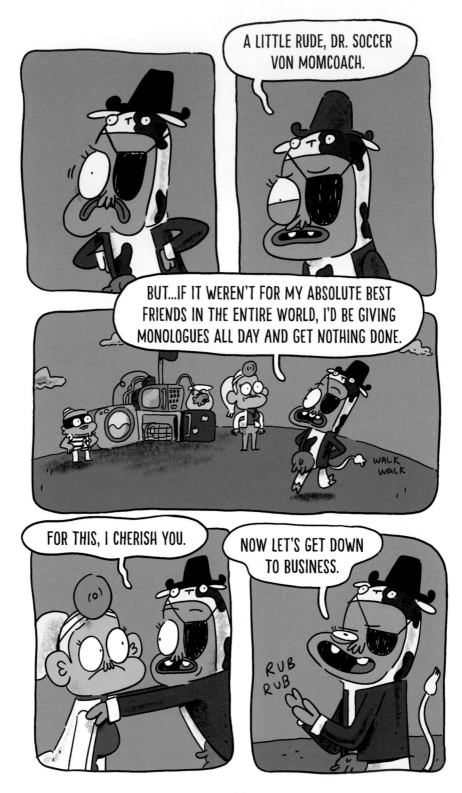

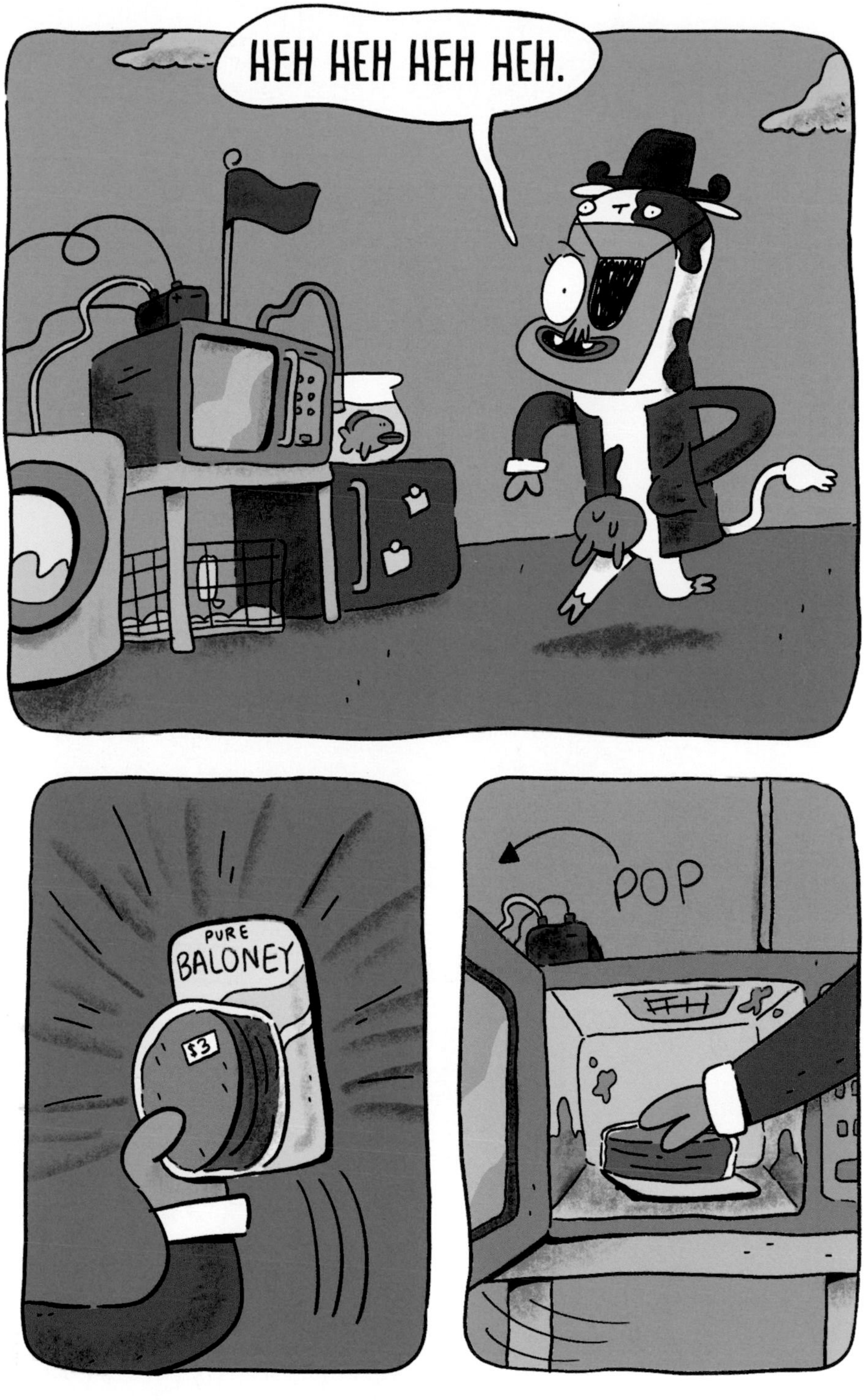
HEH HEH HEH HEH.
PURE
BALONEY
$3
POP

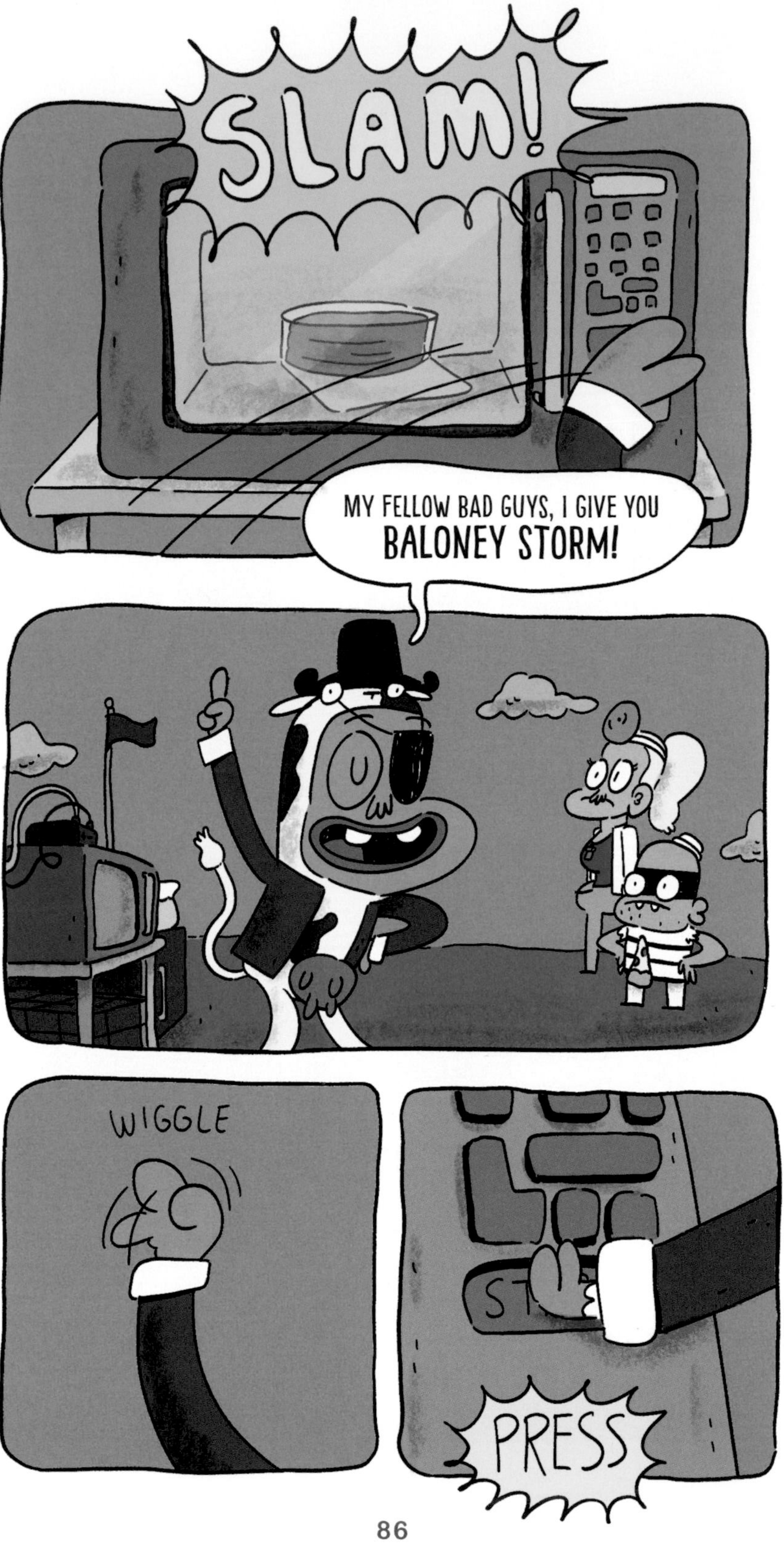
SLAM!
MY FELLOW BAD GUYS, I GIVE YOU BALONEY STORM!
WIGGLE
ST
PRESS

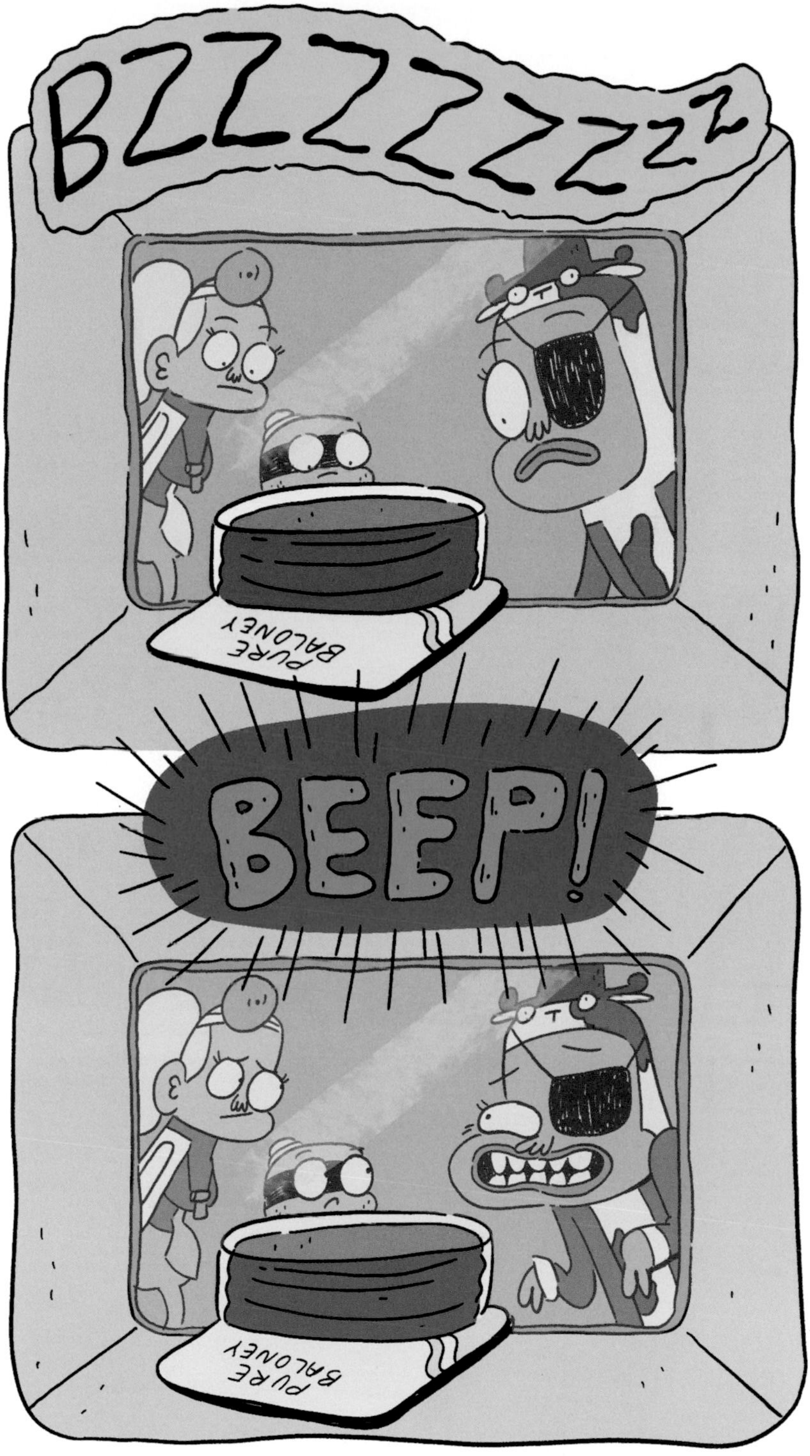
BZZZZZZzz
PURE BALONEY
BEEP!
PURE BALONEY

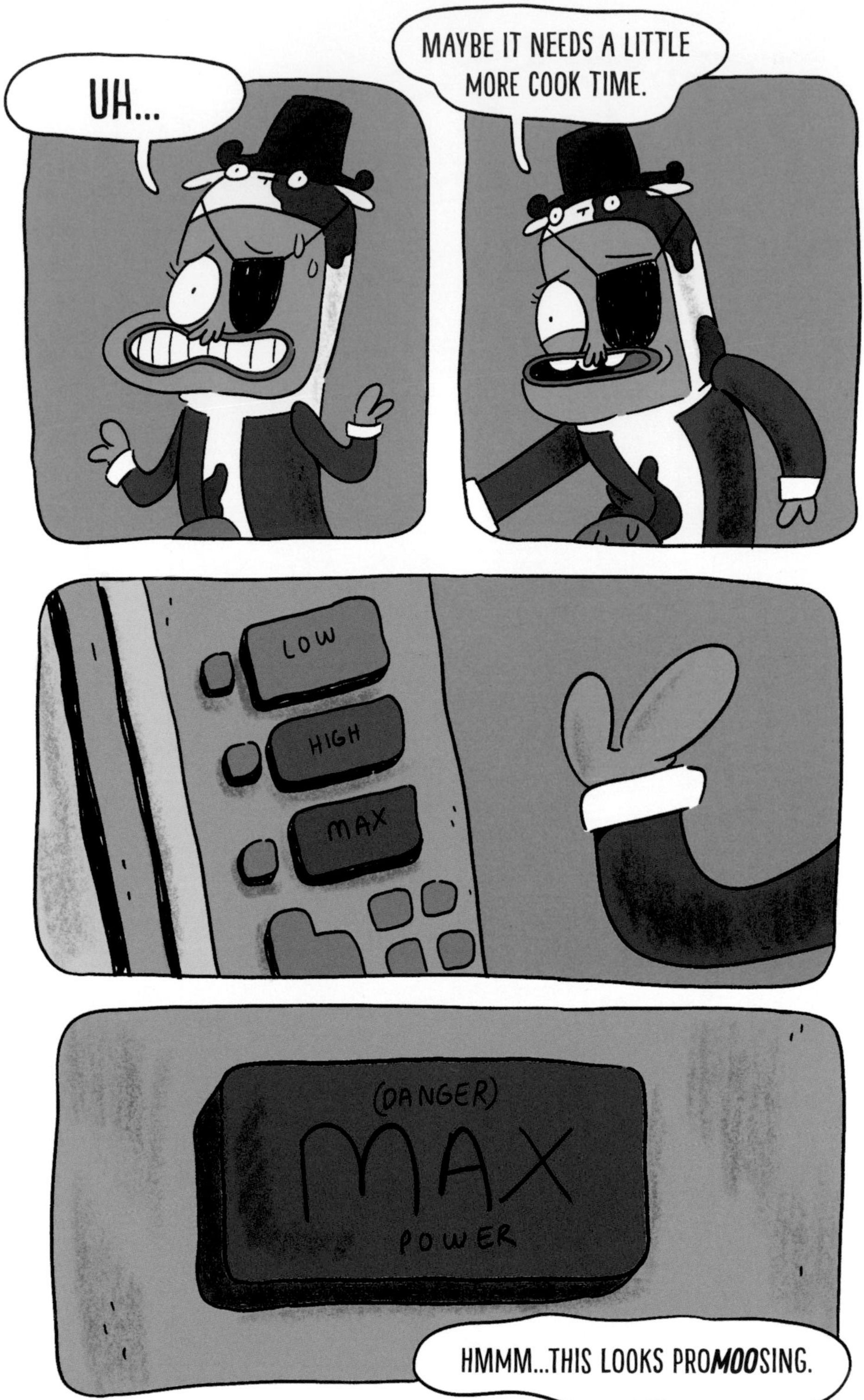
UH...
MAYBE IT NEEDS A LITTLE MORE COOK TIME.
LOW
HIGH
MAX
(DANGER)
MAX
POWER
HMMM...THIS LOOKS PROMOOSING.

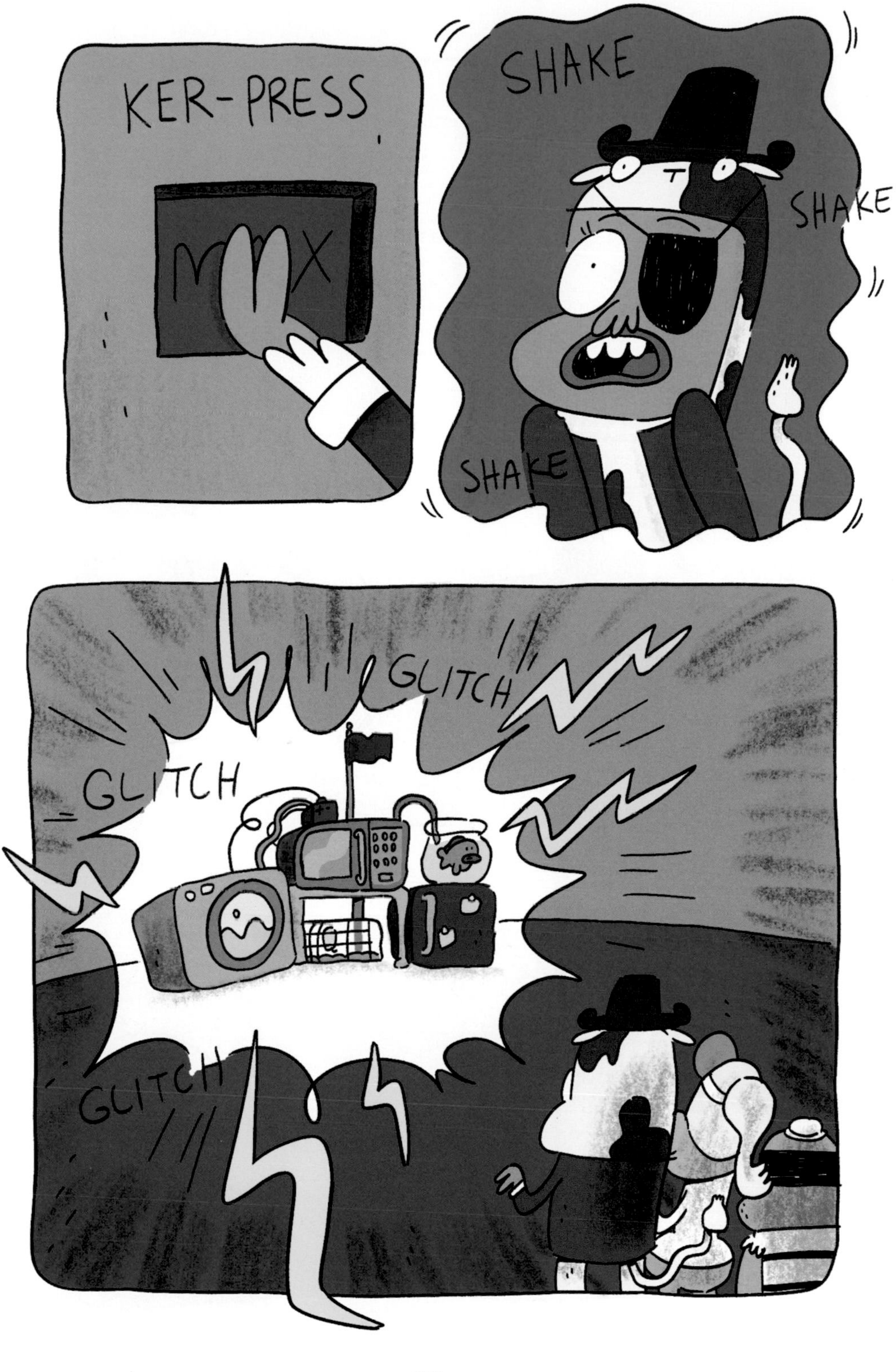
KER-PRESS
MAX
SHAKE
SHAKE
SHAKE
GLITCH
GLITCH
GLITCH

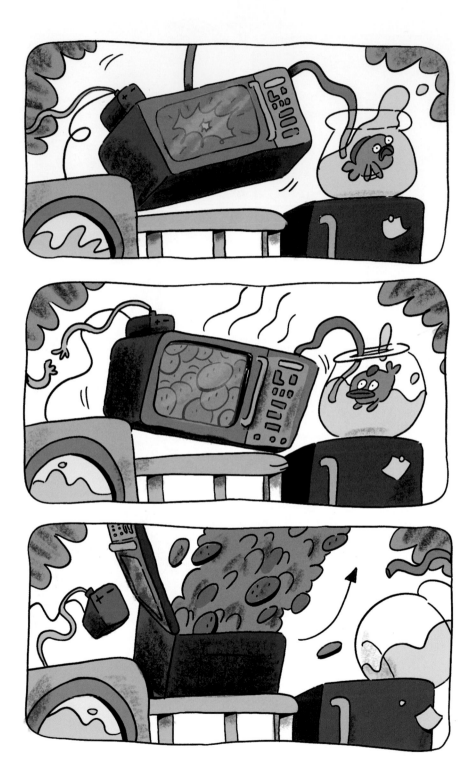

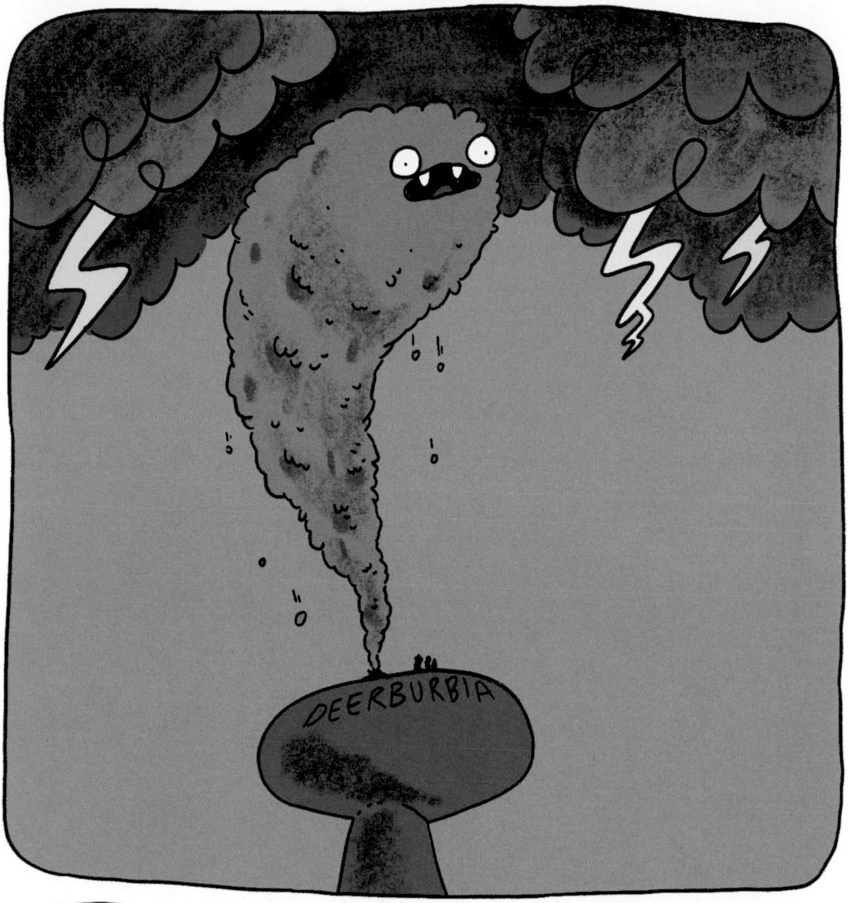
DEERBURBIA

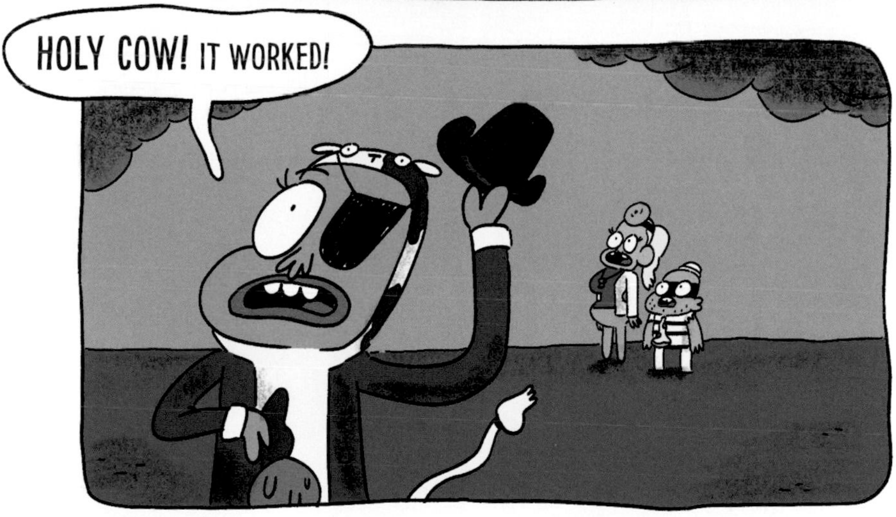
HOLY COW! IT WORKED!

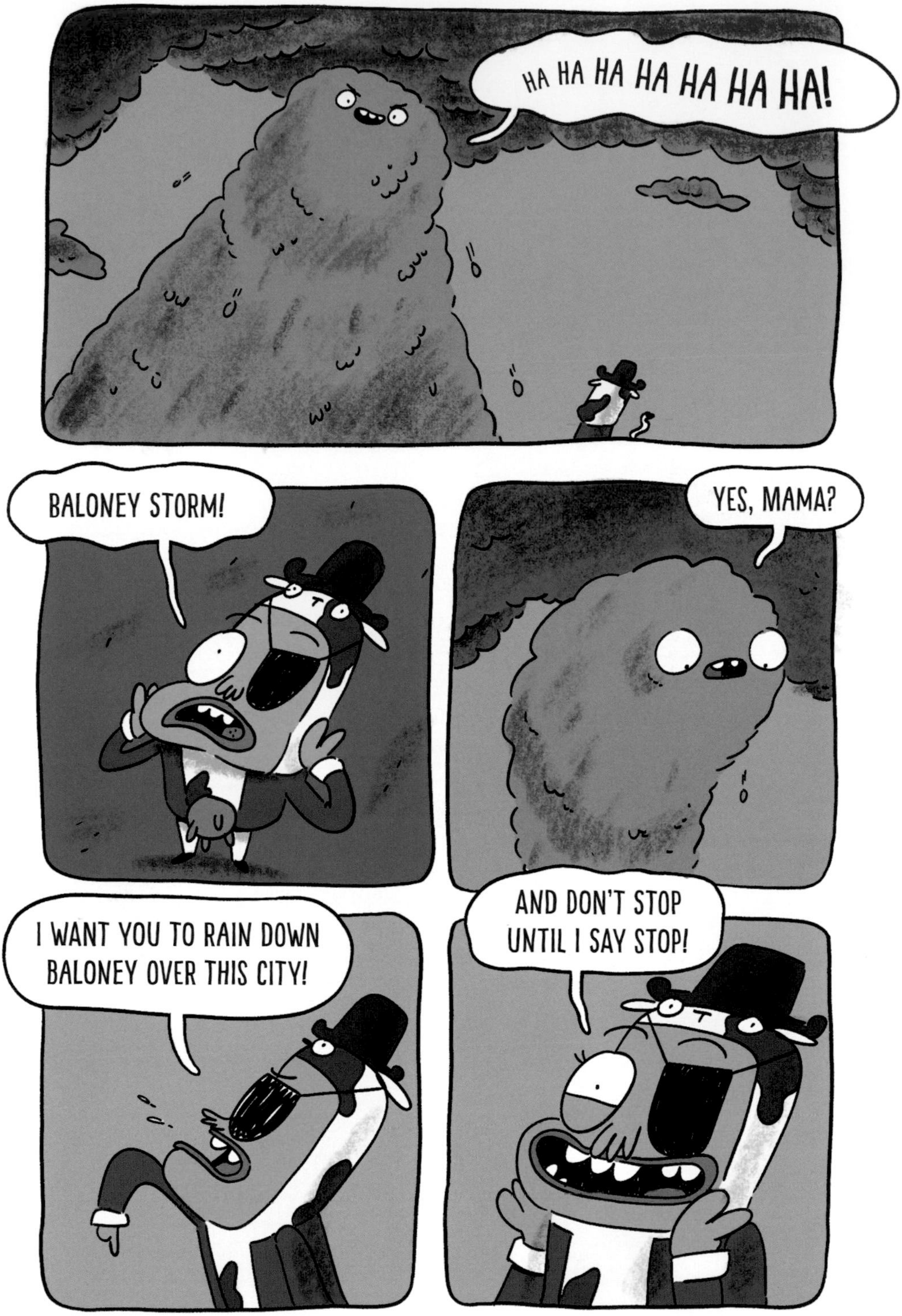
HA HA HA HA HA HA HA!
BALONEY STORM!
YES, MAMA?
I WANT YOU TO RAIN DOWN BALONEY OVER THIS CITY!
AND DON'T STOP UNTIL I SAY STOP!

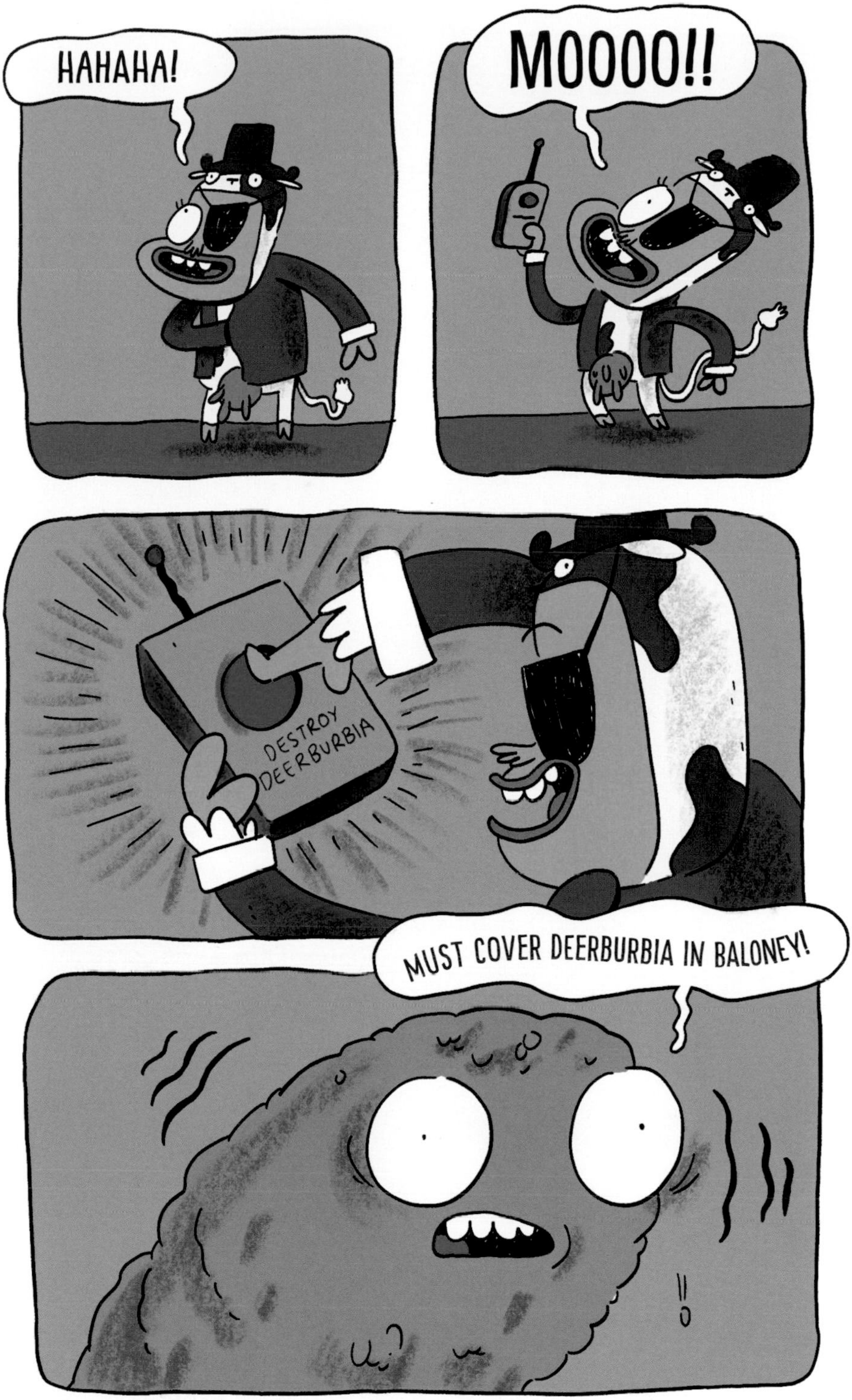
HAHAHA!
MOOOO!!
DESTROY DEERBURBIA
MUST COVER DEERBURBIA IN BALONEY!
!!

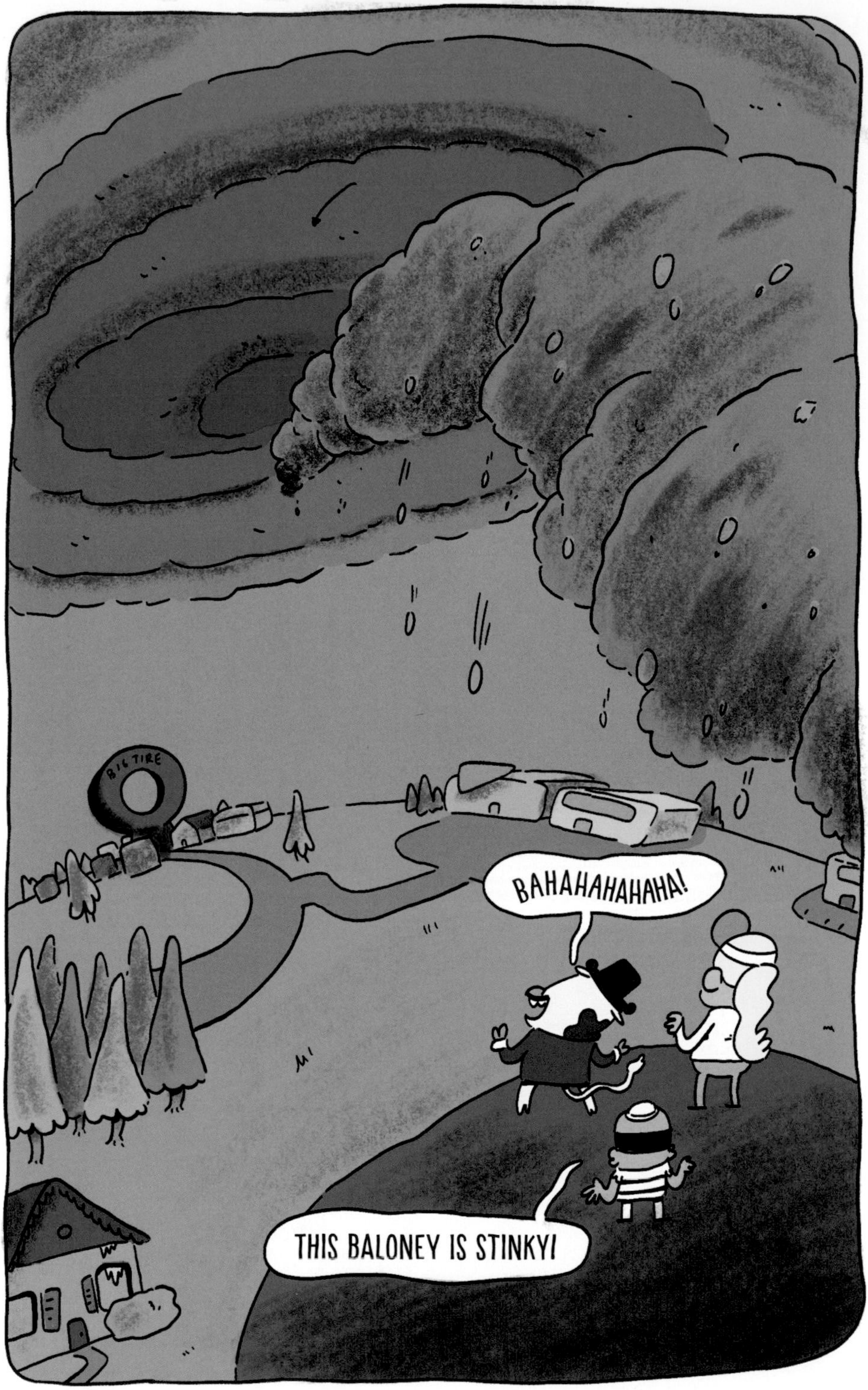
BIG TIRE
BAHAHAHAHAHA!
THIS BALONEY IS STINKY!

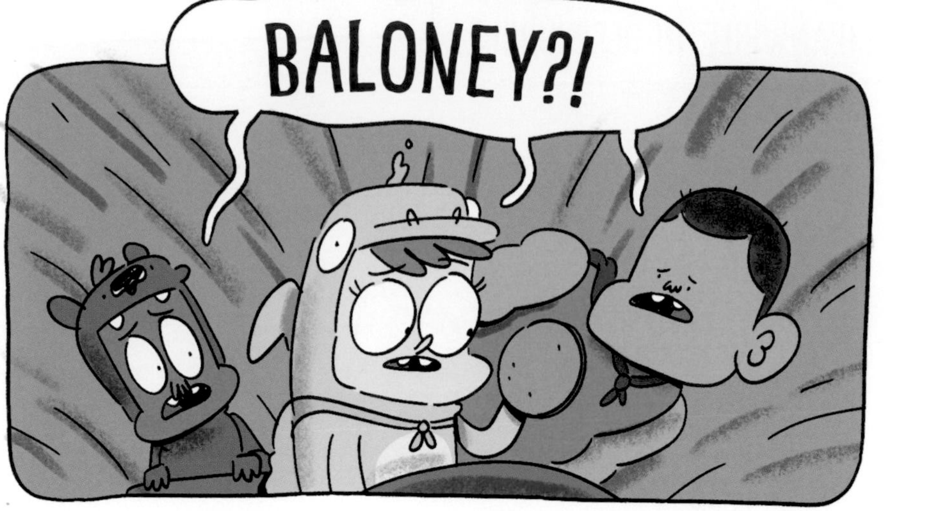
BALONEY?!

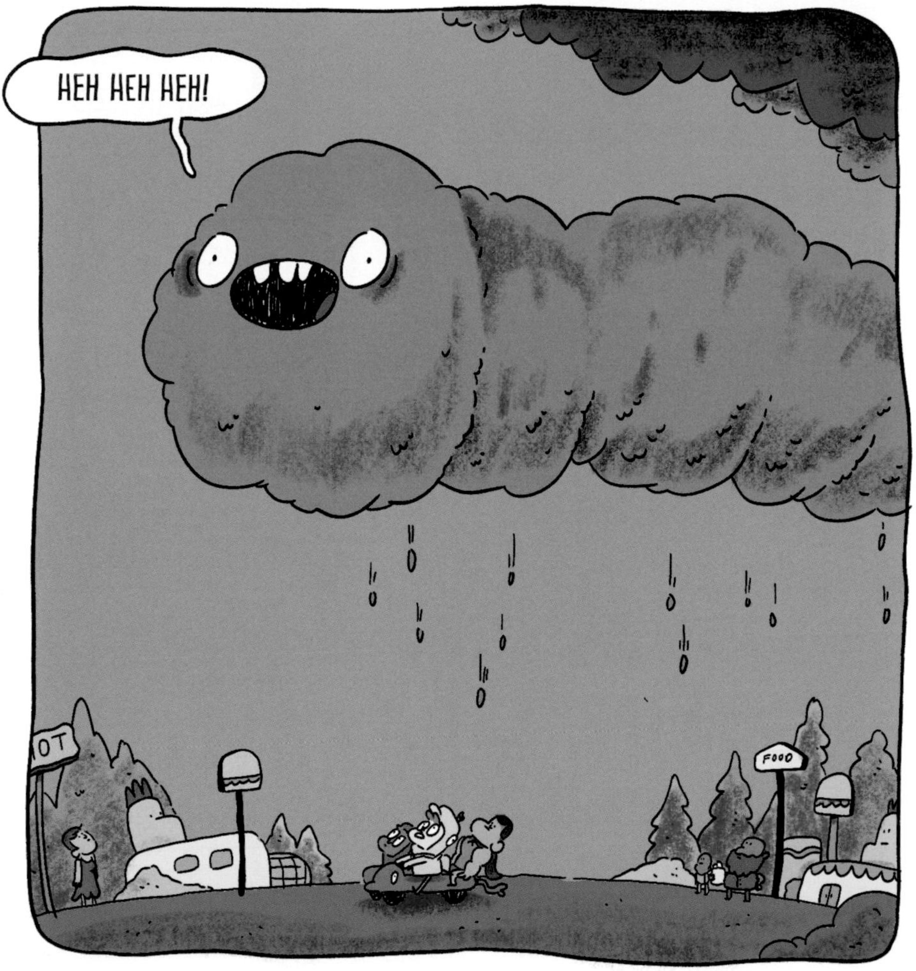
HEH HEH HEH!
FOOD

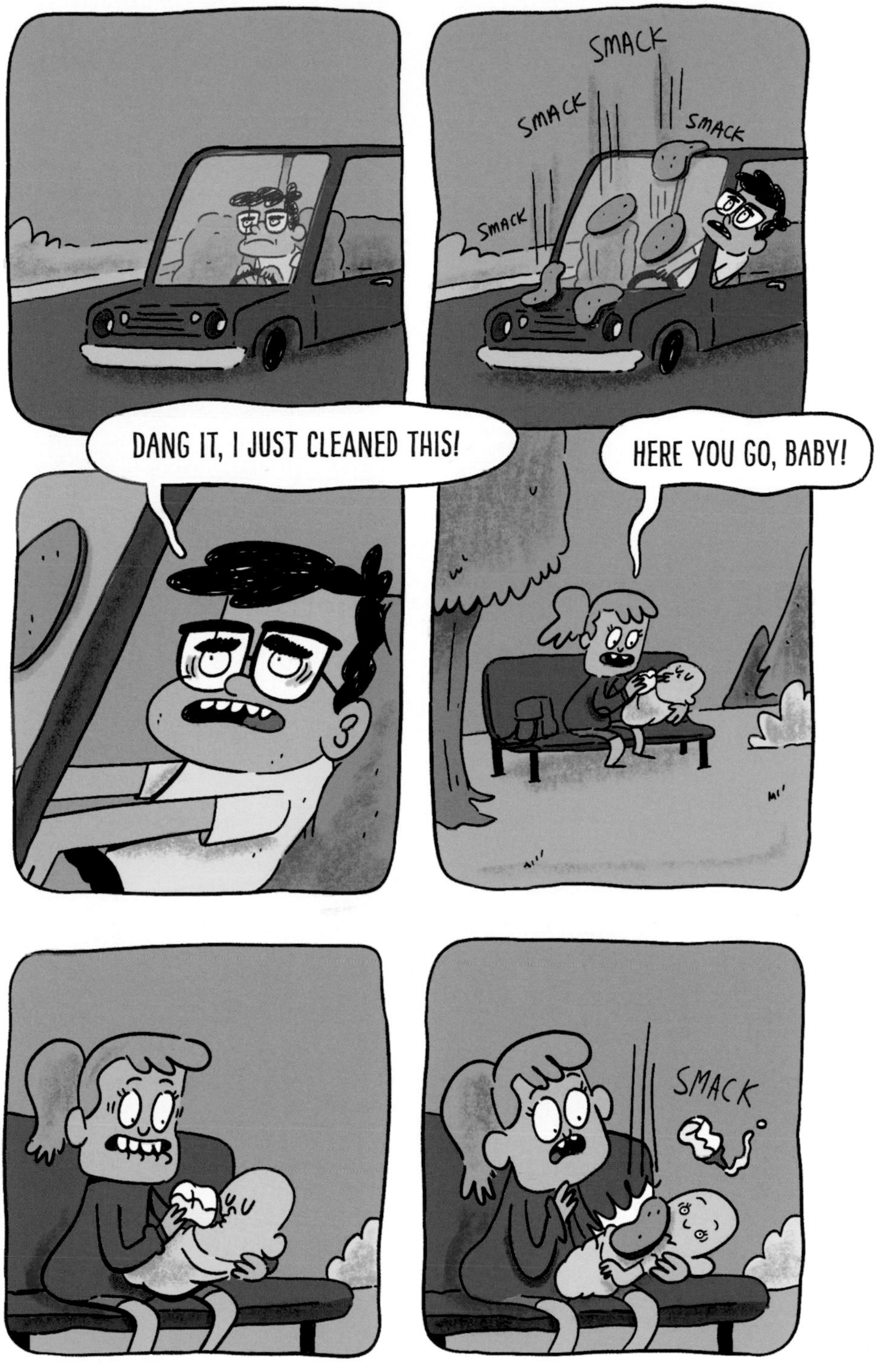
SMACK
SMACK
SMACK
SMACK
DANG IT, I JUST CLEANED THIS!
HERE YOU GO, BABY!
SMACK

100

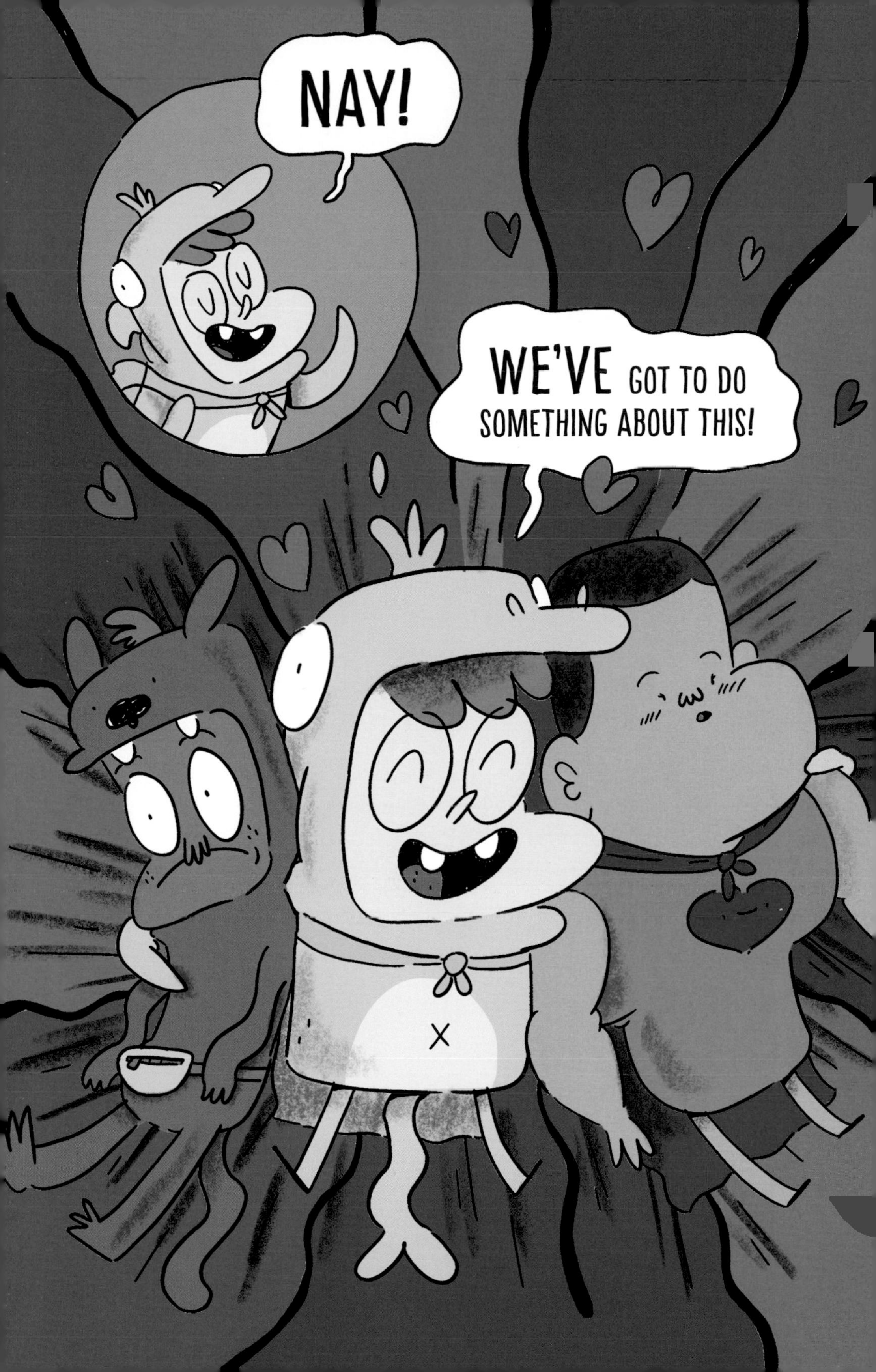
NAY!
WE'VE GOT TO DO SOMETHING ABOUT THIS!

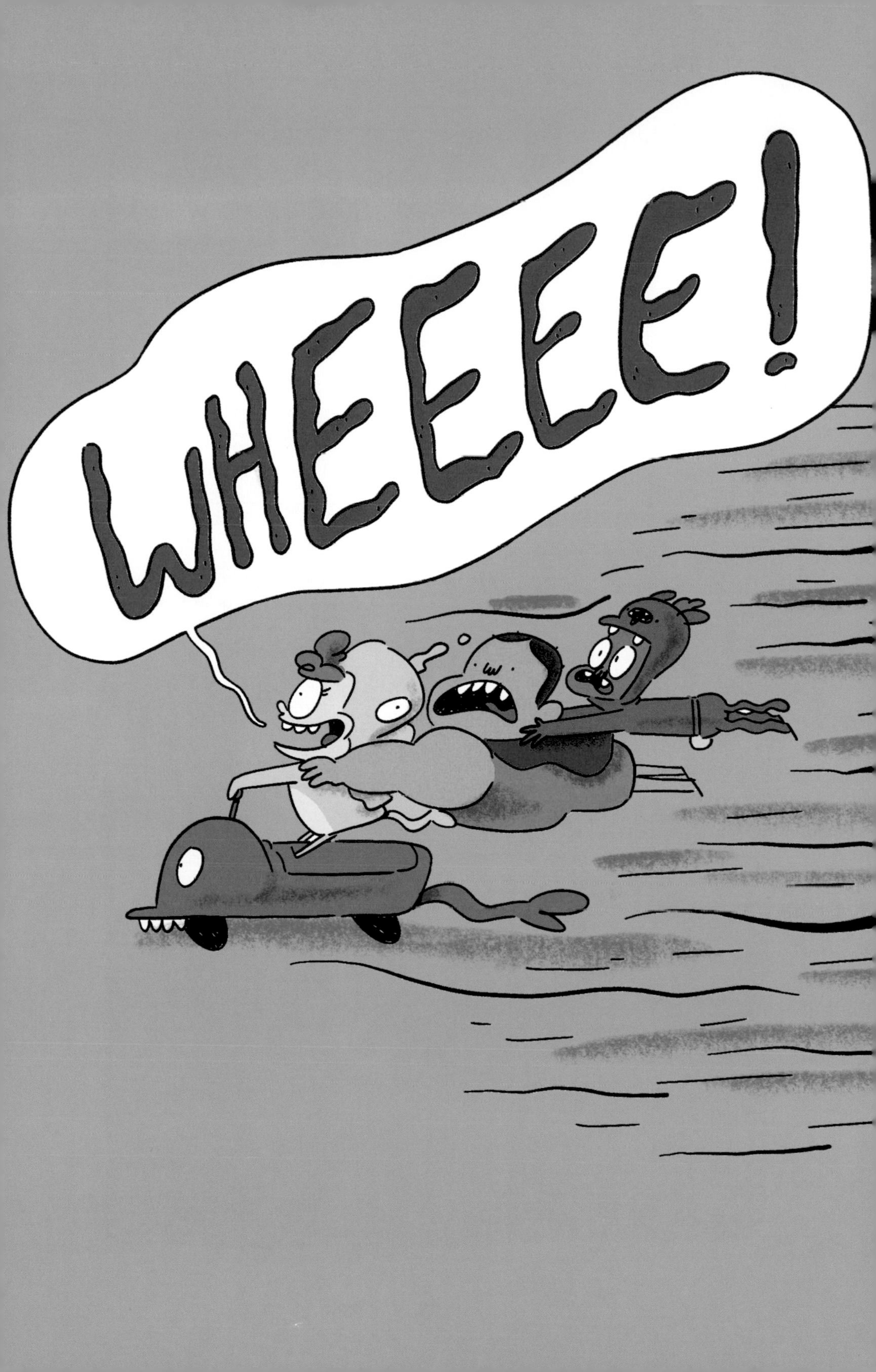
WHEEEE!

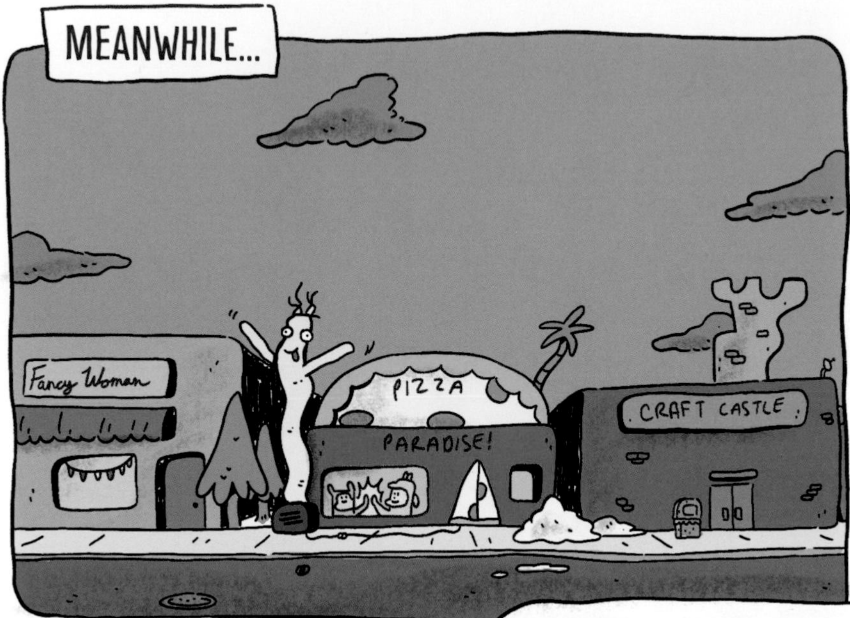
MEANWHILE...
Fancy Woman
PIZZA
PARADISE!
CRAFT CASTLE

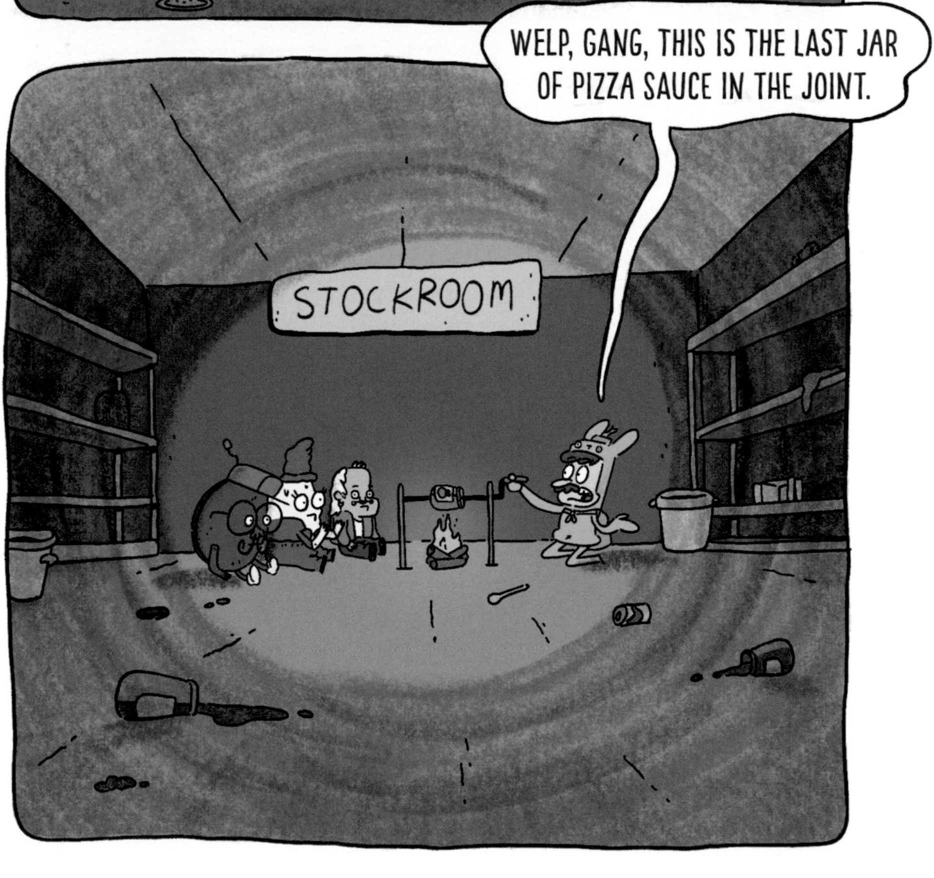
WELP, GANG, THIS IS THE LAST JAR OF PIZZA SAUCE IN THE JOINT.
STOCKROOM

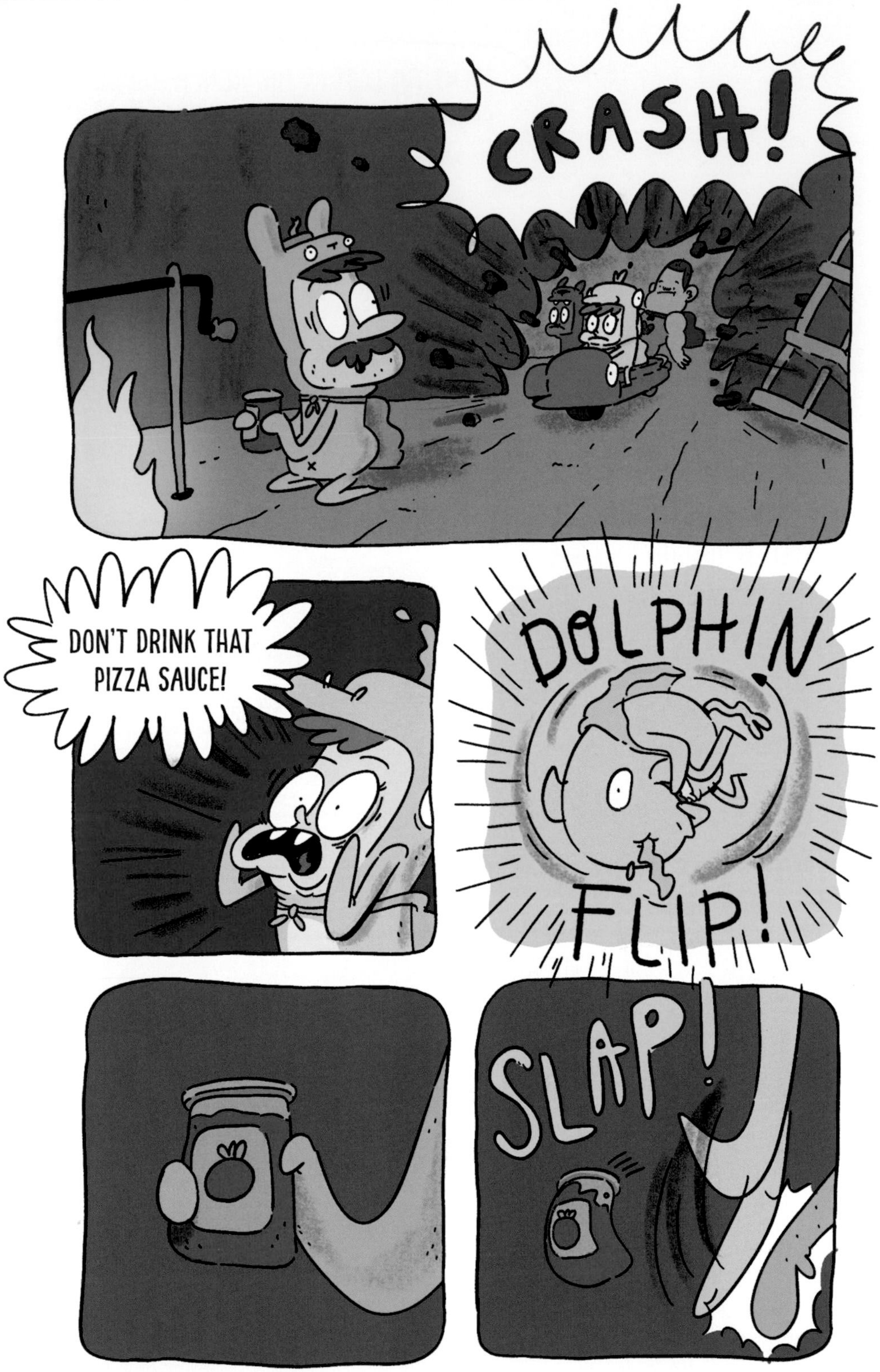
CRASH!
DON'T DRINK THAT PIZZA SAUCE!
DOLPHIN FLIP!
SLAP!

108

111

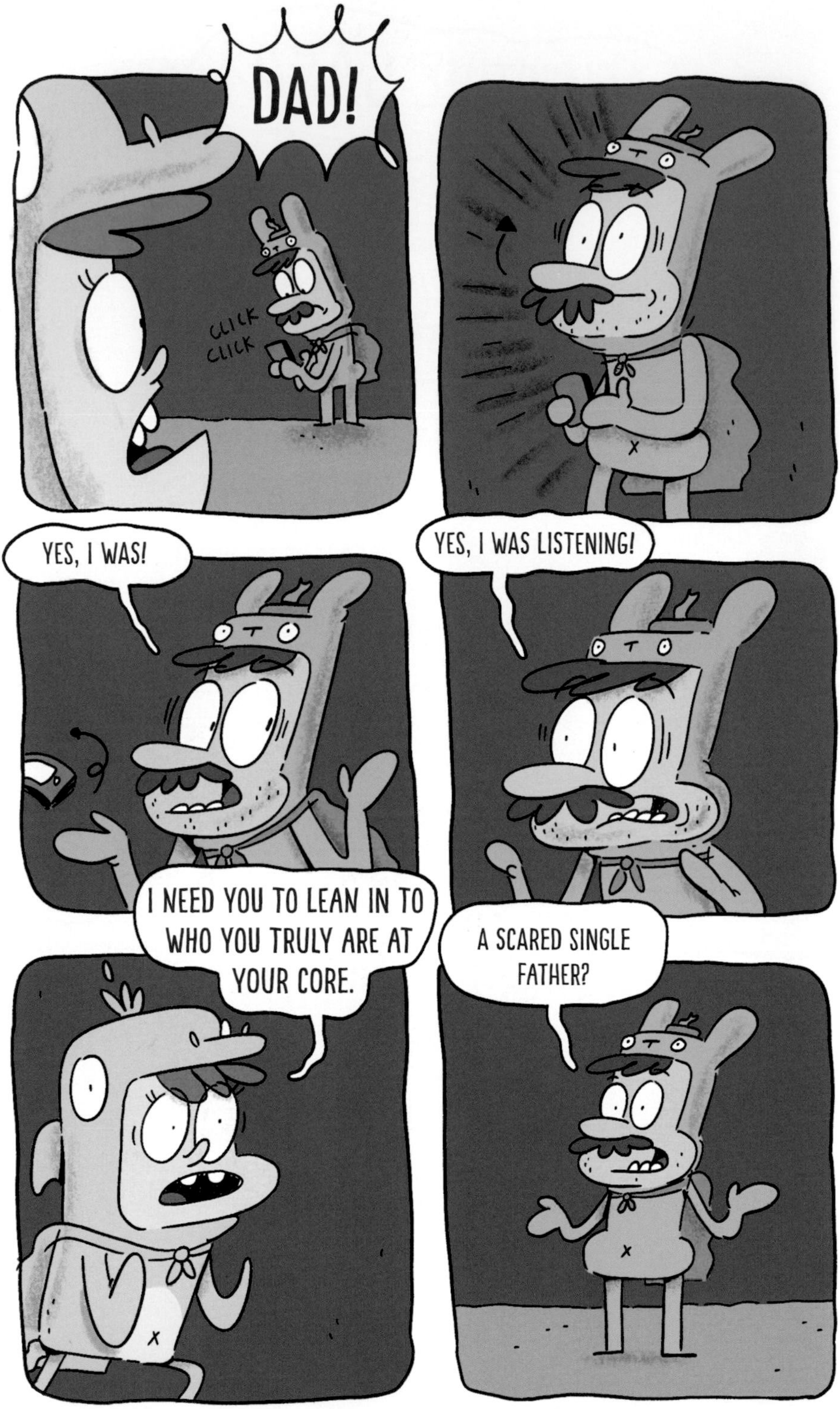
DAD!
CLICK
CLICK
YES, I WAS!
YES, I WAS LISTENING!
I NEED YOU TO LEAN IN TO WHO YOU TRULY ARE AT YOUR CORE.
A SCARED SINGLE FATHER?

113

116

117

118

(JUST AN OUTDATED COMPUTER ON A FOLDING TABLE)

119

120

121

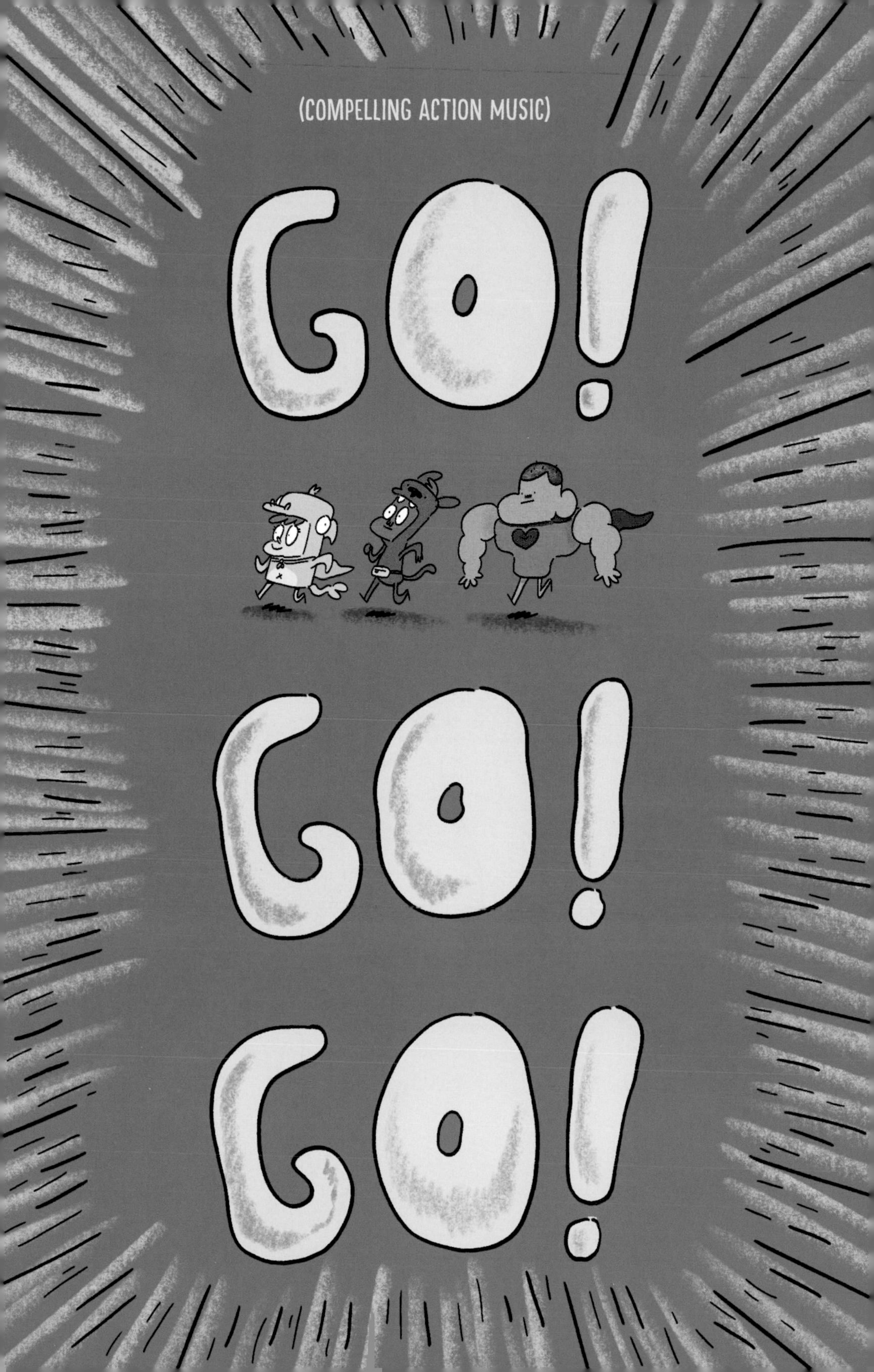
(COMPELLING ACTION MUSIC)
GO!
GO!
GO!

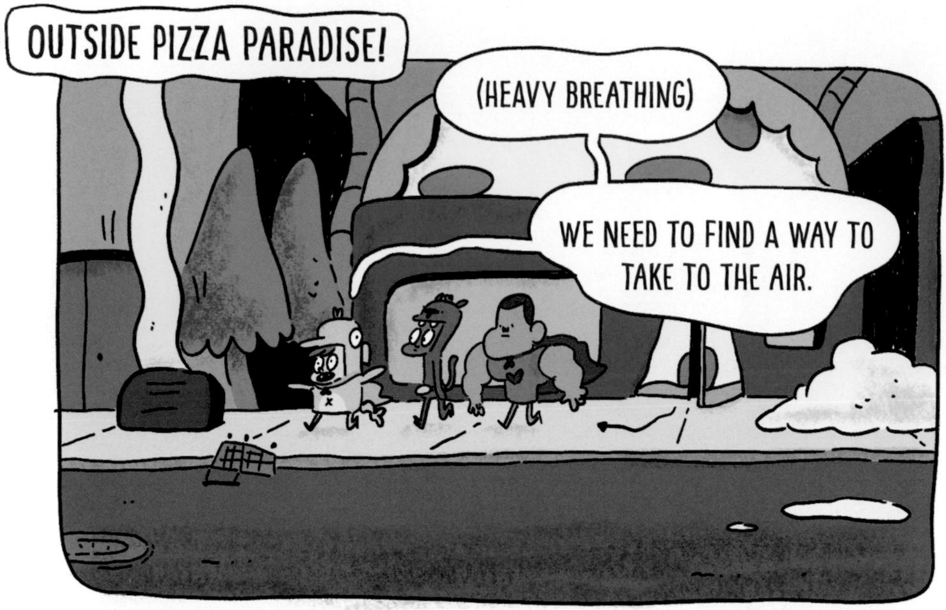
OUTSIDE PIZZA PARADISE!
(HEAVY BREATHING)
WE NEED TO FIND A WAY TO TAKE TO THE AIR.

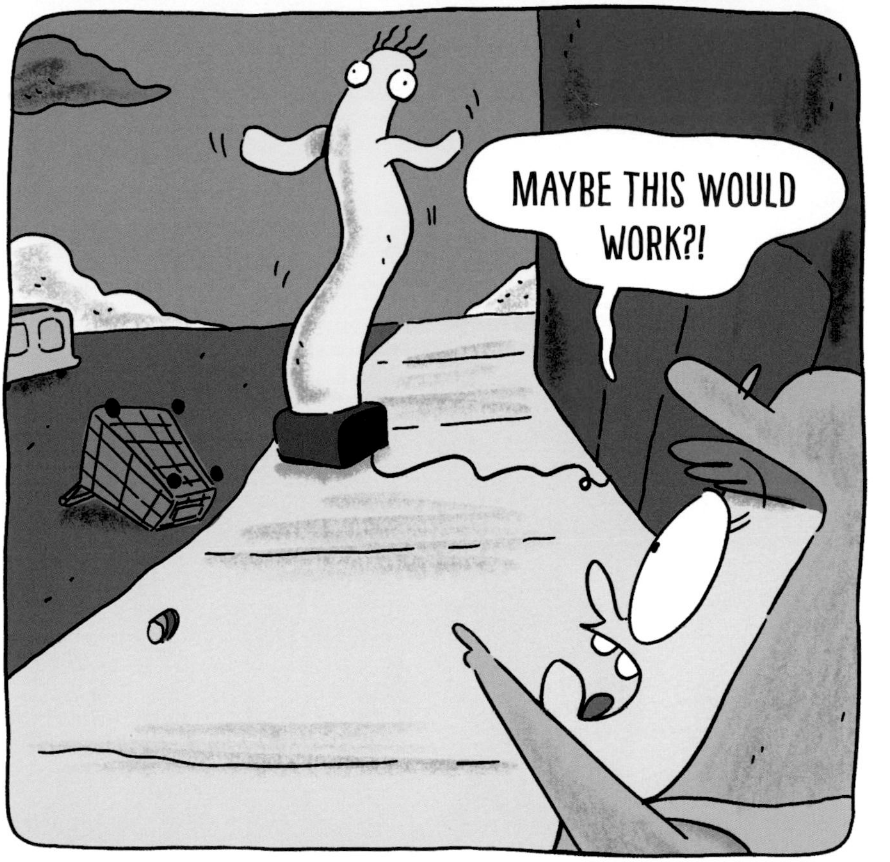
MAYBE THIS WOULD WORK?!

126

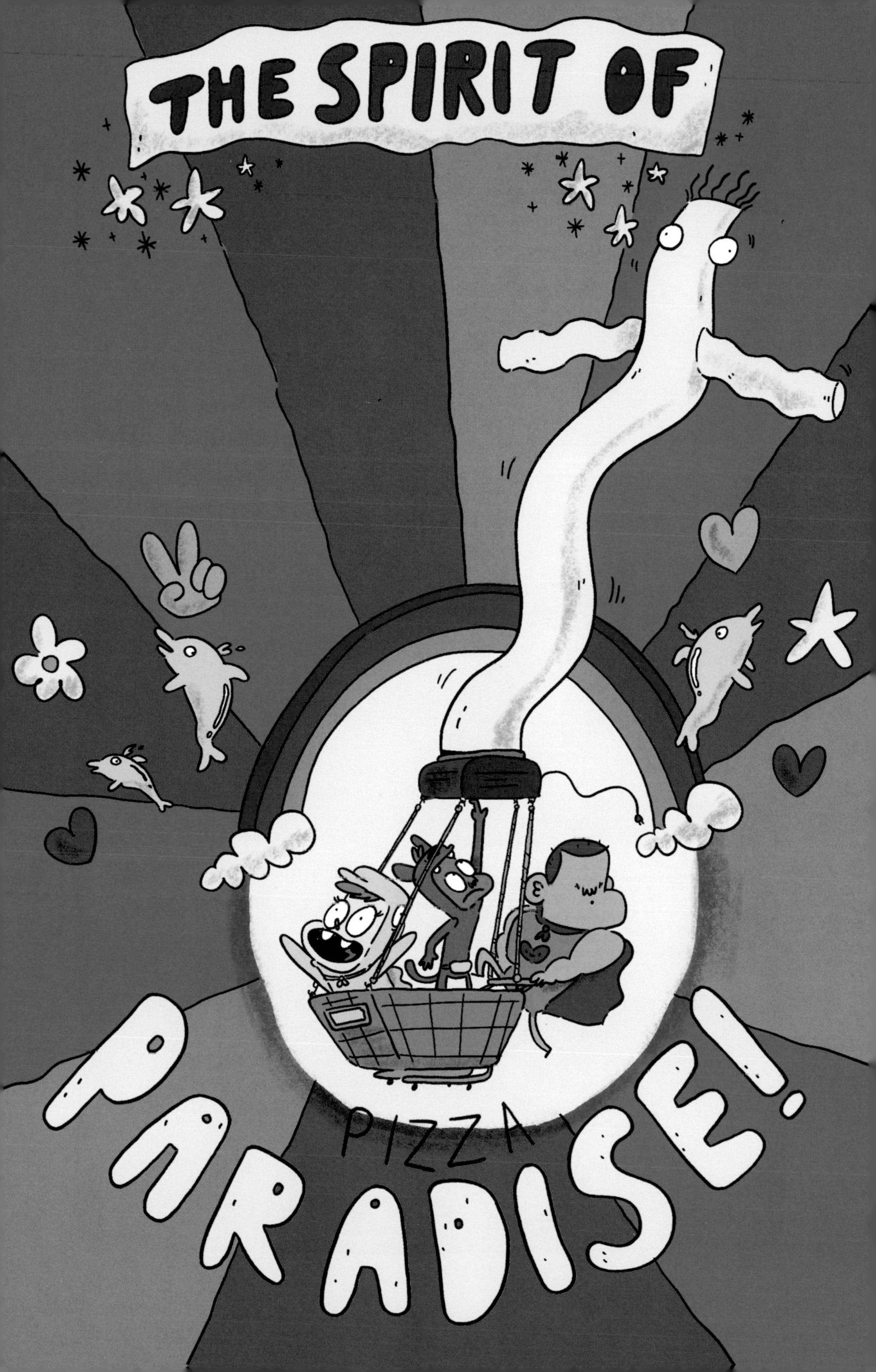
THE SPIRIT OF
PIZZA
PARADISE!

129

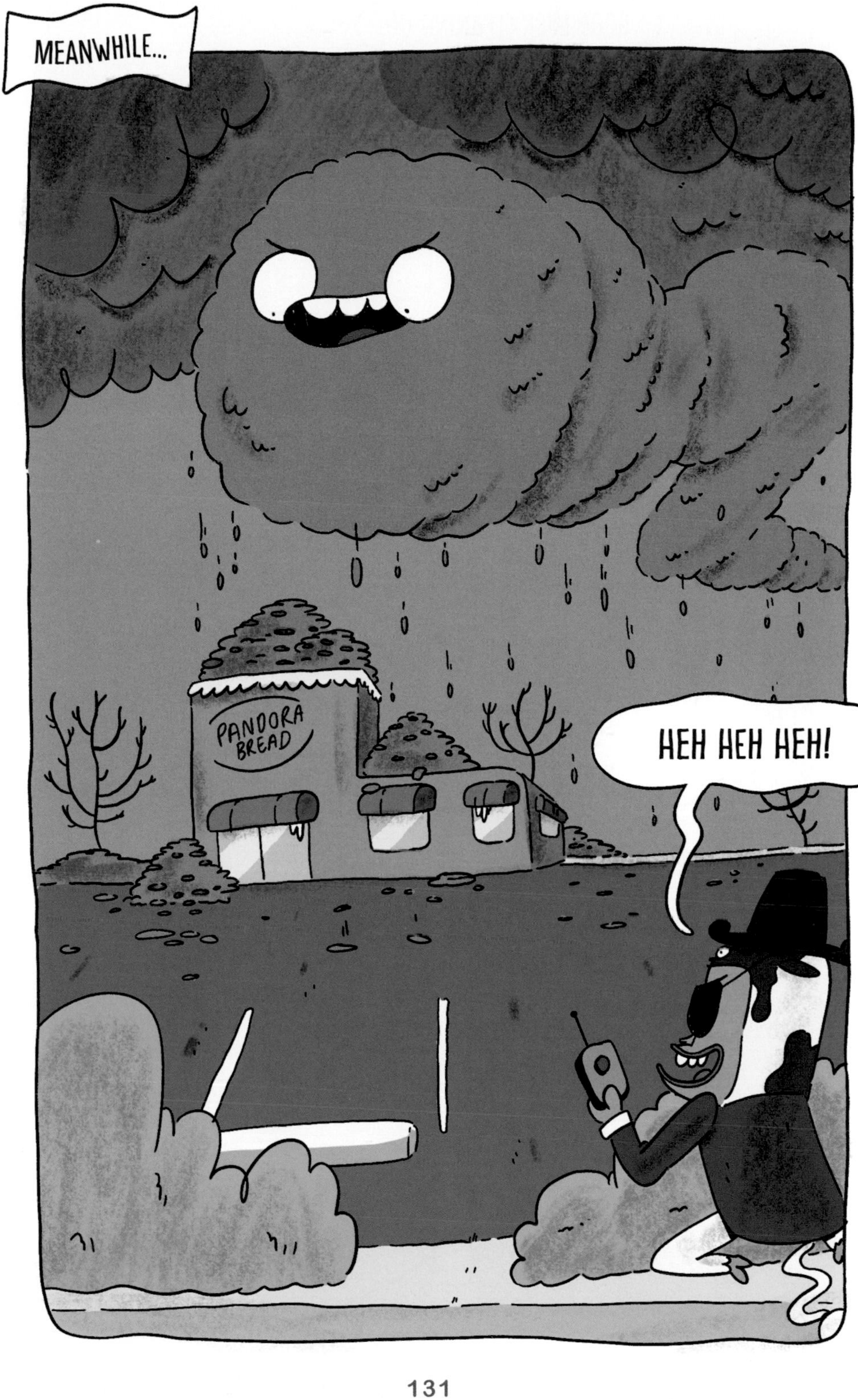
MEANWHILE...
PANDORA BREAD
HEH HEH HEH!

133

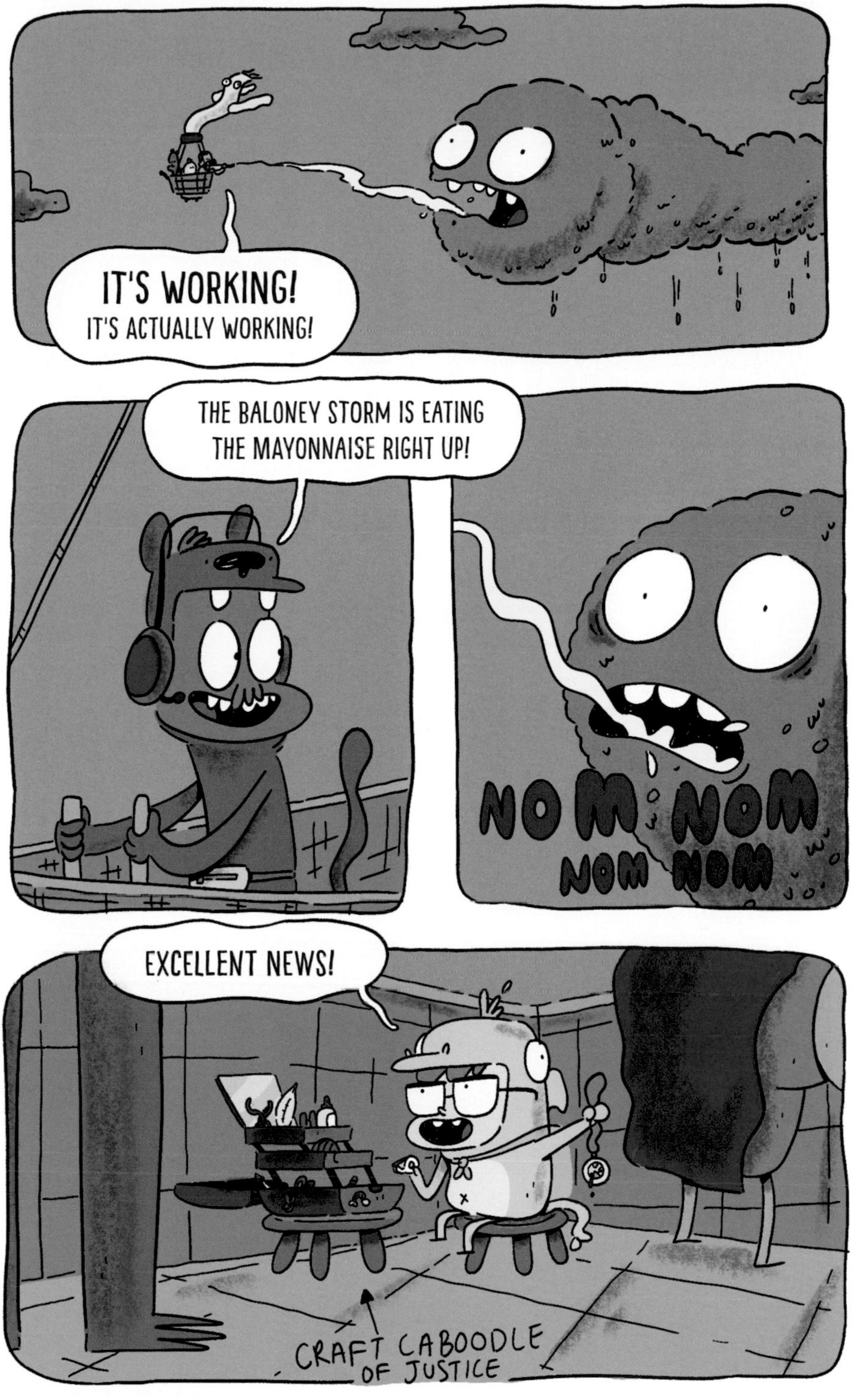
IT'S WORKING!
IT'S ACTUALLY WORKING!
THE BALONEY STORM IS EATING THE MAYONNAISE RIGHT UP!
NOM NOM
NOM NOM
EXCELLENT NEWS!
CRAFT CABOODLE OF JUSTICE

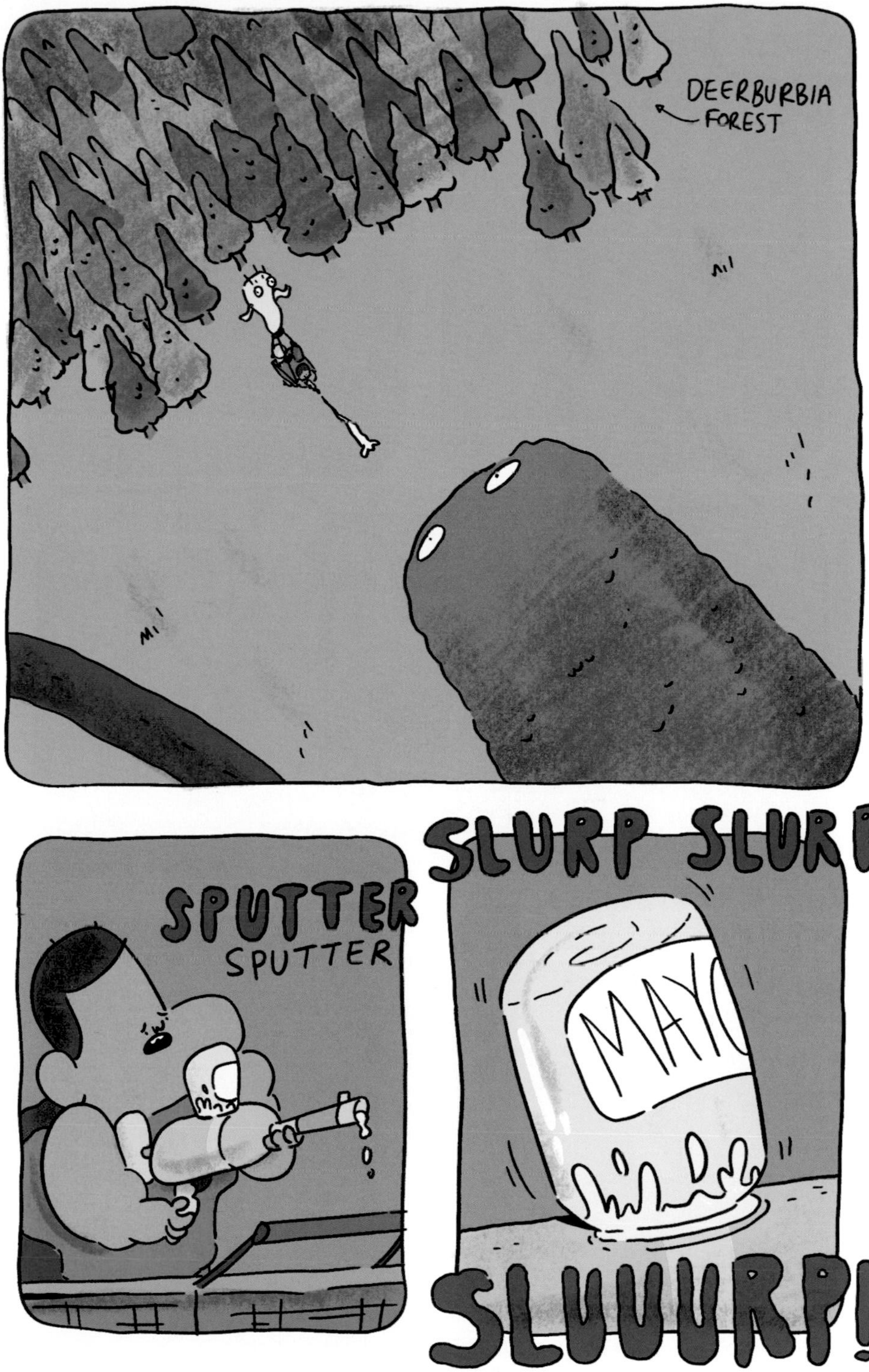
DEERBURBIA FOREST
SPUTTER
SPUTTER
SLURP SLURP
MAYO
SLUUURP!

140

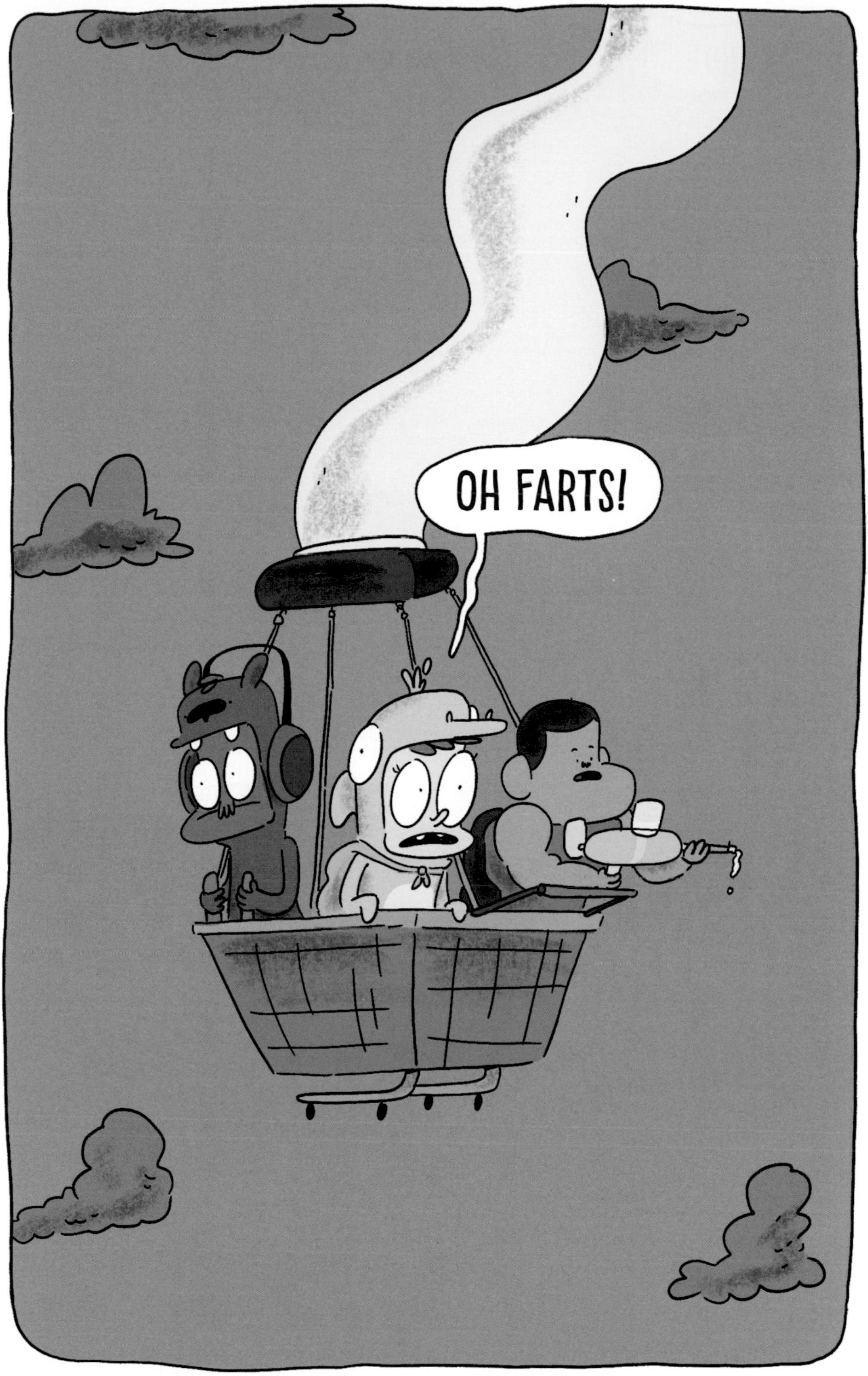
OH FARTS!

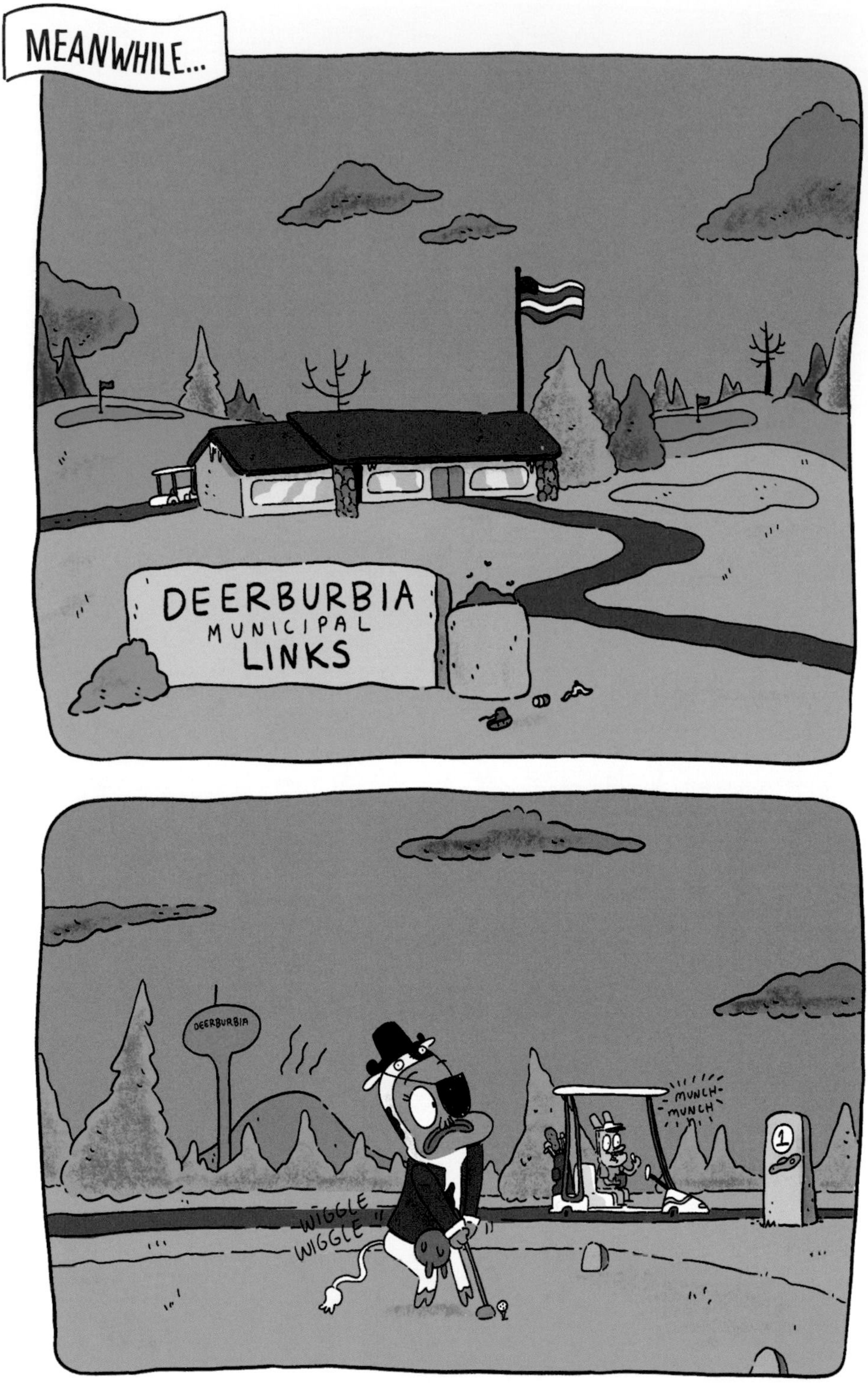
MEANWHILE...
DEERBURBIA MUNICIPAL LINKS
DEERBURBIA
WIGGLE WIGGLE
MUNCH MUNCH
1

145

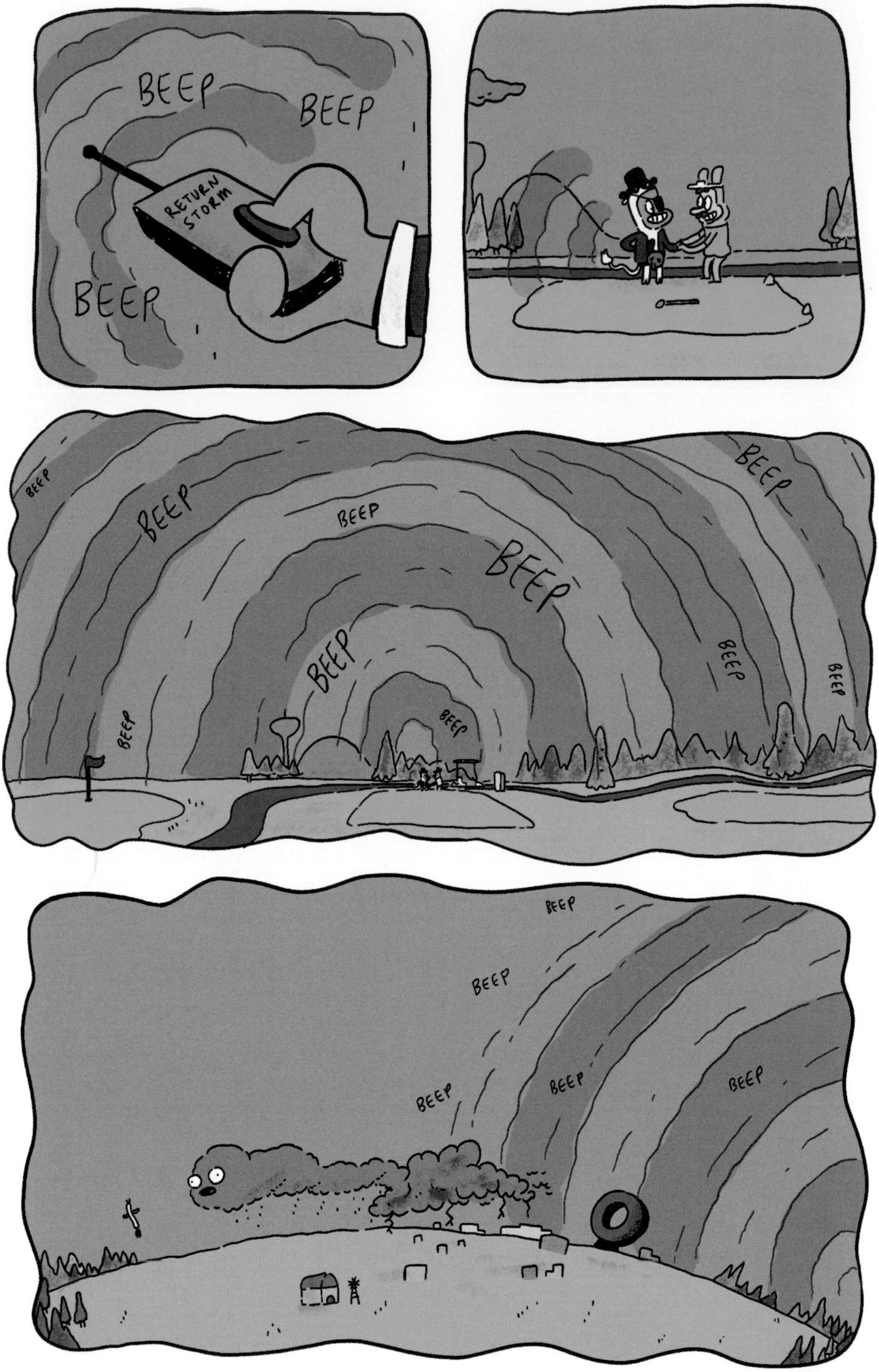
BEEP
BEEP
RETURN STORM
BEEP
BEEP
BEEP
BEEP
BEEP
BEEP
BEEP
BEEP
BEEP
BEEP
BEEP
BEEP
BEEP
BEEP
BEEP
BEEP

151

152

PART THREE

155

157

159

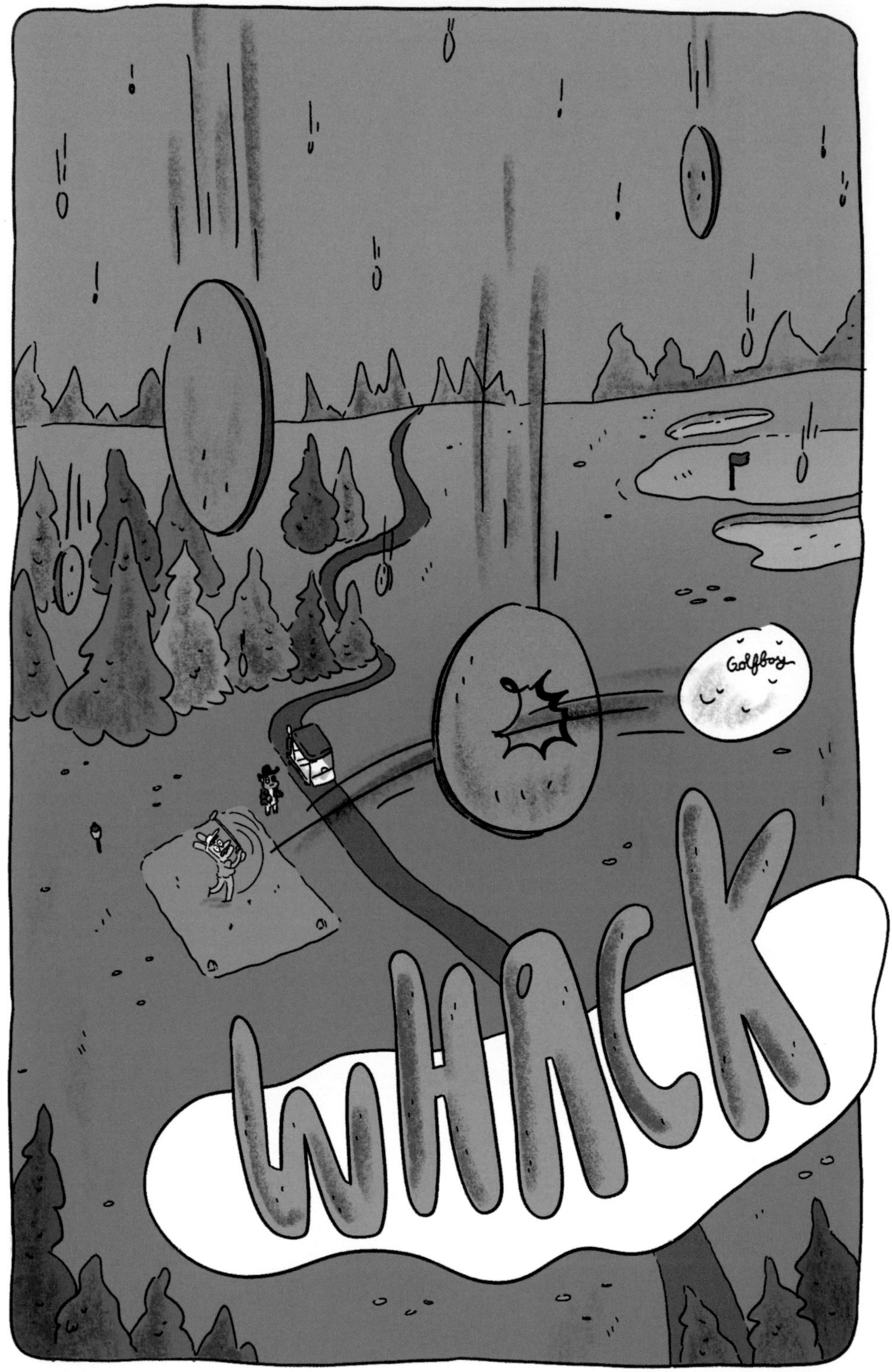
Golfboy
WHACK

161

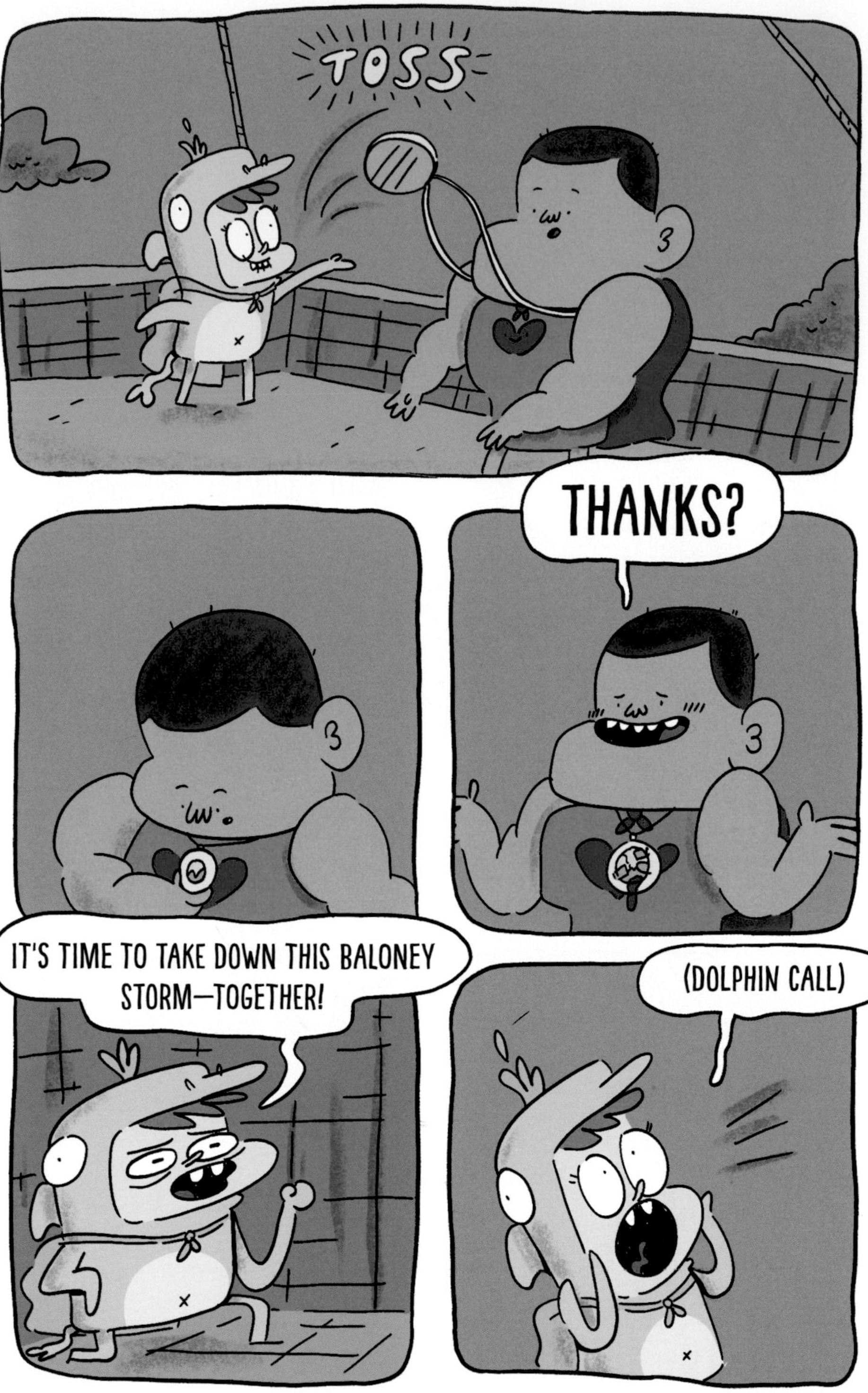
TOSS
THANKS?
IT'S TIME TO TAKE DOWN THIS BALONEY STORM—TOGETHER!
(DOLPHIN CALL)

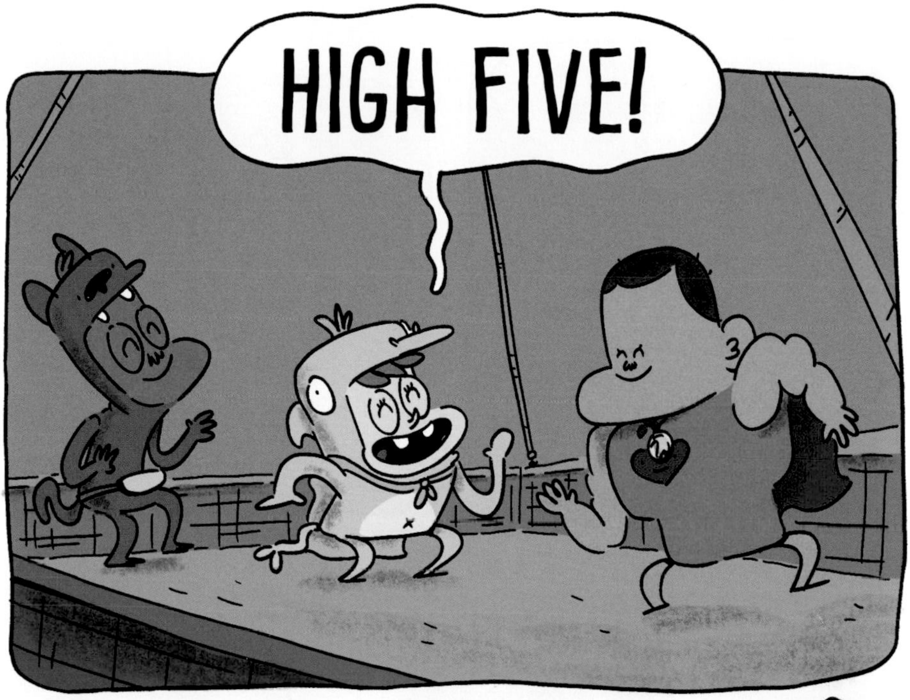
HIGH FIVE!

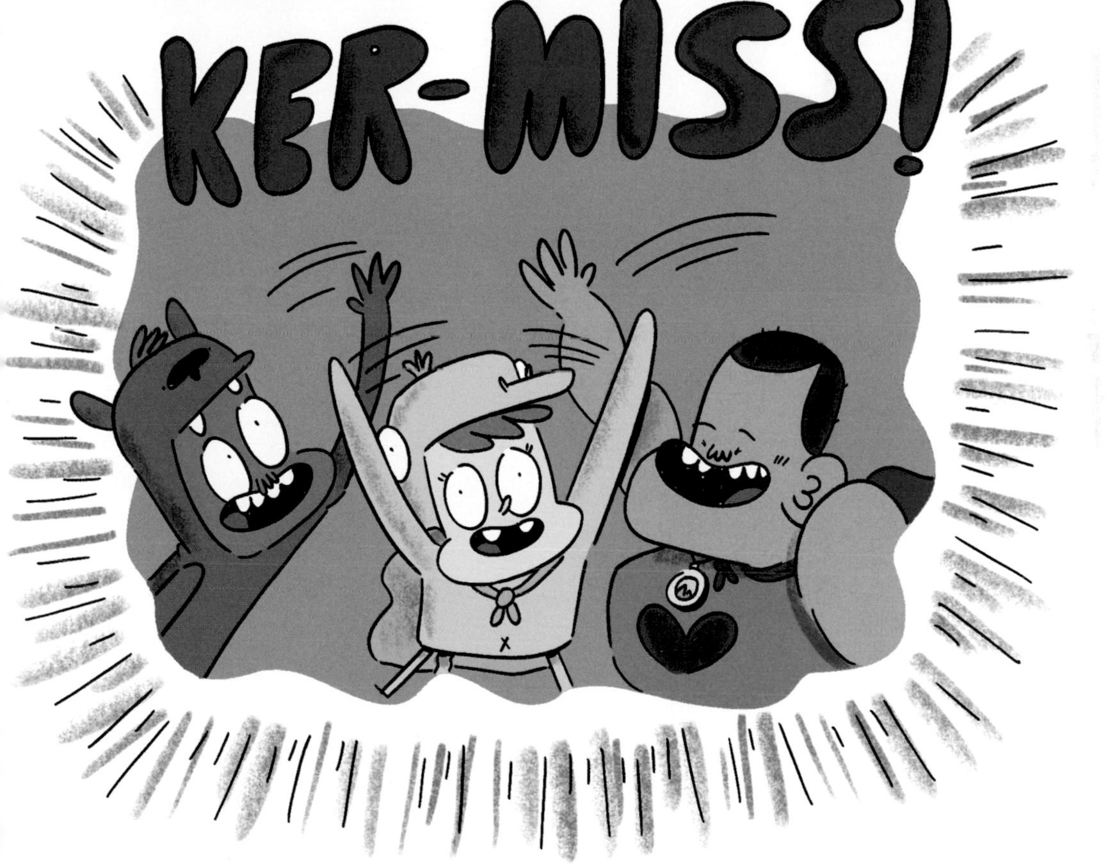
KER-MISS!

164

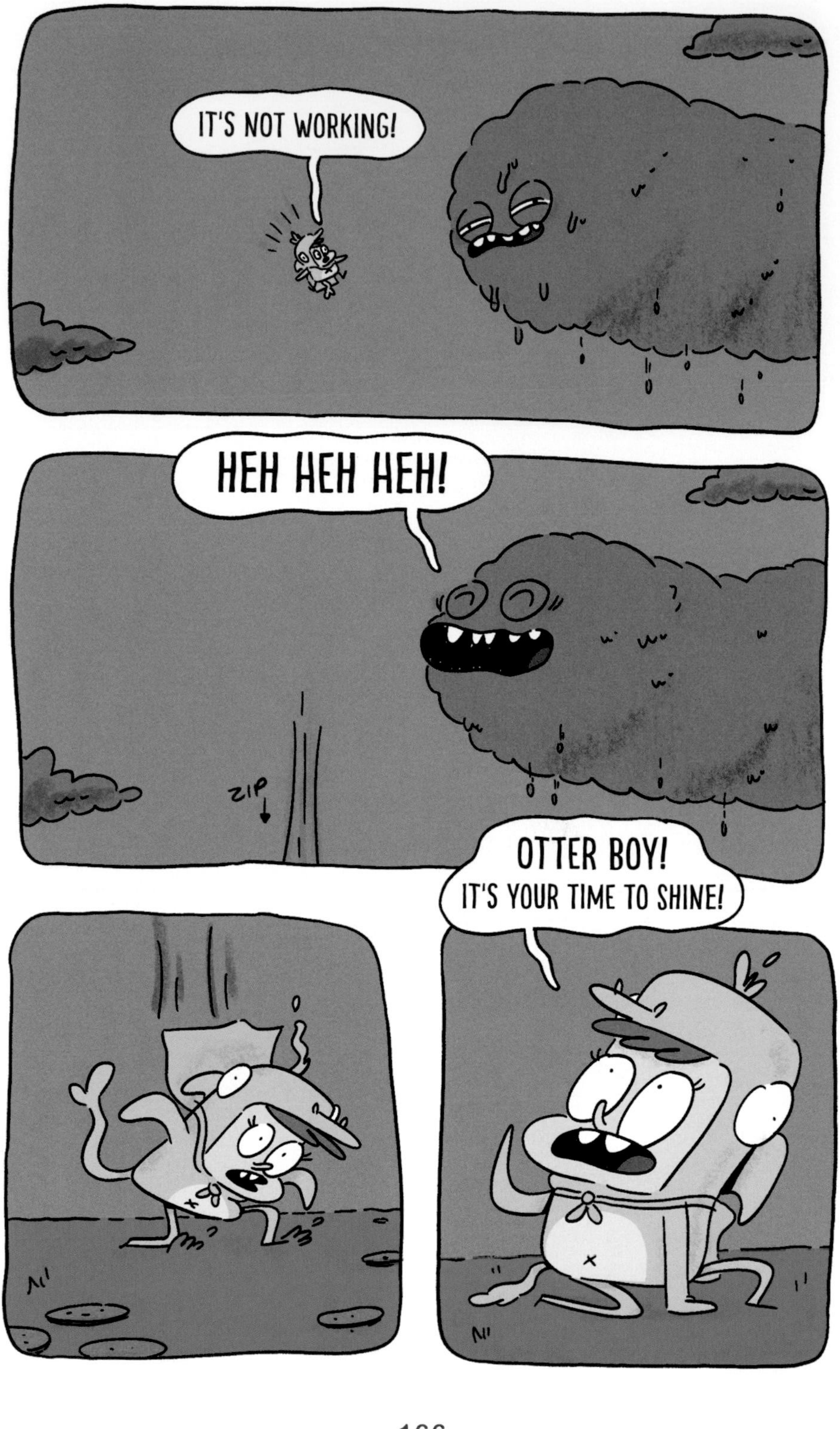
IT'S NOT WORKING!
HEH HEH HEH!
ZIP
OTTER BOY!
IT'S YOUR TIME TO SHINE!

167

168

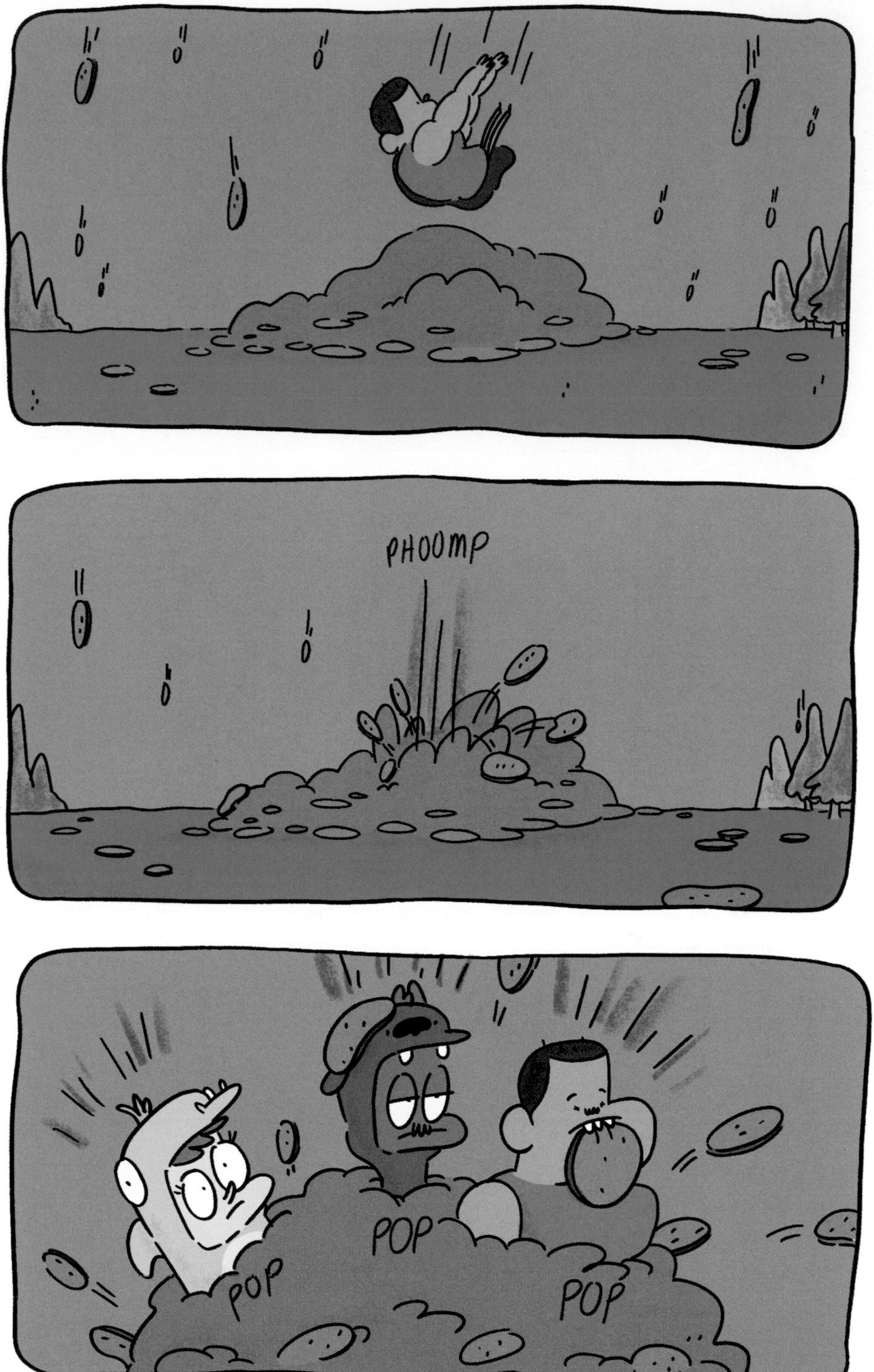
PHOOMP
POP
POP
POP

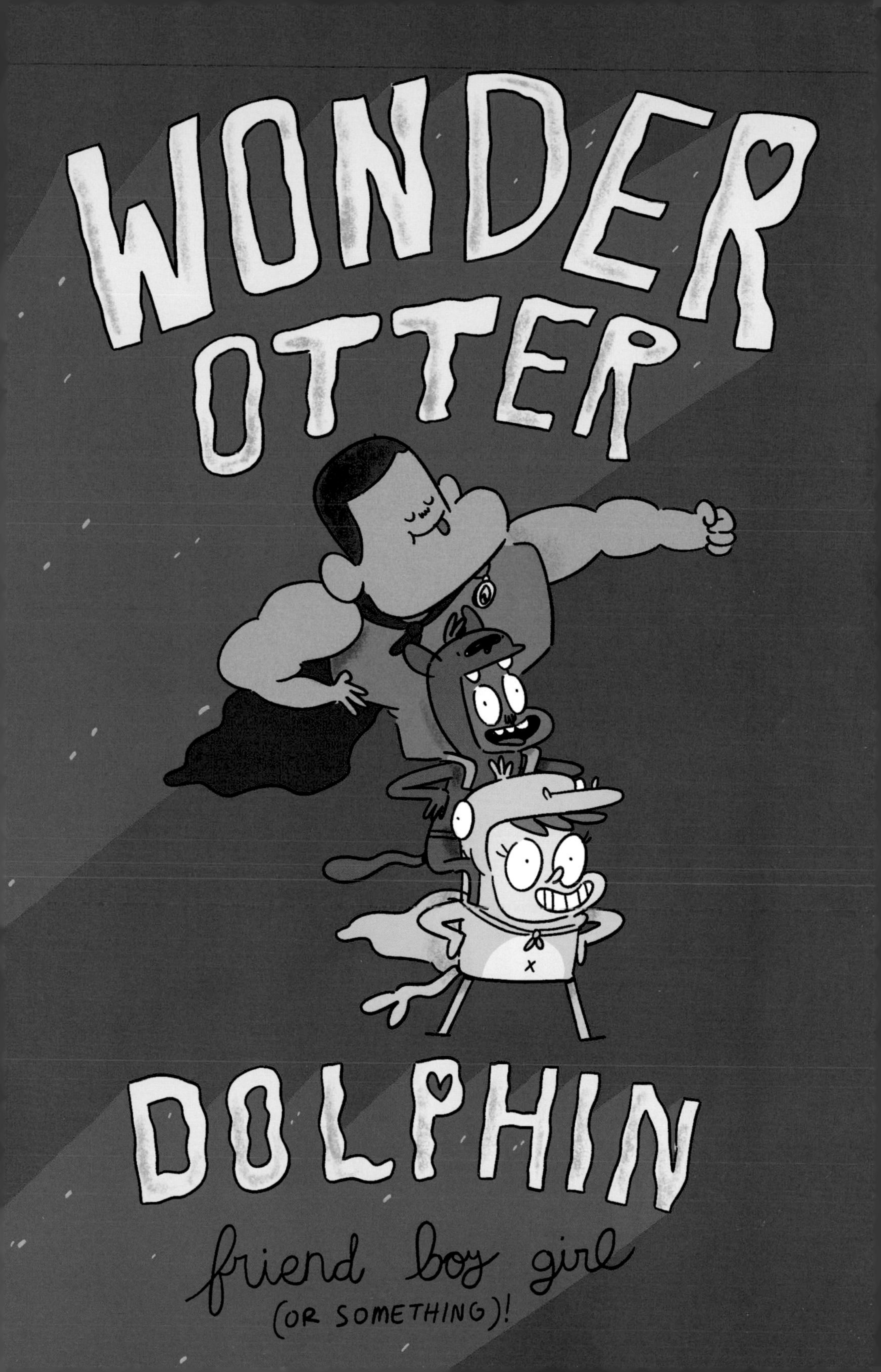
WONDER OTTER
DOLPHIN
friend boy girl
(OR SOMETHING)!

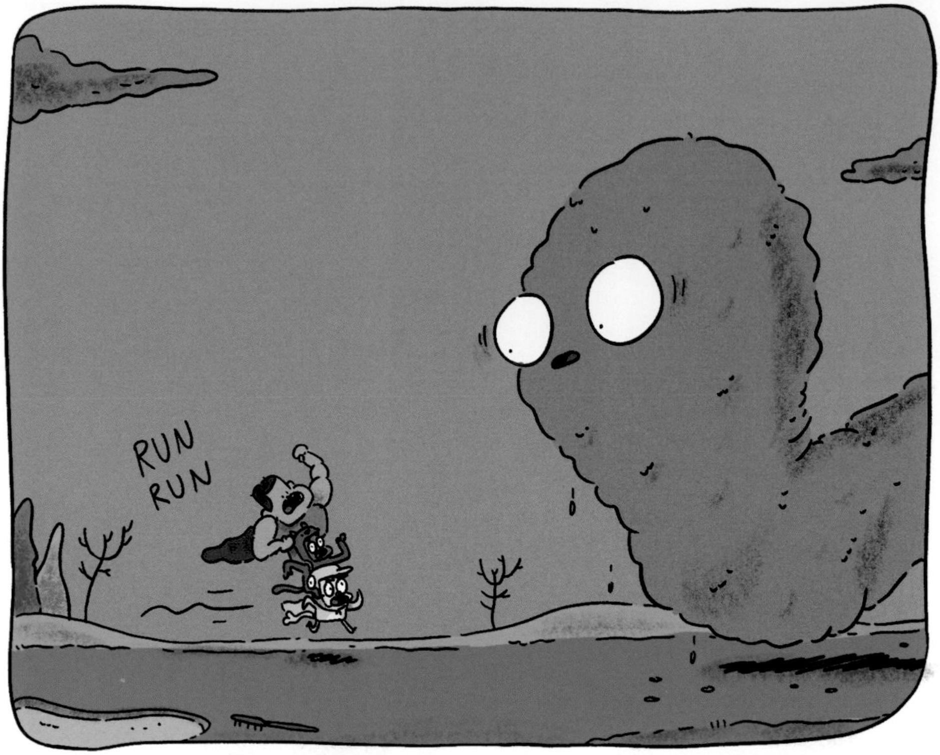
RUN
RUN

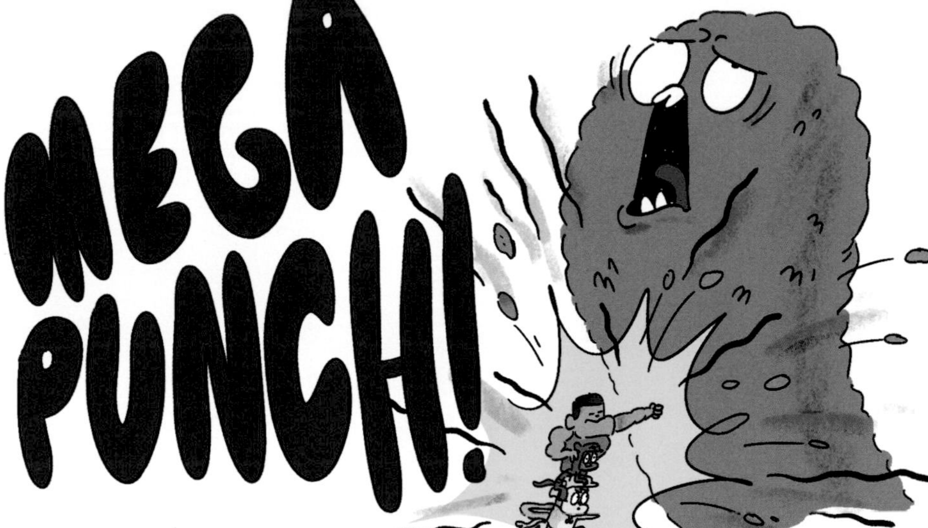
MEGA
PUNCH!!

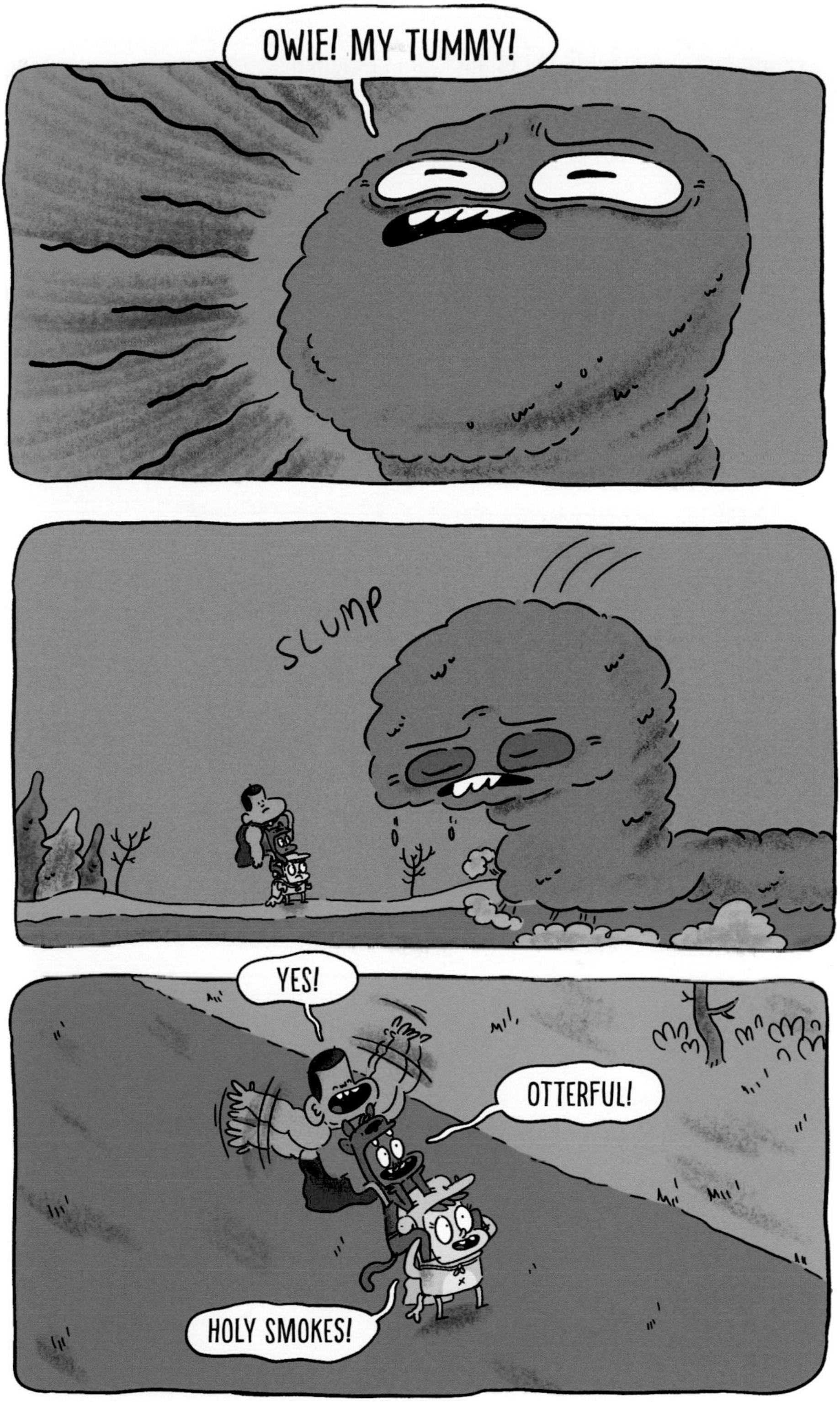
OWIE! MY TUMMY!
SLUMP
YES!
OTTERFUL!
HOLY SMOKES!

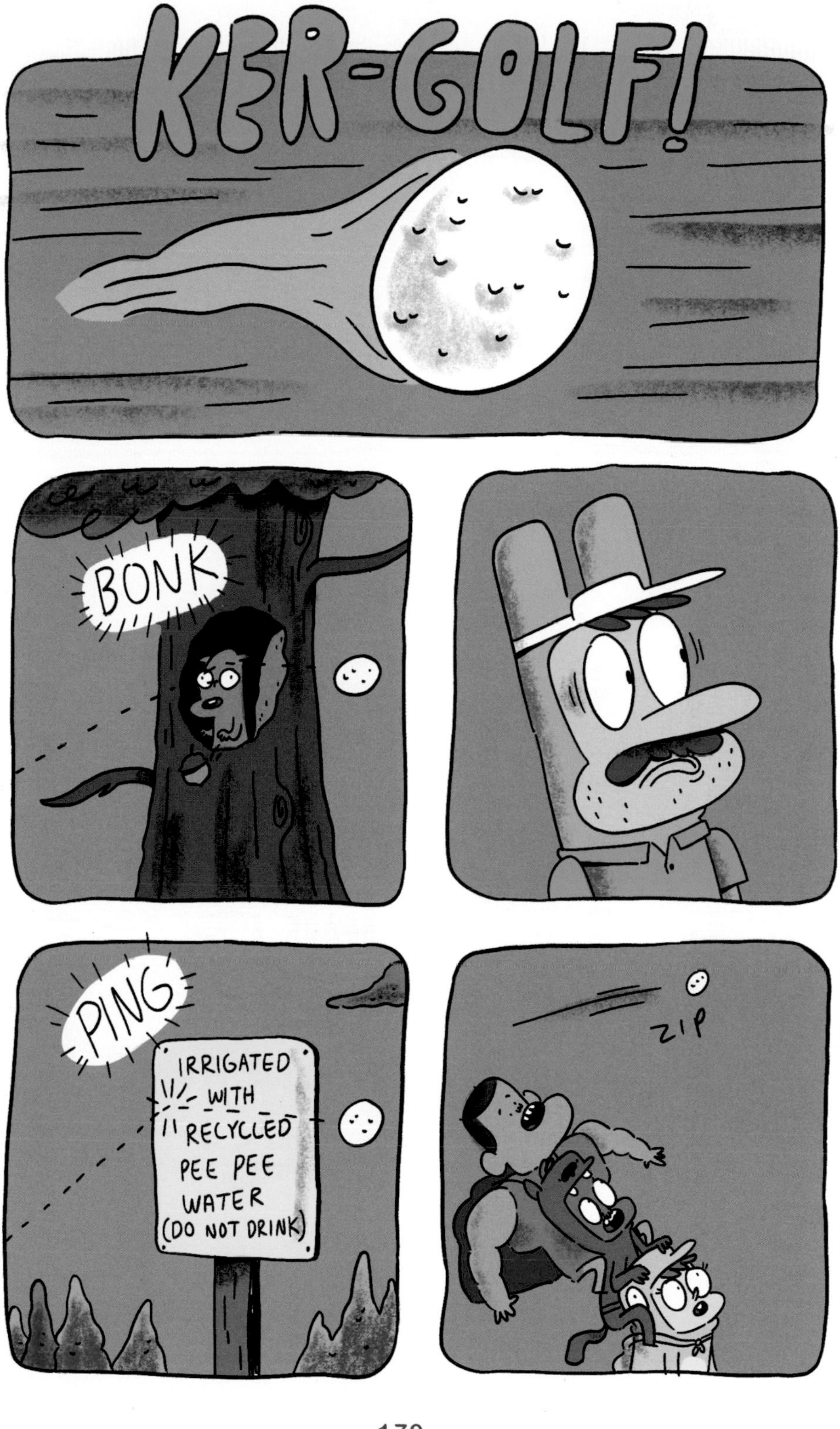
KER-GOLF!
BONK
PING
IRRIGATED WITH RECYCLED PEE PEE WATER (DO NOT DRINK)
ZIP

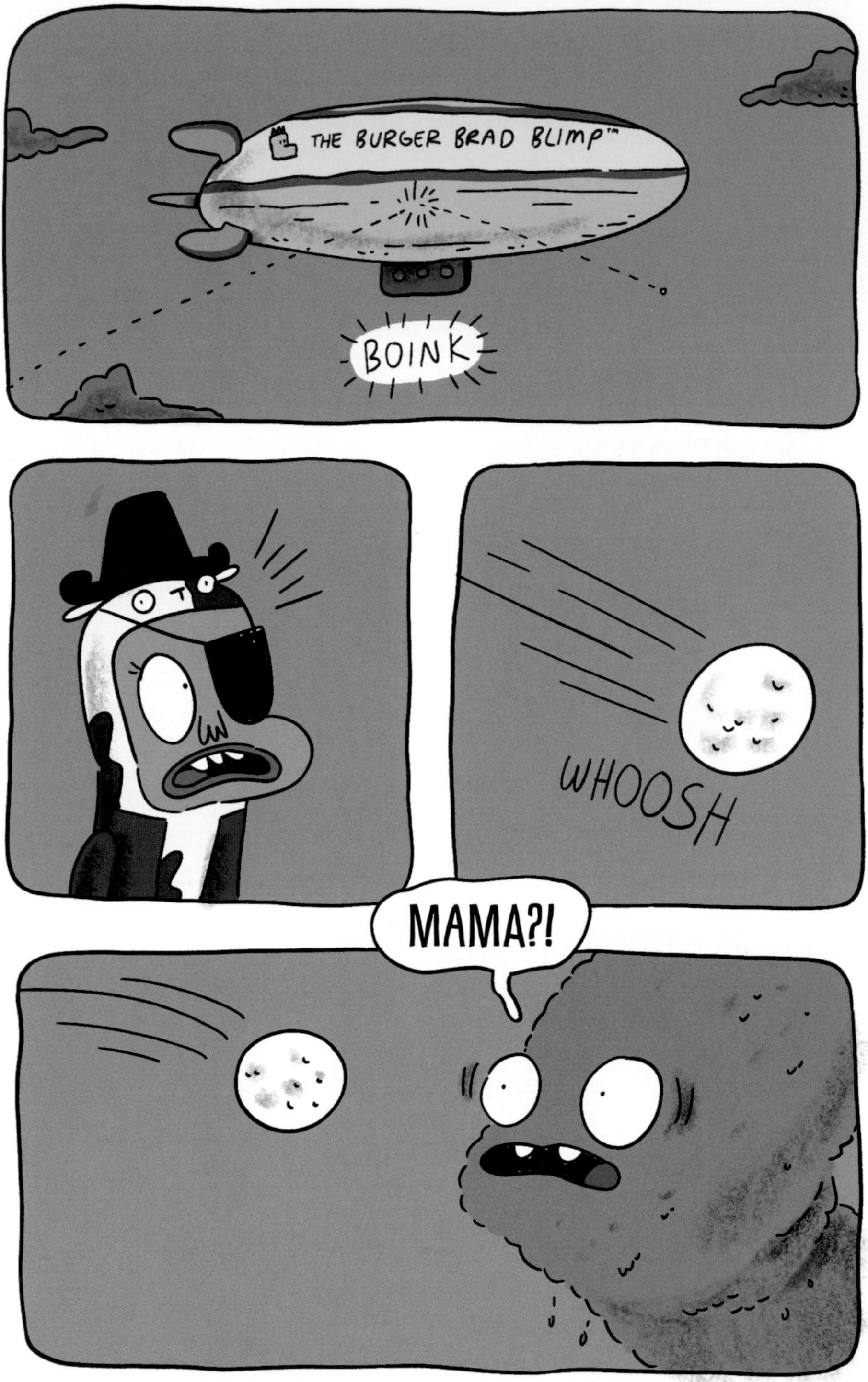
THE BURGER BRAD BLIMP™
BOINK
WHOOSH
MAMA?!

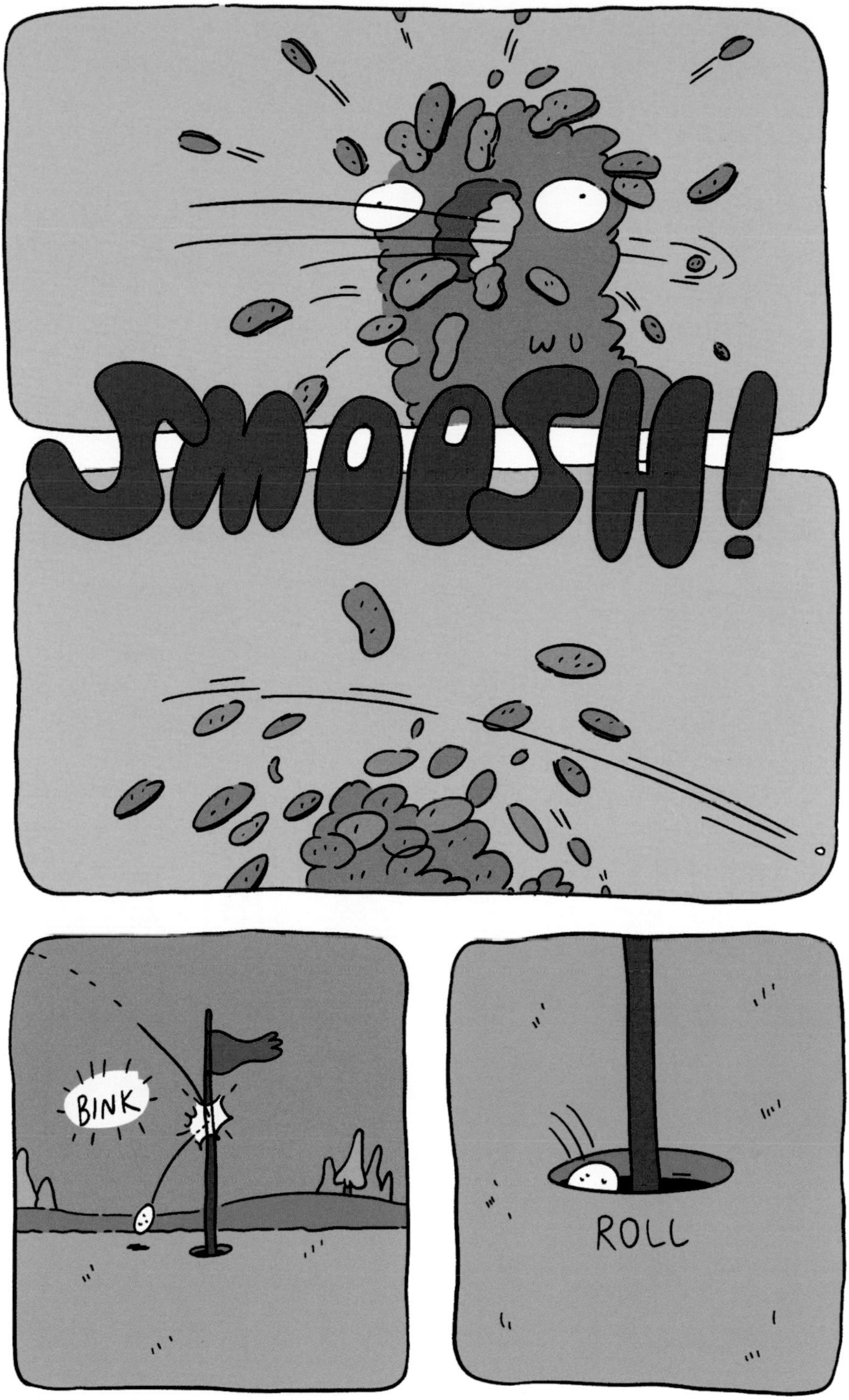
SMOOSH!
BINK
ROLL

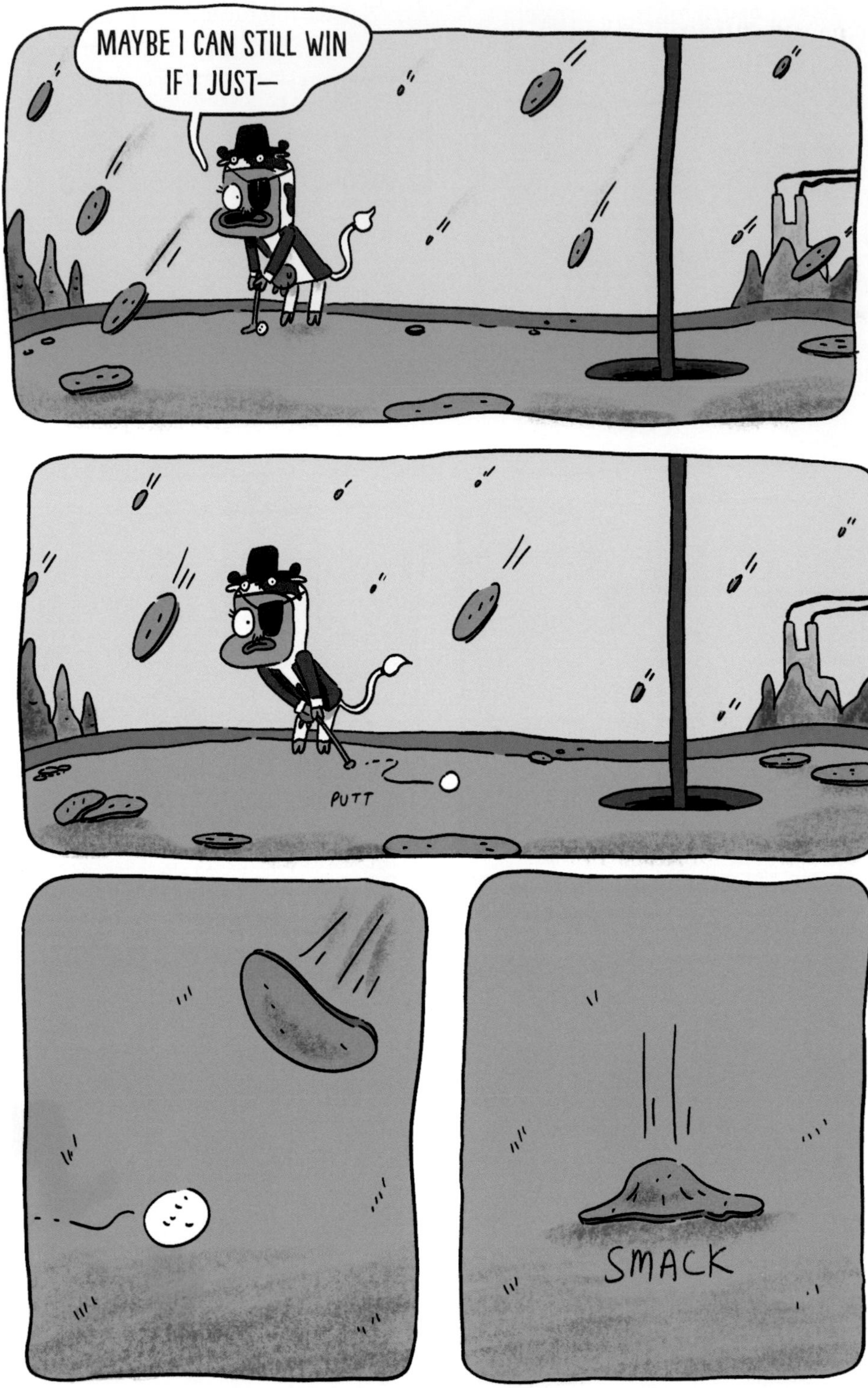
MAYBE I CAN STILL WIN IF I JUST—
PUTT
SMACK

186

189

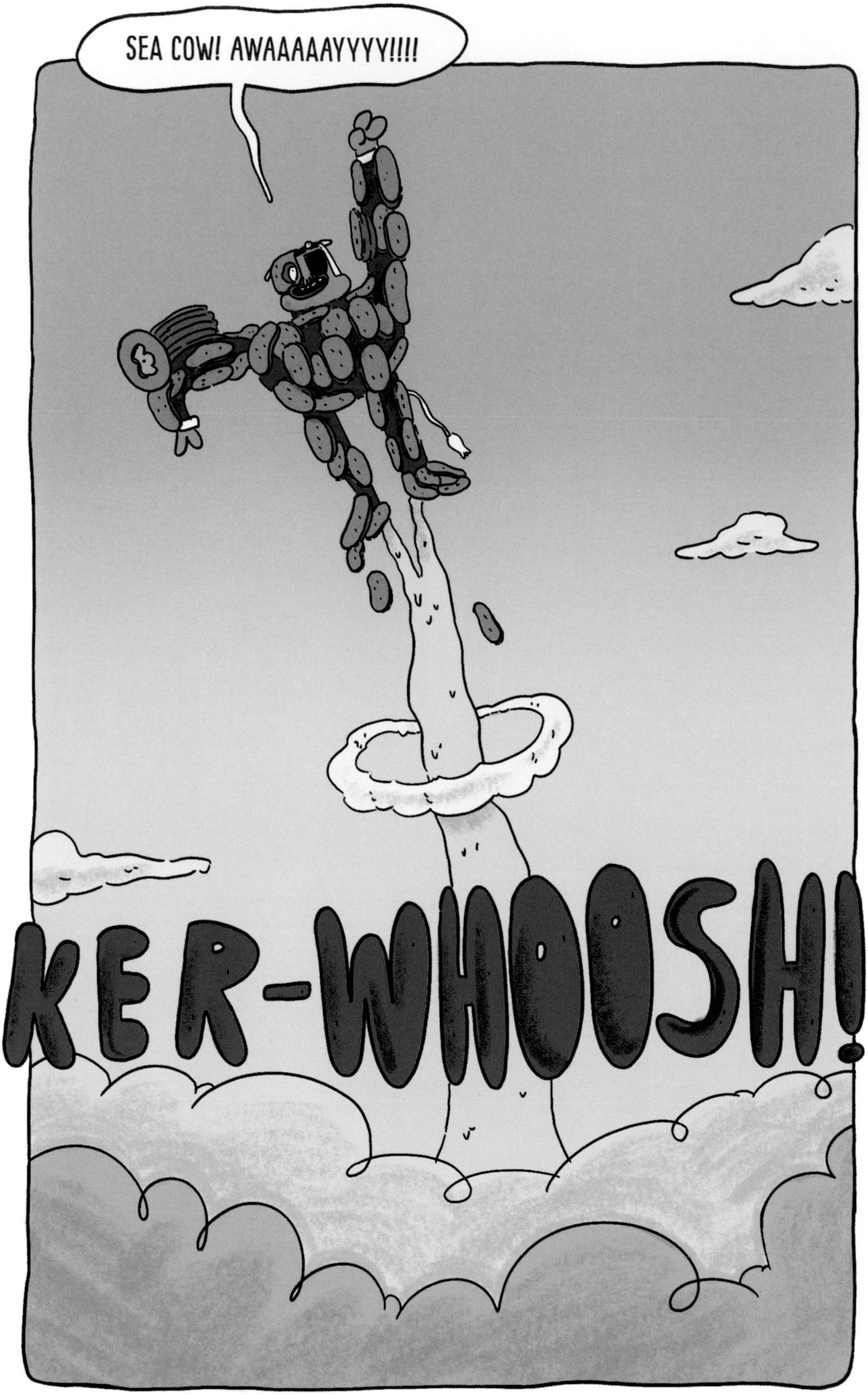
SEA COW! AWAAAAAYYYY!!!!
KER-WHOOSH!

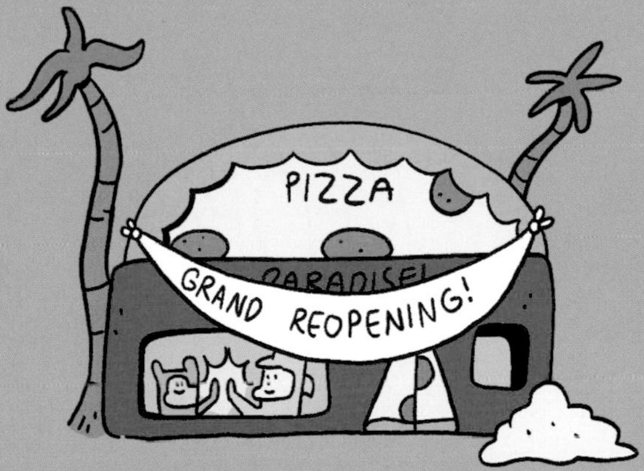
PIZZA
PARADISE!
GRAND REOPENING!

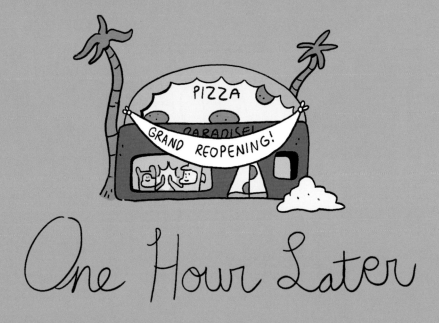

One Hour Later

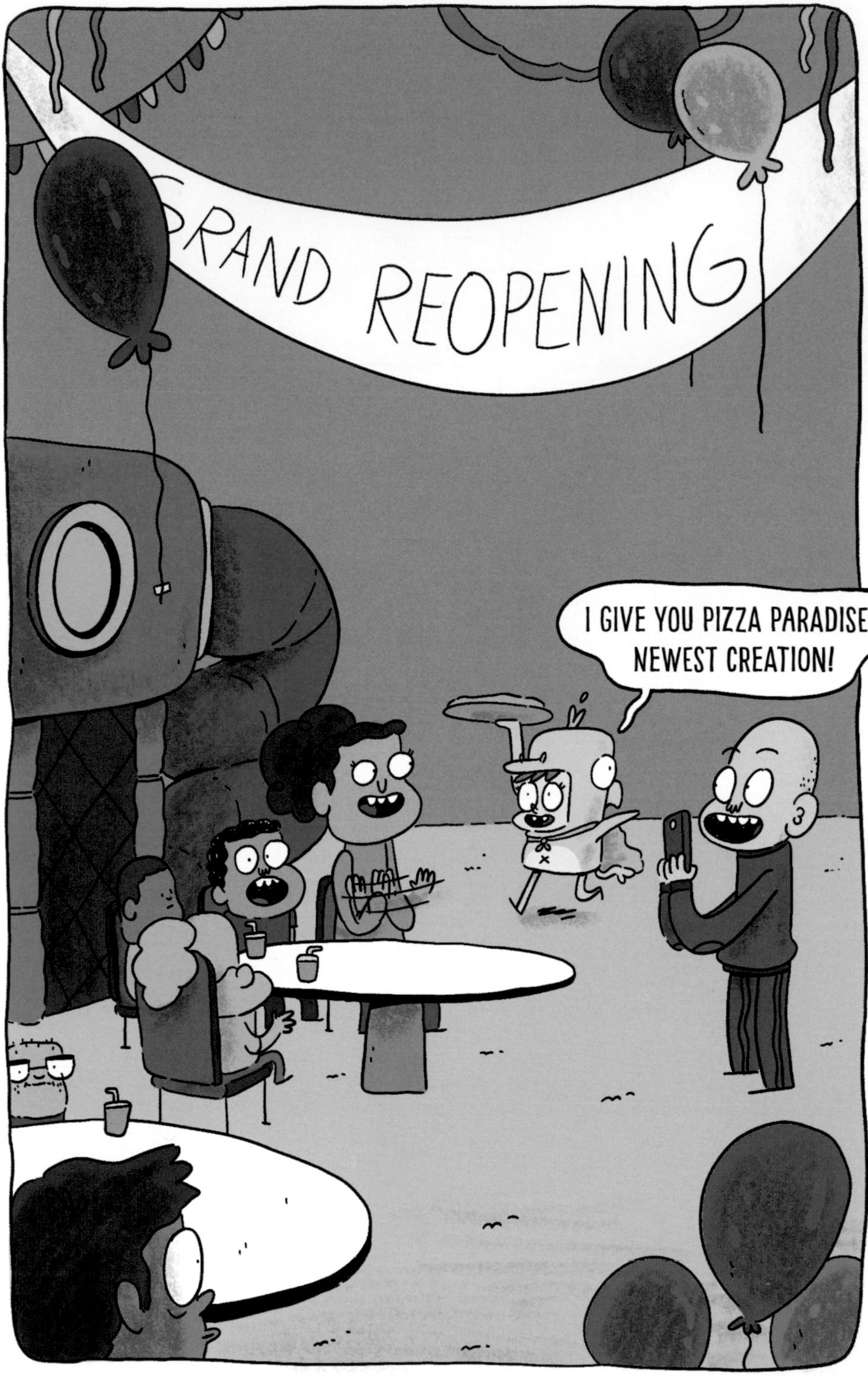
GRAND REOPENING
I GIVE YOU PIZZA PARADISE'S NEWEST CREATION!

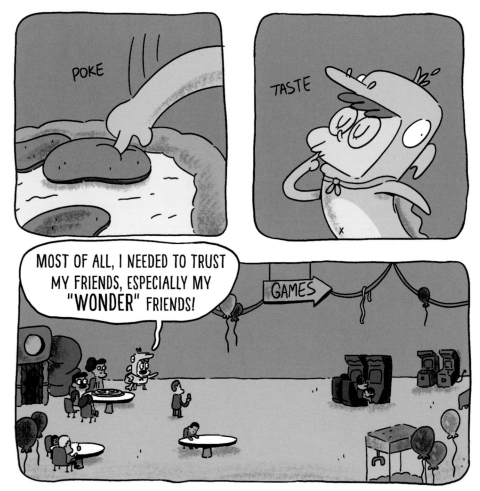

200

202

203

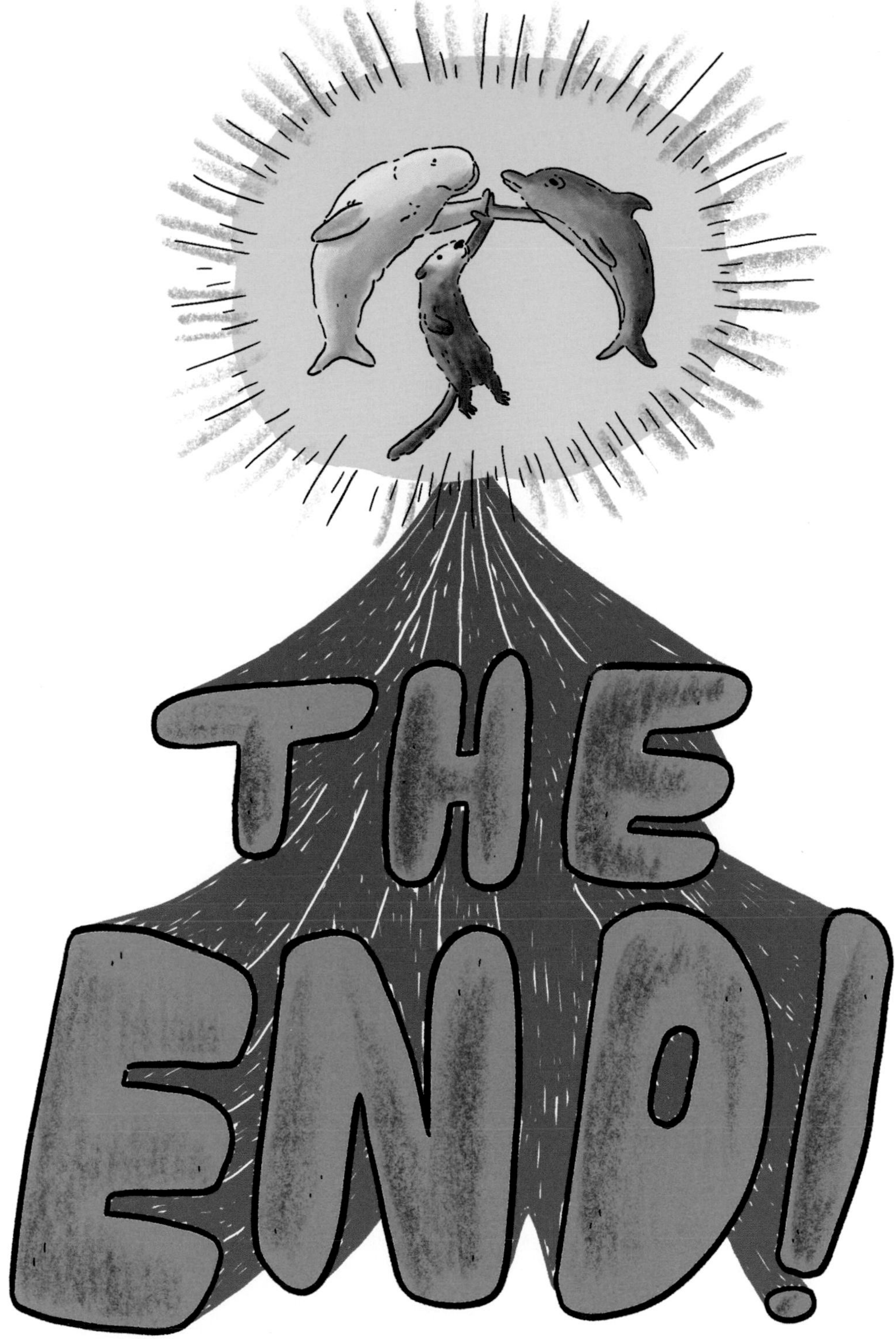
THE END!

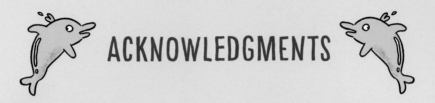

ACKNOWLEDGMENTS

THANKS TO THE WONDERFUL AND PAINFULLY TALENTED LETICIA LACY FOR COLORING THIS BOOK AND ALL OF ITS BROKEN LINEWORK.

THANKS TO ALL THE FINE PEOPLE AT PIXEL+INK AND HOLIDAY HOUSE WHO MADE THIS BOOK POSSIBLE:

BETHANY BUCK, SARA DISALVO, MICHELLE MONTAGUE, TERRY BORZUMATO-GREENBERG, AND THE REST OF THE PUBLICITY AND MARKETING TEAM, WHITNEY MANGER FINE, KELSEY PROVO, ANDREA MILLER, RAINA PUTTER, LISA LEE, HANNAH FINNE, MIRIAM MILLER, JULIA GALLAGHER, MARY BRIGANTE, ALISON WEISS, AND DEREK STORDAHL.

AND THANKS TO THESE PEOPLE (WHO HELPED ME GET THROUGH WRITING A BOOK, DIRECTING A PRE-SCHOOL SHOW, DEVELOPING ANOTHER PRESCHOOL SHOW, LIVING WITH OCD, AND BEING A PARENT DURING A WORLDWIDE PANDEMIC IN THE YEAR 2020): MONIQUE, QUINN, AND ZADIE FOR LOVING ME, SUPPORT-ING ME, AND FILLING MY LIFE WITH LAUGHTER, VISCOUS PURE JOY, WONDER, AND '90S DANCE PARTIES. KYLE BOYD, FOR THE FRIENDSHIP. MY FUNNY FAMILY IN MICHIGAN: MOM, DAD, KRISTIN, KEVIN, LANDON, BENNET, JAKE, AND JESS, AND ALL THE SMITH, THOMPSON, AND COOLEY COUSINS THAT TAUGHT ME HOW TO BE FUNNY AS A KID. AMANDA BERKOWITZ—THERAPY WIZARD! THE LEYSENS BROS (NICK & GREG) FOR BEING AMAZINGLY HUMBLE AND FUNNY PEOPLE TO WORK WITH DURING THE DAY.

THANKS TO THE MUSICIANS THAT HELPED ME THROUGH THE WRITING PROCESS, ESPECIALLY:

JONI MITCHEL, DOLLY PARTON, ANGEL OLSEN, PHOEBE BRIDGERS, BOB DYLAN AND THE SWEET '70S SOUNDS OF THE LAUREL CANYON MUSIC SCENE, WHICH WAS OF GREAT COMFORT DURING A CRAZY YEAR.

AND THESE BOOKS (FOR HELPING ME OPEN MY EYES AND STEP OUTSIDE OF MY OWN HEAD FOR A BIT):

THE METAPHYSICAL CLUB BY LOUIS MENAND, *TURTLES ALL THE WAY DOWN* BY JOHN GREEN, *MAN'S SEARCH FOR HIMSELF* BY ROLLO MAY, *STATION ELEVEN* BY EMILY ST. JOHN MANDEL, AND *KEEP GOING* BY AUSTIN KLEON.

AND THANKS TO YOU, DEAR READER, FOR BUYING THIS BOOK (OR TRADING SOMETHING FOR IT ON THE SCHOOL BLACK MARKET). I AM SO GRATEFUL THAT SOMEONE ACTUALLY WANTS TO READ THIS!

SUPER YEARBOOK!

HEROES:

DOLPHIN GIRL

OTTER BOY

WONDER FRIEND

CAPTAIN DUGONG

THE FUNK MACHINES

GREATER DEERBURBIA, BUT LIKE AS A CHARACTER ITSELF, YOU KNOW?

VILLAINS:

SEA COW

DR. SOCCER VON MOMCOACH

THE MEATLOAF

THE PIZZA PROWLER

BALONEY STORM

AND SOMETIMES CHAD

VOTE :

BEST COUPLE: _____

MOST LIKELY TO SUCCEED: _____

BEST ROBOT BAND: _____

CUTEST LAUGH: _____

MOST CREATIVE: _____

CLASS CLOWN: _____

MOST LIKELY TO BECOME A PART OF A PYRAMID SCHEME: _____

ABOUT THE AUTHOR

ZACH SMITH IS A CARTOONIST, AUTHOR, ILLUSTRATOR, AND SHOW CREATOR. CURRENTLY, HE IS CREATING AN UPCOMING SHOW FOR NICK JR. AND WORKS AS A STORYBOARD ARTIST IN THE ANIMATION INDUSTRY. ZACH LIVES IN THE SUBURBS OF LOS ANGELES WITH HIS WIFE, TWO DAUGHTERS, AND TWO DOGS. BEFORE BECOMING A PROFESSIONAL ARTIST, HE DELIVERED PIZZA FOR A LIVING.